Jacob Faithful

by

Captain Frederick Marryat

Jacob Faithful
by Captain Frederick Marryat

Copyright © 2024

All Rights reserved.

ISBN: 978-93-62204-52-3

Published by

DOUBLE 9 BOOKS

2/13-B, Ansari Road
Daryaganj, New Delhi – 110002
info@double9books.com
www.double9books.com
Tel. 011-40042856

ABOUT THE AUTHOR

Captain Frederick Marryat was both a Royal Navy officer and a novelist. He is now recognized as an early pioneer of nautical fiction, particularly for his semi-autobiographical novel Mr Midshipman Easy (1836). He is especially famous for his children's novel, The Children of the New Forest (1847). In addition, he created a widely used marine flag signalling system known as Marryat's Code. Marryat was born on Great George Street in Westminster, London. His parents were Joseph Marryat, a "merchant prince" and member of Parliament, as well as a slave owner and anti-abolitionist, and Charlotte, née von Geyer. Marryat's time on board the Imperieuse includes action off the Gironde, the rescue of a fellow midshipman who had fallen overboard, the seizure of numerous ships off the Mediterranean coast of Spain, and the capture of Montgat Castle. In 1809, the Imperieuse relocated to operations in the Scheldt, where Marryat caught malaria before returning to England aboard the 74-gun HMS Victorious. After recovering, he returned to the Mediterranean in the 74-gun HMS Centaur and once again rescued a shipmate by plunging into the sea after him. He proceeded as a passenger to Bermuda on the 64-gun HMS Atlas and then to Halifax, Nova Scotia on the schooner HMS Chubb, where he joined the 32-gun frigate HMS Aeolus on April 27, 1811.

CONTENTS

Chapter One

Gentle reader, I was born upon the water—not upon the salt and angry ocean, but upon the fresh and rapid-flowing river. It was in a floating sort of box, called a lighter, and upon the river Thames, at low water, when I first smelt the mud. This lighter was manned (an expression amounting to bullism, if not construed *kind*-ly) by my father, my mother, and your humble servant. My father had the sole charge—he was monarch of the deck: my mother, of course, was queen, and I was the heir-apparent.

Before I say one word about myself, allow me dutifully to describe my parents. First, then, I will portray my queen mother. Report says, that when she first came on board of the lighter, a lighter figure and a lighter step never pressed a plank; but as far as I can tax my recollection, she was always a fat, unwieldy woman. Locomotion was not to her taste—gin was. She seldom quitted the cabin—never quitted the lighter: a pair of shoes may have lasted her for five years for the wear and tear she took out of them. Being of this domestic habit, as all married women ought to be, she was always to be found when wanted; but although always at hand, she was not always on her feet. Towards the close of the day, she lay down upon her bed—a wise precaution when a person can no longer stand. The fact was, that my honoured mother, although her virtue was unimpeachable, was frequently seduced by liquor; and although constant to my father, was debauched and to be found in bed with that insidious assailer of female uprightness—*gin*. The lighter, which might have been compared to another garden of Eden, of which my mother was the Eve, and my father the Adam to consort with, was entered by this serpent who tempted her; and if she did not eat, she drank, which was even worse. At first, indeed—and I may mention it to prove how the enemy always gains admittance under a specious form—she drank it only to keep the cold out of her stomach, which the humid atmosphere from the surrounding water appeared to warrant. My father took his pipe for the same reason; but, at the time that I was born, he smoked and she drank from morning to night, because habit had rendered it almost necessary to their existence. The pipe was always to his lip, the glass incessantly to hers. I would have defied any cold ever to have penetrated into their stomachs;—but I have said enough of my mother for the present; I will now pass on to my father.

My father was a puffy, round-bellied, long-armed, little man, admirably calculated for his station in, or rather out of, society. He could manage a lighter as well as anybody; but he could do no more. He had been brought up to it from his infancy. He went on shore for my mother, and came on board again—the only remarkable event in his life. His whole amusement was his pipe; and, as there is a certain indefinable link between smoking and philosophy, my father, by dint of smoking, had become a perfect philosopher. It is no less strange than true, that we can puff away our cares with tobacco, when, without it, they remain a burden to existence. There is no composing draught like the draught through the tube of a pipe. The savage warriors of North America enjoyed the blessing before we did; and to the pipe is to be ascribed the wisdom of their councils and the laconic delivery of their sentiments. It would be well introduced into our own legislative assembly. Ladies, indeed, would no longer peep down through the ventilator; but we should have more sense and fewer words. It is also to tobacco that is to be ascribed the stoical firmness of those American warriors, who, satisfied with the pipes in their mouths, submitted with perfect indifference to the torture of their enemies. From the well-known virtues of this weed arose that peculiar expression when you irritate another, that you "put his pipe out."

My father's pipe, literally and metaphorically, was never put out. He had a few apophthegms which brought every disaster to a happy conclusion; and as he seldom or never indulged in words, these sayings were deeply impressed upon my infant memory. One was, "*It's no use crying; what's done can't be helped.*" When once these words escaped his lips, the subject was never renewed. Nothing appeared to move him: the abjurations of those employed in the other lighters, barges, vessels, and boats of every description, who were contending with us for the extra foot of water, as we drifted up or down with the tide, affected him not, further than an extra column or two of smoke rising from the bowl of his pipe. To my mother he used but one expression, "*Take it coolly;*" but it always had the contrary effect with my mother, as it put her more in a passion. It was like pouring oil upon flame; nevertheless, the advice was good, had it ever been followed. Another favourite expression of my father's when anything went wrong, and which was of the same pattern as the rest of his philosophy, was, "*Better luck next time.*" These aphorisms were deeply impressed upon my memory; I continually recalled them to mind, and thus I became a philosopher long before my wise teeth were in embryo, or I had even shed the first set with which kind Nature presents us, that in the petticoat age we may fearlessly indulge in lollipop.

My father's education had been neglected. He could neither write nor read; but although he did not exactly, like Cadmus, invent letters, he had accustomed himself to certain hieroglyphics, generally speaking sufficient for his purposes, and which might be considered as an artificial memory. "I can't write nor read, Jacob," he would say; "I wish I could; but look, boy, I means this mark for three quarters of a bushel. Mind you recollects it when I axes you, or I'll be blowed if I don't wallop you." But it was only a case of peculiar difficulty which would require a new hieroglyphic, or extract such a long speech from my father. I was well acquainted with his usual scratches and dots, and having a good memory, could put him right when he was puzzled with some misshapen x or z, representing some unknown quantity, like the same letters in algebra.

I have said that I was heir-apparent, but I did not say that I was the only child born to my father in his wedlock. My honoured mother had had two more children; but the first, who was a girl, had been provided for by a fit of the measles; and the second, my elder brother, by stumbling over the stern of the lighter when he was three years old. At the time of the accident my mother had retired to her bed, a little the worse for liquor; my father was on deck forward, leaning against the windlass, soberly smoking his evening pipe. "What was that?" exclaimed my father, taking his pipe out of his mouth, and listening; "I shouldn't wonder if that wasn't Joe." And my father put in his pipe again, and smoked away as before.

My father was correct in his surmises. It *was* Joe who had made the splash which roused him from his meditations, for the next morning Joe was nowhere to be found. He was, however, found some days afterwards; but, as the newspapers say, and as may well be imagined, the vital spark was extinct; and, moreover, the eels and chubs had eaten off his nose and a portion of his chubby face, so that, as my father said, "he was of no use to nobody." The morning after the accident my father was up early, and had missed poor little Joe. He went into the cabin, smoked his pipe, and said nothing. As my brother did not appear as usual for his breakfast, my mother called out for him in a harsh voice; but Joe was out of hearing, and as mute as a fish. Joe opened not his mouth in reply, neither did my father. My mother then quitted the cabin, and walked round the lighter, looked into the dog-kennel to ascertain if he was asleep with the great mastiff—but Joe was nowhere to be found.

"Why, what can have become of Joe?" cried my mother, with maternal alarm in her countenance, appealing to my father, as she hastened back to the cabin. My father spoke not, but taking the pipe out of his mouth, dropped the bowl of it in a perpendicular direction till it landed softly on the deck, then put it into his mouth again, and puffed mournfully. "Why, you don't mean to say he is overboard?" screamed my mother.

My father nodded his head, and puffed away at an accumulated rate. A torrent of tears, exclamations, and revilings succeeded to this characteristic announcement. My father allowed my mother to exhaust herself. By the time when she had finished, so was his pipe; he then knocked out the ashes, and quietly observed, "It's no use crying; what's done can't be helped," and proceeded to refill the bowl.

"Can't be helped!" cried my mother; "but it might have been helped."

"Take it coolly," replied my father.

"Take it coolly!" replied my mother in a rage—"take it coolly! Yes, you're for taking everything coolly: I presume, if I fell overboard you would be taking it coolly."

"You would be taking it coolly, at all events," replied my imperturbable father.

"O dear! O dear!" cried my poor mother; "two poor children, and lost them both!"

"Better luck next time," rejoined my father; "so, Sall, say no more about it."

My father continued for some time to smoke his pipe, and my mother to pipe her eye, until at last my father, who was really a kind-hearted man, rose from the chest upon which he was seated, went to the cupboard, poured out a teacupful of *gin*, and handed it to my mother. It was kindly done of him, and my mother was to be won by kindness. It was a pure offering in the spirit, and taken in the spirit in which it was offered. After a few repetitions, which were rendered necessary from its potency being diluted with her tears, grief and recollection were drowned together, and disappeared like two lovers who sink down entwined in each other's arms.

With this beautiful metaphor, I shall wind up the episode of my unfortunate brother Joe.

It was about a year after the loss of my brother that I was ushered into the world, without any other assistants or spectators than my father and Dame Nature, who I believe to be a very clever midwife if not interfered with. My father, who had some faint ideas of Christianity, performed the baptismal rites by crossing me on the forehead with the end of his pipe, and calling me Jacob: as for my mother being churched, she had never been but once to church in her life. In fact, my father and mother never quitted the lighter, unless when the former was called out by the superintendent or proprietor, at the delivery or shipment of a cargo, or was once a month for a few minutes on shore to purchase necessaries. I cannot recall much of my infancy; but I recollect that the lighter was often very brilliant with blue and red paint, and that my mother used to point it out to me as "so pretty," to keep me quiet. I shall therefore pass it over, and commence at the age of five years, at which early period I was of some little use to my father. Indeed I was almost as forward as some boys at ten. This may appear strange; but the fact is, that my ideas although bounded, were concentrated. The lighter, its equipments, and its destination were the microcosm of my infant imagination; and my ideas and thoughts being directed to so few objects, these objects were deeply impressed, and their value fully understood. Up to the time that I quitted the lighter, at eleven years old, the banks of the river were the boundaries of my speculations. I certainly comprehended something of the nature of trees and houses; but I do not think that I was aware that the former *grew*. From the time that I could recollect them on the banks of the river, they appeared to be exactly of the same size as they were when first I saw them, and I asked no questions. But by the time that I was ten years old, I knew the name of the reach of the river, and every point — the depth of water, and the shallows, the drift of the current, and the ebb and flow of the tide itself. I was able to manage the lighter as it floated down with the tide; for what I lacked in strength I made up with dexterity arising from constant practice.

It was at the age of eleven years that a catastrophe took place which changed my prospects in life, and I must, therefore, say a little more about my father and mother, bringing up their history to that period. The propensity of my mother to ardent spirits had, as always is the case, greatly increased upon her, and her corpulence had increased in the same ratio. She was now a most unwieldy, bloated mountain of flesh, such a form as I have never since beheld, although, at the time, she did not appear to me to be disgusting, accustomed to witness imperceptibly her increase, and not seeing any other females, except at a distance. For the last two years she had seldom quitted her bed — certainly she did not crawl out of the cabin more than five minutes during the week — indeed, her obesity and habitual intoxication rendered her incapable. My father went on shore for a quarter of an hour once a month, to purchase gin, tobacco, red herrings, and decayed ship-biscuits; — the latter was my principal fare, except when I could catch a fish over the sides, as we lay at anchor. I was, therefore, a great water-drinker, not altogether from choice, but from the salt nature of my food, and because my mother had still sense enough left to discern that "Gin wasn't good for little boys." But a great change had taken place in my father.

I was now left almost altogether in charge of the deck, my father seldom coming up except to assist me in shooting the bridges, or when it required more than my exertions to steer clear of the crowds of vessels which we encountered when between them. In fact, as I grew more capable, my father became more incapable, and passed most of his time in the cabin, assisting my mother in emptying the great stone bottle. The woman had prevailed upon the man, and now both were guilty in partaking of the forbidden fruit of the Juniper Tree. Such was the state of affairs in our little kingdom when the catastrophe occurred which I am now about to relate.

One fine summer's evening we were floating up with the tide, deeply laden with coals, to be delivered at the proprietor's wharf, some distance above Putney Bridge; a strong breeze sprang up and checked our progress, and we could not, as we expected, gain the wharf that night. We were about a mile and a half above the bridge when the tide turned against us, and we dropped our anchor. My father who, expecting to arrive that evening, had very unwillingly remained sober, waiting until the lighter had swung to the stream, and then saying to me, "Remember, Jacob, we must be at the wharf early tomorrow morning, so keep alive," went into the cabin to indulge in his potations, leaving me in possession of the deck, and also of my supper, which I never ate below, the little cabin being so unpleasantly close. Indeed, I took all my meals *al fresco*, and, unless the nights were intensely cold, slept on deck, in the capacious dog-kennel abaft, which had once been tenanted by the large mastiff; but he had been dead some years, was thrown overboard, and, in all probability, had been converted into savoury sausages at 1 shilling per pound weight. Some time after his decease, I had taken possession of his apartment and had performed his duty. I had finished my supper, which was washed down with a considerable portion of Thames water, for I always drank more when above the bridges, having an idea that it tasted more pure and fresh. I had walked forward and looked at the cable to see if all was right, and then, having nothing more to do, I lay down on the deck, and indulged in the profound speculations of a boy of eleven years old. I was watching the stars above me, which twinkled faintly, and appeared to me ever and anon to be extinguished and then relighted. I was wondering what they could be made of, and how they came there, when of a sudden I was interrupted in my reveries by a loud shriek, and perceived a strong smell of something burning. The shrieks were renewed again and again, and I had hardly time to get upon my legs when my father burst up from the cabin, rushed over the side of the lighter, and disappeared under the water. I caught a glimpse of his features as he passed me, and observed fright and intoxication blended together. I ran to the side where he had disappeared, but could see nothing but a few eddying circles as the tide rushed quickly past. For a few seconds I remained staggered and stupefied at his sudden disappearance and evident death, but I was recalled to recollection by the smoke which encompassed me, and the shrieks of my mother, which were now fainter and fainter, and I hastened to her assistance.

A strong, empyreumatic, thick smoke ascended from the hatchway of the cabin, and, as it had now fallen calm, it mounted straight up the air in a dense column. I attempted to go in, but so soon as I encountered the smoke I found that it was impossible; it would have suffocated me in half a minute. I did what most children would have done in such a situation of excitement and distress—I sat down and cried bitterly. In about ten minutes I moved my hands, with which I had covered up my face, and looked at the cabin hatch. The smoke had disappeared, and all was silent. I went to the hatchway, and although the smell was still overpowering, I found that I could bear it. I descended the little ladder of three steps, and called "Mother!" but there was no answer. The lamp fixed against the after bulk-head, with a glass before it, was still alight, and I could see plainly to every corner of the cabin. Nothing was burning—not even the curtains to my mother's bed appeared to be singed. I was astonished—breathless with fear, with a trembling voice, I again called out "Mother!" I remained more than a minute panting for breath, and then ventured to draw back the curtains of the bed—my mother was not there! but there appeared to be a black mass in the centre of the bed. I put my hand fearfully upon it—it was a sort of unctuous, pitchy cinder. I screamed with horror—my little senses reeled—I staggered from the cabin and fell down on the deck in a state amounting almost to insanity: it was followed by a sort of stupor, which lasted for many hours.

As the reader may be in some doubt as to the occasion of my mother's death, I must inform him that she perished in that very peculiar and dreadful manner, which does sometimes, although rarely, occur, to those who indulge in an immoderate use of spirituous liquors. Cases of this kind do, indeed, present themselves but once in a century, but the occurrence of them is too well authenticated. She perished from what is termed *spontaneous combustion*, an inflammation of the gases generated from the spirits absorbed into the system. It is to be presumed that the flames issuing from my mother's body completely frightened out of his senses my father, who had been drinking freely; and thus did I lose both my parents, one by fire and the other by water, at one and the same time.

Chapter Two

It was broad daylight when I awoke from my state of bodily and mental imbecility. For some time I could not recall to my mind all that had happened: the weight which pressed upon my feelings told me that it was something dreadful. At length, the cabin hatch, still open, caught my eye; I recalled all the horrors of the preceding evening, and recollected that I was left alone in the lighter. I got up and stood on my feet in mute despair. I looked around me—the mist of the morning was hanging over the river, and the objects on shore were with difficulty to be distinguished. I was chilled from lying all night in the heavy dew, and, perhaps, still more from previous and extraordinary excitement. Venture to go down into the cabin I dare not. I had an indescribable awe, a degree of horror at what I had seen, that made it impossible; still I was unsatisfied, and would have given worlds, if I had had them, to explain the mystery. I turned my eyes from the cabin hatch to the water, thought of my father, and then, for more than half an hour, watched the tide as it ran up—my mind in a state of vacancy. As the sun rose, the mist gradually cleared away; trees, houses, and green fields, other barges coming up with the tide, boats passing and repassing, the barking of dogs, the smoke issuing from the various chimneys, all broke upon me by degrees; and I was recalled to the sense that I was in a busy world, and had my own task to perform. The last words of my father—and his injunctions had ever been a law to me—were, "Mind, Jacob, we must be up at the wharf early to-morrow morning." I prepared to obey him. Purchase the anchor I could not; I therefore slipped the cable, lashing a broken sweep to the end of it, as a buoy-rope, and once more the lighter was at the mercy of the stream, guided by a boy of eleven years old. In about two hours I was within a hundred yards of the wharf, and well in-shore, I hailed for assistance, and two men, who were on board of the lighters moored at the wharf, pushed off in a skiff to know what it was that I wanted. I told them that I was alone in the lighter, without anchor or cable, and requested them to secure her. They came on board, and in a few minutes the lighter was safe alongside of the others. As soon as the lashings were passed, they interrogated me as to what had happened, but although the fulfilling of my father's last injunctions had borne up my spirits, now that they were obeyed a reaction took place. I could not answer them; I threw myself down on the deck in a paroxysm of grief, and cried as if my heart would break.

The men, who were astonished, not only at my conduct but at finding me alone in the lighter, went on shore to the clerk, and stated the circumstances. He returned with them, and would have interrogated me, but my paroxysm was not yet over, and my replies, broken my sobs, were unintelligible. The clerk and the two men went down into the cabin, returned hastily, and quitted the lighter. In about a quarter of an hour I was sent for, and conducted to the house of the proprietor—the first time in my life that I had ever put my foot on *terra firma*. I was led into the parlour, where I found the proprietor at breakfast with his wife and his daughter, a little girl nine years old. By this time I had recovered myself, and on being interrogated, told my story clearly and succinctly, while the big tears coursed each other down my dirty face.

"How strange and how horrible!" said the lady to her husband; "I cannot understand it even now."

"Nor can I; but still it is true, from what Johnson the clerk has witnessed."

In the meantime my eyes were directed to every part of the room, which appeared to my ignorance as a Golcondo of wealth and luxury. There were few things which I had seen before, but I had an innate idea that they were of value. The silver tea-pot, the hissing urn, the spoons, the pictures in their frames, every article of furniture caught my wondering eye, and for a short time I had forgotten my father and my mother; but I was recalled from my musing speculations by the proprietor inquiring how far I had brought the lighter without assistance.

"Have you any friends, my poor boy?" inquired the lady.

"No."

"What! no relations onshore?"

"I never was on shore before in my life."

"Do you know that you are a destitute orphan?"

"What's that?"

"That you have no father or mother," said the little girl.

"Well," replied I, in my father's words, having no answer more appropriate, "it's no use crying; what's done can't be helped."

"But what do you intend to do now?" inquired the proprietor, looking hard at me after my previous answer.

"Don't know, I'm sure. Take, it coolly," replied I, whimpering.

"What a very odd child!" observed the lady. "Is he aware of the extent of his misfortune?"

"Better luck next time, missus," repled I, wiping my eyes with the back of my hand.

"What strange answers from a child who has shown so much feeling," observed the proprietor to his wife. "What is your name."

"Jacob Faithful."

"Can you write or read?"

"No," replied I, again using my father's words: "No, I can't—I wish I could."

"Very well, my poor boy, we'll see what's to be done," said the proprietor.

"I know what's to be done," rejoined I; "you must send a couple of hands to get the anchor and cable, afore they cut the buoy adrift."

"You are right, my lad, that must be done immediately," said the proprietor; "but now you had better go down with Sarah into the kitchen; cook will take care of you. Sarah, my love, take him down to cook."

The little girl beckoned me to follow her. I was astonished at the length and variety of the *companion-ladders*, for such I considered the stairs, and was at last landed below, when little Sarah, giving cook the injunction to take care of me, again tripped lightly up to her mother.

I found the signification of "take care of any one" very different on shore from what it was on the river, where taking care of you means getting out of your way, and giving you a wide berth; and I found the shore reading much more agreeable. Cook did take care of me; she was a kind-hearted, fat woman who melted at a tale of woe, although the fire made no impression on her. I not only beheld, but I devoured, such things as never before entered into my mouth or my imagination. Grief had not taken away my appetite. I stopped occasionally to cry a little, wiped my eyes, and sat down again. It was more than two hours before I laid down my knife, and not until strong symptoms of suffocation played round the regions of my trachea did I cry out, "Hold, enough." Somebody has made an epigram about the vast ideas which a miser's horse must have had of corn. I doubt, if such ideas were existent, whether they were at all equal to my astonishment at a leg of mutton. I never had seen such a piece of meat before, and wondered if it were fresh or otherwise. After such reflection I naturally felt inclined to sleep; in a few minutes I was snoring upon two chairs, cook having covered me up with her apron to keep away the flies. Thus was I fairly embarked upon a new element to me—my mother earth; and it may be just as well to examine now into the capital I possessed for my novel enterprise. In person

I was well-looking; I was well-made, strong, and active. Of my habiliments the less said the better; I had a pair of trousers with no seat to them; but this defect, when I stood up, was hid by my jacket, composed of an old waistcoat of my father's, which reached down as low as the morning frocks worn in those days. A shirt of coarse duck, and a fur cap, which was as rough and ragged as if it had been the hide of a cat pulled to pieces by dogs, completed my attire. Shoes and stockings I had none; these supernumerary appendages had never confined the action of my feet. My mental acquisitions were not much more valuable; they consisted of a tolerable knowledge of the depth of water, names of points and reaches in the River Thames, all of which was not very available on dry land—of a few hieroglyphics of my father's, which, as the crier says sometimes, winding up his oration, were of "no use to nobody but the owner." Add to the above the three favourite maxims of my taciturn father, which were indelibly imprinted upon my memory, and you have the whole inventory of my stock-in-trade. These three maxims were, I may say, incorporated into my very system, so continually had they been quoted to me during my life; and before I went to sleep that night they were again conned over. "What's done can't be helped," consoled me for the mishaps of my life; "Better luck next time," made me look forward with hope and, "Take it coolly," was a subject of great reflection, until I feel into a deep sleep; for I had sufficient penetration to observe that my father had lost his life by not adhering to his own principles; and this perception only rendered my belief in the infallibility of these maxims to be even still more steadfast.

I have stated what was my father's legacy, and the reader will suppose that from the maternal side the acquisition was *nil*. Directly such was the case, but indirectly she proved a very good mother to me, and that was by the very extraordinary way in which she had quitted the world. Had she met with a common death, she would have been worth nothing. Burke himself would not have been able to dispose of her; but dying as she did, her ashes were the source of wealth. The bed, with her remains lying in the centre, even the curtains of the bed, were all brought on shore, and locked up in an outhouse. The coroner came down in a post-chaise and four, charged to the country; the jury was empanelled, my evidence was taken, surgeons and apothecaries attended from far and near to give their opinions, and after much examination, much arguing, and much disagreement, the verdict was brought in that she died through "the visitation of God." As this, in other phraseology, implies that "God only knows how she died," it was agreed to *nemine contradicente*, and gave universal satisfaction. But the extraordinary circumstance was spread everywhere, with all due amplifications, and thousands flocked to the wharfinger's yard to witness the effects of spontaneous combustion. The proprietor immediately perceived that he could avail himself of the public curiosity to my advantage. A plate, with some silver and gold, was placed at the foot of my poor mother's flock mattress, with, "For the benefit of the orphan," in capital text, placarded above it; and many were the shillings, half-crowns, and even larger sums which were dropped into it by the spectators, who shuddered as they turned away from this awful specimen of the effects of habitual intoxication. For many days did the exhibition continue, during which time I was domiciled with the cook, who employed me in scouring her saucepans, and any other employment in which my slender services might be useful, little thinking at the time that my poor mother was holding her levée for my advantage. On the eleventh day the exhibition was closed, and I was summoned upstairs by the proprietor, whom I found in company with a little gentleman in black. This was a surgeon who had offered a sum of money for my mother's remains, bed and curtains, in a lot. The proprietor was willing to get rid of them in so advantageous a manner, but did not conceive that he was justified in taking this step, although for my benefit, without first consulting me, as heir-at-law.

"Jacob," said he, "this gentleman offers 20 pounds, which is a great deal of money, for the ashes of your poor mother. Have you any objection to let him have them?"

"What do you want 'em for?" inquired I.

"I wish to keep them, and take great care of them," answered he.

"Well," replied I, after a little consideration, "if you'll take care of the old woman, you may have her," — and the bargain was concluded. Singular that the first bargain I ever made in my life should be that of selling my own mother. The proceeds of the exhibition and sale amounted to 47 pounds odd, which the worthy proprietor of the lighter, after deducting for a suit of clothes, laid up for my use. Thus ends the history of my mother's remains, which proved more valuable to me than ever she did when living. In her career she somewhat reversed the case of Semele, who was first visited in a shower of gold, and eventually perished in the fiery embraces of the god: whereas my poor mother perished first by the same element, and the shower of gold descended to her only son. But this is easily explained. Semele was very lovely and did not drink gin — my mother was her complete antithesis.

When I was summoned to my master's presence to arrange the contract with the surgeon, I had taken off the waistcoat which I wore as a garment over all, that I might be more at my ease in chopping some wood for the cook, and the servant led me up at once, without giving me time to put it on. After I had given my consent, I turned away to go downstairs again, when having, as I before observed, no seat to my trousers, the solution of continuity was observed by a little spaniel, who jumped from the sofa, and arriving at a certain distance, stood at bay, and barked most furiously at the exposure. He had been bred among respectable people, and had never seen such an exposé. Mr Drummond, the proprietor, observed the defect pointed out by the dog, and forthwith I was ordered to be suited with a new suit— certainly not before they were required. In twenty-four hours I was thrust into a new garment by a bandy-legged tailor, assisted by my friend the cook, and turn or twist whichever way I pleased, decency was never violated. A new suit of clothes is generally an object of ambition, and flatters the vanity of young and old; but with me it was far otherwise. Encumbered with my novel apparel, I experienced at once feelings of restraint and sorrow. My shoes hurt me, my worsted stockings irritated the skin, and as I had been accustomed to hereditarily succeed to my father's cast-off skins, which were a world too wide for my shanks, having but few ideas, it appeared to me as if I had swelled out to the size of the clothes which I had been accustomed to wear, not that they had been reduced to my dimensions. I fancied myself a man, but was very much embarrassed with my manhood. Every step that I took I felt as if I was checked back by strings. I could not swing my arms as I was wont to do, and tottered in my shoes like a rickety child. My old apparel had been consigned to the dust-hole by cook, and often during the day would I pass, casting a longing eye at it, wishing that I dare recover it, and exchange it for that which I wore. I knew the value of it, and, like the magician in Aladdin's tale, would have offered new lamps for old ones, cheerfully submitting to ridicule, that I might have repossessed my treasure.

With the kitchen and its apparatus I was now quite at home: but at every other part of the house and furniture I was completely puzzled. Everything appeared to me foreign, strange, and unnatural, and Prince Le Boo, or any other savage, never stared or wondered more than I did. Of most things I knew not the use, of many not even the names. I was literally a savage, but still a kind and docile one. The day after my new clothes had been put on, I was summoned into the parlour. Mr Drummond and his wife surveyed me in my altered habiliments, and amused themselves at my awkwardness, at the same time that they admired my well-knit, compact, and straight figure, set off by a fit, in my opinion much too straight. Their little daughter Sarah, who often spoke to me, went up and whispered to her mother. "You must ask papa," was the reply. Another whisper, and a kiss, and Mr Drummond told me I should dine with them. In a few minutes I followed them into the dining-room and for the first time I was seated to a repast which could boast of some of the supernumerary comforts of civilised life. There I sat, perched on a chair with my feet swinging close to the carpet, glowing with heat from the compression of my clothes and the novelty of my situation, and all that was around me. Mr Drummond helped me to some scalding soup, a silver spoon was put into my hand, which I twisted round and round, looking at my face reflected in miniature on its polish.

"Now, Jacob, you must eat the soup with the spoon," said little Sarah, laughing; "we shall all be done. Be quick."

"Take it coolly," replied I, digging my spoon into the burning preparation, and tossing it into my mouth. It burst forth from my tortured throat in a diverging shower, accompanied with a howl of pain.

"The poor boy has scalded his mouth," cried the lady, pouring out a tumbler of water.

"It's no use crying," replied I, blubbering with all my might; "what's done can't be helped."

"Better that you had not been helped," observed Mr Drummond, wiping off his share of my liberal spargification from his coat and waistcoat.

"The poor boy has been shamefully neglected," observed the good-natured Mrs Drummond. "Come, Jacob, sit down and try it again; it will not burn you now."

"Better luck next time," said I, shoving in a portion of it, with a great deal of tremulous hesitation, and spilling one-half of it in its transit. It was now cool, but I did not get on very fast; I held my spoon awry, and soiled my clothes.

Mrs Drummond interfered, and kindly showed me how to proceed; when Mr Drummond said, "Let the boy eat it after his own fashion, my dear—only be quick, Jacob, for we are waiting."

"Then I see no good losing so much of it, taking it in tale," observed I, "when I can ship it all in bulk in a minute." I laid down my spoon, and stooping my head, applied my mouth to the edge of the plate, and sucked the remainder down my throat without spilling a drop. I looked up for approbation, and was very much astonished to hear Mrs Drummond quietly observe, "That is not the way to eat soup."

I made so many blunders during the meal that little Sarah was in a continued roar of laughter; and I felt so miserable, that I heartily wished myself again in my dog-kennel on board of the lighter, gnawing biscuit in all the happiness of content and dignity of simplicity. For the first time I felt the pangs of humiliation. Ignorance is not always debasing. On board of the lighter, I was sufficient for myself, my company, and my duties. I felt an elasticity of mind, a respect for myself, and a consciousness of power, as the immense mass was guided through the waters by my single arm. There, without being able to analyse my feelings, I was a spirit guiding a little world; and now, at this table, and in company with rational and well-informed beings, I felt humiliated and degraded; my heart was overflowing with shame, and at one unusual loud laugh of the little Sarah, the heaped up measure of my anguish overflowed, and I burst into a passion of tears. As I lay with my head upon the table-cloth, regardless of those decencies I had so much feared, and awake only to a deep sense of wounded pride, each sob coming from the very core of my heart, I felt a soft breathing warm upon my cheek, that caused me to look up timidly, and I beheld the glowing and beautiful face of little Sarah, her eyes filled with tears, looking so softly and beseechingly at me, that I felt at once I was of some value, and panted to be of more.

"I won't laugh at you any more," said she; "so don't cry, Jacob."

"No more I will," replied I, cheering up. She remained standing by me, and I felt grateful. "The first time I get a piece of wood," whispered I, "I'll cut you out a barge."

"That boy has a heart," said Mr Drummond to his wife.

"But will it swim, Jacob?" inquired the little girl.

"Yes, and if it's *lopsided*, call me a lubber."

"What's lopsided, and what's a lubber?" replied Sarah.

"Why, don't you know?" cried I; and I felt my confidence return when I found that in this little instance I knew more than she did.

Chapter Three

Before I quitted the room, Sarah and I were in deep converse at the window, and Mr and Mrs Drummond employed likewise at the table. The result of the conversation between Sarah and me was the intimacy of children; that of Mr and Mrs Drummond, that the sooner I was disposed of, the more it would be for my own advantage. Having some interest with the governors of a charity school near Brentford, Mr Drummond lost no time in procuring me admission; and before I had quite spoiled my new clothes, having worn them nearly three weeks, I was suited afresh in a formal attire—a long coat of pepper and salt, yellow leather breeches tied at the knees, a worsted cap with a tuft on the top of it, stockings and shoes to match, and a large pewter plate upon my breast, marked with Number 63, which, as I was the last entered boy, indicated the sum total of the school. It was with regret that I left the abode of the Drummonds, who did not think it advisable to wait for the completion of the barge, much to the annoyance of Miss Drummond, and before we arrived met them all out walking. I was put into the ranks, received a little good advice from my worthy patron, who then walked away one way, while we walked another, looking like a regiment of yellow-thighed field-fares straightened in human perpendiculars. Behold, then, the last scion of the Faithfuls, peppered, salted, and plated, that all the world might know that he was a charity-boy, and that there was charity in this world. But if heroes, kings, great and grave men, must yield to destiny, lighter-boys cannot be expected to escape; and I was doomed to receive an education, board, lodging, raiment, etcetera, free, gratis, and for nothing.

Every society has it chief; and I was about to observe that every circle has it centre, which certainly would have been true enough, but the comparison is of no use to me, as our circle had two centres, or, to follow up the first idea, had two chiefs—the chief schoolmaster and the chief domestic—the chief masculine and the chief feminine—the chief with the ferula, and the chief with the brimstone and treacle—the master and the matron, each of whom had their appendages—the one in the usher, the other in the assistant housemaid. But of this quartette, the master was not only the most important, but the most worthy of description; and as he will often appear in the pages of my narrative, long after my education was complete, I shall be very particular in my description of Dominie Dobiensis, as he delighted to be called, or Dreary Dobs, as his dutiful scholars delighted to call him. As in our school it was necessary that we should be instructed in reading, writing, and ciphering, the governors had selected the Dominie as the most fitting person that had offered for the employment, because he had, in the first place, written a work that nobody could understand upon the Greek particles; secondly, he had proved himself a great mathematician, having, it is said, squared the circle by algebraical false quantities, but would never show the operation for fear of losing the honour by treachery. He had also discovered as many errors in the demonstrations of Euclid as ever did Joey Hume in army and navy estimates, and with as much benefit to the country at large. He was a man who breathed certainly in the present age, but the half of his life was spent in antiquity or algebra. Once carried away by a problem, or a Greek reminiscence, he passed away, as it were, from his present existence, and everything was unheeded. His body remained, and breathed on his desk, but his soul was absent. This peculiarity was well known to the boys, who used to say, "Dominie is in his dreams, and talks in his sleep."

Dominie Dobiensis left reading and writing to the usher, contrary to the regulations of the school, putting the boys, if possible, into mathematics, Latin, and Greek. The usher was not over competent to teach the two first; the boys not over willing to learn the latter. The master was too clever, the usher too ignorant; hence the scholars profited little. The Dominie was grave and irascible, but he possessed a fund of drollery and the kindest heart. His features could not laugh, but his trachea did. The chuckle rose no higher than the rings of the wind-pipe, and then it was vigorously thrust back again by the impulse of gravity into the region of his heart, and gladdened it with hidden mirth in its dark centre. The Dominie loved a pun; whether it was let off in English, Greek, or Latin. The last two were made by nobody but himself, and not being understood, were, of course, relished by himself alone. But his love of a pun was a serious attachment: he loved it with a solemn affection—with him it was no laughing matter.

In person Dominie Dobiensis was above six feet, all bone and sinews. His face was long and his lineaments large; but his predominant feature was his nose, which, large as were the others, bore them down into insignificance. It was a prodigy—a ridicule; but he consoled himself—Ovid was called Naso. It was not an aquiline nose, nor was it an aquiline nose reversed. It was not a nose snubbed at the extremity, gross, heavy, or carbuncled, or fluting. In all its magnitude of proportions, it was an intellectual nose. It was thin, horny, transparent, and sonorous. Its snuffle was consequential and its sneeze oracular. The very sight of it was impressive; its sound, when blown in school hours, was ominous. But the scholars loved the nose for the warning which it gave: like the rattle of the dreaded snake, which announces its presence, so did the nose indicate to the scholars that they were to be on their guard. The Dominie would attend to this world and its duties for an hour or two, and then forget his scholars and his school-room, while he took a journey into the world of Greek or algebra. Then, when he marked x, y, and z, in his calculations, the boys knew that he was safe, and their studies were neglected.

Reader, did you ever witness the magic effects of a drum in a small village, when the recruiting party, with many-coloured ribbons, rouse it up with a spirit-stirring tattoo? Matrons leave their domestic cares, and run to the cottage door: peeping over their shoulders, the maidens admire and fear. The shuffling clowns raise up their heads gradually, until they stand erect and proud; the slouch in the back is taken out, their heavy walk is changed to a firm yet elastic tread, every muscle appears more braced, every nerve, by degrees, new strung; the blood circulates rapidly: pulses quicken, hearts throb, eyes brighten, and as the martial sound pervades their rustic frames, the Cimons of the plough are converted, as if by magic, into incipient heroes for the field;—and all this is produced by beating the skin of the most gentle, most harmless animal of creation.

Not having at hand the simile synthetical, we have resorted to the antithetical. The blowing of the Dominie's nose produced the very contrary effects. It was a signal that he had returned from his intellectual journal, and was once more in his school-room—that the master had finished with his x, y, z's, and it was time for scholars to mind their p's and q's. At this note of warning, like the minute-roll among the troops, every one fell into his place; half-munched apples were thrust into the first pocket—popguns disappeared—battles were left to be decided elsewhere—books were opened, and eyes directed to them—forms that were fidgeting and twisting in all directions, now took one regimental inclined position over the desk— silence was restored, order resumed her reign, and Mr Knapps, the usher, who always availed himself of these interregnums, as well as the scholars, by deserting to the matron's room, warned by the well-known sound, hastened to the desk of toil; such were the astonishing effects of a blow from Dominie Dobiensis' sonorous and peace-restoring nose.

"Jacob Faithful, draw near," were the first words which struck upon my tympanum the next morning, when I had taken my seat at the further end of the school-room. I rose and threaded my way through two lines of boys, who put out their legs to trip me up in my passage through their ranks; and surmounting all difficulties, found myself within three feet of the master's high desk, or pulpit, from which he looked down upon me like the Olympian Jupiter upon mortals, in ancient time.

"Jacob Faithful, canst thou read?"

"No, I can't," replied I; "I wish I could."

"A well-disposed answer, Jacob; thy wishes shall be gratified. Knowest thou thine alphabet?"

"I don't know what that is."

"Then thou knowest it not. Mr Knapps shall forthwith instruct thee. Thou shall forthwith go to Mr Knapps, who inculcateth the rudiments. *Levior Puer*, lighter-boy, thou hast a *crafty* look." And then I heard a noise in his throat that resembled the "cluck, cluck" when my poor mother poured the gin out of the great stone bottle.

"My little navilculator," continued he, "thou art a weed washed on shore, one of Father Thames' cast-up wrecks. '*Fluviorum rex Eridanus,*' (Chuck, cluck.) To thy studies; be thyself—that is, be Faithful. Mr Knapps, let the Cadmean art proceed forthwith." So saying, Dominie Dobiensis thrust his large hand into his right coat pocket, in which he kept his snuff loose, and taking a large pinch (the major part of which, the stock being low, was composed of hair and cotton abrasions which had collected in the corners of his pocket), he called up the first class, while Mr Knapps called me to my first lesson.

Mr Knapps was a thin, hectic-looking young man, apparently nineteen or twenty years of age, very small in all his proportions, red ferret eyes, and without the least sign of incipient manhood; but he was very savage, nevertheless. Not being permitted to pummel the boys when the Dominie was in the school-room, he played the tyrant most effectually when he was left commanding officer. The noise and hubbub certainly warranted his interference—the respect paid to him was positively *nil*. His practice was to select the most glaring delinquent, and let fly his ruler at him, with immediate orders to bring it back. These orders were complied with for more than one reason; in the first place, was the offender hit, he was glad that another should have his turn; in the second, Mr Knapps being a very bad shot (never having drove a Kamschatdale team of dogs), he generally missed the one he aimed at, and hit some other, who, if he did not exactly deserve it at that moment, certainly did for previous, or would for subsequent, delinquencies. In the latter case, the ruler was brought back to him because there was no injury inflicted, although intended. However, be it as it may, the ruler was always returned to him; and thus did Mr Knapps pelt the boys as if they were cocks on Shrove Tuesday, to the great risk of their heads and limbs. I have little further to say of Mr Knapps, except that he wore a black shalloon loose coat; on the left sleeve of which he wiped his pen, and upon the right, but too often, his ever-snivelling nose.

"What is that, boy?" said Mr Knapps, pointing to the letter A.

I looked attentively, and recognising, as I thought, one of my father's hieroglyphics, replied, "That's half-a-bushel;" and I was certainly warranted in my supposition.

"Half-a-bushel! You're more than half a fool. That's the letter *A*."

"No; it's half-a-bushel; father told me so."

"Then your father was as big a fool as yourself."

"Father knew what half-a-bushel was, and so do I: that's half-a-bushel."

"I tell you it's the letter A," cried Mr Knapps, in a rage.

"It's half-a-bushel," replied I, doggedly. I persisted in my assertion: and Mr Knapps, who dared not punish me while the Dominie was present, descended his throne of one step, and led me up to the master.

"I can do nothing with this boy, sir," said he, red as fire; "he denies the first letter in the alphabet, and insists upon it that the letter A is not A, but half-a-bushel."

"Dost thou, in thine ignorance, pretend to teach when thou comest here to learn, Jacob Faithful?"

"Father always told me that that thing there meant half-a-bushel."

"Thy father might, perhaps, have used that letter to signify the measure which thou speakest of, in the same way as I, in my mathematics, use divers letters for known and unknown quantities; but thou must forget that which thy father taught thee, and commence *de novo*. Dost thou understand?"

"No, I don't."

"Then, little Jacob, that represents the letter A, and whatever else Mr Knapps may tell thee, thou wilt believe. Return, Jacob, and be docile."

Chapter Four

I did not quit Mr Knapps until I had run through the alphabet, and then returned to my place, that I might con it over at my leisure, puzzling myself with the strange complexity of forms of which the alphabet was composed. I felt heated and annoyed by the constraint of my shoes, always an object of aversion from the time I had put them on. I drew my foot out of one, then out of the other, and thought no more of them for some time. In the meanwhile the boys next me had passed them on with their feet to the others, and thus were they shuffled along until they were right up to the master's desk. I missed them, and perceiving that there was mirth at my expense, I narrowly and quietly watched up and down till I perceived one of the head boys of the school, who sat nearest the Dominie, catch up one of my shoes, and the Dominie being then in an absent fit, drop it into his coat-pocket. A short time afterwards he got up, went to Mr Knapps, put a question to him, and while it was being answered, he dropped the other into the pocket of the usher, and tittering to the other boys, returned to his seat. I said nothing; but when the hours of school were over, the Dominie looked at his watch, blew his nose, which made the whole of the boys pop up their heads, like the clansmen of Roderick Dhu, when summoned by his horn, folded up his large pocket-hankerchief slowly and reverently, as if it were a banner, put it into his pocket, and uttered in a solemn tone, "*Tempus est ludendi.*" As this Latin phrase was used every day at the same hour, every boy in the school understood so much Latin. A rush from all the desks ensured, and amidst shouting, yelling, and leaping every soul disappeared except myself, who remained fixed to my form. The Dominie rose from his pulpit and descended, the usher did the same, and both approached me on their way to their respective apartments.

"Jacob Faithful, why still porest thou over thy book—didst thou not understand that the hours of recreation had arrived? Why risest thou not upon thy feet like the others?"

"'Cause I've got no shoes."

"And where are thy shoes, Jacob?"

"One's in your pocket," replied I "and t'other's in his'n."

Each party placed their hands behind, and felt the truth of the assertion.

"Expound, Jacob," said the Dominie, "who hath done this?"

"The big boy with the red hair, and a face picked all over with holes like the strainers in master's kitchen," replied I.

"Mr Knapps, it would be *infra dig* on my part, and also on yours, to suffer this disrespect to pass unnoticed. Ring in the boys."

The boys were rung in, and I was desired to point out the offender, which I immediately did, and who as stoutly denied the offence; but he had abstracted my shoe-strings, and put them into his own shoes. I recognised them and it was sufficient.

"Barnaby Bracegirdle," said the Dominie, "thou art convicted, not only of disrespect towards me and Mr Knapps, but further of the grievous sin of lying. Simon Swapps, let him be hoisted."

He was hoisted: his nether garments descended, and then the birch descend with all the vigour of the Dominie's muscular arm. Barnaby Bracegirdle showed every symptom of his disapproval of the measures taken; but Simon Swapps held fast, and the Dominie flogged fast. After a minute's flagellation, Barnaby was let down, his yellow tights pulled up, and the boys dismissed. Barnaby's face was red, but the antipodes were redder. The Dominie departed, leaving us together,—he adjusting his inexpressibles, I putting in my shoe-strings. By the time Barnaby had buttoned up and wiped his eyes, I had succeeded in standing in my shoes. There we were *tête-à-tête*.

"Now, then," said Barnaby, holding one fist to my face, while, with the other open hand he rubbed behind, "come out in the play-ground, Mr *Cinderella*, and see if I won't drub you within an inch of your life."

"It's no use crying," said I, soothingly: for I had not wished him to be flogged. "What's done can't be helped. Did it hurt you much?"

This intended consolation was taken for sarcasm. Barnaby stormed.

"Take it coolly," observed I.

Barnaby waxed even more wroth.

"Better luck next time," continued I, trying to soothe him.

Barnaby was outrageous—he shook his fist and ran into the play-ground, daring me to follow him. His threats had no weight with me; not wishing to remain indoors, I followed him in a minute or two, when I found him surrounded by the other boys, to whom he was in loud and vehement harangue.

"Cinderella, where's your glass slippers?" cried the boys, as I made my appearance.

"Come out, you water-rat," cried Barnaby, "you son of a cinder!"

"Come out and fight him, or else you're a coward!" exclaimed the whole host, from Number 1 to Number 62, inclusive.

"He has had beating enough already to my mind," replied I; "but he had better not touch me—I can use my arms."

A ring was formed, in the centre of which I found Barnaby and myself. He took off his clothes, and I did the same. He was much older and stronger than I, and knew something about fighting. One boy came forward as my second. Barnaby advanced and held out his hand, which I shook heartily, thinking it was all over: but immediately received a right and left on the face, which sent me reeling backwards. This was a complete mystery, but it raised my bile, and I returned it with interest. I was very strong in my arms, as may be supposed; and I threw them about like sails of a windmill, never hitting straight out, but with semicircular blows, which descended on or about his ears. On the contrary, his blows were all received straightforward, and my nose and face were soon covered with blood. As I warmed with pain and rage I flung out my arms at random, and Barnaby gave me a knock-down blow. I was picked up and sat upon my second's knee, who whispered to me as I spat the blood out of my mouth, "Take it coolly, and make sure when you hit."

My own—my father's maxim—coming from another, it struck with double force, and I never forgot it during the remainder of the fight. Again we were standing up face to face; again I received it right and left, and returned it upon his right and left ears. Barnaby rushed in—I was down again.

"Better luck next time," said I to my second, as cool as a cucumber.

A third and a fourth round succeeded, all apparently in Barnaby's favour, but really in mine. My face was beat to a mummy, but he was what is termed groggy, from the constant return of blows on the side of the head. Again we stood up panting and exhausted. Barnaby rushed at me, and I avoided him: before he could return to the attack I had again planted two severe blows upon his ears, and he reeled. He shook his head, and with his fists in the attitude of defence, asked me whether I had had enough.

"*He* has," said my second; "stick to him now, Jacob, and you'll beat him."

I did stick to him; three or four more blows applied to the same part finished him, and he fell senseless on the ground.

"You've settled him," cried my second.

"What's done can't be helped," replied I. "Is he dead?"

"What's all this?" cried Mr Knapps, pressing his way through the crowd, followed by the matron.

"Barnaby and Cinderella having it out, sir," said one of the elder boys.

The matron, who had already taken a liking for me, because I was good-looking, and because I had been recommended to her care by Mrs Drummond, ran to me.

"Well," says she, "if the Dominie don't punish that big brute for this, I'll see whether I'm anybody or not;" and taking me by the hand, she led me away. In the meantime Mr Knapps surveyed Barnaby, who was still senseless; and desired the other boys to bring him in and lay him on his bed. He breathed hard, but still remained senseless, and a surgeon was sent for, who found it necessary to bleed him copiously. He then, at the request of the matron, came to me; my features were indistinguishable, but elsewhere I was all right. As I stripped he examined my arms.

"It seemed strange," observed he, "that the bigger boy should be so severely punished; but this boy's arms are like little *sledge-hammers*. I recommend you," said he to the other boys, "not to fight with him, for some day or other he'll kill one of you."

This piece of advice was not forgotten by the other boys, and from that day I was the cock of the school. The name of Cinderella, given me by Barnaby, in ridicule of my mother's death, was immediately abandoned, and I suffered no more persecution. It was the custom of the Dominie, whenever two boys fought, to flog them both; but in this instance it was not followed up, because I was not the aggressor, and my adversary narrowly escaped with his life. I was under the matron's care for a week, and Barnaby under the surgeon's hands for about the same time.

Neither was I less successful in my studies. I learnt rapidly, after I had conquered the first rudiments; but I had another difficulty to conquer, which was my habit of construing everything according to my refined ideas; the force of association had become so strong that I could not overcome it for a considerable length of time. Mr Knapps continually complained of my being obstinate, when, in fact, I was anxious to please as well as to learn. For instance, in spelling, the first syllable always produced the association with something connected with my former way of life. I recollect the Dominie once, and only once, gave me a caning, about a fortnight after I went to the school.

I had been brought up by Mr Knapps as contumelious.

"Jacob Faithful, how is this? thine head is good yet wilt thou refuse learning. Tell me now, what does *c-a-t* spell?"

It was the pitch-pipe to *cat-head*, and answered I accordingly.

"Nay, Jacob, it spells *cat*; take care of thy head on the next reply. Understand me, head is not understood. Jacob, thy head is in jeopardy. Now, Jacob, what does *m-a-t* spell?"

"*Chafing-mat*," replied I.

"It spells mat only, silly boy; the chafing will be on my part directly. Now, Jacob, what does *d-o-g* spell?"

"Dog-kennel."

"Dog, Jacob, without the kennel. Thou art very contumelious, and deservest to be rolled in the kennel. Now, Jacob, this is the last time that thou triflest with me; what does *h-a-t* spell?"

"Fur cap," replied I, after some hesitation.

"Jacob, I feel the wrath rising within me, yet would I fain spare thee; if *h-a-t* spell fur-cap, pray advise me, what doth *c-a-p* spell, then?"

"*Capstern.*"

"Indeed, Jacob, thy stern as well as thy head are in danger; and I suppose, then, *w-i-n-d* spells windlass, does it not?"

"Yes, sir," replied I, pleased to find that he agreed with me.

"Upon the same principle, what does *r-a-t* spell?"

"*Rat*, sir," replied I.

"Nay, Jacob, *r-a-t* must spell *rattan*, and as thou hast missed thine own mode of spelling, thou shalt not miss the cane." The Dominie then applied it to my shoulders with considerable unction, much to the delight of Mr Knapps, who thought the punishment was much too small for the offence. But I soon extricated myself from these associations as my ideas extended, and was considered by the Dominie as the cleverest boy in the school. Whether it were from natural intellect, or from my brain having lain fallow, as it were, for so many years, or probably from the two causes combined, I certainly learned almost by instinct. I read my lessons once over and laid my book aside, for I knew it all. I had not been six months at the school before I discovered that, in a thousand instances, the affection of a father appeared towards me under the rough crust of the Dominie. I think it was on the third day of the seventh month that I afforded him a day of triumph and warming of his heart, when he took me for the first time into his little study, and put the Latin Accidence into my hands. I learnt my first lesson in a quarter of an hour; and I remember well how that unsmiling, grave man looked into my smiling eyes, parting the chestnut curls, which the matron would not cut off, from my brows, and saying, "*Bene fecisti, Jacobe.*" Many times afterwards, when the lesson was over, he would fix his eyes upon me, fall back on his chair, and make me recount all I could remember of my former life, which was really nothing but a record of perceptions and feelings. He *could* attend to *me*, and as I related some early and singular impression, some conjecture of what I saw, yet could not comprehend, on the shore which I had never touched, he would rub his hands with enthusiasm, and exclaim, "I have found a new book—an album, whereon I may write the deeds of heroes and the words of sages. *Carissime Jacobe*! how happy shall we be when we get into Virgil!" I hardly need say that I loved him—I did so from my heart, and learned with avidity to please him. I felt that I was of consequence—my confidence in myself was unbounded. I walked proudly, yet I was not vain. My school-fellows hated me, but they feared me as much for my own prowess as my interest with the master; but still many were the bitter gibes and innuendoes which I was obliged to hear as I sat down with them to our meals. At other times I held communion with the Dominie, the worthy old matron, and my books. We walked out every day, at first attended by Mr Knapps the usher. The boys would not walk with me without they were ordered, and if ordered, most unwillingly. Yet I had given no cause of offence. The matron found it out, told the Dominie, and after that the Dominie attended the boys and led me by the hand.

This was of the greatest advantage to me, as he answered all my questions, which were not few, and each day I advanced in every variety of knowledge. Before I had been eighteen months at school, the Dominie was unhappy without my company, and I was equally anxious for his presence. He was a father to me, and I loved him as a son should love a father, and as it will hereafter prove, he was my guide through life.

But although the victory over Barnaby Bracegirdle, and the idea of my prowess procured me an enforced respect, still the Dominie's goodwill towards me was the occasion of a settled hostility. Affront me, or attack me openly, they dare not; but supported as the boys were by Mr Knapps the usher, who was equally jealous of my favour, and equally mean in spirit, they caballed to ruin me, if possible, in the good opinion of my master. Barnaby Bracegirdle had a talent for caricature, which was well-known to all but the Dominie. His first attempt against me was a caricature of my mother's death, in which she was represented as a lamp supplied from a gin-bottle, and giving flame out of her mouth. This was told to me, but I did not see it. It was given by Barnaby to Mr Knapps, who highly commended it, and put it into his desk. After which, Barnaby made an oft-repeated caricature of the Dominie, with a vast nose, which he shewed to the usher as *my* performance. The usher understood what Barnaby was at, and put it into his desk without comment. Several other ludicrous caricatures were made of the Dominie and of the matron, all of which were consigned to Mr Knapps by the boys as being the productions of my pencil; but this was not sufficient—it was necessary I should be more clearly identified. It so happened that one evening, when sitting with the Dominie at my Latin, the matron and Mr Knapps being in the adjoining room, the light, which had burned close down, fell in the socket and went out. The Dominie rose to get another; the matron also got up to fetch away the candlestick with the same intent. They met in the dark, and ran their heads together pretty hard. As this event was only known to Mr Knapps and myself, he communicated it to Barnaby, wondering whether I should not make it a subject of one of my caricatures. Barnaby took the hint; in the course of a few hours this caricature was added to the others. Mr Knapps, to further his views, took an opportunity to mention with encomium my talent for drawing, added that he had seen several of my performances. "The boy hath talent," replied the Dominie; "he is a rich mine, from which much precious metal is to be obtained."

"I hear that thou hast the talent for drawing, Jacob," said he to me, a day or two afterwards.

"I never had in my life, sir," replied I.

"Nay, Jacob; I like modesty but modesty should never lead to a denial of the truth. Remember, Jacob, that thou do not repeat the fault."

I made no answer, as I felt convinced that I was not in fault; but that evening I requested the Dominie to lend me a pencil, as I wished to try and draw. For some days, various scraps of my performances were produced, and received commendation. "The boy draweth well," observed the Dominie to Mr Knapps, as he examined my performance through his spectacles.

"Why should he have denied his being able to draw?" observed the usher.

"It was a fault arising from modesty or want of confidence—even a virtue, carried to excess, may lead us into error."

The next attempt of Barnaby was to obtain the Cornelius Nepos which I then studied. This was effected by Mr Knapps, who took it out of the Dominie's study, and put it into Barnaby's possession, who drew on the fly-leaf, on which was my name, a caricature head of the Dominie; and under my own name, which I had written on the leaf, added, in my hand, *fecit*, so that it appeared, Jacob Faithful *fecit*. Having done this, the leaf was torn out of the book, and consigned to the usher with the rest. The plot was now ripe; and the explosion soon ensued. Mr Knapps told the Dominie that I drew caricatures of my school-fellows. The Dominie taxed me, and I denied it. "So you denied drawing," observed the usher.

A few days passed away, when Mr Knapps informed the Dominie that I had been caricaturing him and Mrs Bately, the matron, and that he had proofs of it. I had then gone to bed; the Dominie was much surprised, and thought it impossible that I could be so ungrateful. Mr Knapps said that should make the charge openly, and prove it the next morning in the school-room; and wound up the wrong by describing me in several points, as a cunning, good-for-nothing, although clever boy.

Chapter Five

Ignorant of what had passed, I slept soundly; and the next morning found the matron very grave with me, which I did not comprehend. The Dominie also took no notice of my morning salute: but supposing him to be wrapt in Euclid at the time, I thought little of it. The breakfast passed over, and the bell rang for school. We were all assembled; the Dominie walked in with a very magisterial air, followed by Mr Knapps, who, instead of parting company when he arrived at his own desk, continued his course with the Dominie to his pulpit. We all knew that there was something in the wind; but of all, perhaps, I was the least alarmed. The Dominie unfolded his large handkerchief, waved it, and blew his nose, and the school was into profound silence. "Jacob Faithful, draw near," said he, in a tone which proved that the affair was serious. I drew near, wondering. "Thou hast been accused by Mr Knapps of caricaturing, and holding up to the ridicule of the school, me—thy master. Upon any other boy such disrespect should be visited severely; but from thee, Jacob, I must add in the words of Caesar, '*Et tu Brute,*' I expected, I had a right to expect, otherwise. *In se animi ingrati crimen vitia omnia condit.* Thou understandest me, Jacob—guilty or not guilty?"

"Not guilty, sir," replied I, firmly.

"He pleadeth net guilty, Mr Knapps; proceed, then, to prove thy charge."

Mr Knapps then went to his desk, and brought out the drawings with which he had been supplied by Barnaby Bracegirdle and the other boys. "These drawings, sir, which you will please to look over, have all been given up to me as the performance of Jacob Faithful. At first I could not believe it to be true; but you will perceive, at once, that they are all by the same hand."

"That I acknowledge," said the Dominie; "and all reflect upon my nose. It is true that my nose is of large dimensions, but it was the will of Heaven that I should be so endowed; yet are the noses of these figures even larger than mine own could warrant, if the limner were correct, and not malicious. Still have they merit," continued the Dominie, looking at some of them; and I heard a gentle *cluck, cluck*, in his throat, as he laughed at his own misrepresentations. "*Artis adumbratae meruit cum sedula laudem,* as Prudentius hath it. I have no time to finish the quotation."

"Here is one drawing, sir," continued Mr Knapps, "which proves to me that Jacob Faithful is the party; in which you and Mrs Bately are shown up to ridicule. Who would have been aware that the candle went out in your study, except Jacob Faithful?"

"I perceive," replied the Dominie, looking at it through his spectacles, when put into his hand, "the arcana of the study have been violated."

"But, sir," continued Mr Knapps, "here is a more convincing proof. You observe this caricature of yourself, with his own name put to it—his own handwriting. I recognised it immediately; and happening to turn over his Cornelius Nepos, observed the first blank leaf torn out. Here it is, sir, and you will observe that it fits on to the remainder of the leaf in the book exactly."

"I perceive that it doth; and am grieved to find that such is the case. Jacob Faithful, thou are convicted of disrespect and of falsehood. Where is Simon Swapps?"

"If you please, sir, may I not defend myself?" replied I. "Am I to be flogged unheard?"

"Nay, that were an injustice," replied the Dominie; "but what defence canst thou offer? *O puer infelix et sceleratus!*"

"May I look at those caricatures, sir?" said I.

The Dominie handed them to me in silence. I looked them all over, and immediately knew them to be drawn by Barnaby Bracegirdle. The last particularly struck me. I had felt confounded and frightened with the strong evidence brought against me; but this re-assured me, and I spoke boldly. "These drawings are by Barnaby Bracegirdle, sir, and not by me. I never drew a caricature in my life."

"So didst thou assert that thou couldst not draw, and afterwards provedst by thy pencil to the contrary, Jacob Faithful."

"I knew not that I was able to draw when I said so; but I wished to draw when you supposed I was able—I did not like that you should give me credit for what I could not do. It was to please you, sir, that I asked for the pencil."

"I wish it were as thou statest, Jacob—I wish from my inmost soul that thou wert not guilty."

"Will you ask Mr Knapps from whom he had these drawings, and at what time? There are a great many of them."

"Answer, Mr Knapps, to the questions of Jacob Faithful."

"They have been given to me by the boys at different times during this last month."

"Well, Mr Knapps, point out the boys who gave them."

Mr Knapps called out eight or ten boys, who came forward. "Did Barnaby Bracegirdle give you none of them, Mr Knapps?" said I, perceiving that Barnaby was not summoned.

"No," replied Mr Knapps.

"If you please, sir," said I to the Dominie, "with respect to the leaf out of my Nepos, the Jacob Faithful was written on it by me on the day that you gave it to me; but the *fecit*, and the caricature of yourself, is not mine. How it came there I don't know."

"Thou hast disproved nothing, Jacob," replied the Dominie.

"But I have proved something, sir. On what day was it that I asked you for the pencil to draw with? Was it not on a Saturday?"

"Last Saturday week, I think it was."

"Well, then, sir, Mr Knapps told you the day before that I could draw?"

"He did; and thou deniedst it."

"How, then, does Mr Knapps account for not producing those caricatures of mine, which he says he has collected for a whole month? Why didn't he give them to you before?"

"Thou puttest it shrewdly," replied the Dominie. "Answer, Mr Knapps, why didst thou, for a fortnight at the least, conceal thy knowledge of his offence?"

"I wished to have more proofs," replied the usher.

"Thou hearest, Jacob Faithful."

"Pray, sir, did you ever hear me speak of my poor mother but with kindness?"

"Never, Jacob, thou hast ever appeared dutiful."

"Please, sir, to call up John Williams."

"John, Number 37, draw near."

"Williams," said I, "did you not tell me that Barnaby Bracegirdle had drawn my mother flaming at the mouth?"

"Yes, I did."

My indignation now found vent in a torrent of tears. "Now, sir," cried I, "if you believe that I drew the caricatures of you and Mrs Bately—did I draw this, which is by the same person?" And I handed up to the Dominie the caricature of my mother, which Mr Knapps had inadvertently produced at the bottom of the rest. Mr Knapps turned white as a sheet.

The Dominie looked at the caricature, and was silent for some time. At last he turned to the usher.

"From whom didst thou obtain this, Mr Knapps?"

Mr Knapps replied in his confusion, "From Barnaby Bracegirdle."

"It was but this moment thou didst state that thou hadst received none from Barnaby Bracegirdle. Thou hast contradicted thyself, Mr Knapps. Jacob did not draw his mother; and the pencil is the same as that which drew the rest—ergo, he did not, I really believe, draw one of them. *Ite procul fraudes*. God, I thank thee, that the innocent have been protected. Narrowly hast thou escaped these toils, O Jacob—*Cum populo et duce fraudulento*. And now for punishment. Barnaby Bracegirdle, thou gavest this caricature to Mr Knapps; from whence hadst thou it? Lie not."

Barnaby turned red and white, and then acknowledged that the drawing was his own.

"You boys," cried the Dominie, waving his rod which he had seized, "you gave these drawings to Mr Knapps; tell me from whom they came."

The boys, frightened at the Dominie's looks, immediately replied in a breath, "From Barnaby Bracegirdle."

"Then, Barnaby Bracegirdle, from whom didst thou receive them?" inquired the Dominie. Barnaby was dumbfounded.

"Tell the truth; didst thou not draw them thyself, since thou didst not receive them from other people?"

Barnaby fell upon his knees, and related the whole circumstances, particularly the way in which the Cornelius Nepos had been obtained through the medium of Mr Knapps. The indignation of the Dominie was now beyond all bounds. I never had seen him so moved before. He appeared to rise at least a foot more in stature, his eyes sparkled, his great nose turned red, his nostrils dilated, and his mouth was more than half open, to give vent to the ponderous breathing from his chest. His whole appearance was withering to the culprits.

"For thee, thou base, degraded, empty-headed, and venomous little abortion of a man, I have no words to signify my contempt. By the governors of this charity I leave thy conduct to be judged; but until they meet, thou shalt not pollute and contaminate the air of this school by thy presence. If thou hast one spark of good feeling in thy petty frame, beg pardon of this poor boy, whom thou wouldst have ruined by thy treachery. If not, hasten to depart, lest in my wrath I apply to the teacher the punishment intended for the scholar, but of which thou art more deserving than even Barnaby Bracegirdle."

Mr Knapps said nothing, hastened out of the school, and that evening quitted his domicile. When the governors met he was expelled with ignominy. "Simon Swapps, hoist up Barnaby Bracegirdle." Most strenuously and most indefatigably was the birch applied to Barnaby, a second time, through me. Barnaby howled and kicked, howled and kicked, and kicked again. At last the Dominie was tired. "*Consonat omne nemus strepitu*" (for *nemus* read schoolroom), exclaimed the Dominie, laying down the rod, and pulling out his handkerchief to wipe his face. "*Calcitrat, ardescunt germani coede bimembres*, that last quotation is happy." (cluck, cluck.) He then blew his nose, addressed the boys in a long oration—paid me a handsome compliment upon my able defence—proved to all those who chose to listen to him that innocence would always confound guilt—intimated to Barnaby that he must leave the school, and then finding himself worn out with exhaustion, gave the boys a holiday, that they might reflect upon what had passed, and which they duly profited by in playing at marbles and peg in the ring. He then dismissed the school, took me by the hand, and led me into his study, where he gave vent to his strong and affectionate feelings towards me, until the matron came to tell us that dinner was ready.

After this everything went on well. The Dominie's kindness and attention were unremitting, and no one ever thought of caballing against me. My progress became most rapid; I had conquered Virgil, taken Tacitus by storm, and was reading the Odes of Horace. I had passed triumphantly through decimals, and was busily employed in mensuration of solids, when one evening I was seized with a giddiness in my head. I complained to the matron; she felt my hands, pronounced me feverish, and ordered me to bed. I passed a restless night the next morning I attempted to rise, but a heavy burning ball rolled as it were in my head, and I fell back on my pillow. The matron came, was alarmed at my state, and sent for the surgeon, who pronounced that I had caught the typhus fever, then raging through the vicinity. This was the first time in my life that I had known a day's sickness—it was a lesson I had yet to learn. The surgeon bled me, and giving directions to the matron, promised to call again. In a few hours I was quite delirious—my senses ran wild. One moment I thought I was with little Sarah Drummond, walking in green fields, holding her by the hand. I turned round, and she was no longer there, but I was in the lighter, and my hand grasped the cinders of my mother; my father stood before me, again jumped overboard and disappeared; again the dark black column ascended from the cabin, and I was prostrate on the deck. Then I was once more alone on the placid and noble Thames, the moon shining bright, and the sweep in my hand, tiding up the reach, and admiring the foliage which hung in dark shadows over the banks. I saw the slopes of green, so pure and so fresh by that sweet light, and in the distance counted the numerous spires of the great monster city, and beheld the various bridges spanning over the water. The faint ripple of the tide was harmony, the reflection of the moon, beauty; I felt happiness in my heart; I was no longer the charity-boy, but the pilot of the barge. Then, as I would survey the scene, there was something that invariably presented itself between my eyes and the object of my scrutiny; whichever way I looked, it stood in my way, and I could not remove it. It was like a cloud, yet transparent, and with a certain undefined shape. I tried for some time, but in vain, to decipher it, but could not. At last it appeared to cohere into a form—it was the Dominie's great nose, magnified into that of the Scripture, "As the tower which looketh towards Damascus." My temples throbbed with agony—I burned all over. I had no exact notions of death in bed, except that of my poor mother, and I thought that I was to die like her; the horrible fear seized me that all this burning was but prefatory to bursting out into flame and consuming into ashes. The dread hung about my young heart and turned that to ice, while the rest of my body was on fire. This was my last recollection, and then all was blank. For many days I lay unconscious of either pain or existence: when I awoke from my stupor, my wandering senses gradually returning, I opened my eyes, and dimly perceived something before me that cut across my vision in a diagonal line. As the mist cleared away, and I recovered myself, I made out that it was the nose of Dominie Dobiensis, who was kneeling at the bed-side, his nose adumbrating the coverlid of my bed, his spectacles dimmed with tears, and his long grey locks falling on each side, and shadowing his eyes. I was not frightened, but I was too weak to stir or speak. His prayer-book was in his hand, and he still remained on his knees. He had been praying for me. Supposing me still insensible, he broke out in the following soliloquy:—

"*Naviculator larvus pallidus*—how beautiful even in death! My poor lighter-boy, that hath mastered the rudiments, and triumphed over the Accidence—but to die! *Levior puer*, a puerile conceit, yet I love it, as I do thee. How my heart bleeds for thee! The icy breath of death hath whitened thee, as the hoar-frost whitens the autumnal rose. Why wert thou transplanted from thine own element? Young prince of the stream—lord of the lighter— '*Ratis rex et magister'*—heir apparent to the tiller—betrothed to the sweep— wedded to the deck—how art thou laid low! Where is the blooming cheek, ruddy with the browning air? where the bright and swimming eye? Alas where? *'Tum breviter dirae mortis aperta via est,'* as sweet Tibullus hath it;" and the Dominie sobbed anew. "Had this stroke fallen upon me, the aged, the ridiculed, the little regarded, the ripe one for the sickle, it would have been well—yet fain would I have instructed thee still more before I quitted the scene—fain have left thee the mantle of learning. Thou knowest, Lord, that I walk wearily, as in the desert, that I am heavily burdened, and that my infirmities are many. Must I then mourn over thee, thou promising one— must I say with the epigrammatist—

> "'Hoc jacet in tumulo, raptus puerilibus annis,
> Jacob Faithful domini cura, doloroque sui?'

"True, most true. Thou hast quitted the element thou so joyously controlledst, thou hast come upon the terra firma for thy grave?

> "'Sis licet inde sibi tellus placata, levisque,
> Artifices levior non potes esse manu.'

"Earth, lay light upon the lighter-boy—the lotus, the water-lily, that hath been cast on shore to die. Hadst thou lived, Jacob, I would have taught thee the Humanities; we would have conferred pleasantly together. I would have poured out my learning to thee, my Absalom, my son!"

He rose and stood over me; the tears coursed down his long nose from both his eyes, and from the point of it poured out like a little rain-gutter upon the coverlid. I understood not all his words, but I understood the spirit of them—it was love. I feebly stretched forth my arms, and articulated "Dominie!"

The old man clasped his hands, looked upwards, and said, "O God, I thank thee—he will live. Hush, hush, my sweet one, thou must not prate;" and he retired on tiptoe, and I heard him mutter triumphantly, as he walked away, "He called me 'Dominie!'"

From that hour I rapidly recovered, and in three weeks was again at my duties. I was now within six months of being fourteen years old, and Mr Drummond, who had occasionally called to ascertain my progress, came to confer with the Dominie upon my future prospects. "All that I can do for him, Mr Dobbs," said my former master, "is to bind him apprentice to serve his time on the River Thames, and that cannot be done until he is fourteen. Will the rules of the school permit his remaining?"

"The regulations do not exactly, but I will," replied the Dominie. "I have asked nothing for my long services, and the governors will not refuse me such a slight favour; should they, I will charge myself with him, that he may not lose his precious time. What sayest thou, Jacob, dost thou feel inclined to return to thy father Thames?"

I replied in the affirmative, for the recollections of my former life were those of independence and activity.

"Thou hast decided well, Jacob—the tailor at his needle, the shoemaker at his last, the serving boy to an exacting mistress, and all those apprenticed to the various trades, have no time for improvement; but afloat there are moments of quiet and peace—the still night for reflection, the watch for meditation; and even the adverse wind or tide leaves moments of leisure which may be employed to advantage. Then wilt thou call to mind the stores of learning which I have laid up in thy garner, and wilt add to them by perseverance and industry. Thou hast yet six months to profit by, and, with the blessing of God, those six months shall not be thrown away."

Mr Drummond having received my consent to be bound apprentice, wished me farewell, and departed. During the six months the Dominie pressed me hard, almost too hard, but I worked for *love*, and to please him I was most diligent. At last the time had flown away, the six months had more than expired, and Mr Drummond made his appearance, with a servant carrying a bundle under his arm. I slipped off my pepper-and-salt, my yellows and badge, dressed myself in a neat blue jacket and trousers, and with many exhortations from the Dominie, and kind wishes from the matron, I bade farewell to them and to the charity-school, and in an hour was once more under the roof of the kind Mrs Drummond.

But how different were my sensations to those which oppressed me when I had before entered. I was no longer a little savage, uneducated and confused in my ideas. On the contrary, I was full of imagination, confident in myself, and in my own powers, cultivated in mind, and proud of my success. The finer feelings of my nature had been called into play. I felt gratitude, humility, and love, at the same time that I was aware of my own capabilities. In person I had much improved, as well as much increased in stature. I walked confident and elastic, joying in the world, hoping, anticipating, and kindly disposed towards my fellow-creatures. I knew, I felt my improvement, my total change of character, and it was with sparkling eyes that I looked up at the window, where I saw Mrs Drummond and little Sarah watching my return and reappearance after an absence of three years.

Mrs Drummond had been prepared by her husband to find a great change; but still she looked for a second or two with wonder as I entered the door, with my hat in my hand, and paid my obeisance. She extended her hand to me, which I took respectfully.

"I should not have known you, Jacob; you have grown quite a man," said she, smiling. Sarah held back, looking at me with pleased astonishment; but I went up to her, and she timidly accepted my hand. I had left her as my superior—I returned, and she soon perceived that I had a legitimate right to the command. It was some time before she would converse, and much longer before she would become intimate; but when she did so, it was no longer the little girl encouraging the untutored boy by kindness, or laughing at his absurdities, but looking up to him with respect and affection, and taking his opinion as a guide for her own. I had gained the *power of knowledge*.

By the regulations of the Waterman's Company, it is necessary that every one who wishes to ply on the river on his own account should serve as an apprentice from the age of fourteen to twenty-one; at all events, he must serve an apprenticeship for seven years, and be fourteen years old before he signs the articles. This apprenticeship may be served in any description of vessel which sails or works on the river, whether it be barge, lighter, fishing smack, or a boat of larger dimensions, and it is not until that apprenticeship is served that he can work on his own account, either in a wherry or any other craft. Mr Drummond offered to article me on board of one of his own lighters free of all expense, leaving me at liberty to change into any other vessel that I might think proper. I gratefully accepted the proposal, went with him to Watermen's Hall, signed the papers, and thus was, at the age of fourteen, "*Bound 'prentice to a Waterman.*"

Chapter Six

"Jacob, this is Marables, who has charge of the Polly barge," said Mr Drummond, who had sent for me into his office, a few days after my arrival at his house. "Marables," continued my protector, addressing the man, "I have told you that this lad is bound 'prentice to the Polly; I expect you will look after him, and treat him kindly. No blows or ill treatment. If he does not conduct himself well (but well I'm sure he will), let me know when you come back from your trip."

During this speech I was scrutinising the outward man of my future controller. He was stout and well-built, inclining to corpulence, his features remarkably good, although his eyes were not large. His mouth was very small, and there was a good-natured smile on his lips as he answered, "I never treated a cat ill, master."

"I believe not," replied Mr Drummond; "but I am anxious that Jacob should do well in the world, and therefore let you know that he will always have my protection, so long as he conducts himself properly."

"We shall be very good friends, sir, I'll answer for it, if I may judge from the cut of his jib," replied Marables, extending to me an immense hand, as broad as it was long.

After this introduction, Mr Drummond gave him some directions, and left us together.

"Come and see the craft, boy," said Marables and I followed him to the barge, which was one of those fitted with a mast which lowered down and hauled up again, as required. She plied up and down the river as far as the Nore, sometimes extending her voyage still farther: but that was only in the summer months. She had a large cabin abaft, and a cuddy forward. The cabin was locked, and I could not examine it.

"This will be your berth," said Marables, pointing to the cuddy-hatch forward; "you will have it all to yourself. The other man and I sleep abaft."

"Have you another man, then?"

"Yes, I have, Jacob," replied he; and then muttering to himself, "I wish I had not—I wish the barge was only between us, Jacob, or that you had not been sent on board," continued he, gravely. "It would have been better—much better." And he walked aft, whistling in a low tone, looking down sadly on the deck.

"Is your cabin large?" inquired I, as he came forward.

"Yes, large enough; but I cannot show it to you now—he has the key."

"What, the other man under you?"

"Yes," replied Marables, hastily. "I've been thinking, Jacob, that you may as well remain on shore till we start. You can be of no use here."

To this I had no objection; but I often went on board during the fortnight that the barge remained, and soon became very partial to Marables. There was a kindness about him that won me, and I was distressed to perceive that he was often very melancholy. What surprised me most was to find that during the first week the cabin was constantly locked, and that Marables had not the key; it appeared so strange that he, as master of the barge, should be locked out of his own cabin by his inferior.

One day I went early on board, and found not only the cabin doors open, but the other man belonging to her walking up and down the deck with Marables. He was a well-looking, tall, active young man, apparently not thirty, with a general boldness of countenance strongly contrasted with a furtive glance of the eye. He had a sort of blue smock-frock over-all, and the trousers which appeared below were of a finer texture than those usually worn by people of his condition.

"This is the lad who is bound to the barge," said Marables. "Jacob, this is Fleming."

"So, younker," said Fleming, after casting an inquiring eye upon me, "you are to sail with us, are you? It's my opinion that your room would be better than your company. However, if you keep your eyes open, I'd advise you to keep your mouth shut. When I don't like people's company, I sometimes give them a hoist into the stream—so keep a sharp look out, my joker."

Not very well pleased with this address, I answered, "I thought Marables had charge of the craft, and that I was to look to him for orders."

"Did you, indeed!" replied Fleming, with a sneer. "I say, my lad, can you swim?"

"No, I can't," replied I—"I wish I could."

"Well, then, take my advice—learn to swim as fast as you can for I have a strong notion that one day or other I shall take you by the scruff of the neck, and send you to look after your father."

"Fleming! Fleming! pray be quiet!" said Marables, who had several times pulled him by the sleeve. "He's only joking, Jacob," continued Marables to me, as, indignant at the mention of my father's death, I was walking away to the shore, over the other lighters.

"Well," replied I, turning round, "if I am to be tossed overboard, it's just as well to let Mr Drummond know, that if I'm missing he may guess what's become of me."

"Pooh! nonsense!" said Fleming, immediately altering his manner, and coming to me where I stood in the barge next to them. "Give us your hand, my boy; I was only trying what stuff you were made of. Come, shake hands; I wasn't in earnest."

I took the proffered hand, and went on shore. "Nevertheless," thought I, "I'll learn to swim; for I rather think he was in earnest." And I took my first lesson that day; and by dint of practice soon acquired that very necessary art. Had it not been for the threat of Fleming, I probably should not have thought of it; but it occurred to me that I might tumble, even if I were not thrown overboard, and that a knowledge of swimming would do no harm.

The day before the barge was to proceed down the river to Sheerness, with a cargo of bricks, I called upon my worthy old master, Dominie Dobiensis.

"*Salve puer!*" cried the old man, who was sitting in his study. "Verily, Jacob, thou art come in good time. I am at leisure, and will give thee a lesson. Sit down, my child."

The Dominie opened the Aeneid of Virgil, and commenced forthwith. I was fortunate enough to please him with my off-hand translation; and as he closed the book, I told him that I had called to bid him farewell, as we started at daylight the next morning.

"Jacob," said he, "thou hast profited well by the lessons which I have bestowed upon thee: now take heed of that advice which I am now about to offer to thee. There are many who will tell thee that thy knowledge is of no use, for what avail can the Latin tongue be to a boy on board of a lighter. Others may think that I have done wrong thus to instruct thee, as thy knowledge may render thee vain—*nil exactius eruditiusque est*—or discontented with thy situation in life. Such is too often the case, I grant; but it is because education is not as general as it ought to be. Were all educated, the superiority acquired or presumed upon by education would be lost, and the nation would not only be wiser but happier. It would judge more rightly, would not condemn the measures of its rulers, which at present it cannot understand, and would not be led away by the clamour and misrepresentation of the disaffected. But I must not digress, as time is short. Jacob, I feel that thou wilt not be spoilt by the knowledge instilled into thee; but mark me, parade it not, for it will be vanity, and make thee enemies. Cultivate thyself as much as thou canst, but in due season—thy duties to thy employer must be first attended to—but treasure up what thou hast, and lay up more when thou canst. Consider it as hidden wealth, which may hereafter be advantageously employed. Thou art now but an apprentice in a barge; but what mayest thou not be, Jacob, if thou art diligent—if thou fear God, and be honest? I will now call to my mind some examples to stimulate thee in thy career."

Here the Dominie brought forward about forty or fifty instances from history, in which people from nothing had risen to the highest rank and consideration; but although I listened to them very attentively, the reader will probably not regret the omission of the Dominie's catalogue. Having concluded, the Dominie gave me a Latin Testament, the Whole Duty of Man, and his blessing. The matron added to them a large slice of seed-cake and by the time that I had returned to Mr Drummond's, both the Dominie's precepts and the matron's considerate addition had been well digested.

It was six o'clock the next morning that we cast off our fastenings and pulled into the stream. The day was lovely, the sun had risen above the trees, which feathered their boughs down on the sloping lawns in front of the many beautiful retreats of the nobility and gentry which border the river; and the lamp of day poured a flood of light upon the smooth and rapidly ebbing river. The heavy dew which had fallen during the night studded the sides of the barge, and glittered like necklaces of diamonds; the mist and the fog had ascended, except here and there, where it partially concealed the landscape; boats laden with the produce of the market-gardens in the vicinity were hastening down with the tide to supply the metropolis; the watermen were in their wherries, cleaning and mopping them out, ready for their fares; the smoke of the chimneys ascended in a straight line to heaven; and the distant chirping of the birds in the trees added to the hilarity and lightness of heart with which I now commenced my career as an apprentice.

I was forward, looking down the river, when Marables called me to take the helm, while they went to breakfast. He commenced giving me instructions; but I cut them short by proving to him that I knew the river as well as he did. Pleased at the information, he joined Fleming, who was preparing the breakfast in the cabin, and I was left on the deck by myself. There, as we glided by every object which for years I had not seen, but which was immediately recognised and welcomed as an old friend, with what rapidity did former scenes connected with them flash into my memory! There was the inn at the water-side, where my father used to replenish the stone bottle; it was just where the barge now was that I had hooked and pulled up the largest chub I had ever caught. Now I arrived at the spot where we had ran foul of another craft; and my father, with his pipe in his mouth and his "Take it coolly," which so exasperated the other parties, stood as alive before me. Here—yes, it was here—exactly here—where we anchored on that fatal night when I was left an orphan—it was here that my father disappeared; and as I looked down at the water, I almost thought I could perceive it again close over him, as it eddied by: and it was here that the black smoke—The whole scene came fresh to my memory, my eyes filled with tears, and, for a little while, I could not see to steer. But I soon recovered myself; the freshness of the air, the bright sky overhead, the busy scene before me, and the necessity of attending to my duty, chased away my painful remembrances; and when I had passed the spot I was again cheerful and content.

In half-an-hour I had shot Putney Bridge, and was sweeping clear of the shallows on the reach below, when Marables and Fleming came up. "How!" exclaimed Marables; "have we passed the bridge? Why did you not call us?"

"I have shot it without help many and many a time," replied I, "when I was but ten years old. Why should I call you from your breakfast? But the tides are high now, and the stream rapid; you had better get a sweep out on the bow, or we may tail on the bank."

"Well!" replied Fleming, with astonishment; "I had no idea that he would have been any help to us; but so much the better." He then spoke in a low tone to Marables.

Marables shook his head. "Don't try it Fleming, it will never do."

"So you said once about yourself," replied Fleming, laughing.

"I did—I did!" replied Marables, clenching both his hands, which at the time were crossed on his breast, with a look of painful emotion; "but I say again, don't try it; nay, I say more, you *shall* not."

"Shall not?" replied Fleming, haughtily.

"Yes," replied Marables, coolly; "I say shall not, and I'll stand by my words. Now, Jacob, give me the helm, and get your breakfast."

I gave up the helm to Marables, and was about to enter the cabin, when Fleming caught me by the arm, and *slewed* me round. "I say, my joker, we may just as well begin as we leave off. Understand me, that into that cabin you never enter; and understand further, that if ever I find you in that cabin, by day or night, I'll break every bone in your body. Your berth is forward; and as for your meals, you may either take them down there or you may eat them on deck."

From what I had already witnessed, I knew that for some reason or other, Fleming had the control over Marables; nevertheless I replied, "If Mr Marables says it is to be so, well and good; but he has charge of this barge." Marables made no reply; he coloured up, seemed very much annoyed, and then looked up to the sky.

"You'll find," continued Fleming, addressing me in a low voice, "that I command here—so be wise. Perhaps the day may come when you may walk in and out the cabin as you please, but that depends upon yourself. By-and-by, when we know more of each other—"

"Never, Fleming, never!" interrupted Marables, in a firm and loud tone. "It *shall* not be."

Fleming muttered what I could not hear, and going into the cabin, brought me out my breakfast which I despatched with good appetite; and soon afterwards I offered to take the helm; which offer was accepted by Marables, who retired to the cabin with Fleming, where I heard them converse for a long while in a low tone.

The tide was about three-quarters ebb when the barge arrived abreast of Millbank. Marables came on deck, and taking the helm, desired me to go forward and see the anchor clear for letting go.

"Anchor clear!" said I. "Why, we have a good hour more before we meet the flood."

"I know that, Jacob, as well as you do; but we shall not go farther to-night. Be smart, and see all clear."

Whether Fleming thought that it was necessary to blind me, or whether it was true that they were only obeying their orders, he said to Marables in my hearing, "Will you go on shore and give the letters to Mr Drummond's correspondent, or shall I go for you?"

"You had better go," replied Marables, carelessly; and shortly after they went to dinner in the cabin, Fleming bringing me mine out on deck.

The flood tide now made, and we rode to the stream. Having nothing to do, and Marables as well as Fleming appearing to avoid me, I brought the Dominie's Latin Testament, and amused myself with reading it. About a quarter of an hour before dusk, Fleming made his appearance to go on shore. He was genteelly, I may say fashionably, dressed in a suit of black, with a white neckcloth. At first I did not recognise him, so surprised was I at his alteration; and my thoughts, as soon as my surprise was over, naturally turned upon the singularity of a man who worked in a barge under another now assuming the dress and appearance of a gentleman. Marables hauled up the little skiff which lay astern. Fleming jumped in and shoved off. I watched him till I perceived him land at the stairs, and then turned round to Marables: "I can't understand all this," observed I.

"I don't suppose you can," replied Marables: "but still I could explain it if you will promise me faithfully not to say a word about it."

"I will make that promise if you satisfy me that all is right," answered I.

"As to all being right, Jacob, that's as may be; but if I prove to you that there is no harm done to our master, I suppose you will keep the secret. However, I must not allow you to think worse of it than it really is; no, I'll trust to your good nature. You wouldn't harm me, Jacob?" Marables then told me that Fleming had once been well-to-do in the world, and during the long illness and subsequent death of Marables' wife, had lent him money; that Fleming had been very imprudent, and had run up a great many debts, and that the bailiffs were after him. On this emergency he had applied to Marables to help him, and that, in consequence, he had received him on board of the barge, where they never would think of looking for him; that Fleming had friends, and contrived to go on shore at night to see them, and get what assistance he could from them in money: in the meantime his relations were trying what they could do to arrange with his creditors. "Now," said Marables, after this narration, "how could I help assisting one who has been so kind to me? And what harm does it do Mr Drummond? If Fleming can't do his work, or won't, when we unload, he pays another man himself; so Mr Drummond is not hurt by it."

"That may be all true," replied I; "but I cannot imagine why I am not to enter the cabin, and why he orders about here as master."

"Why, you see, Jacob, I owe him money, and he allows me so much per week for the cabin, by which means I pay it off. Do you understand now?"

"Yes, I understand what you have said," replied I.

"Well, then, Jacob, I hope you'll say nothing about it. It would only harm me, and do no good."

"That depends upon Fleming's behaviour towards me," replied I. "I will not be bullied and made uncomfortable by him, depend upon it; he has no business on board the barge, that's clear, and I am bound 'prentice to her. I don't wish to hurt you; and as I suppose Fleming won't be long on board, I shall say nothing unless he treats me ill."

Marables then left me, and I reflected upon what he had said. It appeared all very probable; but still I was not satisfied. I resolved to watch narrowly, and if anything occurred which excited more suspicions, to inform Mr Drummond upon our return. Shortly afterwards Marables came out again, and told me I might go to bed, and he would keep the deck till Fleming's return. I assented, and went down to the cuddy; but I did not much like this permission. It appeared to me as if he wanted to get rid of me, and I laid awake, turning over in my mind all that I had heard and seen. About two o'clock in the morning I heard the sound of oars, and the skiff strike the side of the barge. I did not go up, but I put my head up the scuttle to see what was going on. It was broad moonlight, and almost as clear as day. Fleming threw up the painter of the skiff to Marables, and, as he held it, lifted out of the boat a blue bag, apparently well filled. The contents jingled as it was landed on the deck. He then put out a yellow silk handkerchief full of something else, and having gained the deck, Marables walked aft with the painter in his hand until the skiff had dropped astern, where he made it fast, and returned to Fleming, who stood close to the blue bag. I heard Fleming ask Marables, in a low voice, if I were in bed, and an answer given in the affirmative. I dropped my head immediately, that I might not be discovered, and turned into my bed-place. I was restless for a long while; thought upon thought, surmise upon surmise, conjecture upon conjecture, and doubt upon doubt, occupied my brain, until at last I went fast asleep— so fast, that I did not wake until summoned by Fleming. I rose, and when I came on deck found that the anchor had been weighed more than two hours, and that we were past all the bridges. "Why, Jacob, my man, you've had a famous nap," said Fleming, with apparent good humour; "now go aft, and get your breakfast, it has been waiting for you this half-hour." By the manner of Fleming I took it for granted that Marables had acquainted him with our conversation, and, indeed, from that time, during our whole trip, Fleming treated me with kindness and familiarity. The veto had not, however, been taken off the cabin, which I never attempted to enter.

Chapter Seven

On our arrival off the Medway, I had just gone down to bed and was undressing, when I heard Fleming come on deck and haul up the boat. I looked up the hatchway; it was very dark, but I could perceive Marables hand him the bag and handkerchief, with which he pulled on shore. He did not return until the next morning at daylight, when I met him as he came up the side. "Well, Jacob," said he, "you've caught me, I've been on shore to see my sweetheart; but you boys ought to know nothing about these things. Make the boat fast, there's a good lad."

When we were one night discharging our cargo, which was for government, I heard voices alongside. From habit, the least noise now awoke me: a boat striking the side was certain so to do. It was then about twelve o'clock. I looked up the hatchway, perceived two men come on board and enter the cabin with packages. They remained there about ten minutes, and then, escorted to the side by Fleming, left the barge. When the barge was cleared, we hauled off to return, and in three days were again alongside of Mr Drummond's wharf. The kindness both of Marables and of Fleming had been very great. They lived in a style very superior to what they could be expected to do, and I fared well in consequence.

On our arrival at the wharf, Marables came up to me, and said, "Now, Jacob, as I have honestly told you the secret, I hope you won't ruin me by saying a word to Mr Drummond." I had before made up my mind to say nothing to my master until my suspicions were confirmed, and I therefore gave my promise; but I had also resolved to impart my suspicions, as well as what I had seen, to the old Dominie. On the third day after our arrival I walked out to the school, and acquainted him with all that had passed, and asked him for his advice.

"Jacob," said he, "thou hast done well, but thou mightest have done better; hadst thou not given thy promise, which is sacred, I would have taken thee to Mr Drummond, that thou mightest impart the whole, instanter. I like it not. Evil deeds are done in darkness. *Noctem peccatis et fraudibus objice nubem.* Still, as thou sayest, nought is yet proved. Watch, therefore, Jacob—watch carefully over thy master's interests, and the interests of society at large. It is thy duty, I may say, *Vigilare noctesque diesque*. It may be as Marables hath said—and all may be accounted for; still, I say, be careful, and be honest."

I followed the suggestions of the Dominie: we were soon laden with another cargo of bricks, to be delivered at the same place, and proceeded on our voyage. Marables and Fleming, finding that I had not said a word to Mr Drummond, treated me with every kindness. Fleming once offered me money, which I refused, saying that I had no use for it. I was on the best terms with them, at the same time that I took notice of all that passed, without offering a remark to excite their suspicions. But not to be too prolix, it will suffice to say that we made many trips during several months, and that during that time I made the following observations:— that Fleming went on shore at night at certain places, taking with him bags and bundles; that he generally returned with others, which were taken into the cabin; that sometimes people came off at night, and remained some time in the cabin with him; and that all this took place when it was supposed that I was asleep. The cabin was invariably locked when the barge was lying at the wharfs, if Fleming was on shore, and at no time was I permitted to enter it. Marables was a complete cipher in Fleming's hands, who ordered everything as he pleased; and in the conversations which took place before me, with much less restraint than at first, there appeared to be no idea of Fleming's leaving us. As I felt convinced that there was no chance of discovery without further efforts on my part, and my suspicions increasing daily, I resolved upon running some hazard. My chief wish was to get into the cabin and examine its contents; but this was not easy, and would, in all probability, be a dangerous attempt. One night I came on deck in my shirt. We were at anchor off Rotherhithe: it was a dark night, with a drizzling rain. I was hastening below, when I perceived a light still burning in the cabin, and heard the voices of Marables and Fleming. I thought this a good opportunity, and having no shoes, walked softly on the wet deck to the cabin-door, which opened forward, and peeped through the crevices. Marables and Fleming were sitting opposite each other at the little table. There were some papers before them, and they were dividing some money. Marables expostulated at his share not being sufficient, and Fleming laughed and told him he had earned no more. Fearful of being discovered, I made a silent retreat, and gained my bed. It was well that I had made the resolution; for just as I was putting my head below the hatch, and drawing it over the scuttle, the door was thrown open and Fleming came out, I pondered over this circumstance, and the remark of Fleming that Marables had not earned any more, and I felt convinced that the story told me by Marables relative to Fleming was all false. This conviction stimulated me more than ever to discover the secret, and many and many a night did I watch, with a hope of being able to examine the cabin; but it was to no purpose, either Fleming or Marables was always on board. I continued to report to the Dominie all I had discovered, and he agreed at last that it was better that I should not say anything to Mr Drummond until there was the fullest proof of the nature of their proceedings.

The cabin was now the sole object of my thoughts, and many were the schemes resolved in my mind to obtain an entrance. Fatima never coveted admission to the dreadful chamber of Bluebeard as I did to ascertain the secrets of this hidden receptacle. One night Fleming had quitted the barge, and I ascended from my dormitory. Marables was on deck, sitting upon the water-cask, with his elbow resting on the gunwale, his hand supporting his head, as if in deep thought. The cabin-doors were closed, but the light still remained in it. I watched for some time, and perceiving that Marables did not move, walked gently up to him. He was fast asleep; I waited for some little time alongside of him. At last he snored. It was an opportunity not to be lost. I crept to the cabin-door; it was not locked. Although I did not fear the wrath of Marables, in case of discovery, as I did that of Fleming, it was still with a beating heart and a tremulous hand that I gently opened the door, pausing before I entered, to ascertain if Marables were disturbed. He moved not, and I entered, closing the door after me. I caught up the light, and held it in my hand as I hung over the table. On each side were the two bed-places of Marables and Fleming, which I had before then had many a partial glimpse of. In front of the two bed-places were two lockers to sit down upon. I tried them—they were not fast—they contained their clothes. At the after part of the cabin were three cupboards; I opened the centre one; it contained crockery, glass, and knives and forks. I tried the one on the starboard side; it was locked, but the key was in it. I turned it gently, but being a good lock, it snapped loud. I paused in fear—but Marables still slept. The cupboard had three shelves, and every shelf was loaded with silver spoons, forks, and every variety of plate, mixed with watches, bracelets, and ornaments of every description. There was, I perceived, a label on each, with a peculiar mark. Wishing to have an accurate survey, and encouraged by my discovery, I turned to the cupboard opposite, on the larboard side, and I opened it. It contained silk handkerchiefs in every variety, lace veils, and various other articles of value; on the lower shelf were laid three pairs of pistols. I was now satisfied, and closing the last cupboard, which had not been locked, was about to retreat, when I recollected that I had not re-locked the first cupboard, and that they might not, by finding it open, suspect my visit, I turned the key. It made a louder snap than before. I heard Marables start from his slumber on deck; in a moment I blew out the lamp, and remained quiet. Marables got up, took a turn or two, looked at the cabin doors, which were shut, and opened them a little. Perceiving that the lamp had, as he thought, gone out, he shut them again, and, to my consternation, turned the key. There I was, locked up, until the arrival of Fleming—then to be left to his mercy. I hardly knew how to act: at last I resolved upon calling to Marables, as I dreaded his anger less than Fleming's. Then it occurred to me that Marables might come in, feel for the lamp to re-light it, and that, as he came in on one side of the cabin, I might, in the dark, escape by the other. This all but forlorn hope prevented me for some time from applying to him. At last I made up my mind that I would, and ran from the locker to call through the door, when I heard the sound of oars. I paused again—loitered—the boat was alongside, and I heard Fleming jump upon the deck.

"Quick," said he to Marables, as he came to the cabin-door, and tried to open it; "We've no time to lose—we must get up the sacks and sink everything. Two of them have 'peached, and the fence will be discovered."

He took the keys from Marables and opened the door; I had replaced the lamp upon the table. Fleming entered, took a seat on the locker on the larboard side, and felt for the lamp. Marables followed him, and sat down on the starboard locker;—escape was impossible. With a throbbing heart I sat in silence, watching my fate. In the meantime, Fleming had taken out of his pocket his phosphorus match box. I heard the tin top pulled open—even the slight rustling of the one match selected was perceived. Another second it was withdrawn from the bottle, and a wild flame of light illumined the deck cabin, and discovered me to their view. Staggered at my appearance, the match fell from Fleming's hand, and all was dark as before; but there was no more to be gained by darkness—I had been discovered.

"Jacob!" cried Marables.

"Will not live to tell the tale," added Fleming, with a firm voice, as he put another match into the bottle, and then relighted the lamp. "Come," said Fleming, fiercely; "out of the cabin immediately."

I prepared to obey him. Fleming went out, and I was following him round his side of the table, when Marables interposed.

"Stop: Fleming, what is that you mean to do?"

"Silence him!" retorted Fleming.

"But not murder him, surely?" cried Marables, trembling from head to foot. "You will not, dare not, do that."

"What is it that I dare not do, Marables? but it is useless to talk; it is now his life or mine. One must be sacrificed, and I will not die yet to please him."

"You shall not—by God, Fleming, you shall not!" cried Marables, seizing hold of my other arm, and holding me tight.

I added my resistance to that of Marables; when Fleming, perceiving that we should be masters, took a pistol from his pocket, and struck Marables a blow on the head, which rendered him senseless. Throwing away the pistol, he dragged me out of the cabin. I was strong, but he was very powerful; my resistance availed me nothing: by degrees he forced me to the side of the barge, and lifting me in his arms, dashed me into the dark and rapidly flowing water. It was fortunate for me that the threat of Fleming, upon our first meeting, had induced me to practise swimming, and still more fortunate that I was not encumbered with any other clothes than my shirt, in which I had come on deck. As it was, I was carried away by the tide for some time before I could rise, and at such a distance that Fleming, who probably watched, did not perceive that I came up again. Still, I had but little hopes of saving myself in a dark night, and at nearly a quarter of a mile from shore. I struggled to keep myself afloat, when I heard the sound of oars; a second or two more and I saw them over my head. I grasped at and seized the last, as the others passed me, crying "Help!"

"What the devil! Oars, my men; here's somebody overboard," cried the man, whose oar I had seized.

They stopped pulling; he dragged in his oar till he could lay hold of me, and then they hauled me into the boat. I was exhausted with cold and my energetic struggles in the water; and it was not until they had wrapped me up in a great-coat, and poured some spirits down my throat; that I could speak. They inquired to which of the craft I belonged.

"The Folly barge."

"The very one we are searching for. Where about is she, my lad?"

I directed them: the boat was a large wherry, pulling six oars, belonging to the river police. The officer in the stern sheets, who steered her, then said, "How came you overboard?"

"I was thrown overboard," replied I, "by a man called Fleming."

"The name he goes by," cried the officer. "Give way, my lads. There's murder, it appears, as well as other charges."

In a quarter of an hour we were alongside—the officer and four men sprang out of the boat, leaving the other two with directions for me to remain in the boat. Cold and miserable as I was, I was too much interested in the scene not to rise up from the stern sheets, and pay attention to what passed. When the officer and his men gained the deck, they were met by Fleming in the advance, and Marables about a yard or two behind.

"What's all this?" cried Fleming, boldly. "Are you river pirates, come to plunder us?"

"Not exactly," replied the officer; "but we are just come to overhaul you. Deliver up the key of your cabin," continued he, after trying the door and finding it locked.

"With all my heart, if you prove yourselves authorised to search," replied Fleming; "but you'll find no smuggled spirits here, I can tell you. Marables, hand them the key; I see that they belong to the river guard."

Marables, who had never spoken, handed the key to the officer, who, opening a dark lanthorn, went down into the cabin and proceeded in his search, leaving two of the men to take charge of Fleming and Marables. But his search was in vain; he could find nothing, and he came out on deck.

"Well," said Fleming, sarcastically, "have you made a seizure?"

"Wait a little," said the officer; "how many men have you in this barge?"

"You see them," replied Fleming.

"Yes; but you have a boy; where is he?"

"We have no boy," replied Fleming; "two men are quite enough for this craft."

"Still I ask you, what has become of the boy? for a boy was on your decks this afternoon."

"If there was one, I presume he has gone on shore again."

"Answer me another question; which of you threw him overboard?"

At this query of the officer, Fleming started, while Marables cried out, "It was not I; I would have saved him. O that the boy were here to prove it!"

"I am here, Marables," said I, coming on deck, "and I am witness that you tried to save me, until you were struck senseless by that ruffian, Fleming, who threw me overboard, that I might not give evidence as to the silver and gold which I found in the cabin; and which I overheard him tell you must be put into sacks and sunk, as two of the men had 'peached."

Fleming, when he saw me, turned round, as if not to look at me. His face I could not see; but after remaining a few seconds in that position, he held out his hands in silence for the handcuffs, which the officer had already taken out of his pocket. Marables, on the contrary, sprang forward as soon as I had finished speaking, and caught me in his arms.

"My fine, honest boy! I thank God—I thank God! All that he has said is true, sir. You will find the goods sunk astern, and the buoy-rope to them fastened to the lower pintle of the rudder. Jacob, thank God, you are safe! I little thought to see you again. There, sir," continued he to the officer, holding out his hands, "I deserve it all. I had not strength of mind enough to be honest."

The handcuffs were put on Marables as well as on Fleming, and the officer, allowing me time to go down and put on my clothes, hauled up the sacks containing the valuables, and leaving two hands in charge of the barge, rowed ashore with us all in the boat. It was then about three o'clock in the morning, and I was very glad when we arrived at the receiving-house, and I was permitted to warm myself before the fire. As soon as I was comfortable, I laid down on the bench and fell fast asleep.

Chapter Eight

I did not awake the next morning till roused by the police, who brought us up before the magistrates. The crowd that followed appeared to make no distinction between the prisoners and the witness, and remarks not very complimentary, and to me very annoying, were liberally made. "He's a young hand for such work," cried one. "There's gallows marked in his face," observed another, to whom, when I turned round to look at him, I certainly could have returned the compliment. The station was not far from the magistrates' office, and we soon arrived. The principal officer went into the inner room, and communicated with the magistrates before they came out and took their seats on the bench.

"Where is Jacob Faithful? My lad, do you know the nature of an oath?"

I answered in the affirmative; the oath was administered, and my evidence taken down. It was then read over to the prisoners, who were asked if they had anything to say in their defence. Fleming, who had sent for his lawyer, was advised to make no answer. Marables quietly replied, that all the boy had said was quite true.

"Recollect," said the magistrate, "we cannot accept you as king's evidence; that of the boy is considered sufficient."

"I did not intend that you should," replied Marables. "I only want to ease my conscience, not to try for my pardon."

They were then committed for trial, and led away to prison. I could not help going up to Marables and shaking his hand, before he was led away. He lifted up his two arms, for he was still handcuffed, and wiped his eyes, saying, "Let this be a warning to you, Jacob—not that I think you need it; but still I once was honest as yourself—and look at me now." And he cast his eyes down sorrowfully upon his fettered wrists. They quitted the room, Fleming giving me a look which was very significant of what my chance would be if ever I fell into his clutches.

"We must detain you, my lad," observed one of the magistrates, "without you can procure a sufficient bail for your appearance as witness on the trial."

I replied that I knew of no one except my master, Mr Drummond, and my schoolmaster; and had no means of letting them know of my situation.

The magistrate then directed the officer to go down by the first Brentford coach, acquaint Mr Drummond with what had passed, and that the lighter would remain in charge of the river police until he could send hands on board of her; and I was allowed to sit down on the bench behind the bar. It was not until past noon that Mr Drummond, accompanied by the Dominie, made his appearance. To save time, the magistrates gave them my deposition to read; they put in bail, and I was permitted to leave the court. We went down by the coach, but as they went inside and I was out, I had not many questions asked until my arrival at Mr Drummond's house, when I gave them a detailed account of all that had happened.

"Proh! Deus!" exclaimed the Dominie, when I had finished my story. "What an escape! How narrowly, as Propertius hath it femininely, *'Eripitur nobis jumpridem carus puer.'* Well was it that thou hadst learnt to swim— verily thou must have struggled lustily. *'Pugnat in adversas ire natator aquas,'* yea, lustily for thy life, child. Now, God be praised!"

But Mr Drummond was anxious that the lighter should be brought back to the wharf; he therefore gave me my dinner, for I had eaten nothing that day, and then despatched me in a boat with two men, to bring her up the river. The next morning we arrived; and Mr Drummond, not having yet selected any other person to take her in charge, I was again some days on shore, dividing my time between the Dominie and Mr Drummond's, where I was always kindly treated, not only by him, but also by his wife and his little daughter Sarah.

A master for the lighter was soon found; and as I passed a considerable time under his orders, I must describe him particularly. He had served the best part of his life on board a man-of-war, had been in many general and single actions, and, at the battle of Trafalgar, had wound up his servitude with the loss of both his legs and an out-pension from the Greenwich Hospital, which he preferred to being received upon the establishment, as he had a wife and child. Since that time he had worked on the river. He was very active, and broad-shouldered, and had probably, before he lost his legs, been a man of at least five feet eleven or six feet high; but as he found that he could keep his balance better upon short stumps than long ones, he had reduced his wooden legs to about eight inches in length, which, with his square body, gave him the appearance of a huge dwarf. He bore, and I will say most deservedly, an excellent character. His temper was always cheerful, and he was a little inclined to drink: but the principal feature in him was lightness of heart; he was always singing. His voice was very fine and powerful. When in the service he used to be summoned to sing to the captain and officers, and was the delight of the forecastle. His memory was retentive, and his stock of songs incredible, at the same time, he seldom or ever sang more than one or two stanzas of a song in the way of quotation, or if apt to what was going on, often altering the words to suit the occasion. He was accompanied by his son Tom, a lad of my own age, as merry as his father, and who had a good treble voice and a good deal of humour; he would often take the song up from his father, with words of his own putting in, with ready wit and good tune. We three composed the crew of the lighter; and, as there had already been considerable loss from demurrage, were embarked as soon as they arrived. The name of the father was Tom Beazeley, but he was always known on the river as "old Tom" or, as some more learned wag had christened him, "the *Merman on two sticks.*" As soon as we had put our traps on board, as old Tom called them, he received his orders, and we cast off from the wharf. The wind was favourable. Young Tom was as active as a monkey, and as full of tricks. His father took the helm, while we two, assisted by a dog of the small Newfoundland breed, which Tom had taught to take a rope in his teeth, and be of no small service to two boys in bowsing on a tackle, made sail upon the lighter, and away we went, while old Tom's strain might be heard from either shore.

> "Loose, loose every sail to the breeze,
>   The course of the vessel improve,
> I've done with the toil of the seas,
>   Ye sailors, I'm bound to my love.

"Tom, you beggar, is the bundle ready for your mother? We must drop the skiff, Jacob, at Battersea reach, and send the clothes on shore for the old woman to wash, or there'll be no clean shirts for Sunday. Shove in your shirts, Jacob; the old woman won't mind that. She used to wash for the mess. Clap on, both of you, and get another pull at those haulyards. That'll do, my bantams.

> "Hoist, hoist, every sail to the breeze,
>   Come, shipmates, and join in the song,
> Let's drink while the barge cuts the seas,
>   To the gale that may drive her along.

"Tom, where's my pot of tea? Come, my boy, we must pipe to breakfast. Jacob, there's a rope towing overboard. Now, Tom, hand me my tea, and I'll steer her with one hand, drink with the other, and as for the legs, the less we say about them the better.

"No glory I covet, no riches I want,
Ambition is nothing to me.
But one thing I beg of kind Heaven to grant—"

Tom's treble chimed in, handing him the pot—

"For *breakfast a good cup of tea.*

"Silence, you sea-cook! how dare you shove in your penny whistle! How's tide, Tom?"

"Three quarters ebb."

"No, it a'n't, you thief; how is it Jacob?"

"About half, I think."

"And you're right."

"What water have we down here on the side?"

"You must give the point a wide berth," replied I; "the shoals runs out."

"Thanky, boy, so I thought, but wasn't sure:" and then old Tom burst out in a beautiful air:

"Trust not too much your own opinion,
When your vessel's under weigh,
Let good advice still bear dominion;
That's a compass will not stray."

"Old Tom, is that you?" hallooed a man from another barge.

"Yes; what's left of me, my hearty."

"You'll not fetch the bridges this tide—there's a strong breeze right up the reaches below."

"Never mind, we'll do all we can.

"If unassailed by squall or shower,
Wafted by the gentle gales
Let's not lose the favouring hour,
While success attends our sails."

"Bravo, old Tom! why don't the boys get the lines out, for all the fishes are listening for you," cried the man, as the barges were parted by the wind and tide.

"I did once belong to a small craft called the Anon," observed old Tom, "and they say as how the story was, that that chap could make the fish follow him just when he pleased. I know that when we were in the North Sea the shoals of seals would follow the ship if you whistled; but these brutes have ears—now fish hav'n't got none.

> "Oh well do I remember that cold dreary land,
>   here the northern light,
>   In the winter's night,
>   Shone bright on its snowy strand.

"Jacob, have you finished your breakfast? Here, take the helm, while I and Tom put the craft a little into apple-pie order."

Old Tom then stumped forward, followed by his son and the Newfoundland dog, who appeared to consider himself as one of the most useful personages on board. After coiling down the ropes, and sweeping the decks, they went into the cabin to make their little arrangements.

"A good lock that, Tom," cried the father, turning the key of the cupboard. (I recollected it, and that its snapping so loud was the occasion of my being tossed overboard.) Old Tom continued: "I say, Tom, you won't be able to open that cupboard, so I'll put the sugar and the grog into it, you scamp. It goes too fast when you're purser's steward.

> "For grog is our larboard and starboard,
>   Our main-mast, our mizzen, our log,
> On shore, or at sea, or when harbour'd,
>   The mariner's compass is grog."

"But it arn't a compass to steer steady by, father," replied Tom.

"Then don't you have nothing to do with it, Tom."

"I only takes a little, father, because you mayn't take too much."

"Thanky for nothing; when do I ever take too much, you scamp?"

"Not too much for a man standing on his own pins, but too much for a man on two broomsticks."

"Stop your jaw, Mr Tom, or I'll unscrew one of the broomsticks, and lay it over your shoulders."

"Before it's out of the socket, I'll give you *leg-bail*. What will you do then, father?"

"Catch you when I can, Tom, as the spider takes the fly."

"What's the good o' that, when you can't bear malice for ten minutes?"

"Very true, Tom? then thank your stars that you have two good legs, and that your poor father has none."

"I very often do thank my stars, and that's the truth of it; but what's the use of being angry about a drop of rum, or a handful of sugar?"

"Because you takes more than your allowance."

"Well, do you take less, then all will be right."

"And why should I take less, pray?"

"Because you're only half a man; you haven't any legs to provide for, as I have."

"Now, I tell you, Tom, that's the very reason why I should have more to comfort my old body for the loss of them."

"When you lost your legs you lost your ballast, father, and, therefore, you mustn't carry too much sail, or you'll topple overboard some dark night. If I drink the grog, it's all for your good, you see."

"You're a dutiful son in that way, at all events; and a sweet child, as far as sugar goes; but Jacob is to sleep in the cabin with me, and you'll shake your blanket forward."

"Now that I consider quite unnatural; why part father and son?"

"It's not that exactly, it's only parting son and the grog bottle."

"That's just as cruel; why part two such good friends?"

"'Cause, Tom, he's too strong for you, and floors you sometimes."

"Well, but I forgives him; it's all done in good humour."

"Tom, you're a wag; but you wag your tongue to no purpose. Liquor ain't good for a boy like you, and it grows upon you."

"Well, don't I grow too? we grow together."

"You'll grow faster without it."

"I've no wish to be a tall man cut short, like you."

"If I hadn't been a tall man, my breath would have been cut short for ever; the ball which took my legs would have cut you right in half."

"And the ball that would take your head off, would whistle over mine; so there we are equal again."

"And there's the grog fast," replied old Tom, turning the key, and putting it into his pocket. "That's a stopper over all; so now we'll go on deck."

I have narrated this conversation, as it will give the reader a better idea of Tom, and his way of treating his father. Tom was fond of his father, and although mischievous, and too fond of drinking when he could obtain liquor, was not disobedient or vicious. We had nearly reached Battersea Fields when they returned on deck.

"Do you know, Jacob, how the parish of Battersea came into the possession of those fields?"

"No, I do not."

"Well, then, I'll tell you; it was because the Battersea people were more humane and charitable than their neighbours. There was a time when those fields were of no value; now they're worth a mint of money, they say. The body of a poor devil, who was drowned in the river, was washed on shore on those banks, and none of the parishes would be at the expense of burying it. The Battersea people, though they had least right to be called upon, would not allow the poor fellow's corpse to be lying on the mud, and they went to the expense. Now, when the fields became of value, the other parishes were ready enough to claim them; but the case was tried, and as it was proved that Battersea had buried the body, the fields were decided to belong to that parish. So they were well paid for their humanity, and they deserved it. Mr Drummond says you know the river well, Jacob."

"I was born on it."

"Yes, so I heard, and all about your father and mother's death. I was telling Tom of it, because he's too fond of *bowsing up his jib*."

"Well, father, there's no occasion to remind Jacob; the tear is in his eye already," replied Tom, with consideration.

"I wish you never had any other *drop* in your *eye*,—but never mind, Jacob, I didn't think of what I was saying. Look ye, d'ye see that little house with the two chimneys—that's mine, and there's my old woman.—I wonder what she's about just now." Old Tom paused for a while, with his eyes fixed on the object, and then burst out:—

"I've crossed the wide waters, I've trod the lone strand,
I've triumphed in battle, I've lighted the brand,
I've borne the loud thunder of death o'er the foam;
Fame, riches, ne'er found them,—yet still found a home.

"Tom, boy, haul up the skiff and paddle on shore with the bundle; ask the old woman how she is, and tell her I'm hearty." Tom was in the boat in a moment, and pulling lustily for the shore. "That makes me recollect when I returned to my mother, a'ter the first three years of my sea service. I borrowed the skiff from the skipper.—I was in a Greenland-man, my first ship, and pulled ashore to my mother's cottage under the cliff. I thought the old soul would have died with joy." Here old Tom was silent, brushed a tear from his eye, and, as usual, commenced a strain, *sotto voce*: —

> "Why, what's that to you if my eyes I'm a wiping?
> A tear is a pleasure, d'ye see, in its way.

"How, miserable," continued he, after another pause, "the poor thing was when I would go to sea—how she begged and prayed—boys have no feeling, that's sartin."

> "O bairn, dinna leave me, to gang far away,
> O bairn, dinna leave me, ye're a' that I hae,
> Think on a mither, the wind and the wave,
> A mither set on ye, her feet in the grave.

"However, she got used to it at last, as the woman said when she skinned the ells. Tom's a good boy, Jacob, but not steady, as they say you are. His mother spoils him, and I can't bear to be cross to him neither; for his heart's in the right place, after all. There's the old woman shaking her dish-clout at us as a signal. I wish I had gone on shore myself, but I can't step into these paper-built little boats without my timber toes going through at the bottom."

Chapter Nine

Tom then shoved off the skiff. When half-way between the lighter and the shore, while his mother stood watching us, he lay on his oars. "Tom, Tom!" cried his mother, shaking her fist at him, as he stooped down his head; "if you do, Tom!"

"Tom, Tom!" cried his father, shaking his fist also; "if you dare, Tom!"

But Tom was not within reach of either party; and he dragged a bottle out of the basket which his mother had entrusted to him, and putting it to his mouth, took a long swig.

"That's enough, Tom!" screamed his mother, from the shore.

"That's too much, you rascal!" cried his father, from the barge.

Neither admonition was, however, minded by Tom, who took what he considered his allowance, and then very coolly pulled alongside, and handed up the basket and bundle of clean clothes on deck. Tom then gave the boat's painter to his father, who, I perceived, intended to salute him with the end of it as soon as he came up; but Tom was too knowing—he surged the boat ahead, and was on deck and forward before his father could stump up to him. The main hatch was open, and Tom put that obstacle between his father and himself before he commenced his parley.

"What's the matter, father?" said Tom, smiling, and looking at me.

"Matter, you scamp! How dare you touch the bottle?"

"The bottle—the bottle's there, as good as ever."

"The grog is what I mean—how dare you drink it?"

"I was half-way between my mother and you, and so I drank success and long life to you both. Ain't that being a very dutiful son?"

"I wish I had my legs back again, you rascal!"

"You wish you had the grog back again, you mean, father."

"You have to choose between—for if you had the grog you'd keep your legs."

"For the matter of drinking the grog, you scamp, you seem determined to stand in my shoes."

"Well, shoes are of no use to you now, father—why shouldn't I? Why don't you trust me? If you hadn't locked the cupboard, I wouldn't have helped myself." And Tom, whose bootlace was loose, stooped down to make it fast.

Old Tom, who was still in wrath, thought this a good opportunity, as his son's head was turned the other way, to step over the bricks, with which, as I before said, the lighter had been laden level with the main hatchway, and take his son by surprise. Tom, who had no idea of this manoeuvre, would certainly have been captured, but, fortunately for him, one of the upper bricks turned over, and let his father's wooden leg down between two of the piles, where it was jammed fast. Old Tom attempted to extricate himself, but could not. "Tom, Tom, come here," cried he, "and pull me out."

"Not I," replied Tom.

"Jacob, Jacob, come here; Tom, run and take the helm."

"Not I," replied Tom.

"Jacob, never mind the helm, she'll drift all right for a minute," cried old Tom; "come and help me."

But I had been so amused with the scene, and having a sort of feeling for young Tom, that I declared it impossible to leave the helm without her going on the banks. I therefore remained, wishing to see in what way the two Toms would get out of their respective scrapes.

"Confound these—! Tom, you scoundrel, am I to stick here all day?"

"No, father, I don't suppose you will. I shall help you directly."

"Well, then, why don't you do it?"

"Because I must come to terms. You don't think I'd help myself to a thrashing, do you?"

"I won't thrash you, Tom. Shiver my timbers if I do."

"They're in a fair way of being shivered as it is, I think. Now, father, we're both even."

"How's that?"

"Why you clapped a stopper over all on me this morning, and now you've got one on yourself."

"Well, then, take off mine, and I'll take off yours."

"If I unlock your leg, you'll unlock the cupboard?"

"Yes."

"And you promise me a *stiff one* after dinner?"

"Yes, yes, as stiff as I stand here."

"No, that will be too much, for it would *set me fast*. I only like it about half-and-half, as I took it just now."

Tom, who was aware that his father would adhere to his agreement, immediately went to his assistance, and throwing out some of the upper bricks, released him from his confinement. When old Tom was once more on deck and on his legs, he observed, "It's an ill wind that blows nobody good. The *loss* of my leg has been the *saving* of you many a time, Mr Tom."

It was now time to anchor, as we were meeting the flood. Tom, who officiated as cook, served up the dinner, which was ready; and we were all very pleasant; Tom treating his father with perfect confidence. As we had not to weigh again for some hours, our repast was prolonged, and old Tom, having fulfilled his promise to his son of a *stiff one*, took one or two himself, and became very garrulous.

"Come, spin us a good yarn, father; we've nothing to do, and Jacob will like to hear you."

"Well, then, so I will," answered he; "what shall it be about?"

"Fire and water, of course," replied Tom.

"Well, then, I'll tell you something about both, since you wish it; how I came into his Majesty's sarvice, through *fire*, and how the officer who pressed me went out of it through *water*. I was still 'prentice, and wanted about three months to sarve my time, when, of course, I should no longer be protected from sarving the king, when the ship I was in sailed up the Baltic with a cargo of bullocks. We had at least two hundred on board, tied up on platforms on every deck, with their heads close to the sides, and all their sterns looking in-board. They were fat enough when they were shipped, but soon dwindled away: the weather was very bad, and the poor creatures rolled against each other, and slipped about in a way that it pitied you to see them. However, they were stowed so thick, that they held one another up, which proved of service to them in the heavy gales which tossed the ship about like a pea in a rattle. We had joined a large convoy, and were entering the Sound, when, as usual, it fell calm, and out came the Danish gunboats to attack us. The men-of-war who had charge of the convoy behaved nobly; but still they were becalmed, and many of us were a long way astern. Our ship was pretty well up; but she was too far in-shore; and the Danes made a dash at us with the hope of making a capture. The men-of-war, seeing what the enemy were about, sent boats to beat them off; but it was too late to prevent them boarding, which they did. Not wishing to peep through the bars of the gaol at Copenhagen, we left the ship in our boats on one side, just as the Danes boarded on the other, and pulled towards the men-of-war's armed boats coming to our assistance. The men-of-war's boats pulled right for the ship to retake her, which they did, certainly, but not before the enemy had set fire to the vessel, and had then pulled off towards another. Seeing this, the men-of-war's boats again gave chase to the Danes, leaving us to extinguish the flames, which were now bursting out fore and aft, and climbing like fiery serpents up to the main catharprings. We soon found that it was impossible; we remained as long as the heat and smoke would permit us, and then we were obliged to be off, but I shall never forget the roaring and moaning of the poor animals who were then roasting alive. It was a cruel thing of the Danes to fire a vessel full of these poor creatures. Some had broken loose, and were darting up and down the decks goring others, and tumbling down the hatchways; others remained trembling, or trying to snuff up a mouthful of fresh air amongst the smoke; but the struggling and bellowing, as the fire caught the vessel fore and aft, and was grilling two hundred poor creatures at once, was at last shocking, and might have been heard for a mile. We did all we could. I cut the throats of a dozen, but they kicked and struggled so much, falling down (upon), and treading you under their feet; and one lay upon me, and I expected to be burnt with them, for it was not until I was helped that I got clear of the poor animal. So we stayed as long as we could, and then left them to their fate; and the smell of burnt meat, as we shoved off, was as horrible as the cries and wailings of the poor beasts themselves. The men-of-war's boats returned, having chased away the Danes, and very kindly offered us all a ship, as we had lost our own, so that you see that by *fire* I was forced into his Majesty's sarvice. Now, the boat that took us belonged to one of the frigates who had charge of the convoy, and the lieutenant who commanded the boat was a swearing, tearing sort of a chap, who lived as if his life was to last for ever.

"After I was taken on board, the captain asked me if I would enter, and I thought that I might as well sarve the king handsomely, so I volunteered. It's always the best thing to do, when you're taken, and can't help yourself, for you are more trusted than a pressed man who is obstinate. I liked the sarvice from the first—the captain was not a particular man; according to some people's ideas of the sarvice, she wasn't in quite man-of-war fashion, but she was a happy ship, and the men would have followed and fought for the captain to the last drop of their blood. That's the sort of ship for me. I've seen cleaner decks, but I never saw merrier hearts. The only one of the officers disliked by the men was the lieutenant who pressed me; he had a foul mouth and no discretion; and as for swearing, it was really terrible to hear the words which came out of his mouth. I don't mind an oath rapped out in the heat of the moment, but he invented his oaths when he was cool, and let them out in his rage. We were returning home, after having seen the convoy safe, when we met with a gale of wind in our teeth, one of the very worst I ever fell in with. It had been blowing hard from the South West, and then shifted to the North West, and made a cross sea, which was tremendous. Now, the frigate was a very old vessel, and although they had often had her into dock and repaired her below, they had taken no notice of her upper works, which were as rotten as a medlar. I think it was about three bells in the middle watch, when the wind was howling through the rigging, for we had no canvas on her 'cept a staysail and trysail, when the stay-sail sheet went, and she broached-to afore they could prevent her. The lieutenant I spoke of had the watch, and his voice was heard through the roaring of the wind swearing at the men to haul down the staysail, that we might bend on the sheet, and set it right again; when, she having, I said, broached-to, a wave—ay, a wave as high as the maintop almost, took the frigate right on her broadside, and the bulwarks of the quarter-deck being, as I said, quite rotten, cut them off clean level with the main chains, sweeping them, and guns, and men, all overboard together. The mizzenmast went, but the mainmast held on, and I was under its lee at the time, and was saved by clinging on like a nigger, while for a minute I was under the water, which carried almost all away with it to leeward. As soon as the water passed over me, I looked up and around me—it was quite awful; the quarter-deck was cut off as with a knife—not a soul left there, that I could see; no man at the wheel—mizzen-mast gone—skylights washed away—waves making a clear breach, and no defence; boats washed away from the quarters—all silent on deck, but plenty of noise below and on the main-deck, for the ship was nearly full of water, and all below were hurrying up in their shirts, thinking that we were going down. At last the captain crawled up, and clung by the stancheons, followed by the first lieutenant and the officers, and by degrees all was quiet, the ship was cleared, and the hands were turned up to muster under the half-deck. There were forty-seven men who did not answer to their names—they had been summoned to answer for their lives, poor fellows! and there was also the swearing lieutenant not to be found. Well, at last we got the hands on deck, and put her before the wind, scudding under bare poles. As we went aft to the taffrail, the bulwark of which still remained, with about six feet of the quarter-deck bulwark on each side, we observed something clinging to the stern-ladder, dipping every now and then into the sea, as it rose under her counter, and assisted the wind in driving her before the gale. We soon made it out to be a man, and I went down, slipped a bowling knot over the poor fellow, and with some difficulty we were both hauled up again. It proved to be the lieutenant, who had been washed under the counter, and clung to the stern-ladder, and had thus miraculously been preserved. It was a long while before he came to, and he never did any duty the whole week we were out, till we got into Yarmouth Roads; indeed, he hardly ever spoke a word to any one, but seemed to be always in serious thought. When we arrived, he gave his commission to the captain, and went on shore; went to school again, they say, *bore up for a parson*, and, for all I know, he'll preach somewhere next Sunday. So you see, *water* drove him out of the sarvice, and *fire* forced me in. There's a yarn for you, Jacob."

"I like it very much," replied I.

"And now, father, give us a whole song, and none of your little bits." Old Tom broke out with the "Death of Nelson," in a style that made the tune and words ring in my ears for the whole evening.

The moon was up before the tide served, and we weighed our anchor; old Tom steering, while his son was preparing supper, and I remaining forward, keeping a sharp look-out that we did not run foul of anything. It was a beautiful night; and as we passed through the several bridges, the city appeared as if it were illuminated, from the quantity of gas throwing a sort of halo of light over the tops of the buildings which occasionally marked out the main streets from the general dark mass—old Tom's voice was still occasionally heard, as the scene brought to his remembrance his variety of song.

> "For the murmur of thy lip, love,
>   Comes sweetly unto me,
> As the sound of oars that dip, love,
>   At moonlight on the sea."

I never was more delighted than when I heard these snatches of different songs poured forth in such melody from old Tom's lips, the notes floating along the water during the silence of the night. I turned aft to look at him; his face was directed upwards, looking on the moon, which glided majestically through the heavens, silvering the whole of the landscape. The water was smooth as glass, and the rapid tide had swept us clear of the ranges of ships in the pool; both banks of the river were clear, when old Tom again commenced:—

> "The moon is up, her silver beam
> Shines bower, and grove, and mountain over;

A flood of radiance heaven doth seem
To light thee, maiden, to thy lover."

"Jacob, how does the bluff-nob bear? on the starboard bow?"

"Yes—broad on the bow; you'd better keep up half a point, the tide
sweeps us fast."

"Very true, Jacob; look out, and say when steady it is, boy.

"If o'er her orb a cloud should rest,
    'Tis but thy cheek's soft blush to cover.
He waits to clasp thee to his breast;
    The moon is up—go, meet thy lover.

"Tom, what have you got for supper, boy? What is that frizzing in your
frying-pan? Smells good, anyhow."

"Yes, and I expect will taste good too. However, you look after the
moon, father, and leave me and the frying-pan to play our parts."

"While I sing mine, I suppose, boy.

"The moon is up, round beauty's shine,
    Love's pilgrims bend at vesper hour,
Earth breathes to heaven, and looks divine,
    And lovers' hearts confess her power."

Old Tom stopped and the frying-pan frizzled on, sending forth an
odour which, if not grateful to Heaven, was peculiarly so to us mortals,
hungry with the fresh air.

"How do we go now, Jacob?"

"Steady, and all's right; but we shall be met with the wind next reach,
and had better brail up the mainsail."

"Go, then, Tom, and help Jacob."

"I can't leave the *ingons*, (onions) father, not if the lighter tumbled
overboard; it would bring more tears in my eyes to spoil them, now that they
are frying so merrily, than they did when I was cutting them up. Besides,
the liver would be as black as the bends."

"Clap the frying-pan down on deck, Tom, and brail the sail up with
Jacob, there's a good boy. You can give it another shake or two afterwards.

"Guide on, my bark, how sweet to rove,
    With such a beaming eye above!

"That's right, my boys, belay all that; now to our stations; Jacob on the look-out, Tom to his frying-pan, and I to the helm—

"No sound is heard to break the spell,
Except the water's gentle swell;
While midnight, like a mimic day,
Shines on to guide our moonlight way.

"Well, the moon's a beautiful creature—God bless her! How often have we longed for her in the dark winter, channel-cruising, when the waves were flying over the Eddystone, and trying in their malice to put out the light. I don't wonder at people making songs to the moon, nor at my singing them. We'll anchor when we get down the next reach."

We swept the next reach with the tide which was now slacking fast. Our anchor was dropped and we all went to supper, and to bed. I have been particular in describing the first day of my being on board with my new shipmates, as it may be taken as a sample of our every day life; Tom and his father fighting and making friends, cooking, singing, and spinning yarns. Still, I shall have more scenes to describe. Our voyage was made, we took in a return cargo, and arrived at the proprietor's wharf, when I found that I could not proceed with them the next voyage, as the trial of Fleming and Marables was expected to come on in a few days. The lighter, therefore, took in another cargo, and sailed without me; Mr Drummond, as usual, giving me the run of his house.

Chapter Ten

It was on the 7th of November, if I recollect rightly, that Fleming and Marables were called up to trial at the Old Bailey, and I was in the court, with Mr Drummond and the Dominie, soon after ten o'clock. After the judge had taken his seat, as their trial was first on the list, they were ushered in. They were both clean and well dressed. In Fleming I could perceive little difference; he was pale, but resolute; but when I looked at Marables I was astonished. Mr Drummond did not at first recognise him—he had fallen away from seventeen stone to, at the most, thirteen—his clothes hung loosely about him—his ruddy cheeks had vanished—his nose was becoming sharp, and his full round face had been changed to an oblong. Still there remained that natural good-humoured expression in his countenance, and the sweet smile played upon his lips. His eyes glanced fearfully round the court—he felt his disgraceful situation—the colour mounted to his temples and forehead, and he then became again pale as a sheet, casting down his eyes as if desirous to see no more.

After the indictment had been read over, the prisoners were asked by the clerk whether they pleaded guilty or not guilty.

"Not guilty," replied Fleming, in a bold voice.

"John Marables—guilty or not guilty?"

"Guilty," replied Marables—"guilty, my lord;" and he covered his face with his hands.

Fleming was indicted on three counts;—an assault, with intent to murder; having stolen goods in his possession; and for a burglary in a dwelling-house, on such a date; but I understand that they had nearly twenty more charges against him, had these failed. Marables was indicted for having been an accessary to the last charge, as receiver of stolen goods. The counsel for the crown, who opened the trial, stated that Fleming, *alias* Barkett, *alias* Wenn, with many more *aliases*, had for a long while been at the head of the most notorious gang of thieves which had infested the metropolis for many years; that justice had long been in search of him, but that he had disappeared, and it had been supposed that he had quitted the kingdom to avoid the penalties of the law, to which he had subjected himself by his enormities. It appeared however, that he had taken a step which not only blinded the officers of the police, but at the same time had enabled the gang to carry on their depredations with more impunity than ever. He had concealed himself in a lighter on the river, and appearing in her as one diligently performing his duty, and earning his livelihood as an honest man had by such means been enabled to extend his influence, the number of his associates, and his audacious schemes. The principal means of detection in cases of burglary was by advertising the goods, and the great difficulty on the part of such miscreants was to obtain a ready sale for them—the receivers of stolen goods being aware that the thieves were at their mercy, and must accept what was offered. Now, to obviate these difficulties, Fleming had, as we before observed, concealed himself from justice on board of a river barge, which was made the receptacle for stolen goods: those which had been nefariously obtained at one place being by him and his associates carried up and down the river in the craft, and disposed of at a great distance, by which means the goods were never brought to light, so as to enable the police to recognise or trace them. This system had now been carried on with great success for upwards of twelve months, and would, in all probability, have not been discovered even now, had it not been that a quarrel as to profits had taken place, which had induced two of his associates to give information to the officers; and these two associates had also been permitted to turn king's evidence, in a case of burglary, in which Fleming was a principal, provided that it was considered necessary. But there was a more serious charge against the prisoner,—that of having attempted the life of a boy, named Jacob Faithful, belonging to the lighter, and who, it appeared, had suspicions of what was going on, and, in duty to his master, had carefully watched the proceedings, and given notice to others of what he had discovered from time to time. The lad was the chief evidence against the prisoner Fleming, and also against Marables, the other prisoner, of whom he could only observe, that circumstances would transpire, during the trial, in his favour, which he had no doubt would be well considered by his lordship. He would not detain the gentlemen of the jury any longer, but at once call on his witnesses.

I was then summoned, again asked the same questions as to the nature of an oath, and the judge being satisfied with my replies, I gave my evidence as before; the judge as I perceived, carefully examining my previous disposition, to ascertain if anything I now said was at variance with my former assertions. I was then cross-examined by the counsel for Fleming, but he could not make me vary in my evidence, I did, however, take the opportunity, whenever I was able, of saying all I could in favour of Marables. At last the counsel said he would ask me no more questions. I was dismissed; and the police-officer who had picked me up, and other parties who identified the various property as their own, and the manner in which they had been robbed of it, were examined. The evidence was too clear to admit of doubt. The jury immediately returned a verdict of guilty against Fleming and Marables, but strongly recommended Marables to the mercy of the crown. The judge rose, put on his black cap, and addressed the prisoners as follows. The court was so still, that a pin falling might have been heard:—

"You, William Fleming, have been tried by a jury of your countrymen, upon the charge of receiving stolen goods, to which you have added the most atrocious crime of intended murder. You have had a fair and impartial trial, and have been found guilty; and it appears that, even had you escaped in this instance, other charges, equally heavy, and which would equally consign you to condign punishment, were in readiness to be preferred against you. Your life has been one of guilt, not only in your own person, but also in abetting and stimulating others to crime; and you have wound up your shameful career by attempting the life of a fellow-creature. To hold out to you any hope of mercy is impossible. Your life is justly forfeited to the offended laws of your country; and your sentence is that you be removed from this court to the place from whence you came, and from thence to the place of execution, there to be hanged by the neck till you are dead; and may God, in his infinite goodness, have mercy on your soul!

"You, John Marables, have pleaded guilty to the charges brought against you; and it has appeared, during the evidence brought out on the trial, that, although you have been a party to these nefarious transactions, you are far from being hardened in your guilt." ("No, no!" exclaimed Marables.) "I believe sincerely that you are not, and much regret that one who, from the evidence brought forward, appears to have been, previously to this unfortunate connection, an honest man, should now appear in so disgraceful a situation. A severe punishment is, however, demanded by the voice of justice, and by that sentence of the law you must now be condemned: at the same time I trust that an appeal to the mercy of your sovereign will not be made in vain."

The judge then passed the sentence upon Marables, the prisoners were led out of court, and a new trial commenced; while Mr Drummond and the Dominie conducted me home. About a week after the trial, Fleming suffered the penalty of the law; while Marables was sentenced to transportation for life, which, however, previous to his sailing, was commuted to seven years.

In a few days the lighter returned. Her arrival was announced to me one fine sunny morning as I lay in bed, by a voice whose well-known notes poured into my ear as I was half dozing on my pillow:—

"Bright are the beams of the morning sky,
And sweet the dew the red blossoms sip,
But brighter the glances of dear woman's eye—

"Tom, you monkey, belay the warp, and throw the fenders over the side. Be smart, or old Fuzzle will be growling about his red paint.

"And sweet is the dew on her lip."

I jumped out of my little crib, threw open the window, the panes of which were crystallised with the frost in the form of little trees, and beheld the lighter just made fast to the wharf, the sun shining brightly, old Tom's face as cheerful as the morn, and young Tom laughing, jumping about, and blowing his fingers. I was soon dressed, and shaking hands with my barge-mates.

"Well, Jacob, how do you like the Old Bailey? Never was in it but once in my life, and never mean to go again if I can help it; that was when Sam Bowles was tried for his life, but my evidence saved him. I'll tell you how it was. Tom, look a'ter the breakfast; a bowl of tea this cold morning will be worth having. Come, jump about."

"But I never heard the story of Sam Bowles," answered Tom.

"What's that to you? I'm telling it to Jacob."

"But I want to hear it—so go on, father. I'll start you. Well, d'ye see, Sam Bowles—"

"Master Tom, them as play with *bowls* may meet with *rubbers*. Take care I don't *rub* down your hide. Off, you thief, and get breakfast."

"No, I won't: if I don't have your *Bowles* you shall have no *bowls* of tea. I've made my mind up to that."

"I tell you what, Tom; I shall never get any good out of you until I have both your legs ampitated. I've a great mind to send for the farrier."

"Thanky, father; but I find them very useful."

"Well," said I, "suppose we put off the story till breakfast time; and I'll go and help Tom to get it ready."

"Be it so, Jacob. I suppose Tom must have his way, as I spoiled him myself. I made him so fond of yarns, so I was a fool to be vexed.

"Oh, life is a river, and man is the boat
That over its surface is destined to float;
And joy is a cargo so easily stored,
That he is a fool who takes sorrow on board.

"Now I'll go on shore to master, and find out what's to be done next. Give me my stick, boy, and I shall crawl over the planks a little safer. A safe stool must have three legs, you know."

Old Tom then stumped away on shore. In about a quarter of an hour he returned, bringing half-a-dozen red herrings.

"Here, Tom, grill these sodgers. Jacob, who is that tall old chap, with such a devil of a cutwater, which I met just now with master? We are bound for Sheerness this trip, and I'm to land him at Greenwich."

"What, the Dominie?" replied I, from old Tom's description.

"His name did begin with a D, but that wasn't it."

"Dobbs?"

"Yes, that's nearer; he's to be a passenger on board of us, going down to see a friend who's very ill. Now, Tom, my hearty, bring out the crockery, for I want a little inside lining."

We all sat down to our breakfast, and as soon as old Tom had finished, his son called for the history of Sam Bowles.

"Well, now you shall have it. Sam Bowles was a shipmate of mine on board of the Greenlandman; he was one of our best harpooners, and a good, quiet, honest messmate as ever slung a hammock. He was spliced to as pretty a piece of flesh as ever was seen, but she wasn't as good as she was pretty. We were fitting out for another voyage, and his wife had been living on board with him some weeks, for Sam was devilish spoony on her, and couldn't bear her to be out of his sight. As we 'spected to sail in a few days, we were filling up our complement of men, and fresh hands came on board every day.

"One morning, a fine tall fellow, with a tail as thick as a hawser, came on board and offered himself; he was taken by the skipper, and went on shore again to get his traps. While he was still on deck I went below, and seeing Sam with his little wife on his knee playing with his love-locks, I said that there was a famous stout and good-looking fellow that we should have as a shipmate. Sam's wife, who, like all women, was a little curious, put her head up the hatchway to look at him. She put it down again very quick, as I thought, and made some excuse to go forward in the eyes of her, where she remained some time, and then, when she came aft, told Sam that she would go on shore. Now, as it had been agreed that she should remain on board till we were clear of the river, Sam couldn't think what the matter was; but she was positive, and go away she did, very much to Sam's astonishment and anger. In the evening, Sam went on shore and found her out, and what d'ye think the little Jezebel told him?—why, that one of the men had been rude to her when she went forward, and that's why she wouldn't stay on board. Sam was in a devil of a passion at this, and wanted to know which was the man; but she fondled him, and wouldn't tell him, because she was afraid that he'd be hurt. At last she bamboozled him, and sent him on board again quite content. Well, we remained three days longer, and then dropped down the river to Greenwich, where the captain was to come on board, and we were to sail as soon as the wind was fair. Now, this fine tall fellow was with us when we dropped down the river, and as Sam was sitting down on his chest eating a basin o' soup, the other man takes out a 'baccy pouch of seal-skin;—it was a very curious one, made out of the white and spotted part of a young seal's belly. 'I say, shipmate,' cries Sam, 'hand me over my 'baccy pouch. Where did you pick it up?'

"'Your pouch!' says he to him; 'I killed the seal, and my fancy girl made the pouch for me.'

"'Well, if that ain't cool! you'd swear a man out of his life, mate. Tom,' says he to me, 'ain't that my pouch which my wife gave me when I came back last trip?'

"I looked at it, and knew it again, and said it was. The tall fellow denied it, and there was a devil of a bobbery. Sam called him a thief, and he pitched Sam right down the main hatchway among the casks. After that there was a regular set-to, and Sam was knocked all to shivers, and obliged to give in. When the fight was over, I took up Sam's shirt for him to put on. 'That's my shirt,' cried the tall fellow.

"'That's Sam's shirt,' replied I; 'I know it's his.'

"'I tell you it's mine,' replied the man; 'my lass gave it to me to put on when I got up this morning. The other is his shirt.'

"We looked at the other, and they both were Sam's shirts. Now when Sam heard this, he put two and two together, and became very jealous and uneasy: he thought it odd that his wife was so anxious to leave the ship when this tall fellow came on board; and what with the pouch and the shirt he was puzzled. His wife had promised to come down to Greenwich and see him off. When we anchored, some of the men went on shore—among others the tall fellow. Sam, whose head was swelled up like a pumpkin, told one of his shipmates to say to his wife that he could not come on shore, and that she must come off to him. Well, it was about nine o'clock, dark, and all the stars were twinkling, when Sam says to me, 'Tom, let's go on shore; my black eyes can't be seen in the dark.' As we hauled up the boat, the second mate told Sam to take his harpoon-iron on shore for him, to have the hole for the becket punched larger. Away we went, and the first place, of course, that Sam went to, was the house where he knew that his wife put up at, as before. He went upstairs to her room, and I followed him. The door was not made fast, and in we went. There was his little devil of a wife, fast asleep in the arms of the tall fellow. Sam couldn't command his rage, and having the harpoon-iron in his hand, he drove it right through the tall fellow's body before I could prevent him. It was a dreadful sight: the man groaned, and his head fell over the side of the bed. Sam's wife screamed, and made Sam more wroth by throwing herself on the man's body, and weeping over it. Sam would have pulled out the iron to run her through with, but that was impossible. The noise brought up the people of the house, and it was soon known that murder had been committed. The constable came, Sam was thrown into prison, and I went on board and told the whole story. Well, we were just about to heave up, for we had shipped two more men in place of Sam, who was to be tried for his life, and the poor fellow he had killed, when a lawyer chap came on board with what they call a *suppeny* for me; all I know is, that the lawyer pressed me into his service, and I lost my voyage. I was taken on shore, and well fed till the trial came on. Poor Sam was at the bar for murder. The gentleman in his gown and wig began his yarn, stating that how the late fellow, whose name was Will Errol, was with his own wife when Sam harpooned him.

"'That's a lie!' cried Sam; 'he was with my wife. False papers! Here are mine;' and he pulled out his tin case, and handed them to the court.

"The judge said that this was not the way to try people and that Sam must hold his tongue; so the trial went on, and at first they had it all their own way. Then our turn came, and I was called up to prove what had passed, and I stated how the man was with Sam's wife, and how he, having the harpoon-iron in his hand, had run it through his body. Then they compared the certificates, and it was proved that the little Jezebel had married them both; but she had married Sam first, so he had the most right to her; but fancying the other man afterwards, she thought she might as well have two strings to her bow. So the judge declared that she was Sam's wife, and that any man, even without the harpoon in his hand, would be justified in killing a man whom he found in bed with his own wife. So Sam went scot-free; but the judge wouldn't let off Sam's wife, as she had caused murder by her wicked conduct; he tried her a'terwards for *biggery*, as they call it, and sent her over the water for life. Sam never held up his head a'terwards; what with having killed an innocent man, and the 'haviour of his wife, he was always down. He went out to the fishery, and a whale cut the boat in two with her tail; Sam was stunned, and went down like a stone. So you see the mischief brought about by this little Jezebel, who must have two husbands, and be damned to her."

"Well, that's a good yarn, father," said Tom, as soon as it was finished. "I was right in saying I would hear it. Wasn't I?"

"No," replied old Tom, putting out his large hand, and seizing his son by the collar; "and now you've put me in mind of it, I'll pay you off for old scores."

"Lord love you, father, you don't owe me anything," said Tom.

"Yes, I do; and now I'll give you a receipt in full."

"O Lord! they'll be drowned," screamed Tom, holding up both his hands with every symptom of terror.

Old Tom turned short round to look in the direction, letting go his hold. Tom made his escape, and burst out a-laughing. I laughed also, and so at last did his father.

I went on shore, and found that old Tom's report was correct—the Dominie was at breakfast with Mr Drummond. The new usher had charge of the boys, and the governors had allowed him a fortnight's holiday to visit an old friend at Greenwich. To save expense, as well as to indulge his curiosity, the old man had obtained a passage down in the lighter. "Never yet, Jacob, have I put my feet into that which floateth on the watery element," observed he to me; "nor would I now, but that it saveth money, which thou knowest well is with me not plentiful. Many dangers I expect, many perils shall I encounter; such have I read of in books; and well might Horace exclaim—'*Ille robur et aes triplex,*' with reference to the first man who ventured afloat. Still doth Mr Drummond assure me that the lighter is of that strength as to be able to resist the force of the winds and waves; and, confiding in Providence, I intend to venture, Jacob, '*te duce.*'"

"Nay, sir," replied I, laughing at the idea which the Dominie appeared to have formed of the dangers of river navigation, "old Tom is the *Dux.*"

"Old Tom; where have I seen that name? Now I do recall to mind that I have seen the name painted in large letters upon a cask at the tavern bar of the inn at Brentford; but what it did intend to signify I did not inquire. What connection is there?"

"None," replied I; "but I rather think they are very good friends. The tide turns in half-an-hour, sir; are you ready to go on board?"

"Truly am I, and well prepared, having my habiliments in a bundle, my umbrella and my great-coat, as well as my spencer for general wear. But where I am to sleep hath not yet been made known to me. Peradventure one sleepeth not—'*tanto in periculo.*'"

"Yes, sir, we do. You shall have my berth, and I'll turn in with young Tom."

"Hast thou, then, a young Tom as well as an old Tom on board?"

"Yes, sir; and a dog, also, of the name of Tommy."

"Well, then, we will embark, and thou shalt make me known to this triad of Thomases. '*Inde* Tomos *dictus locus est.*' (*Cluck, cluck.*) Ovid, I thank thee."

Chapter Eleven

The old Dominie's bundle and other paraphernalia being sent on board, he took farewell of Mr Drummond and his family in so serious a manner, that I was convinced that he considered he was about to enter upon a dangerous adventure, and then I led him down to the wharf where the lighter lay alongside. It was with some trepidation that he crossed the plank, and got on board, when he recovered himself and looked round.

"My sarvice to you, old gentleman," said a voice behind the Dominie. It was that of old Tom, who had just come from the cabin. The Dominie turned round, and perceived old Tom.

"This is old Tom, sir," said I to the Dominie, who stared with astonishment.

"Art thou, indeed? Jacob, thou didst not tell me that he had been curtailed of his fair proportions, and I was surprised. Art thou then Dux?" continued the Dominie, addressing old Tom.

"Yes," interrupted young Tom, who had come from forward, "he is *ducks*, because he waddles on his short stumps; and I won't say who be goose. Eh, father?"

"Take care you don't *buy goose*, for your imperance, sir," cried old Tom.

"A forward boy," exclaimed the Dominie.

"Yes," replied Tom "I'm generally forward."

"Art thou forward in thy learning? Canst thou tell me Latin for goose?"

"To be sure," replied Tom; "Brandy."

"Brandy!" exclaimed the Dominie. "Nay, child, it is *anser*."

"Then I was right," replied Tom. "You had your *answer*!"

"The boy is apt." *Cluck cluck.*

"He is apt to be devilish saucy, old gentleman; but never mind that, there's no harm in him."

"This, then, is young Tom, I presume, Jacob?" said the Dominie, referring to me.

"Yes, sir," replied I. "You have seen old Tom, and young Tom, and you have only to see Tommy."

"Want to see Tommy, sir?" cried Tom. "Here, Tommy, Tommy!"

But Tommy, who was rather busy with a bone forward, did not immediately answer to his call, and the Dominie turned round to survey the river. The scene was busy, barges and boats passing in every direction, others lying on shore, with waggons taking out the coals and other cargoes, men at work, shouting or laughing with each other. "'*Populus in fluviis*,' as Virgil hath it. Grand indeed is the vast river, '*Labitur et labetur in omne volubilis aevum*,' as the generations of men are swept into eternity," said the Dominie, musing aloud. But Tommy had now made his appearance, and Tom, in his mischief, had laid hold of the tail of the Dominie's coat, and shown it to the dog. The dog, accustomed to seize a rope when it was shown to him, immediately seized the Dominie's coat, making three desperate tugs at it. The Dominie, who was in one of his reveries, and probably thought it was I who wished to direct his attention elsewhere, each time waved his hand, without turning round, as much as to say, "I am busy now."

"Haul and hold," cried Tom to the dog, splitting his sides, and the tears running down his cheeks with laughing. Tommy made one more desperate tug, carrying away one tail of the Dominie's coat; but the Dominie perceived it not, he was still "*nubibus*," while the dog galloped forward with the fragment, and Tom chased him to recover it. The Dominie continued in his reverie, when old Tom burst out—

"O, England, dear England, bright gem of the ocean,
    Thy valleys and fields look fertile and gay,
The heart clings to thee with a sacred devotion,
    And memory adores when in far lands away."

The song gradually called the Dominie to his recollection; indeed, the strain was so beautiful that it would have vibrated in the ears of a dying man. The Dominie gradually turned round, and when old Tom had finished, exclaimed, "Truly it did delight mine ear, and from such—and," continued the Dominie, looking down upon old Tom—"without legs too!"

"Why, old gentleman, I don't sing with my *legs*," answered old Tom.

"Nay, good *Dux*, I am not so deficient as not to be aware that a man singeth from the mouth; yet is thy voice mellifluous, sweet as the honey of Hybla, strong—"

"As the Latin for goose," finished Tom. "Come, father, old *Dictionary* is in the doldrums; rouse him up with another stave."

"I'll rouse you up with the stave of a cask over your shoulders, Mr Tom. What have you done with the old gentleman's swallow-tail?"

"Leave me to settle that affair, father: I know how to get out of a scrape."

"So you ought, you scamp, considering how many you get into; but the craft are swinging and heaving up. Forward there, Jacob, and sway up the mast; there's Tom and Tommy to help you."

The mast was hoisted up, the sail set, and the lighter in the stream before the Dominie was out of his reverie.

"Are there whirlpools here?" said the Dominie, talking more to himself than to those about him.

"Whirlpools!" replied young Tom, who was watching and mocking him; "yes, that there are, under the bridges. I've watched a dozen *chips* go down, one after the other."

"A dozen *ships*!" exclaimed the Dominie, turning to Tom; "and every soul lost?"

"Never saw them afterwards," replied Tom, in a mournful voice.

"How little did I dream of the dangers of those so near me," said the Dominie, turning away, and communing with himself. "'Those who go down to the sea in ships, and occupy their business in great waters;'—'*Et vastas aperit Syrtes;*'—'These men see the works of the Lord, and his wonders in the deep.'—'*Alternante vorans vasta Charybdis aqua.*'—'For at his word the stormy wind ariseth, which lifteth up the waves thereof.'—'*Surgens a puppi ventus.—Ubi tempestas et caeli mobilis humor.*'—'They are carried up to the heavens, and down again to the deep.'—'*Gurgitibus miris et lactis vertice torrens.*'—'Their soul melteth away because of their troubles.'—'*Stant pavidi. Omnibus ignoiae mortis timor, omnibus hostem.*'—'They reel to and fro, and stagger like a drunken man.'"

"So they do, father, don't they, sometimes?" observed Tom, leering his eye at his father. "That's all I've understood of his speech."

"They are at their wit's end," continued the Dominie.

"Mind the end of your wit, master Tom," answered his father, wroth at the insinuation.

"'So when they call upon the Lord in their trouble'—'*Cujus jurare timent et fallere nomen*'—'He delivereth them out of their distress, for he makest the storm to cease, so that the waves thereof are still;' yea, still and smooth as the peaceful water which now floweth rapidly by our anchored vessel—yet it appeareth to me that the scene hath changed. These fields met not mine eyes before. '*Riparumque toros et prata recentia rivis.*' Surely we have moved from the wharf?"—and the Dominie turned round, and discovered, for the first time, that we were more than a mile from the place at which we had embarked.

"Pray, sir, what's the use of speech, sir?" interrogated Tom, who had been listening to the whole of the Dominie's long soliloquy.

"Thou asketh a foolish question, boy. We are endowed with the power of speech to enable us to communicate our ideas."

"That's exactly what I thought, sir. Then pray what's the use of your talking all that gibberish, that none of us could understand?"

"I crave thy pardon, child; I spoke, I presume, in the dead languages."

"If they're dead, why not let them rest in their graves?"

"Good; thou hast wit." (*Cluck, cluck.*) "Yet, child, know that it is pleasant to commune with the dead."

"Is it? then we'll put you on shore at Battersea churchyard."

"Silence, Tom. He's full of his sauce, sir—you must forgive it."

"Nay, it pleaseth me to hear him talk; but it would please me more to hear thee sing."

"Then here goes, sir, to drown Tom's impudence:—

"Glide on my bark, the morning tide
Is gently floating by thy side;
Around thy prow the waters bright,
In circling rounds of broken light,
Are glittering, as if ocean gave
Her countless gems unto the wave.

"That's a pretty air, and I first heard it sung by a pretty woman; but that's all I know of the song. She sang another—

"I'd be a butterfly, born in a bower."

"You'd be a butterfly!" said the Dominie, taking old Tom literally, and looking at his person.

Young Tom roared, "Yes, sir, he'd be a butterfly, and I don't see why he shouldn't very soon. His legs are gone, and his wings aren't come: so he's a grub now, and that, you know, is the next thing to it. What a funny old beggar it is, father—aren't it?"

"Tom, Tom, go forward, sir; we must shoot the bridge."

"Shoot!" exclaimed the Dominie; "shoot what?"

"You aren't afraid of fire-arms, are ye, sir?" inquired Tom.

"Nay, I said not that I was afraid of fire-arms; but why should you shoot?"

"We never could get on without it, sir; we shall have plenty of shooting, by-and-by. You don't know this river."

"Indeed, I thought not of such doings; or that there were other dangers besides that of the deep waters."

"Go forward, Tom, and don't be playing with your betters," cried old Tom. "Never mind him, sir, he's only humbugging you."

"Explain, Jacob. The language of both old Tom and young Tom are to me as incomprehensible as would be that of the dog Tommy."

"Or as your Latin is to them, sir."

"True, Jacob, true. I have no right to complain; nay, I do not complain, for I am amused, although at times much puzzled."

We now shot Putney Bridge, and as a wherry passed us, old Tom carolled out—

"Did you ever hear tell of a jolly young waterman?"

"No, I never did," said the Dominie, observing old Tom's eyes directed towards him. Tom, amused by this *naïveté* on the part of the Dominie, touched him by the sleeve, on the other side, and commenced with his treble—

"Did you ne'er hear a tale
Of a maid in the vale?"

"Not that I can recollect, my child," replied the Dominie.

"Then, where have you been all your life?"

"My life has been employed, my lad, in teaching the young idea how to shoot."

"So, you're an old soldier, after all, and afraid of fire-arms. Why don't you hold yourself up? I suppose it's that enormous jib of yours that brings you down by the head."

"Tom, Tom, I'll cut you into pork pieces if you go on that gait. Go and get dinner under weigh, you scamp, and leave the gentleman alone. Here's more wind coming.

"A wet sheet and a flowing sea,
    A wind that follows fast,
And fills the white and rustling sail,
    And bends the gallant mast.
And bends the gallant mast, my boys,
    While, like the eagle free,
Away the good ship flies, and leaves
    Old England on the lee."

"Jacob," said the Dominie, "I have heard by the mouth of Rumour, with her hundred tongues, how careless and indifferent are sailors unto danger; but I never could have believed that such lightness of heart could have been shown. Yon man, although certainly not old in years, yet, what is he?—a remnant of a man resting upon unnatural and ill-proportioned support. Yon lad, who is yet but a child, appears as blythe and merry as if he were in possession of all the world can afford. I have an affection for that bold child, and would fain teach him the rudiments, at least, of the Latin tongue."

"I doubt if Tom would ever learn them, sir. He hath a will of his own."

"It grieveth me to hear thee say so, for he lacketh not talent, but instruction; and the Dux, he pleaseth me mightily—a second Palinurus. Yet how that a man could venture to embark upon an element, to struggle through the horrors of which must occasionally demand the utmost exertion of every limb, with the want of the two most necessary for his safety, is to me quite incomprehensible."

"He can keep his legs, sir."

"Nay, Jacob; how can he *keep* what are *already gone*? Even thou speakest strangely upon the water. I see the dangers that surround us, Jacob, yet I am calm: I feel that I have not lived a wicked life—'*Integer vitae, scelerisque purus*,' as Horace truly saith, may venture, even as I have done, upon the broad expanse of water. What is it that the boy is providing for us? It hath an inviting smell."

"Lobscouse, master," replied old Tom, "and not bad lining either."

"I recollect no such word—*unde derivatur*, friend?"

"What's that, master?" inquired old Tom.

"It's Latin for lobscouse, depend upon it, father," cried Tom, who was stirring up the savoury mess with a large wooden spoon. "He be a *deadly* lively old gentleman, with his dead language. Dinner's all ready. Are we to let go the anchor, or pipe to dinner first?"

"We may as well anchor, boys. We have not a quarter of an hour's more ebb, and the wind is heading us."

Tom and I went forward, brailed up the mainsail, cleared away, and let go the anchor. The lighter swung round rapidly to the stream. The Dominie, who had been in a fit of musing, with his eyes cast upon the forests of masts which we had passed below London Bridge, and which were now some way astern of us, of a sudden exclaimed, in a loud voice, "*Parce precor! Periculosum est!*"

The lighter, swinging short round to her anchor, had surprised the Dominie with the rapid motion of the panorama, and he thought we had fallen in with one of the whirlpools mentioned by Tom. "What has happened, good Dux? tell me," cried the Dominie to old Tom, with alarm in his countenance.

"Why, master, I'll tell you after my own fashion," replied old Tom, smiling; and then singing, as he held the Dominie by the button of his spencer—

"Now to her berth the craft draws nigh,
    With slacken'd sail, she feels the tide;
'Stand clear the cable!' is the cry—
    The anchor's gone, we safely ride.

"And now, master, we'll bail out the lobscouse. We sha'n't weigh anchor again until to-morrow morning; the wind's right in our teeth, and it will blow fresh, I'm sartain. Look how the scud's flying; so now we'll have a jolly time of it, and you shall have your allowance of grog on board before you turn in."

"I have before heard of that potation," replied the Dominie, sitting down on the coaming of the hatchway, "and fain would taste it."

Chapter Twelve

We now took our seats on the deck, round the saucepan, for we did not trouble ourselves with dishes, and the Dominie appeared to enjoy the lobscouse very much. In the course of half-an-hour all was over; that is to say, we had eaten as much as we wished; and the Newfoundland dog, who, during our repast, lay close by young Tom, flapping the deck with his tail, and sniffing the savoury smell of the compound, had just licked all our plates quite clean, and was now finishing with his head in the saucepan; while Tom was busy carrying the crockery into the cabin, and bringing out the bottle and tin pannikins, ready for the promised carouse.

"There, now, master, there's a glass o' grog for you that would float a marline-spike. See if that don't warm the *cockles* of your old heart."

"Ay," added Tom, "and set all your *muscles* as taut as weather backstays."

"Master Tom, with your leave, I'll mix your grog for you myself. Hand me back that bottle, you rascal."

"Just as you please, father," replied Tom, handing the bottle; "but recollect, none of your *water bewitched*. Only help me as you love me."

Old Tom mixed a pannikin of grog for Tom, and another for himself. I hardly need say which was the *stiffer* of the two.

"Well, father, I suppose you think the grog will run short. To be sure, one bottle aren't too much 'mong four of us."

"One bottle, you scamp! there's another in the cupboard."

"Then you must see double already, father."

Old Tom, who was startled at this news, and who imagined that Tom must have gained possession of the other bottle, jumped up and made for the cupboard, to ascertain whether what Tom asserted was correct. This was what Tom wished; he immediately changed pannikins of grog with his father, and remained quiet.

"There *is* another bottle, Tom," said his father, coming out and taking his seat again. "I knew there was. You young rascal, you don't know how you frightened me!" And old Tom put the pannikin to his lips. "Drowned the miller, by heavens!" said he, "What could I have been about?" ejaculated he, adding more spirit to his mixture.

"I suppose, upon the strength of another bottle in the locker, you are doubling the strength of your grog. Come, father," and Tom held out his pannikin, "do put a little drop in mine—it's seven-water grog, and I'm not on the black-list."

"No, no, Tom; your next shall be stronger. Well, master, how do you like your liquor?"

"Verily," replied the Dominie, "it is a pleasant and seducing liquor. Lo and behold! I am at the bottom of my utensil."

"Stop till I fill it up again, old gentleman. I see you are one of the right sort. You know what the song says—

"A plague on those musty old lubbers,
    Who tell us to fast and to think,
And patient fall in with life's rubbers,
    With nothing but *water* to *drink*!

"Water, indeed! The only use of water I know is to mix your grog with, and float vessels up and down the world. Why was the sea made salt, but to prevent our drinking too much water. Water, indeed!

"A can of good grog, had they swigg'd it,
    T'would have set them for pleasure agog,
        And in spite of the rules
        Of the schools,
        The old fools
Would have all of them swigg'd it,
And swore there was nothing like grog."

"I'm exactly of your opinion, father," said Tom, holding out his empty pannikin.

"Always ready for two things, Master Tom—grog and mischief; but, however, you shall have one more *dose*."

"It hath, then, medicinal virtues?" inquired the Dominie.

"Ay, that it has, master—more than all the quacking medicines in the world. It cures grief and melancholy, and prevents spirits from getting low."

"I doubt that, father," cried Tom, holding up the bottle "for the more grog we drink, the more the *spirits become low*."

Cluck, cluck, came from the thorax of the Dominie. "Verily, friend Tom, it appeareth, among other virtues, to sharpen the wits. Proceed, friend Dux, in the medicinal virtues of grog."

"Well, master, it cures love when it's not returned, and adds to it when it is. I've heard say it will cure jealousy; but that I've my doubts of. Now I think on it, I will tell you a yarn about a jealous match between a couple of fools. Jacob, aren't your pannikin empty, my boy?"

"Yes," replied I, handing it up to be filled. It was empty, for, not being very fond of it myself, Tom, with my permission, had drunk it as well as his own.

"There, Jacob, is a good dose for you; you aren't always craving after it, like Tom."

"He isn't troubled with low spirits, as I am, father."

"How long has that been your complaint, Tom?" inquired I.

"Ever since I heard how to cure it. Come, father, give us the yarn."

"Well, then, you must mind that an old shipmate o' mine, Ben Leader, had a wife named Poll, a pretty sort of craft in her way—neat in her rigging, swelling-bows, taking sort of figure-head, and devilish well rounded in the counter; altogether, she was a very fancy girl, and all the men were after her. She'd a roguish eye, and liked to be stared at, as most pretty women do, because it flatters their vanities. Now, although she liked to be noticed so far by the other chaps, yet Ben was the only one she ever wished to be handled by; it was 'Paws off, Pompey!' with all the rest. Ben Leader was a good-looking, active, smart chap, and could foot it in a reel, or take a bout at single-stick with the very best o' them; and she was mortal fond of him, and mortal jealous if he talked to any other woman, for the women liked Ben as much as the men liked she. Well, as they returned love for love, so did they return jealousy for jealousy; and the lads and lasses, seeing that, had a pleasure in making them come to a misunderstanding. So every day it became worse and worse between them. Now, I always says that it's a stupid thing to be jealous, *'cause* if there be *cause*, there be no *cause* for love and if there be no *cause*, there be no *cause* for jealousy."

"You're like a row in a rookery, father—nothing but *caws*," interrupted Tom.

"Well, I suppose I am; but that's what I call chop logic—aren't it, master?"

"It was a syllogism," replied the Dominie, taking the pannikin from his mouth.

"I don't know what that is, nor do I want to know," replied old Tom; "so I'll just go on with my story. Well, at last they came to downright fighting. Ben licks Poll 'cause she talked and laughed with other men, and Poll cries and whines all day 'cause he won't sit on her knee, instead of going on board and 'tending to his duty. Well, one night, a'ter work was over, Ben goes on shore to the house where he and Poll used to sleep; and when he sees the girl in the bar, he says, 'Where is Poll?' Now, the girl at the bar was a fresh-comer, and answers, 'What girl?' So Ben describes her, and the bar-girl answers, 'She be just gone to bed with her husband, I suppose;' for, you see, there was a woman like her who had gone up to her bed, sure enough. When Ben heard that, he gave his trousers one hitch, and calls for a quartern, drinks it off with a sigh, and leaves the house, believing it all to be true. A'ter Ben was gone, Poll makes her appearance, and when she finds Ben wasn't in the tap, says, 'Young woman, did a man go upstairs just now?' 'Yes,' replied the bar-girl, 'with his wife, I suppose; they be turned in this quarter of an hour.' When she almost turned mad with rage, and then as white as a sheet, and then she burst into tears, and runs out of the house, crying out, 'Poor misfortunate creature that I am!' knocking everything down undersized, and running into the arms of every man who came athwart her hawse."

"I understood him, but just now, that she was running on foot; yet doth he talk about her *horse*. Expound, Jacob."

"It was a nautical figure of speech, sir."

"Exactly," rejoined Tom; "it meant her figure-head, old gentleman; but my yarn won't cut a figure if I'm brought up all standing in this way. Suppose, master, you hear the story first, and understand it a'terwards?"

"I will endeavour to comprehend by the context," replied the Dominie.

"That is, I suppose, that you'll allow me to stick to my text. Well, then, here's coil away again. Ben, you see, what with his jealousy and what with a whole quartern at a draught, became *somehow nohow*, and he walked down to the jetty with the intention of getting rid of himself, and his wife and all his trouble by giving his soul back to his Creator, and his body to the fishes."

"Bad philosophy," quoth the Dominie.

"I agree with you, master," replied old Tom.

"Pray what sort of a thing is philosophy?" inquired Tom.

"Philosophy," replied old Tom, "is either hanging, drowning, shooting yourself, or, in short, getting out of the world without help."

"Nay," replied the Dominie, "that is *felo de se*."

"Well, I pronounce it quicker than you, master; but it's one and the same thing: but to go on. While Ben was standing on the jetty, thinking whether he should take one more quid of 'baccy afore he dived, who should come down but Poll, with her hair all adrift, streaming and coach-whipping astern of her, with the same intention as Ben—to commit *philo-zoffy*. Ben, who was standing at the edge of the jetty, his eyes fixed upon the water, as it eddied among the piles, looking as dismal as if he had swallowed a hearse and six, with the funeral feathers hanging out of his mouth—"

"A bold comparison," murmured the Dominie.

"Never sees her; and she was so busy with herself, that, although close to him, she never sees he—always remembering that the night was dark. So Poll turned her eyes up, for all the world like a dying jackdaw."

"Tell me, friend Dux," interrupted the Dominie, "doth a jackdaw die in any peculiar way?"

"Yes," replied young Tom; "he always dies black, master."

"Then doth he die as he liveth. (*Cluck, cluck.*) Proceed, good Dux."

"And don't you break the thread of my yarn any more, master, if you wish to hear the end of it. So Poll begins to bludder about Ben. 'O Ben, Ben,' cried she; 'cruel, cruel man; for to come—for to go;—for to go—for to come!'

"'Who's there?' shouted Ben.

"'For to come—for to go,' cried Poll.

"'Ship ahoy!' hailed Ben, again.

"'For to go—for to come,' blubbered Poll; and then she couldn't bring out anything more for sobbing. With that, Ben, who thought he knew the voice, walks up to her, and says, 'Be that you, Poll?'

"'Be that you, Ben?' replied Poll, taking her hands from her face, and looking at him.

"'I thought you were in bed with—with—oh! Poll!' said Ben.

"'And I thought you were in bed with—oh! Ben!' replied Poll.

"'But I wasn't, Poll?'

"'Nor more wasn't I, Ben.'

"'And what brought you here, Poll?'

"'I wanted for to die, Ben. And what brought you here, Ben?'

"'I didn't want for to live, Poll, when I thought you false.'

"Then Polly might have answered in the words of the old song, master; but her poor heart was too full, I suppose." And Tom sang—

"Your Polly has never been false, she declares,
Since last time we parted at Wapping Old Stairs."

"Howsomever, in the next minute they were both hugging and kissing, sobbing, shivering and shaking in each other's arms; and as soon as they had settled themselves a little, back they went, arm-in-arm, to the house, and had a good stiff glass to prevent their taking the rheumatism, went to bed, and were cured of their jealously ever a'terwards—which in my opinion, was a much better *philo-zoffy* than the one they had both been bound on. There, I've wound it all off at last, master, and now we'll fill up our pannikins."

"Before I consent, friend Dux, pr'ythee inform me how much of this pleasant liquor may be taken without inebriating, *vulgo*, getting tipsy."

"Father can drink enough to float a jolly-boat, master," replied Tom; "so you needn't fear. I'll drink pan for pan with you all night long."

"Indeed you won't, mister Tom," replied the father.

"But I will, master."

I perceived that the liquor had already had some effect upon my worthy pedagogue, and was not willing that he should be persuaded into excess. I therefore pulled him by the coat as a hint; but he was again deep in thought, and he did not heed me. Tired of sitting so long, I got up, and walked forward to look at the cable.

"Strange," muttered the Dominie, "that Jacob should thus pull me by the garment. What could he mean?"

"Did he pull you, sir?" inquired Tom.

"Yes, many times; and then he walked away."

"It appears that you have been pulled too much, sir," replied Tom, appearing to pick up the tail of his coat, which had been torn off by the dog, and handing it to him.

"*Eheu! Jacobe—fili dilectissime—quid fecisti?*" cried the Dominie, holding up the fragment of his coat with a look of despair.

"'A long pull, a strong pull, and a pull altogether,'" sang out old Tom: and then looking at Tom, "Now, ain't you a pretty rascal, master Tom?"

"It is done," exclaimed the Dominie, with a sigh, putting the fragment into the remaining pocket; "and it cannot be undone."

"Now, I think it is undone, and can be done, master," replied Tom. "A needle and thread will soon join the pieces of your old coat again—in *holy* matrimony, I may safely say—"

"True. (*Cluck, cluck.*) My housekeeper will restore it; yet will she be wroth, '*Feminae curaeque iraeque;*' but let us think no more about it," cried the Dominie, drinking deeply from his pannikin, and each minute verging fast to intoxication. "'*Nunc est bibendum, nunc pede libero pulsanda tellus.*' I feel as if I were lifted up, and could dance, yea, and could exalt my voice and sing."

"Could you, my jolly old master? then we will both dance and sing—

"Come, let us dance and sing,
While all Barbadoes bells shall ring,
Mars scrapes the fiddle string
While Venus plays the lute.
Hymen gay, trips away,
Jocund at the wedding day.

"Now for chorus—

"Come, let us dance and sing."

Chapter Thirteen

I heard Tom's treble, and a creaking noise, which I recognised to proceed from the Dominie, who had joined the chorus; and I went aft, if possible to prevent further excess; but I found that the grog had mounted into the Dominie's head, and all my hints were disregarded. Tom was despatched for the other bottle, and the Dominie's pannikin was replenished, old Tom roaring out—

"Come, sling the flowing bowl;
　Fond hopes arise,
　The girls we prize
Shall bless each jovial soul;
　The can, boys, bring,
　We'll dance and sing,
While foaming billows roll.

"Now for the chorus again—

"Come, sling the flowing bowl, etcetera.

"Jacob, why don't you join?" The chorus was given by the whole of us. The Dominie's voice was even louder, though not quite so musical, as old Tom's.

"*Evoé!*" cried the Dominie; "*evoé! cantemus.*

"*Amo, amas*—I loved a lass,
　For she was tall and slender;
Amas, amat—she laid me flat,
　Though of the feminine gender.

"Truly do I not forget the songs of my youth, and of my hilarious days: yet doth the potent spirit work upon me like the god in the Cumean sybil; and I shall soon prophecy that which shall come to pass."

"So can I," said Tom, giving me a nudge, and laughing.

"Do thine office of Ganymede, and fill up the pannikin; put not in too much of the element. Once more exalt thy voice, good Dux."

"Always ready, master," cried Tom, who sang out again in praise of his favourite liquor—

"Smiling grog is the sailor's best hope, his sheet anchor,
    His compass, his cable, his log,
That gives him a heart which life's cares cannot canker.
    Though dangers around him,
    Unite to confound him,
He braves them, and tips off his grog.
    'Tis grog, only grog,
Is his rudder, his compass, his cable, his log,
    The sailor's sheet anchor is grog."

"Verily, thou art an Apollo—or, rather, referring to thy want of legs, half an Apollo—that is, a *demi*-god. (*Cluck, cluck.*) Sweet is thy lyre, friend Dux."

"Fair words, master; I'm no liar," cried Tom. "Clap a stopper on your tongue, or you'll get into disgrace."

"*Ubi lapsus quid feci,*" said the Dominie; "I spoke of thy musical tongue; and, furthermore, I spoke alle-gori-cal-ly."

"I know a man lies with his tongue as well as you do, old chap; but as for telling a *hell of a* (something) *lie*, as you states, I say I never did," rejoined old Tom, who was getting cross in his cups.

I now interfered, as there was every appearance of a fray; and in spite of young Tom, who wished, as he termed it, to *kick up a shindy*, prevailed upon them to make friends, which they did, shaking hands for nearly five minutes. When this was ended, I again entreated the Dominie not to drink any more, but to go to bed.

"*Amice, Jacobe,*" replied the Dominie; "the liquor hath mounted into thy brain, and thou wouldst rebuke thy master and thy preceptor. Betake thee to thy couch, and sleep off the effects of thy drink. Verily, Jacob, thou art *plenus Veteris Bacchi*; or, in plain English, thou art drunk. Canst thou conjugate, Jacob? I fear not. Canst thou decline, Jacob? I fear not. Canst thou scan, Jacob? I fear not. Nay, Jacob, methinks that thou art unsteady in thy gait, and not over clear in thy vision. Canst thou hear, Jacob? if so, I will give thee an oration against inebriety, with which thou mayest down on thy pillow. Wilt thou have it in Latin or in Greek?"

"O, damn your Greek and Latin!" cried old Tom; "keep that for to-morrow. Sing us a song, my old hearty; or shall I sing you one? Here goes—

> "For while the grog goes round,
> All sense of danger's drown'd,
> We despise it to a man;
> We sing a little—"

"Sing a little," bawled the Dominie.

"And laugh a little—"

"Laugh a little," chorused young Tom.

"And work a little—"

"Work a little," cried the Dominie.

"And swear a little—"

"Swear *not* a little," echoed Tom.

"And fiddle a little—"

"Fiddle a little," hiccuped the Dominie.

"And foot it a little—"

"Foot it a little," repeated Tom.

> "And swig the flowing can,
> And fiddle a little,
> And foot it a little,
> And swig the flowing can—"

roared old Tom, emptying his pannikin.

"And swig the flowing can—"

followed the Dominie, tossing off his.

"And swig the flowing can—"

cried young Tom turning up his pannikin empty.

"Hurrah! that's what I calls glorious. Let's have it over again, and then we'll have another dose. Come, now, all together." Again was the song repeated; and when they came to "foot it a little," old Tom jumped on his stumps, seizing hold of the Dominie, who immediately rose, and the three danced round and round for a minute or two, singing the song and chorus, till old Tom, who was very far gone, tripped against the coamings of the hatchway, pitching his head into the Dominie's stomach, who fell backwards, clinging to young Tom's hand; so that they all rolled on the deck together—my worthy preceptor underneath the other two.

"Foot it *rather too much* that time, father," said young Tom, getting up the first, and laughing. "Come, Jacob, let's put father on his pins again; he can't rise without a purchase." With some difficulty, we succeeded. As soon as he was on his legs again, old Tom put a hand upon each of our shoulders, and commenced, with a drunken leer—

"What though his timbers they are gone,
 And he's a slave to tipple,
No better sailor e'er was born
 Than Tom, the jovial cripple."

"Thanky, my boys, thanky; now rouse up the old gentleman. I suspect we knocked the wind out of him. Hollo, there, are you hard and fast?"

"The bricks are hard, and verily my senses are fast departing," quoth the Dominie, rousing himself, and sitting up, staring around him.

"Senses going, do you say, master?" cried old Tom. "Don't throw them overboard till we have made a finish. One more pannikin apiece, one more song, and then to bed. Tom, where's the bottle?"

"Drink no more, sir, I beg; you'll be ill to-morrow," said I to the Dominie.

"*Deprome quadrimum,*" hiccuped the Dominie. "*Carpe diem—quam minimum—creula postero.*—Sing, friend Dux—*Quem virum—sumes celebrare—music amicus.*—Where's my pattypan?—We are not Thracians—*Natis in usum—laetitae scyphis pugnare—*(hiccup)*—Thracum est*—therefore we—will not fight—but we will drink—*recepto dulce mihi furere est amico*—Jacob, thou art drunk—sing, friend Dux, or shall I sing?

"*Propria quae maribus* had a little dog,
 Quae genus was his name—

"My memory faileth me—what was the tune?"

"That tune was the one the old cow died of, I'm sure," replied Tom. "Come, old Nosey, strike up again."

"Nosey, from *nasus*—truly, it is a fair epithet; and it remindeth me that my nose—suffered in the fall which I received just now. Yet I cannot sing—having no words—"

"Nor tune, either, master," replied old Tom; "so here goes for you —

"Young Susan had lovers, so many that she
　Hardly knew upon which to decide;
They all spoke sincerely, and promised to be
　All worthy of such a sweet bride.
In the morning she'd gossip with William, and then
　The noon will be spent with young Harry,
The evening with Tom; so, amongst all the men,
　She never could tell which to marry.
　　Heigho! I am afraid
　Too many lovers will puzzle a maid.

"It pleaseth me — it ringeth in mine ears — yea, most pleasantly. Proceed, — the girl was as the Pyrrha of Horace —

"Quis multa gracillis — te puer in rosa —
Perfusis liquidis urgit odoribus.
Grate, Pyrrha — sub antro?"

"That's all high Dutch to me, master; but I'll go on if I can. My memory box be a little out of order. Let me see — oh!

"Now William grew jealous, and so went away;
　Harry got tired of wooing;
And Tom having teased her to fix on the day,
　Received but a frown for so doing;
So, 'mongst all her lovers, quite left in the lurch,
　She pined every night on her pillow;
And meeting one day a pair going to church,
　Turned away, and died under a willow.
　　Heigho! I am afraid
　Too many lovers will puzzle a maid.

"Now, then, old gentleman, tip off your grog. You've got your allowance, as I promised you."

"Come, master, you're a cup too low," said Tom, who, although in high spirits, was not at all intoxicated; indeed, as I afterwards found, he could carry more than his father. "Come, shall I give you a song?"

"That's right, Tom; a volunteer's worth two pressed men. Open your mouth wide, an' let your whistle fly away with the gale. You whistles in tune, at all events."

Tom then struck up, the Dominie see-sawing as he sat, and getting very sleepy—

> "Luck in life, or good or bad,
>   Ne'er could make me melancholy;
> Seldom rich, yet never sad,
>   Sometimes poor, yet always jolly.
> Fortune's in my scale, that's poz,
>   Of mischance put more than half in;
> Yet I don't know how it was,
>   I could never cry for laughing—
>   Ha! ha! ha! Ha! ha! ha!
>   I could never cry for laughing.

"Now for chorus, father—

> "Ha! ha! ha! Ha! ha! ha!
> I could never cry for laughing.

"That's all I know; and that's enough, for it won't wake up the old gentleman."

But it did. "Ha, ha, ha—ha, ha, ha! I could never die for laughing," bawled out the Dominie, feeling for his pannikin; but this was his last effort. He stared round him. "Verily, verily, we are in a whirlpool—how everything turneth round and round! Who cares? Am I not an ancient mariner—'*Qui videt mare turgidum—et infames scopulos.*' Friend Dux, listen to me—*favet linguis.*"

"Well," hiccuped old Tom, "so I will—but speak—plain English—as I do."

"That I'll be hanged if he does," said Tom to me. "In half an hour more I shall understand old Nosey's Latin just as well as his—plain English, as he calls it."

"I will discuss in any language—that is—in any tongue—be it in the Greek or the Latin—nay, even—(hiccups)—friend Dux—hast thou not partaken too freely—of—dear me! *Quo me, Bacche, rapis tui—plenum*—truly I shall be tipsy—and will but finish my pattypan—*dulce periculum est*—Jacob—can there be two Jacobs?—and two old Toms?—nay—*mirabile dictu*—there are two young Toms, and two dog Tommies—each with—two tails. *Bacche, parce—precor—precor*—Jacob, where art thou?—*Ego sum tu es*—

thou art—*sumus*, we are—where am I? *Procumbit humi bos*—for Bos—read Dobbs—*amo, amas*—I loved a lass. *Tityre, tu patulae sub teg-mine*—nay—I quote wrong—then must I be—I do believe that—I'm drunk."

"And I'm cock sure of it," cried Tom, laughing, as the Dominie fell back in a state of insensibility.

"And I'm cock sure of it," said old Tom, rolling himself along the deck to the cabin hatch "that I've as much—as I can stagger—under, at all events—so I'll sing myself to sleep—'cause why—I'm happy. Jacob—mind you keep all the watches to-night—and Tom may keep the rest." Old Tom then sat up, leaning his back against the cabin hatch, and commenced one of those doleful ditties which are sometimes heard on the forecastle of a man-of-war; he had one or two of the songs that he always reserved for such occasions. While Tom and I dragged the Dominie to bed, old Tom drawled out his ditty—

> "Oh! we sailed to Virgi-ni-a, and thence to Fy-al,
> Where we water'd our shipping, and so then weigh-ed all,
> Full in view, on the seas—boys—seven sail we did es-py,
> O! we man-ned our capstern, and weighed spee-di-ly.

"That's right, my boys, haul and hold—stow the old Dictionary away—for he can't command the parts of speech.

> "The very next morning—the engagement proved—hot,
> And brave Admiral Benbow received a chain-shot.
> O when he was wounded to his merry men—he—did—say,
> Take me up in your arms, boys, and car-ry me a-way.

"Now, boys, come and help me—Tom—none of your foolery—for your poor old father is—drunk—."

We assisted old Tom into the other "bed-place" in the cabin. "Thanky, lads—one little bit more, and then I'm done—as the auctioneer says—going—going—

> "O the guns they did rattle, and the bul-lets—did—fly,
> When brave Benbow—for help loud—did cry, Carry me
> down to the cock-pit—there is ease for my smarts, If my
> merry men should see me—'twill sure—break—their—
> hearts.

"Going,—old swan-hopper—as I am—going—gone."

Tom and I were left on deck.

"Now, Jacob, if you have a mind to turn in. I'm not sleepy—you shall keep the morning watch."

"No, Tom, you'd better sleep first. I'll call you at four o'clock. We can't weigh till tide serves; and I shall have plenty of sleep before that."

Tom went to bed, and I walked the deck till the morning, thinking over the events of the day, and wondering what the Dominie would say when he came to his senses. At four o'clock, as agreed, I roused Tom out, and turned into his bed, and was soon as fast asleep as old Tom and the Dominie, whose responsive snores had rung in my ears during the whole time that I had walked the deck.

Chapter Fourteen

About half-past eight the next morning, I was called up by Tom to assist in getting the lighter under weigh. When on deck I found old Tom as fresh as if he had not drunk a drop the night before, very busily stumping about the windlass, with which we hove up first the anchor, and then the mast. "Well, Jacob, my boy, had sleep enough? Not too much, I dare say; but a bout like last night don't come often, Jacob—only once in a way; now, and then I do believe it's good for my health. It's a great comfort to me, my lad, to have you on board with me, because as you never drinks, I may now indulge a *little* oftener. As for Tom, I can't trust him—too much like his father—had nobody to trust to for the look-out, except the dog Tommy, till you came with us. I can trust Tommy as far as keeping off the river sharks; he'll never let them take a rope-yarn off the deck, night or day; but a dog's but a dog, after all. Now we're brought to; so clap on, my boy, and let's heave up with a will."

"How's the old gentleman, father?" said Tom, as we paused a moment from our labour at the windlass.

"Oh! he's got a good deal more to sleep off yet. There he lies, flat on his back, blowing as hard as a grampus. Better leave him as long as we can. We'll rouse him as soon as we turn Greenwich reach. Tom, didn't you think his nose loomed devilish large yesterday?"

"Never seed such a devil of a cutwater in my life, father."

"Well, then, you'll see a larger when he gets up, for it's swelled bigger than the brandy bottle. Heave and haul! Now bring to the fall, and up with the mast, boys, while I goes aft and takes the helm."

Old Tom went aft. During the night the wind had veered to the north, and the frost had set in sharp, the rime covered the deck of the barge, and here and there floating ice was to be seen coming down with the tide. The banks of the river and fields adjacent were white with hoar frost, and would have presented but a cheerless aspect, had not the sun shone out clear and bright. Tom went aft to light the fire, while I coiled away and made all snug forward. Old Tom as usual carolled forth—

"Oh! for a soft and gentle wind,
     I heard a fair one cry
But give to me the roaring breeze,
     And white waves beating high,
And white waves beating high, my boys,
     The good ship tight and free,
The world of waters is our own,
     And merry men are we."

"A nice morning this for cooling a hot head, that's sartain. Tommy, you rascal, you're like a court lady, with her velvet *gownd*, covered all over with diamonds," continued old Tom, looking at the Newfoundland dog, whose glossy black hair was besprinkled with little icicles, which glittered in the sun.

"You and Jacob were the only sensible ones of the party last night, for you both were sober."

"So was I, father. I was as sober as a judge," observed Tom, who was blowing up the fire.

"May be, Tom, as a judge a'ter dinner; but a judge on the bench be one thing, and a judge over a bottle be another, and not bad judges in that way either. At all events, if you warn't *sewed up*, it wasn't your fault."

"And I suppose," replied Tom, "it was only your misfortune that you were."

"No, I don't say that; but still, when I look at the dog, who's but a beast by nature, and thinks of myself, who wasn't meant to be a beast, why, I blushes, that's all."

"Jacob, look at father—now, does he blush?" cried Tom.

"I can't say that I perceive it," replied I, smiling.

"Well, then, if I don't it's the fault of my having no legs. I'm sure when they were knocked off I lost half the blood in my body, and that's the reason, I suppose. At all events, I meant to blush, so we'll take the will for the deed."

"But do you mean to keep sober in future, father?" said Tom.

"Never do you mind that—mind your own business, Mr Tom. At all events, I sha'n't get tipsy till next time, and that's all I can say with safety, 'cause, d'ye see, I knows my failing. Jacob, did you ever see that old gentleman sail too close to the wind before?"

"I never did—I do not think that he was ever tipsy before last night."

"Then I pities him—his headache, and his repentance. Moreover, there be his nose and the swallow-tail of his coat to make him unhappy. We shall be down abreast of the Hospital in half-an-hour. Suppose you go and give him a shake, Jacob. Not you, Tom; I won't trust you—you'll be doing him a mischief; you haven't got no fellow-feeling, not even for dumb brutes."

"I'll thank you not to take away my character that way, father," replied Tom. "Didn't I put you to bed last night when you were speechless?"

"Suppose you did—what then?"

"Why, then, I had a feeling for a dumb brute. I only say that, father, for the joke of it, you know," continued Tom, going up to his father and patting his rough cheek.

"I know that, my boy; you never were unkind, that's sartain; but you must have your joke—

> "Merry thoughts are link'd with laughter,
>   Why should we bury them?
> Sighs and tears may come hereafter,
>   No need to hurry them.
> They who through a spying-glass,
>   View the minutes as they pass,
> Make the sun a gloomy mass,
>   But the fault's their own, Tom."

In the meantime I was vainly attempting to rouse the Dominie. After many fruitless attempts, I put a large quantity off snuff on his upper lip, and then blew it up his nose. But, merciful powers! what a nose it had become—larger than the largest pear that I ever saw in my life. The whole weight of old Tom had fallen on it, and instead of being crushed by the blow, it appeared as if, on the contrary, it had swelled up, indignant at the injury and affront which it had received. The skin was as tight as the parchment of a drum, and shining as if it had been oiled, while the colour was a bright purple. Verily, it was the Dominie's nose in a rage.

The snuff had the effect of partially awakening him from his lethargy. "Six o'clock—did you say, Mrs Bately? Are the boys washed—and in the schoolroom? I will rise speedily—yet I am overcome with much heaviness. *Delapsus somnus* ab—" and the Dominie snored again. I renewed my attempts, and gradually succeeded. The Dominie opened his eyes, stared at the deck and carlines above him, then at the cupboard by his side; lastly, he looked at and recognised me.

"*Eheu, Jacobe!*—where am I? And what is that which presses upon my brain? What is it so loadeth my cerebellum, even as if it were lead? My memory—where is it? Let me recall my scattered senses." Here the Dominie was silent for some time. "Ah me! yea, and verily, I do recollect—with pain of head and more pain of heart—that which I would fain forget, which is, that I did forget myself; and indeed have forgotten all that passed the latter portion of the night. Friend Dux hath proved no friend, but hath led me into the wrong path: and as or the potation called *Grog—Eheu, Jacobe!* how have I fallen—fallen in my own opinion—fallen in thine—how can I look thee in the face! O, Jacob! what must thou think of him who hath hitherto been thy preceptor and thy guide!" Here the Dominie fell back on the pillow, and turned away his head.

"It is not your fault, sir," replied I, to comfort him; "you were not aware of what you were drinking—you did not know that the liquor was so strong. Old Tom deceived you."

"Nay, Jacob, I cannot lay that flattering unction to my wounded heart. I ought to have known, nay, now I recall to mind, that thou wouldst have warned me—even to the pulling off of the tail of my coat—yet I heeded thee not, and I am humbled—even I, the master over seventy boys!"

"Nay, sir, it was not I who pulled off the tail of your coat; it was the dog."

"Jacob, I have heard of the wonderful sagacity of the canine species, yet could not I ever have believed that a dumb brute would have perceived my folly, and warned me from intoxication. *Mirabile dictu!* Tell me, Jacob, thou who hast profited by these lessons which thy master could give—although he could not follow up his precept by example—tell me, what did take place? Let me know the full extent of my backsliding."

"You fell asleep, sir, and we put you to bed."

"Who did me that office, Jacob?"

"Young Tom and I, sir; as for old Tom, he was not in a state to help anybody."

"I am humbled, Jacob—"

"Nonsense, old gentleman; why make a fuss about nothing?" said old Tom, who, overhearing our conversation came into the cabin. "You had a *drop* too much, that's all, and what o' that? It's a poor heart that never rejoiceth. Rouse a bit, wash your face with old Thames water, and in half-an-hour you'll be as fresh as a daisy."

"My head acheth!" exclaimed the Dominie, "even as if there were a ball of lead rolling from one temple to the other; but my punishment is just."

"That is the punishment of making too free with the bottle, for sartain; but if it is an offence, then it carries its own punishment and that's quite sufficient. Every man knows that when the heart's over light at night, that the head's over heavy in the morning. I have known and proved it a thousand times. Well, what then? I puts the good against the bad, and I takes my punishment like a man."

"Friend Dux, for so I will still call thee, thou lookest not at the offence in a moral point of vision."

"What's moral?" replied old Tom.

"I would point out that intoxication is sinful."

"Intoxication sinful! I suppose that means that it's a sin to get drunk. Now, master, it's my opinion that as God Almighty has given us good liquor, it was for no other purpose than to drink it; and therefore it would be ungrateful to him, and a sin, not to get drunk—that is, with discretion."

"How canst thou reconcile getting drunk with discretion, good Dux?"

"I mean, master, when there's work to be done, the work should be done; but when there's plenty of time, and everything is safe, and all ready for a start the next morning, I can see no possible objection to a jollification. Come, master, rouse out; the lighter's abreast of the Hospital almost by this time, and we must put you on shore."

The Dominie, whose clothes were all on, turned out of his bed-place and went with us on deck. Young Tom, who was at the helm, as soon as we made our appearance, wished him a good-morning very respectfully. Indeed, I always observed that Tom, with all his impudence and waggery, had a great deal of consideration and kindness. He had overheard the Dominie's conversation with me, and would not further wound his feelings with a jest. Old Tom resumed his place at the helm, while his son prepared the breakfast, and I drew a bucket of water for the Dominie to wash his face and hands. Of his nose not a word was said; and the Dominie made no remarks to me on the subject, although I am persuaded it must have been very painful, from the comfort he appeared to derive in bathing it with the freezing water. A bowl of tea was a great solace to him, and he had hardly finished it when the lighter was abreast the Hospital stairs. Tom jumped into the boat and hauled it alongside. I took the other oar, and the Dominie, shaking hands with old Tom, said, "Thou didst mean kindly, and therefore I wish thee a kind farewell, good Dux."

"God be with you, master," replied old Tom; "shall we call for you as we come back?"

"Nay, nay," replied the Dominie, "the travelling by land is more expensive, but less dangerous. I thank thee for thy songs, and—for all thy kindness, good Dux. Are my paraphernalia in the boat, Jacob?"

I replied in the affirmative. The Dominie stepped in, and we pulled him on shore. He landed, took his bundle and umbrella under his arm, shook hands with Tom and then with me, without speaking, and I perceived the tears start in his eyes as he turned and walked away.

"Well, now," said Tom, looking after the Dominie, "I wish I had been drunk instead of he. He does so take it to heart, poor old gentleman!"

"He has lost his self-esteem, Tom," replied I. "It should be a warning to you. Come, get your oar to pass."

"Well, some people he fashioned one way and some another. I've been tipsy more than once, and I never lost anything but my reason, and that came back as soon as the grog left my head. I can't understand that fretting about having had a glass too much. I only frets when I can't get enough. Well, of all the noses I ever saw, his bests them by chalks; I did so want to laugh at it, but I knew it would pain him."

"It is very kind of you, Tom, to hold your tongue, and I thank you very much."

"And yet that old dad of mine swears I've got no fellow-feeling, which I consider a very undutiful thing for him to say. What's the reason, Jacob, that sons be always cleverer than their fathers?"

"I didn't know that was the case, Tom."

"But it is so *now*, if it wasn't in *olden time*. The proverb says, 'Young people *think* old people to be fools, but old people *know* young people to be fools.' We must alter that, for I says, 'Old people *think* young people to be fools, but young people *know* old people to be fools.'"

"Have it your own way, Tom, that will do, rowed of all."

We tossed in our oars, made the boat fast, and gained the deck, where old Tom still remained at the helm. "Well," said he, "Jacob, I never thought I should be glad to see the old gentleman clear of the lighter, but I was—devilish glad; he was like a load on my conscience this morning; he was trusted to my charge by Mr Drummond, and I had no right to persuade him to make a fool of himself. But, however, what's done can't be helped, as you say sometimes; and it's no use crying; still it was a pity, for he be, for all the world, like a child. There's a fancy kind of lass in that wherry, crossing *our* bows; look at the streamers from her top-gallant.

> "Come o'er the sea,
>   Maiden, to me,
> Mine through sunshine, storm, and snows,
>   Seasons may roll,
>   But the true soul
> Burns the same wherever it goes
>   Then come o'er the sea,
>   Maiden, with me."

"See you hanged first, you underpinned old hulk!" replied the female in the boat, which was then close under our bows.

"Well, that be civil, for certain," said old Tom, laughing.

Chapter Fifteen

We arrived at Sheerness the next morning, landed the bricks, which were for the Government buildings, and returned in ballast to the wharf. My first inquiry was for the Dominie; but he had not yet returned; and Mr Drummond further informed me that he had been obliged to send away his under-clerk and wished me to simply take his place until he could procure another. The lighter therefore took in her cargo, and sailed without me, which was of consequence, as my apprenticeship still went on. I now lived with Mr Drummond as one of his own family, and wanted for nothing. His continual kindness to me made me strive all I could to please him by diligence and attention, and I soon became very expert at accounts, and, as he said, very useful. The advantages to me, I hardly need observe were considerable, and I gained information every day. Still, although I was glad to be of any use to Mr Drummond, the confinement at the desk was irksome, and I anxiously looked for the arrival of the new clerk to take my place and leave me free to join the lighter. Mr Drummond did not appear to me to be in any hurry; indeed, I believe that he would have retained me altogether, had he not perceived that I still wished to be on the river.

"At all events, Jacob, I shall keep you here until you are master of your work; it will be useful to you hereafter," he said to me one day; "and you do not gain much by sailing up and down the river."

This was true; and I also derived much advantage from the evenings spent with Mrs Drummond, who was a very sensible good woman, and would make me read aloud to her and little Sarah as they sat at their needle. I had no idea, until I was employed posting up the book, that Mr Drummond's concern was so extensive, or that there was so much capital employed in the business. The Dominie returned a few days after my arrival. When we met his nose had resumed its former appearance, and he never brought up the subject of the evening on board of the lighter. I saw him frequently, mostly on Sundays after I had been to church with the family; and half-an-hour, at least, was certain to be dedicated to our reading together one of the classics.

As I was on shore several months, I became acquainted with many families, one or two of which were worth noticing. Among the foremost was Captain Turnbull, at least such was his appellation until within the last two months previous to my making his acquaintance, when Mr Turnbull sent out his cards, *George Turnbull, Esquire.* The history of Captain Turnbull was as follows:— He had, with his twin brother, been hung up at the knocker, and afterwards had been educated at the Foundling Hospital; they had both been apprenticed to the sea; grown up thorough-bred, capital, seamen in the Greenland fishery; rose to be mates then captains; had been very successful, owned part, then the whole of the ship, afterwards two or three ships; and had wound up with handsome fortunes. Captain Turnbull was a married man without a family; his wife, fine in person, vulgar in speech, a would-be fashionable lady, against which fashion Captain T had for years pleaded poverty; but his brother, who had remained a bachelor, died, leaving him forty thousand pounds—a fact which could not be concealed. Captain Turnbull had not allowed his wife to be aware of the extent of his own fortune, more from a wish to live quietly and happily than from any motive of parsimony, for he was liberal to excess; but now he had no further excuse to plead, and Mrs Turnbull insisted upon *fashion.* The house they had lived in was given up, and a marine villa on the borders of the Thames to a certain degree met the views of both parties; Mrs Turnbull anticipating dinners and fêtes, and the captain content to watch what was going on in the river, and amuse himself in a wherry. They had long been acquaintances of Mr and Mrs Drummond; and Captain Turnbull's character was such as always to command the respect of Mr Drummond, as he was an honest, friendly man. Mrs Turnbull had now set up her carriage, and she was, in her own opinion, a very great personage. She would have cut all her former acquaintance; but on that point the captain was inflexible, particularly as regarded the Drummonds. As far as they were concerned, Mrs Turnbull gave way, Mrs Drummond being a lady-like woman, and Mr Drummond universally respected as a man of talent and information. Captain, or rather, Mr Turnbull, was a constant visitor at our house, and very partial to me. He used to scold Mr Drummond for keeping me so close to my desk, and would often persuade him to give me a couple of hours' run. When this was obtained, he would call a waterman, throw him a crown, and tell him to get out of his wherry as fast as he could. We then embarked, and amused ourselves pulling up and down the river, while Mrs Turnbull, dressed in the extremity of the fashion, rode out in the carriage and left her cards in every direction.

One day Mr Turnbull called upon the Drummonds, and asked them to dine with him on the following Saturday; they accepted the invitation. "By-the-by," said he, "I got what my wife calls a *remind* in my pocket;" and he pulled out of his coat-pocket a large card, "with Mr and Mrs Turnbull's compliments," etcetera, which card he had doubled in two by his sitting down upon it, shortly after he came in. Mr Turnbull straightened it again as well as he could, and laid it on the table. "And Jacob," said he, "you'll come too. You don't want a remind; but if you do, my wife will send you one."

I replied, "that I wanted no remind for a good dinner."

"No, I dare say not, my boy; but recollect that you come an hour or two before the dinner-hour, to help me; there's so much fuss with one thing or another, that I'm left in the lurch; and as for trusting the keys of the spirit-room to that long-togged rascal of a butler, I'll see him harpoon'd first; so do you come and help me, Jacob."

This having been promised, he asked Mr Drummond to lend me for an hour or so, as he wished to take a row up the river. This was also consented to; we embarked and pulled away for Kew Bridge. Mr Turnbull was as good a hand at a yarn as old Tom, and many were the adventures he narrated to me of what had taken place during the vicissitudes of his life, more especially when he was employed in the Greenland fishery. He related an accident that morning, which particularly bore upon the marvellous, although I do not believe that he was at all guilty of indulging in a traveller's licence.

"Jacob," said he, "I recollect once when I was very near eaten alive by foxes, and that in a very singular manner. I was then mate of a Greenland ship. We had been on the fishing ground for three months, and had twelve fish on board. Finding we were doing well, we fixed our ice-anchors upon a very large iceberg, drifting up and down with it, and taking fish as we fell in with them. One morning we had just cast loose the carcass of a fish which we had cut up, when the man in the crow's nest, on the look-out for another 'fall,' cried out that a large polar bear and her cub were swimming over to the iceberg, against the side of which, and about half-a-mile from us, the carcass of a whale was beating. As we had nothing to do, seven of us immediately started in chase we had intended to have gone after the foxes, which had gathered there also in hundreds, to prey upon the dead whale. It was then quite calm: we soon came up with the bear, who at first was for making off; but as the cub could not get on over the rough ice as well as the old one, she at last turned round to bay. We shot the cub to make sure of her, and it did make sure of the dam not leaving us till either she or we perished in the conflict. I never shall forget her moaning over the cub, as it lay bleeding on the ice, while we fired bullet after bullet into her. At last she turned round, gave a roar and a gnashing snarl, which you might have heard a mile, and, with her eyes flashing fire, darted upon us. We received her in a body, all close together, with our lances to her breast; but she was so large and strong, that she beat us all back, and two of us fell; fortunately the others held their ground, and as she was then on end, three bullets were put into her chest, which brought her down. I never saw so large a beast in my life. I don't wish to make her out larger than she really was, but I have seen many a bullock at Smithfield which would not weigh two-thirds of her. After that, we had some trouble in despatching her; and while we were so employed, the wind blew up in gusts from the northward, and the snow fell heavy. The men were for returning to the ship immediately, which certainly was the wisest thing for us all to do; but I thought that the snowstorm would blow over in a short time, and not wishing to lose so fine a skin, resolved to remain and flay the beast; for I knew that if left there a few hours, as the foxes could not get hold of the carcass of the whale, which had not grounded, they would soon finish the bear and the cub, and the skins be worth nothing. Well, the other men went back to the ship, and as it was, the snow-storm came on so thick that they lost their way, and would never have found her, if it was not that the bell was kept tolling for a guide to them. I soon found that I had done a very foolish thing; instead of the storm blowing over, the snow came down thicker and thicker; and before I had taken a quarter of the skin off, I was becoming cold and numbed, and then I was unable to regain the ship, and with every prospect of being frozen to death before the storm was over. At last, I knew what was my only chance. I had flayed all the belly of the bear, but had not cut her open. I ripped her up, tore out all her inside, and then contrived to get into her body, where I lay, and, having closed up the entrance hole, was warm and comfortable, for the animal heat had not yet been extinguished. This manoeuvre, no doubt, saved my life: and I have heard that the French soldiers did the same in their unfortunate Russian campaign, killing their horses and getting inside to protect themselves from the dreadful weather. Well, Jacob, I had not lain more than half-an-hour, when I knew by sundry jerks and tugs at my newly invented hurricane-house that the foxes were busy—and so they were sure, enough. There must have been hundreds of them, for they were at work in all directions, and some pushed their sharp noses into the opening where I had crept in; but I contrived to get out my knife and saw their noses across whenever they touched me, otherwise I should have been eaten up in a very short time. There were so many of them, and they were so ravenous, that they soon got through the bear's thick skin, and were tearing away at the flesh. Now I was not so much afraid of their eating me, as I thought that if I jumped up and discovered myself they would have all fled. No saying, though; two or three hundred ravenous devils take courage when together; but I was afraid that they would devour my covering from the weather, and then I should perish with the cold; and I was also afraid of having pieces nipped out of me, which would of course oblige me to quit my retreat. At last daylight was made through the upper part of the carcass, and I was only protected by the ribs of the animal, between which every now and then their noses dived and nipped my sealskin jacket. I was just thinking of shouting to frighten them away, when I heard the report of half-a-dozen muskets, and some of the bullets struck the carcass, but fortunately did not hit me. I immediately halloed as loud as I could, and the men, hearing me, ceased firing. They had fired at the foxes, little thinking that I was inside of the bear. I crawled out; the storm was over, and the men of the ship had come back to look for me. My brother, who was also a mate on board of the vessel, who had not been with the first party, had joined them in the search, but with little hopes of finding me alive. He hugged me in his arms, covered as I was with blood, as soon as he saw me. He's dead now, poor fellow—That's the story, Jacob."

"Thank you, sir," replied I; but perceiving that the memory of his brother affected him, I did not speak again for a few minutes. We then resumed our conversation, and pulling back with the tide, landed at the wharf.

On the day of the dinner party I went up to Mr Turnbull's at three o'clock as he had proposed. I found the house in a bustle; Mr and Mrs Turnbull, with the butler and footman, in the dining-room, debating as to the propriety of *this* and *that* being placed *here* and *there*, both servants giving their opinion, and arguing on a footing of equality, contradicting and insisting, Mr Turnbull occasionally throwing in a word, and each time snubbed by his wife, although the servants dare not take any liberty with him. "Do, pray, Mr Turnbull, leave *h*us to settle these matters. Get *h*up your wine; that is your department. Leave the room, Mr Turnbull, *h*if you please. Mortimer and I know what we are about, without your *h*interference."

"Oh! by the Lord, I don't wish to interfere; but I wish you and your servants not to be squabbling, that's all. If they gave me half the *cheek*—"

"Do, pray, Mr Turnbull, leave the room, and allow me to regulate my own '*ouse*hold."

"Come, Jacob, we'll go down into the cellar," said Mr Turnbull; and accordingly we went.

I assisted Mr Turnbull in his department as much as I could, but he grumbled very much. "I can't bear all this nonsense, all this finery and foolery. Everything comes up cold, everything is out of reach. The table's so long, and so covered with uneatables, that my wife is hardly within hail and, by jingo, with her the servants are masters. Not with me, at all events; for if they spoke to me as they do to Mrs Turnbull, I would kick them out of the house. However, Jacob, there's no help for it. All one asks for is quiet; and I must put up with all this sometimes, or I should have no quiet from one year's end to another. When a woman will have her way, there's no stopping her: you know the old verse—

"A man's a fool who strives by force or skill
To stem the torrent of a woman's will;
For if she will, she will, you may depend on't,
And if she won't, she won't—and there's an end on't.

"Now let's go up into my room, and we will chat while I wash my hands."

As soon as Mr Turnbull was dressed, we went down into the drawing-room, which was crowded with tables loaded with every variety of ornamental articles. "Now this is what my wife calls fashionable. One might as well be steering through an ice-floe as try to come to an anchor here without running foul of something. It's *hard-a-port* or *hard-a-starboard* every minute; and if your coat-tail *jibes*, away goes something, and whatever it is that smashes, Mrs T always swears it was the *most valuable* thing in the room. I'm like a bull in a china-shop. One comfort is, that I never come in here except when there's company. Indeed, I'm not allowed, thank God. Sit on a chair, Jacob, one of those spider-like French things, for my wife won't allow *blacks*, as she calls them, to come to an anchor upon her sky-blue silk sofas. How stupid to have furniture that one's not to make use of! Give me comfort but it appears that's not to be bought for money."

Chapter Sixteen

Six o'clock was now near at hand, and Mrs Turnbull entered the drawing-room in full dress. She certainly was a very handsome woman, and had every appearance of being fashionable; but it was her language which exposed her. She was like the peacock. As long as she was silent you could but admire the plumage, but her voice spoilt all. "Now, Mr Turnbull," said she, "I wish to *h*explain to you that there are certain *h*improprieties in your behaviour which I cannot put *h*up with, particularly that *h*of talking about when you were before the mast."

"Well, my dear, is that anything to be ashamed of?"

"Yes, Mr Turnbull, that *h*is—one *h*always sinks them ere particulars in fashionable society. To wirtuperate in company a'n't pleasant, and *H*i've thought of a plan which may *h*act as an *h*impediment to your vulgarity. Recollect, Mr T, when*h*ever I say that *H*i've an 'eadache, it's to be a sign for you to 'old your tongue; and, Mr T, *h*oblige me by wearing kid gloves all the evening."

"What! at dinner time, my dear?"

"Yes, Mr T, at dinner time; your 'ands are not fit to be touched."

"Well, I recollect when you thought otherwise."

"When, Mr T? 'ave I not often told you so?"

"Yes, lately; but I referred to the time when one Poll Bacon of Wapping took my hand for better or for worse."

"Really, Mr T, you quite shock me. My name was Mary, and the Bacons are a good old *H*inglish name. You 'ave their *h*arms quartered on the carriage in right o' me. That's something, I can tell you."

"Something I had to pay for pretty smartly, at all events."

"The payment, Mr T, was on account of granting *h*arms to you, who never 'ad any."

"And never wished for them. What do I care for such stuff?"

"And when you did choose, Mr Turnbull, you might have consulted me, instead of making yourself the laughing-stock of Sir George Naylor and all the 'eralds. Who but a madman would have chosen three harpoons *saluims*, and three barrels *couchants*, with a spouting whale for a crest? Just to point out to everybody what should *h*ever be buried in *h*oblivion; and then your beastly motto—which I *would have* changed—'*Blubber for ever!*' Blubber indeed! *h*enough to make *h*any one *blubber* for ever."

"Well, the heralds told me they were just what I ought to have chosen, and very apposite, as they termed it."

"They took your money and laughed at you. Two pair of griffins, a lion, half-a-dozen leopards, and a hand with a dagger, wouldn't 'ave cost a farthing more. But what can you *h*expect from an '*og*?"

"But if I was *cured*, I should be what you *were*—Bacon."

"I won't *demean* myself, Mr Turnbull."

"That's right, my dear, don't; there's no curing you. Recollect the motto you chose in preference to mine."

"Well, and a very proper one—'*Too much familiarity breeds contempt*'—is it not so, Master Faithful?"

"Yes, madam, it was one of our copies at school."

"I beg your pardon, sir, it was my *h*own *h*invention."

Rap, tap, rap, tap, tap, tap, tap.

"Mr and Mrs Peters, of Petercumb Hall," announced the butler. Enter Mrs Peters first, a very diminutive lady, and followed by Mr Peters, six feet four inches without his shoes, deduct for stooping and curved shoulders seven inches. Mr Peters had retired from the Stock Exchange with a competence, bought a place, named it Petercumb Hall, and set up his carriage. Another knock, and Mr and Mrs Drummond were announced. Compliments exchanged, and a pastile lighted by Mrs Turnbull.

"Well, Drummond," said Mr Turnbull, "what are coals worth now?"

"Mr Turnbull, I've got such an '*eadache*."

This was of course a matter of condolence from all present, and a stopper upon Mr Turnbull's tongue.

Another sounding rap, and a pause. "Monsieur and Madame de Tagliabue coming up." Enter Monsieur and Madame de Tagliabue. The former, a dapper little Frenchman, with a neat pair of legs, and stomach as round as a pea. Madame sailing in like an outward-bound East Indiaman, with studding sails below and aloft; so large in her dimensions, that her husband might be compared to the pilot-boat plying about her stern.

"Charmée de vous voir, Madame Tom-bulle. Vous vous portez bien; n'est-ce pas?"

"*Ve*," replied Mrs Turnbull, who thus exhausted her knowledge of the French language while the Monsieur tried in vain, first on one side, and then on the other, to get from under the lee of his wife and make his bow. This was not accomplished until the lady had taken possession of a sofa, which she filled most comfortably.

Who these people were, and how they lived, I never could find out: they came in a fly from Brentford.

Another announcement. "My Lord Babbleton and Mr Smith coming up."

"Mr T, pray go down and receive his lordship. (There are two wax candles for you to light on the hall table, and you must walk up with them before his lordship," said the lady aside.)

"I'll be hanged if I do," replied Mr Turnbull; "let the servants light him."

"O, Mr T, I've such an 'eadache?"

"So you may have," replied Mr T, sitting down doggedly.

In the meantime Mr Smith entered, leading Lord Babbleton, a boy of twelve or thirteen years old, shy, awkward, red-haired, and ugly, to whom Mr Smith was tutor. Mrs T had found out Mr Smith, who was residing near Brentford with his charge, and made his acquaintance on purpose to have a lord on her visiting list, and, to her delight, the leader had not forgotten to bring his bear with him. Mrs Turnbull sprang to the door to receive them, making a prepared courtesy to the aristocratical cub, and then shaking him respectfully by the hand. "Won't your lordship walk to the fire? Isn't your lordship cold? I hope your lordship's sty is better in your lordship's eye. Allow me to introduce to your lordship's notice Mr and Mrs Peters— Madame and Mounsheer Tagleebue—Mr and Mrs Drummond, the Right Honourable Lord Viscount Babbleton." As for Mr Turnbull and myself, we were left out as unworthy of introduction. "We are ready for dinner, Mr Turnbull."

"Snobbs, get dinner dressed up," said Mr T to the butler.

"O, Mr T, I've such an 'eadache."

This last headache was produced by Mr T forgetting himself, and calling the butler by his real name, which was Snobbs; but Mrs Turnbull had resolved that it should be changed to *Mortimer*—or rather, to Mr Mortimer, as the household were directed to call him, on pain of expulsion.

Dinner was announced. Madame Tagliabue, upon what pretence I know not, was considered the first lady in the room, and Lord Babbleton was requested by Mrs Turnbull to hand her down. Madame rose, took his lordship's hand, and led him away. Before they were out of the room, his lordship had disappeared among the ample folds of Madame's gown, and was seen no more until she pulled him out, on their arrival at the dinner-table. At last we were all arranged according to Mrs Turnbull's wishes, although there were several chops and changes about, until the order of precedence could be correctly observed. A French cook had been sent for by Mrs Turnbull; and not being mistress of the language, she had a card with the names of the dishes to refresh her memory, Mr Mortimer having informed her that such was always the custom among great people, who, not ordering their own dinners, of course they could not tell what there was to eat.

"Mrs Turnbull, what soup have you there?"

"*Consummy* soup, my lord. Will your lordship *make use* of that or of this here, which is *o'juss.*"

His lordship stared, made no answer; looked foolish; and Mr Mortimer placed some soup before him.

"Lord Babbleton takes soup," said Mr Smith, pompously; and the little right honourable supped soup, much to Mrs Turnbull's satisfaction.

"Madame, do you soup? or do you fish?"

"Merci, no soup—*poisson.*"

"Don't be afraid, madame; we've a French cook: you won't be *poisoned* here," replied Mrs Turnbull, rather annoyed.

"Comment, my chère madame, I meant to say dat I prefer de cod."

"Mr T, some soup for Madame. John, a *clean* plate for Lord Babbleton. What will your lordship condescend to *make use* of now?" (Mrs Turnbull thought the phrase, *make use*, excessively refined and elegant.)

"Ah, madame, votre cuisine est superbe," exclaimed Monsieur Tagliabue, tucking the corner of his napkin into his button-hole, and making preparations for well filling his little rotundity.

"*Ve,*" replied Mrs Turnbull. "Mrs Peters, will you try the dish next Mr Turnbull? What is it?" (*looking at her card*)—"*Agno roty.* Will you, my lord? If your lordship has not yet got into your French—it means roast quarter of lamb."

"His lordship is very partial to lamb," said Mr Smith, with emphasis.

"Mr Turnbull, some lamb for Lord Babbleton, and for Mr Peters."

"Directly, my dear.—Well, Jacob, you see, when I was first mate—"

"Dear! Mr Turnbull—I've such an 'eadache. Do, pray, cut the lamb. (*Aside*.) Mr Mortimer, do go and whisper to Mr Turnbull that I beg he will put on his gloves."

"Mrs Peters, you're doing nothing. Mr Mortimer, 'and round the side dishes, and let John serve out the champagne."

"Mrs Peters, there's a *wolley went o' weaters*. Will you make use of some? Mrs Drummond, will you try the dish coming round? It is—let me see— *chew farsy*. My Lord Babbleton, I 'ope the lamb's *to your liking*? Monshere Tagliabue—William, give Monshere a clean plate. What will you take next?"

"Vraiment, madame, tout est excellent, superbe! Je voudrais embrasser votre cuisinier—c'est un artiste comme il n'y a pas?"

"*Ve*," replied Mrs Turnbull.

The first course was removed; and the second, after some delay, made its appearance. In the interim, Mr Mortimer handed round one or two varieties of wine.

"Drummond, will you take a glass of wine with me?" said Mr Turnbull. "I hate your sour French wines. Will you take Madeira? I was on shore at Madeira once for a few hours, when I was before the mast, in the—"

"Mr Turnbull, I've such an 'eadache," cried his lady, in an angry tone. "My lord, will you take some of this?—it is *ding dong o' turf*—a turkey, my lord."

"His lordship is fond of turkey," said Mr Smith, dictatorially.

Monsieur Tagliabue, who sat on the other side of Mrs T, found that the turkey was in request—it was some time before he could help himself.

"C'est superbe?" said Monsieur, thrusting a truffle into his mouth. "Apparemment, madame, n'aime pas la cuisine Anglaise?"

"*Ve*," replied Mrs Turnbull. "Madame, what will you be *h*assisted to?" continued Mrs T.

"Tout de bon, madame."

"*Ve*; what are those by you, Mr Peters?" inquired the lady in continuation.

"I really cannot exactly say; but they are fritters of some sort."

"Let me see—hoh! bidet du poms. Madame, will you eat some *bidet du poms*?"

"Comment, madame, je ne vous comprends pas—"

"*Ve.*"

"Monsieur Tagliabue, expliquez donc;" said the foreign lady, red as a quarter of beef.

"Permettez," said Monsieur, looking at the card. "Ah, c'est impossible, ma chère," continued he, laughing. "Madame Turnbull se trompait; elle voudrait dire *Beignets de pommes.*"

"Vous trouvez notre langue fort difficile, n'est-ce pas?" continued madame, who recovered her good humour, and smiled graciously at Mrs T.

"*Ve,*" replied Mrs Turnbull, who perceived that she had made some mistake, and was anxiously awaiting the issue of the dialogue. It had, however, the effect of checking Mrs T, who said little more during the dinner and dessert.

At last the ladies rose from the dessert, and left the gentlemen at the table; but we were not permitted to remain long before coffee was announced, and we went up stairs. A variety of French liqueurs were handed about, and praised by most of the company. Mr Turnbull, however, ordered a glass of brandy as a *settler.*

"Oh! Mr Turnbull, I've such an 'eadache!"

After that the party became very dull. Lord Babbleton fell asleep on the sofa. Mr Peters walked round the room, admiring the pictures, and asking the names of the masters.

"I really quite forget; but, Mr Drummond, you are a judge of paintings I hear. Who do you think this is painted by?" said the lady, pointing to a very inferior performance. "I am not quite sure; but I think it is Van—Van *Daub.*"

"I should think so too," replied Mr Drummond, drily; "we have a great many pictures in England by the same hand."

The French gentleman proposed *écarté*, but no one knew how to play it except his wife; who sat down with him to pass away the time. The ladies sauntered about the room, looking at the contents of the tables, Mrs Peters occasionally talking of Petercumb Hall; Mr Smith played at patience in one corner; while Mr Turnbull and Mr Drummond sat in another in close conversation; and the lady of the house divided her attentions, running from one to the other, and requesting them not to talk so loud as to awake the Right Honourable Lord Viscount Babbleton. At last the vehicles were announced, and the fashionable party broke up, much to the satisfaction of everybody, and to none more than myself.

I ought to observe that all the peculiar absurdities I have narrated did not strike me so much at the time; but it was an event to me to dine out, and the scene was well impressed upon my memory. After what occurred to me in my after life, and when I became better able to judge of fashionable pretensions, the whole was vividly brought back to my recollection.

Chapter Seventeen

I remained with Mr Drummond about eight months, when at last the new clerk made his appearance—a little fat fellow, about twenty, with a face as round as a full moon, thick lips, and red cheeks. During this time I frequently had the pleasure of meeting with old and young Tom, who appeared very anxious that I should rejoin them; and I must say that I was equally willing to return to the lighter. Still Mr Drummond put his veto on it, and Mrs Drummond was also constantly pointing out the very desirable situation I might have on shore as a clerk in the office; but I could not bear it—seated nearly the whole day—perched up on a high stool—turning over Debtors, contra Creditors, and only occasionally interrupted by the head clerk, with his attempt to make rhymes. The new clerk came, I expected my release, but I was disappointed. Mr Drummond discovered him to be so awkward, and the head clerk declared that the time was so busy, that he could not spare me. This was true; Mr Drummond had just come to a final arrangement, which had been some time pending, by which he purchased a wharf and large warehouses, with a house adjoining, in Lower Thames Street—a very large concern, for which he had paid a considerable sum of money. What with the valuations, winding up of the Brentford concern on the old account, etcetera, there was much to do, and I toiled at the desk until the removal took place; and when the family were removed, I was still detained, as there was no warehouseman to superintend the unloading and hoisting up of goods. Mr Tomkins, the head clerk, who had been many years a faithful servant to Mr Drummond, was admitted a partner, and had charge of the Brentford wharf, a species of promotion which he and his wife resolved to celebrate with a party. After a long debate, it was resolved that they should give a ball, and Mrs Tomkins exerted all her taste and ingenuity on the occasion. My friend Tomkins lived at a short distance from the premises, in a small house, surrounded with half an acre of garden, chiefly filled with gooseberry-bushes, and perambulated by means of four straight gravel walks. Mr and Mrs Drummond were invited, and accepted the invitation, which was considered by the Tomkinses as a great mark of condescension. As a specimen of Mr Tomkins's poetical talents, I shall give his invitation to Mr Drummond, written in the very best German text:—

"Mr and Mrs T—
Sincerely hope to see
Mr and Mrs Drum-
Mond, to a very hum-
Ble party that they in-
Tend to ask their kin
To, on the Saturday
Of the week ensuing:
When fiddles they will play,
And other things be doing."

Belle Vue House.

To which *jeu d'esprit* Mr Drummond answered with a pencil on a card—

"Mr and Mrs Drum-
Mond intend to come."

"Here, give Tomkins that, Jacob; it will please him better than any formal acceptation." Mr and Mrs Turnbull were also asked; the former accepted, but the latter indignantly refused.

When I arrived with Mr and Mrs Drummond many of the company were there; the garden was what they called illuminated, that is, every gooseberry-bush had one variegated lamp suspended above the centre; and, as Mr Tomkins told me afterwards, the lamps were red and yellow, according to the fruit they bore. It was a cold, frosty, clear night, and the lamps twinkled as brightly among the bare boughs of the gooseberry trees as the stars did in the heavens. The company in general were quite charmed with the novelty. "Quite a *minor Wauxhall*," cried one lady, whose exuberance of fat kept her warm enough to allow her to stare about in the open air. The entrance porch had a dozen little lamps, backed with laurel twigs, and looked very imposing. Mrs Tomkins received her company upon the steps outside, that she might have the pleasure of hearing their praises of her external arrangements; still it was freezing, and she shivered not a little. The drawing-room, fourteen feet by ten, was fitted up as a ballroom, with two fiddlers and a fifer sitting in a corner and a country-dance was performing when we arrived. Over the mantle-piece was a square of laurel twigs, inclosing as a frame this couplet from the poetical brain of the master of the house, cut out in red paper, and bespangled with blue and yellow tinsel—

"Here we are to dance so gay,
While the fiddlers play away."

Other appropriate distichs, which I have now forgotten, were framed in the same way on each of the other compartments. But the dining-room was the *chef d'oeuvre*. It was formed into a bower, with evergreens, and on the evergreen boughs were stuck real apples and oranges in all directions, so that you could help yourself.

"Vell, I do declare, this is a paradise!" exclaimed the fat lady who entered with me.

"In all but one thing, ma'am," replied Mr Turnbull, who, with his coat off, was squeezing lemons for the punch—"there's no *forbidden* fruit. You may help yourself."

The bon-mot was repeated by Mr Tomkins to the end of his existence, not only for its own sake, but because it gave him an opportunity of entering into a detail of the whole *fête*—the first he had ever given in his life. "Ah, Jacob, my boy, glad to see you—come and help here—they'll soon be thirsty, I'll warrant," said Mr Turnbull, who was in his glory. The company, although not so very select, were very happy; they danced, drank punch, laughed, and danced again; and it was not till a late hour, long after Mr and Mrs Drummond had gone home, that I quitted the "festive scene;" Mr Turnbull, who walked away with me, declaring that it was worth a dozen of his party, although they had not such grand people as Mrs Tagliabue, or the Right Honourable Lord Viscount Babbleton. I thought so too; every one was happy, and every one at their ease; and I do believe they would have stayed much longer, but the musicians took so much punch that one fiddler broke his fiddle, the other broke his head in going down the steps into the garden, and the fifer swore he could blow no longer; so, as there was an end to the music, clogs, pattens, and lanterns were called for, the shawls were brought out of the kitchen, and every one went away. Nothing could *go off better*. Mrs Tomkins had a cold and rheumatism the next day; but that was not surprising, a *minor Wauxhall* not being seasonable in the month of December.

A week after this party we removed to Thames Street, and I performed the duty of warehouseman. Our quantity of lighters was now much increased, and employed in carrying dry goods, etcetera. One morning old Tom came under the crane to discharge his lighter, and wishing to see me, when the fall had been overhauled down to heave up the casks with which the lighter was laden, instead of hooking on a cask, held on by his hands, crying, "Hoist away," intending to be hoisting himself up to the door of the warehouse where I was presiding. Now, there was nothing unusual in this whim of old Tom's, but still he ran a very narrow chance, in consequence of an extra whim of young Tom's, who, as soon as his father was suspended in the air, caught hold of his two wooden stumps, to be hoisted up also; and as he caught hold of them, standing on tiptoe, they both swung clear of the lighter, which could not approach to within five feet of the buildings. The crane was on the third story of the warehouse, and very high up. "Tom, Tom, you rascal, what the devil are you about?" cried the old man, when he felt the weight of his son's body hanging to him.

"Going up along with you, father—hope we shall go to heaven the same way."

"More likely to go to the devil together, you little fool; I never can bear your weight. Hoist away, there, quick."

Hearing the voices, I looked out of the door, and perceiving their situation, ordered the men to hoist as fast as they could, before old Tom's strength should be exhausted; but it was a compound moving crane, and we could not hoist very fast, although we could hoist very great weights. At last, as they were wound up higher and higher, old Tom's strength was going fast. "O Tom, Tom, what must be done? I can't—I can't hold on but a little longer, and we shall be both dashed to pieces. My poor boy?"

"Well, then, I'll let go, father; it was all my folly, and I'll be the sufferer."

"Let go!" cried old Tom; "no, no, Tom—don't let go, my boy; I'll try a little longer. Don't let go, my dear boy—don't let go!"

"Well, father, how much longer can you hold on?"

"A little—very little longer," replied the old man, struggling. "Well, hold fast now," cried young Tom, who, raising his head above his arms, with great exertion shifted one of his hands to his father's thigh, then the other; raising himself as before, he then caught at the seat of his father's trousers with his teeth; old Tom groaned, for his son had taken hold of more than the garments; he then shifted his hands round his father's body—from thence he gained the collar of his jacket—from the collar he climbed on his father's shoulders, from thence he seized hold of the fall above, and relieved his father of the weight. "Now, father, are you all right?" cried Tom, panting as he clung to the fall above him.

"I can't hold on ten seconds more, Tom—no longer—my clutch is going now."

"Hang on by your eyelids, father, if you love me," cried young Tom, in agony.

It was indeed an awful moment; they were now at least sixty feet above the lighter, suspended in the air; the men whirled round the wheel, and I had at last the pleasure of hauling them both in on the floor of the warehouse; the old man so exhausted that he could not speak for more than a minute. Young Tom, as soon as all was safe, laughed immoderately. Old Tom sat upright. "It might have been no laughing matter, Mr Tom," said he, looking at his son.

"What's done can't be helped, father, as Jacob says. After all, you're more frightened than hurt."

"I don't know that, you young scamp," replied the old man, putting his hand behind him, and rubbing softly; "you've bit a piece clean out of my *starn*. Now, let this be a warning to you, Tom. Jacob, my boy, couldn't you say that I've met with an *accident*, and get a drop of something from Mr Drummond?"

I thought, after his last observation, I might honestly say that he had met with an accident, and I soon returned with a glass of brandy, which old Tom was drinking off when his son interrupted him for a share.

"You know, father, I shared the danger."

"Yes, Tom, I know you did," replied the father; "but this was sent to me on account of my *accident*, and as I had that all to myself, I shall have all this too."

"But, father, you ought to give me a drop, if it were only to *take the taste out of my mouth*."

"Your own flesh and blood, Tom," replied his father, emptying his glass.

"Well, I always heard it was quite unnatural not to like your own flesh and blood," replied Tom; "but I see now that there may be reasons for it."

"Be content, Tom," replied his father, putting down the glass; "we're now just square. You've had your *raw nip*, and I've had mine."

Mr Drummond now came up, and asked what had been the matter. "Nothing, sir—only an accident. Tom and I had a bit of a *hoist*."

As this last word had a double meaning, Mr Drummond thought that a cask had surged, when coming out of the lighter, and struck them down. He desired old Tom to be more careful, and walked away, while we proceeded to unload the lighter. The new clerk was a very heavy, simple young man, plodding and attentive certainly, but he had no other merit; he was sent into the lighter to rake the marks and numbers of the casks as they were hoisted up, and soon became a butt to young Tom, who gave him the wrong marks and numbers of all the casks, to his interrogations.

"What's that, boy?" cried the pudding-faced fellow, with his pencil in one hand and his book in the other.

"Pea soup, 13," replied Tom; "ladies' bonnets, 24. Now, then, master, chalk again, pipe-clay for sodgers, 3; red herrings, 26." All of which were carefully noted down by Mr Grubbins who, when the lighter was cleared, took the memoranda to Mr Drummond.

Fortunately, we had checked the number of the casks as they were received above—their contents were flour. Mr Drummond sent for young Tom, and asked him how he dared play such a trick. Tom replied very boldly, "that it was meant as a good lesson to the young man, that in future he did his own work, and did not trust to others." To this Mr Drummond agreed, and Master Tom was dismissed without punishment.

As the men had all gone to dinner, I went down into the lighter to have a little chat with my old shipmates. "Well, Jacob," said old Tom, "Tom's not a bit wiser than he was before—two scrapes to-day, already."

"Well, father, if I prove my folly by getting into scrapes, I prove my wit by getting out of them."

"Yes, that may be true, Tom; but suppose we had both come down with a run, what would you have thought then?"

"I suspect, father, that I should have been past thinking."

"I once did see a thing of that kind happen," said old Tom, calling to mind former scenes in his life; "and I'll tell you a yarn about it, boys, because they say danger makes friends."

We sat down by old Tom, who narrated as follows "When I was captain of the main-top in the *La Minerve*, forty-four gun frigate, we were the smartest ship up the Mediterranean; and many's the exercise we were the means of giving to other ship's companies, because they could not beat us—no, not even hold a candle to us. In both fore and main-top we had eight-and-twenty as smart chaps as ever put their foot to a rattling, or slid down by an a'ter backstay. Now, the two captains of the foretop were both prime young men, active as monkeys, and bold as lions. One was named Tom Herbert, from North Shields, a dark, good-looking chap, with teeth as white as a nigger's, and a merry chap he was, always a-showing them. The other was a cockney chap. Your Lunnuners arn't often good seamen; but when they are seamen, there's no better; they never allow any one to show them the way, that's for sartin, being naturally spunky sort of chaps, and full of tricks and fun. This fellow's name was Bill Wiggins, and between him and Herbert there was always a jealousy who should be the smartest man. I've seen both of them run out on the yard, in fine weather, without holding on nothing, seize the lift, and down to their station, haul up the earing, in no time; up by the lift again, and down on deck, by the backstay, before half the men had time to get clear of the top. In fact, they often risked their lives in bad weather, when there was no occasion for it, that one might outdo the other. Now, this was all very well, and a good example to the other men: the captain and officers appeared to like these contests for superiority, but it ended in their hating each other, and not being even on speaking terms, which, as the two captains of the top, was bad. They had quarrelled often, and fought five times, neither proving the better man; either both done up, or parted by the master-at-arms, and reported to the first lieutenant, so that at last they were not so much countenanced by the officers, and were out of favour with the captain, who threatened to disrate them both if ever they fought again. We were cruising off the Gulf of Lyons, where sometimes it blows hard enought to blew the devil's horns off, though the gales never last very long. We were under close reefed fore- and main-top sails, storm stay-sail and trysail, when there was a fresh hand at the bellows, and the captain desired the officers of the watch, just before dinner to take in the fore-top sail. Not to disturb the watch below, the main-top men were ordered up forward to help the fore-top men of the watch; and I was of course aloft, ready to lie out on the lee yard-arm—when Wiggins, who had the watch below, came up in the top, not liking that Herbert should be at work in such weather without he being there too.

"'Tom,' says to me, 'I'll take the yard-arm.'

"'Very well,' say I, 'with all my heart; then I'll look to the bunt.'

"Just at that time there came on a squall with rain, which almost blinded us; the sail was taken in very neatly, the clew-lines, chock-a-block, bunt-lines and leech-lines well up, reef-tackles overhauled, rolling-tackles taut, and all as it should be. The men lied out on the yard, the squall wore worse and worse, but they were handing in the leech of the sail, when snap went one bunt-line, then the other; the sail flapped and flagged, till away went the leech-lines, and the men clung to the yards for their lives; for the sail mastered them, and they could do nothing. At last it split like thunder, buffeting the men on the yard-arms till they were almost senseless, until to windward it wore away into long coach whips, and the whole of the canvas left was at the lee yard-arm. The men laid in at last with great difficulty, quite worn out by fatigue and clinging for their existence; all but Wiggins, who was barred by the sail to leeward from making his footing good on the horse, and there he was, poor fellow, completely in irons, and so beaten by the canvas that he could hardly be said to be sensible. It takes a long while to tell all this, but it wasn't the work of a minute. At last he made an attempt to get up by the lift, but was struck down, and would have been hurled overboard if it hadn't been that his leg fell over the horse, and there he was, head downwards, hanging over a raging sea, ready to swallow him up as soon as he dropt into it. As every one expected he would be beat off before any assistance could be given, you may guess that it was an awful moment to those below who were looking up at him, watching for his fall and the roll of the ship, to see if he fell clear into the sea, or was dashed to pieces in the fore-chains.

"I couldn't bear to see a fellow-creature, and good seaman in the bargain, in that state, and although the captain dare not *order* any one to help him, yet there were one or two midshipmen hastening up the fore-rigging, with the intent, I have no doubt, of trying to save him (for midshipmen don't value their lives at a quid of tobacco), so I seizes the studding sail halyards, and runs up the topmast rigging, intending to go down by the lift, and pass a bowling knot round him before he fell, when who should I meet at the cross-trees but Tom Herbert, who snatched the rope out of my hand, bawling to me through the gale, 'This is my business, Tom.'

"Down he goes by the lift, the remainder of the canvas flapped over him, and I seed no more until I heard a cry from all below, and away went Herbert and Wiggins, both together, flying to leeward just as the ship was taking her recovery to windward. Fortunately they both fell clear of the ship about two feet, not more, and as their fall was expected, they had prepared below. A master's mate, of the name of Simmonds, and the captain of the forecastle, both went overboard in bowling knots, with another in their hands, and in a minute or two they were all four on board again; but Herbert and were both senseless, and a long while coming to again. Well, now, what do you think was the upshot of it? Why, they were the best friends in the world ever afterwards, and would have died for one another; and if one had a glass of grog from the officers for any little job, instead of touching his forelock and drinking it off to the officer's health, he always took it out of the gun-room, that he might give half of it to the other. So, d'ye see my boys, as I said before I began my yarn, that danger makes friends.

> "'Tis said we vent'rous die hard,
>   When we leave the shore,
> Our friends may mourn, lest we return
>   To bless their sight no more.
> But this is all a notion
>   Bold Jack can't understand;
> Some die upon the ocean.
>   And some die upon dry land."

"And if we had tumbled, father, we should have just died betwixt and between, not water enough to float us. It would have been *woolez wous parlez wous*, plump in the mud, as you say sometimes."

"Why, yes, Tom. I've a notion that I should have been planted too deep ever to have struck," replied the old man, looking at his wooden stumps.

"Why, yes, father, *legs* are *legs*, when you tumble into six foot of mud. How you would have *dibbled* down, if your *daddles* hadn't held on."

"Well then, Tom, recollect that you never *sell* your father for a *lark* again."

Tom laughed, and catching at the word, although used in a different sense, sung—

"Just like the *lark* high poised in air.

"And so were you, father, only you didn't sing as he does, and you didn't leave your young one below in the nest."

"Ay, it is the young uns which prevent the old ones from rising in the world—that's very true, Tom. Holla, who have we got here? My service to you, at all events."

Chapter Eighteen

It was the captain of the American schooner, from out of which we were then taking the casks of flour.

"We've no *sarvice* in our country, I've a notion, my old bobtail roarer," said he. "When do you come alongside of my schooner, for tother lading with this raft of yours? Not to-night, I guess."

"Well, you've guessed right this time," replied old Tom; "we shall lie on the mud till to-morrow morning, with your permission."

"Yes, for all the world like a Louisiana alligator. You take things coolly, I've a notion, in the old country. I don't want to be hanging head and starn in this little bit of a river of your'n. I must be back to New York afore fever time."

"She be a pretty craft, that little thing of yours," observed old Tom; "how long may she take to make the run?"

"How long? I expect in just no time; and she'd go as fast again, only she won't wait for the breeze to come up with her."

"Why don't you heave-to for it?" said young Tom.

"Lose too much time, I guess. I have been chased by an easterly wind all the way from your Land's End to our Narrows, and it never could overhaul me."

"And I presume the porpoises give it up in despair, don't they?" replied old Tom, with a leer; "and yet I've seen the creatures playing across the bows of an English frigate at her speed, and laughing at her."

"They never play their tricks with me, old snapper; if they do, I cuts them in halves, and a-starn they go, head part floating on one side, and tail part on the other."

"But don't they join together again when they meet in your wake?" inquired Tom.

"Shouldn't wonder," replied the American captain.

"Pray, captain, what may be that vessel they talk so much about at New York?" Old Tom referred to the first steam vessel, whose qualities at that time had been tried, and an exaggerated report of which had been copied from the American papers. "That ship, or whatever she may be, that sails without masts, yards, or canvas; it is quite above my comprehension."

"Old country heads can't take it in. I'll tell you what—she goes slick through the water, a-head or a-starn, broadside on, or up or down, or any way; and all you have to do is to poke the fire and warm your fingers; and the more you poke, the faster she goes 'gainst wind and tide."

"Well, I must see that to believe it, though," replied old Tom.

"No fear of a capsize, I calculate. My little craft did upset with me one night, in a pretty comfortable heavy *gal*; but she's *smart*, and came up again on the other side in a moment, all right as before. Never should have known anything about it, if the man at the wheel had not found his jacket wet, and the men below had a round turn in all the clews of their hammocks."

"After that round turn, you may belay," cried young Tom, laughing.

"Yes, but don't let's have a stopper over all, Tom," replied his father. "I consider all this excessively *divarting*. Pray, captain, does everything else go fast in the new country."

"Everything with us *clean slick*, I guess."

"What sort of horses have you in America?" inquired I.

"Our Kentucky horses, I've a notion, would surprise you. They're almighty goers; at a trot, beat a *North West gal* of wind. I once took an Englishman with me in a gig up Allibama country, and he says, 'What's this great churchyard we are passing through?' 'And stranger,' says I, 'I calculate it's nothing but the milestones we are passing so *slick*.' But I once had a horse, who, I expect, was a deal quicker than that. I once seed a flash of lightning chase him for half-an-hour round the clearance, and I guess it couldn't catch him. But I can't wait no longer. I expect you'll come alongside to-morrow afore meridian."

"Ay, ay, master," replied old Tom, tuning up—

"'Twas post meridian, half-past four,
    By signal I from Nancy parted,
At five she lingered on the shore,
    With uplift eyes and broken-hearted."

"I calculate you are no fool of a screamer," said the American, shoving off his boat from the barge, and pulling to his vessel.

"And I calculate you're no fool of a liar," said young Tom.

"Well, so he is; but I do like a good lie, Jacob, there's some fun in it. But what the devil does the fellow mean by calling a gale of wind—*a gal*?"

"I don't know," replied Tom, "unless for the same reason that we call a girl *a blowing*."

Our conversation was here interrupted by Mr Hodgson, the new head clerk, of whom I have hitherto said nothing. He came into the establishment in the place of Mr Tomkins, when we quitted the Battersea wharf, and had taken an evident dislike to me, which appeared to increase every day, as Mr Drummond gave me fresh marks of his approbation. "You, Faithful, come out of that barge directly, and go to your desk. I will have no eye-servers under me. Come out, sir, directly."

"I say, Mr Quilldriver," cried old Tom, "do you mean for to say that Jacob is an eye-sarver?"

"Yes, I do; and want none of your impertinence, or I'll unship you, you old blackguard."

"Well, then, for the first part of your story, my sarvice to you and you *lies*; and as for the second, that remains to be proved."

Mr Hodgson's temper was not softened by this reply of old Tom. My blood was also up, for I had borne much already; and young Tom was bursting with impatience to take my part. He walked carelessly by the head clerk, saying to me as he passed by, "Why, I thought, Jacob, you were 'prentice to the river; but it seems that you're bound to the counting-house. How long do you mean to sarve?"

"I don't know," replied I, as I walked away sulkily; "but I wish I was out of my time."

"Very well, sir, I shall report your behaviour to Mr Drummond. I'll make him know your tricks."

"Tricks! you won't let him know his tricks. His duty is to take his trick at the wheel," replied old Tom; "not to be brought up at your cheating tricks at the desk."

"Cheating tricks, you old scoundrel, what do you mean by that?" replied Mr Hodgson, in a rage.

"My father means *ledger*demain, I suppose," replied young Tom.

This repartee from a quarter so little expected sent off the head clerk more wroth than ever.

"You seemed to hit him hard there, Tom," said his father; "but I can't say that I understand how."

"You've had me taught to read and write, father," replied young Tom; "and a'ter that, a lad may teach himself everything. I pick up every day, here and there; and I never see a thing or a word that I don't understand but I find out the meaning when I can. I picked up that hard word at Bartlemy fair."

"And very hard you hit him with it."

"Who wouldn't to serve a friend? But mark my words, father, this won't last long. There's a squall blowing up, and Jacob, quiet as he seems to be, will show his teeth ere long."

Tom was correct in his surmise. I had not taken my seat at my desk more than a minute, when Mr Hodgson entered, and commenced a tirade of abuse, which my pride could no longer allow me to submit to. An invoice, perfectly correct and well-written, which I had nearly completed, he snatched from before me, tore into fragments, and ordered me to write it over again. Indignant at this treatment, I refused, and throwing down my pen, looked at him determinedly in the face. Irritated at this defiance, he caught up a directory, and threw it at my head. No longer able to command myself, I seized a ruler and returned the salute. It was whizzing through the air as Mr Drummond entered the room; and he was just in time to witness Mr Hodgson struck on the forehead and felled to the ground, while I remained with my arm raised, standing upon the cross-bar of my high stool, my face glowing with passion.

Appearances were certainly against me. Assistance was summoned, and the head clerk removed to his chamber, during all which time I remained seated on my stool before the desk, my breast heaving with tumultuous feelings. How long I remained there I cannot say, it might have been two hours; feelings long dormant had been aroused, and whirled round and round in a continual cycle in my feverish brains. I should have remained probably much longer in this state of absorption, had I not been summoned to attend Mr Drummond. It appeared that in the meantime Mr Hodgson had come to his own senses, and had given his own version of the fracas, which had been, to an unjustifiable degree, corroborated by the stupid young clerk, who was no friend of mine, and who sought favour with his principal. I walked up to the drawing-room, where I found Mr and Mrs Drummond, and little Sarah, whose eyes were red with crying. I entered without any feeling of alarm, my breast was too full of indignation. Mrs Drummond looked grave and mournful, Mr Drummond severe.

"Jacob Faithful, I have sent for you to tell you that in consequence of your disgraceful conduct to my senior clerk, you can no longer remain under my roof. It appears that what I have been a witness to this day has been but a sequel to behaviour equally improper and impertinent; that so far from having, as I thought, done your duty, you have constantly neglected it; and that the association you have formed with that drunken old man and his insolent son has led you into this folly. You may say that it was not your wish to remain on shore, and that you preferred being on the river. At your age it is too often the case that young people consult their wishes rather than their interests; and it is well for them if they find those who are older, and wished them well, to decide for them. I had hoped to have been able to place you in a more respectable situation in society than was my original intention when you were thrown upon me, a destitute orphan; but I now perceive my error. You have proved yourself not only deceitful but ungrateful."

"I have not," interrupted I, calmly.

"You have. I have been a witness myself to your impropriety of conduct, which, it appears, has long been concealed from me; but no more of that. I bound you apprentice to the river, and you must now follow up your apprenticeship; but expect nothing farther from me. You must now work your own way up in the world, and I trust that you will reform and do well. You may return to the lighter until I can procure you a situation in another craft, for I consider it my duty to remove you from the influence of those who have led you astray, and with the old man and his son you will not remain. I have one thing more to say. You have been in my counting-house for some months, and you are now about to be thrown upon the world. There are ten pounds for your services," (and Mr Drummond laid the money on the table). "You may also recollect that I have some money belonging to you, which has been laid by until you shall be out of your apprenticeship. I consider it my duty still to retain that money for you; as soon as your apprenticeship is expired you may demand it, and it shall be made over to you. I trust, sincerely trust, Jacob, that the severe lesson you are now about to receive will bring you to a sense of what is right, and that you will forget the evil counsel you have received from your late companions. Do not attempt to justify yourself; it is useless." Mr Drummond then rose and left the room.

I should have replied, had it not been for this last sentence of Mr Drummond's, which again roused the feeling of indignation, which, in their presence, had been gradually giving way to softer emotions. I therefore stood still, and firmly met the glance of Mr Drummond as he passed me. My looks were construed into hardness of heart.

It appeared that Mr Drummond had left the room by previous arrangement, that he might not be supposed to be moved from this purpose, and that Mrs Drummond was then to have talked to me, and to have ascertained how far there was a chance of my pleading guilty, and begging for a mitigation of my sentence; but the firm composure of innocence was mistaken for defiance; and the blood mounting to my forehead from a feeling of injustice—of injustice from those I loved and venerated—perhaps the most poignant feeling in existence to a sensitive and generous mind—was falsely estimated as proceeding from impetuous and disgraceful sources. Mrs Drummond looked upon me with a mournful face, sighed, and said nothing; little Sarah watching me with her large black eyes, as if she would read my inmost soul.

"Have you nothing to say, Jacob," at last observed Mrs Drummond, "that I can tell Mr Drummond when his anger is not so great?"

"Nothing, madam," replied I, "except that I'll try to forgive him."

This reply was offensive even to the mild Mrs Drummond. She rose from her chair. "Come, Sarah," said she: and she walked out of the room, wishing me, in a kind, soft voice, a "good-bye, Jacob," as she passed me.

My eyes swam with tears. I tried to return the salutation, but I was too much choked by my feelings; I could not speak, and my silence was again looked upon as contumacy and ingratitude. Little Sarah still remained—she had not obeyed her mother's injunctions to follow her. She was now nearly fourteen years old, and I had known her as a companion and a friend for five years. During the last six months that I had resided in the house we had become more intimately acquainted. I joined her in the evening in all her pursuits, and Mr and Mrs Drummond appeared to take a pleasure in our intimacy. I loved her as a dear sister; my love was based on gratitude. I had never forgotten her kindness to me when I first came under her father's roof, and a long acquaintance with the sweetness of her disposition had rendered the attachment so firm, that I felt I could have died for her. But I never knew the full extent of the feeling until now that I was about to leave her, perhaps for ever. My heart sank when Mr Drummond left the room—a bitter pang passed through it as the form of Mrs Drummond vanished from my sight; but now was to be the bitterest of all. I felt it, and I remained with the handle of the door in my hand, gasping for breath—blinded with the tears that coursed each other rapidly down my cheeks. I remained a minute in this state, when I felt that Sarah touched my other listless hand.

"Jacob!" she would have said, but before half my name was out she burst into tears, and sobbed on my shoulder. My heart was too much surcharged not to take the infection—my grief found vent, and I mingled my sobs with those of the affectionate girl. When we were more composed, I recounted to her all that had passed, and one, at least, in the world acknowledged that I had been treated unjustly. I had but just finished, when the servant interrupted us with a message to Sarah, that her mother desired her presence. She threw herself into my arms, and bade me farewell. I released her, she hastened to obey her mother, but perceiving the money still upon the table, she pointed to it. "Your money, Jacob!"

"No Sarah, I will not accept it. I would accept of anything from those who treat me kindly, and feel more and more grateful to them; but that I will not accept—I cannot, and you must not let it be left here. Say that I could not take it."

Sarah would have remonstrated, but perceiving that I was firm, and at the same time, perhaps, entering into my feelings, she again bade me farewell, and hastened away.

The reader may easy imagine that I did not put off my departure. I hastened to pack up my clothes, and in less than ten minutes after Sarah had quitted me, I was on board the lighter, with old Tom and his son, who were then going to supper. They knew a part of what had happened, and I narrated the rest.

"Well," replied old Tom, after I had finished my story, "I didn't know that I have done you any harm, Jacob, and I'm sorry that Mr Drummond should suppose so. I'm fond of a drop, that's true; but I appeals to you, whether I ever force it on you—and whether I don't check that boy as much as I can; but then, d'ye see, although I preach, I don't practise, that's the worst of it; and I know I've to answer for making Tom so fond of grog; and though I never says anything about it, I often think to myself, that if Tom should chance to be pressed some of these days, and be punished for being in liquor, he'll think of his old father, and curse him in his heart, when he eyes the cat flourishing round before it strikes."

"I'll curse the cat, father, or the boatswain's mate, or the officer who complained of me, or the captain who flogs me, or my own folly, but I'll be hanged if ever I curse you, who have been so kind to me," replied Tom, taking his father's hand.

"Well, we must hope for the best, my dear boy," replied old Tom; "but, Jacob, you've not had fair play, that sartain. It's very true that master did take you as an orphan, and help you to an education; but that's no reason why he should take away your free will, and after binding you 'prentice to the river, perch you up on a high stool, and grind your nose down to the desk. If so be he was so kind to you only to make you a slave, why, then, there was no kindness at all, in my opinion: and as for punishment without hearing what a man has to say in his own defence—there's ne'er a Tartar in the sarvice but would allow a man to speak before he orders him to strip. I recollect a story about that in the sarvice, but I'm in no humour to spin a yarn now. Now, you see, Jacob, Master Drummond has done a great deal for you, and now he has undone a great deal! I can't pretend to balance the account, but it does appear to me that you don't owe him much; for what thanks is there if you take a vessel in tow, and then cast her off, half-way, when she most needs your assistance? But what hurts me most is his saying that you sha'n't stay in the lighter with us; if you had, you shouldn't have wanted, as long as pay and pension are forthcoming. Never mind—Tom, my boy, bring out the bottle—hang care: it killed the cat."

The grog did not, however, bring back old Tom's spirits; the evening passed heavily, and we retired to our beds at a seasonable hour, as we were to drop down to the schooner early the next morning. That night I did not close my eyes. I ran over, in my mind, all that had occurred, and indignation took full possession of my soul. My whole life passed in review before me. I travelled back to my former days—to the time which had been almost obliterated from my memory, when I had navigated the barge with my father. Again was the scene of his and my mother's death presented to my view; again I saw him disappear, and the column of black smoke ascend to the sky. The Dominie, the matron, Marables, and Fleming, the scene in the cabin—all passed in rapid succession. I felt that I had done my duty, and that I had been unjustly treated; my head ached with tumultuous and long suppressed feelings. Reader, I stated that when I was first taken in hand by Mr Drummond I was a savage, although a docile one, to be reclaimed by kindness, and kindness only. You may have been surprised at the rapid change which took place in a few years; that change was produced by kindness. The conduct of Mr Drummond, of his amiable wife and daughter, had been all kindness; the Dominie and the worthy old matron had proved equally beneficent. Marables had been kind; and, although now and then, as in the case of the usher at the school, and Fleming on board the lighter, I had received injuries, still, these were but trifling checks to the uninterrupted series of kindness with which I had been treated by everybody. Thus was my nature rapidly formed by a system of kindness assisted by education; and had this been followed up, in a few years my new character would have been firmly established. But the blow was now struck, injustice roused up the latent feelings of my nature, and when I rose the next morning I was changed. I do not mean to say that all that precept and education had done for me was overthrown; but if not overthrown, it was so shaken to the base, so rent from the summit to the foundation, that, at the slightest impulse in a wrong direction, it would have fallen in and left nothing but a mixed chaos of ruined prospects. If anything could hold it together it was the kindness and affection of Sarah, to which I would again and again return in my revolving thoughts, as the only bright star to be discovered in my clouded horizon.

How dangerous, how foolish, how presumptuous it is in adults to suppose that they can read the thoughts and the feelings of those of a tender age! How often has this presumption on their part been the ruin of a young mind, which, if truly estimated and duly fostered, would have blossomed and produced good fruit! The blush of honest indignation is as dark as the blush of guilt, and the paleness of concentrated courage as marked as that of fear, the firmness of conscious innocence is but too often mistaken as the effrontery of hardened vice, and the tears springing from a source of injury, the tongue tied from the oppression of a wounded heart, the trembling and agitation of the little frame convulsed with emotion have often and often been ascribed by prejudging and self-opinionated witnesses to the very opposite passions to those which have produced them. Youth should never be judged harshly, and even when judged correctly, should it be in an evil course, may always be reclaimed;—those who decide otherwise, and leave it to drift about the world, have to answer for the *cast-away*.

Chapter Nineteen

"Hollo! in the lighter there—I say, you *lighter boy*!" were words I heard, as I was pacing the deck of the vessel in deep cogitation Tom and his father were both in the cabin; there could be no doubt but that they were addressed to me. I looked up, and perceived the grinning, stupid, sneering face of the young clerk, Gubbins. "Why don't you answer when you're called to, heh?" continued the numbskull. "You're wanted up here! Come up directly."

"Who wants me?" replied I, reddening with anger.

"What's that to you? Do you mean to obey *my* order or not?"

"No, I do not," replied I; "I'm not under the orders of such a fool, thank God; and if you come within my reach, I'll try if I can't break your head, thick as it is, as well as your master's."

The lout disappeared, and I continued to pace up and down.

As I afterwards discovered, the message was from Mrs Drummond, who requested to speak to me. Sarah had communicated the real facts of my case, and Mrs Drummond had been convinced that what I had said was correct. She had talked with her husband; she pointed out to him that my conduct under Mr Tomkins had been so exemplary that there must have been some reason for so sudden a change. Sarah had gone down into the counting-house, and obtained the invoice which the senior clerk had torn up. The correctness of it established the fact of one part of my assertions, and that nothing but malice could have warranted its having been destroyed. Mr Drummond felt more than he chose to acknowledge; he was now aware that he had been too precipitate; even my having refused the money assumed a different appearance; he *was* puzzled and mortified. Few people like to acknowledge that they have been in error. Mr Drummond, therefore, left his wife to examine further into the matter, and gave her permission to send for me. The message given, and the results of it have been stated. The answer returned was that I would not come, and that I had threatened to break the clerk's head as well as that of Mr Drummond; for although the scoundrel knew very well that in making use of the word "master," I referred to the senior clerk, he thought it proper to substitute that of Mr Drummond. The effect of this reply may easily be imagined. Sarah was astonished, Mrs

Drummond shocked, and Mr Drummond was almost pleased to find that he could not have been in the wrong. Thus was the breach made even wider than before, and all communication broken off. Much depends in this world upon messages being correctly given.

In half-an-hour we had hauled out of the tier and dropped down to the American schooner, to take out a cargo of flour, which old Tom had directions to land at the Battersea wharf; so that I was, for the time, removed from the site of my misfortune. I cannot say that I felt happy, but I certainly felt glad that I was away. I was reckless to a degree that was insupportable. I had a heavy load on my mind which I could not shake off—a prey upon my spirits—a disgust at almost everything. How well do I recollect with what different feelings I looked upon the few books which Mr Drummond and the Dominie had given me to amuse my leisure hours. I turned from them with contempt, and thought I would never open them again. I felt as if all ties were now cut off, and that I was again wedded to the Thames; my ideas, my wishes, extended no farther, and I surveyed the river and its busy scene as I did before I had been taken away from it, as if all my energies, all my prospects were in future to be bounded by its shores. In the course of four-and-twenty hours a revulsion had taken place, which again put me on the confines of barbarism.

My bargemates were equally dull as I was; they were too partial to me, and had too much kindness of heart, not to feel my situation, and anger at the injustice with which I had been treated. Employment, however, for a time relieved our melancholy thoughts. Our cargo was on board of the lighter, and we were again tiding it through the bridges.

We dropped our anchor above Putney Bridge a little after twelve o'clock, and young Tom, with the wish of amusing me, proposed that we should go on shore and walk. "Ah! do my lads, do—it will do you good, Jacob; no use moping here a whole tide. I'll take care of the 'barkey. Mind you make the boat well fast, and take the sculls into the public-house there. I'll have the supper under weigh when you come back, and then we'll have a night on't. It's a poor heart that never rejoices; and, Tom, take a bottle on shore, get it filled, and bring it off with you. Here's the money. But I say, Tom, honour bright."

"Honour bright, father;" and to do Tom justice, he always kept his promise, especially after the word had passed of "honour bright." Had there been gallons of spirits under his charge he would not have tasted a drop after that pledge.

"Haul up the boat, Jacob, quick," said Tom, as his father went into the cabin to fetch an empty bottle. Tom hastened down below forward and brought up an old gun, which he put under the stern sheets before his father came out on the deck. We then received the bottle from him, and Tom called out for the dog Tommy.

"Why, you're not going to take the dog. What's the use of that? I want him here to keep watch with me," said old Tom.

"Pooh! father; why can't you let the poor devil have a run on shore? He wants to eat grass, I am sure, for I watched him this day or two. We shall be back before dark."

"Well, well, just as you please, Tom." Tommy jumped into the boat, and away we went.

"And now, Tom, what are you after?" said I, as soon as we were ten yards from the lighter.

"A'ter, Jacob, going to have a little shooting on Wimbledon Common; but father can't bear to see a gun in my hand, because I once shot my old mother. I did pepper her, sure enough; her old flannel petticoat was full of shot, but it was so thick that it saved her. Are you anything of a shot?"

"Never fired a gun in my life."

"Well, then, we'll fire in turns, and toss up, if you like, for first shot."

We landed, carried the sculls up to the public-house, and left the bottle to be filled, and then, with Tommy bounding before us, and throwing about his bushy tail with delight, ascended Putney Hill, and arrived at the Green Man public-house, at the corner of Wimbledon Common. "I wonder where green men are to be found?" observed Tom, laughing; "I suppose they live in the same country with the *blue* dogs my father speaks about sometimes. Now, then, its time to load."

The bowl of a tobacco pipe, full of powder, was then inserted, with an equal dose of shot, and all being ready we were soon among the furze. A half penny decided it was my first shot, and fate further decided that a water-wagtail should be the mark. I took good aim, as I thought, at least I took sufficient time, for I followed him with the muzzle of the gun for three or four minutes at least, as he ran to and fro; at last I fired. Tommy barked with delight, and the bird flew away. "I think I must have hit it," said I; "I saw it wag its tail."

"More proof of a miss than a hit," replied Tom. "Had you hit it he'd never have wagged his tail again."

"Never mind," said I, "better luck next time."

Tom then knocked a blackbird off a furze bush, and loading the gun, handed it to me. I was more successful than before; a cock sparrow, three yards distant, yielded to the prowess of my arm, and I never felt more happy in my life than in this first successful attempt at murder.

Gaily did we trudge over the common, sometimes falling in with gravel-pits half full of water, at others bogs and swampy plains, which obliged us to make a circuit. The gun was fired again and again; but our game-bag did not fill very fast. However, if we were not quite so well pleased when we missed as when we hit, Tommy was, every shot being followed up with a dozen bounds, and half a minute's barking. At last we began to feel tired, and agreed to repose a while in a cluster of furze bushes. We sat down, pulled out our game, and spread it in a row before us. It consisted of two sparrows, one greenfinch, one blackbird, and three tomtits. All of a sudden we heard a rustling in the furze, and then a loud squeal. It was the dog, who, scenting something, had forced its way into the bush, and had caught a hare, which having been wounded in the loins by some other sportsman, had dragged itself there to die. In a minute we had taken possession of it, much to the annoyance of Tommy, who seemed to consider that there was no co-partnership in the concern, and would not surrender his prize until after sundry admonitory kicks. When we had fairly beaten him off we were in an ecstasy of delight. We laid the animal out between us, and were admiring it from the ear to the tip of his tail, when we were suddenly saluted with a voice close to us. "Oh, you blam'd young poachers, so I've caught you, have I?" We looked up, and beheld the common-keeper. "Come—come along with me; we've a nice clink at Wandsworth to lock you up in. I've been looking a'rter you some time. Hand your gun here."

"I should rather think not," replied I. "The gun belongs to us, and not to you;" and I caught up the gun, and presented the muzzle at him.

"What! do you mean to commit murder? Why, you young villains!"

"Do you want to commit a robbery?" retorted I, fiercely; "because if you do, I mean to commit murder. Then I shoot him. Tom."

"No, Jacob, no; you mustn't shoot men," replied Tom, who perceived that I was in a humour to keep my word with the common-keeper. "Indeed, you can't," continued he, whispering to me; "the gun's not loaded."

"Do you mean to refuse to give me up your gun?" repeated the man.

"Yes I do," replied I, cocking the lock; "so keep off."

"Oh! you young reprobates—you'll come to the gallows before long, that's certain. Do you refuse to come with me?"

"I should rather think we do," replied I.

"You refuse, do you? Recollect I've caught you in the fact, poaching, with a dead hare in your possession."

"Well, it's no use crying about it. What's done can't be helped," replied I.

"Don't you know that all the game, and all the turf, and all the bog, and all the gravel, and all the furze on this common belong to the Right Honourable Earl Spencer?"

"And all the blackbirds, and all the greenfinches, and all the sparrows, and all the tomtits too, I suppose?" replied I.

"To be sure they do—and I'm common-keeper. Now you'll give me up that hare immediately."

"Look you," replied Tom, "we didn't kill that hare, the dog caught it, and it is his property. We sha'n't interfere in the matter. If Tommy chooses to let you have it, well and good. Here, Tommy, this here gentleman says," (and Tom pointed to the keeper) "that this hare," (and Tom pointed to the hare) "is not yours; now will you 'watch it,' or let him have it?"

At the word 'watch it,' Tommy laid down with his fore-paws over the hare, and showing a formidable set of ivories, looked fiercely at the man, and growled.

"You see what he says; now you may do as you please," continued Tom, addressing the man.

"Yes—very well—you'll come to the gallows, I see that; but I'll just go and fetch half-a-dozen men to help me, and then we'll have you both in gaol."

"Then, be smart," replied I, jumping up and levelling the gun. Tommy jumped up also to fly at the man, but Tom caught him by the neck and restrained him. The common-keeper took to his heels, and as soon as he was out of gun-shot, turned round, shook his fist, and then hastened away to obtain the reinforcement he desired.

"I wish the gun had been loaded," said I.

"Why, Jacob, what's come over you? Would you have fired at him? The man is only doing his duty—we have no business here."

"I think otherwise," replied I. "A hare on a common is as much mine as Lord Spencer's. A common belongs to everybody."

"That's my opinion, too; but, nevertheless, if he gets hold of us, he'll have us in gaol; and therefore I propose we make off as fast as we can in the opposite way to which he is gone."

We started accordingly, and as the keeper proceeded in the direction of Wandsworth, we took the other direction; but it so happened that on turning round, after a quarter of an hour's walk, we perceived the man coming back with three or four others. "We must run for it," cried Tom, "and then hide ourselves." After ten minutes' hard run we descended into a hollow and swampy place, looking round to see if they could perceive us, and finding that they were not in sight, we plunged into a thick cluster of furze bushes, which completely concealed us. Tommy followed us, and there we lay. "Now they never will find us," said Tom, "if I can only keep the dog quiet. Lie down, Tommy. Watch, and lie down." The dog appeared to understand what was required; he lay between us perfectly still.

We had remained there about half-an-hour when we heard voices. I motioned to Tom to give me the powder to load the gun, but he refused. The voices came nearer; Tommy gave a low growl. Tom held his mouth with his hands. At last they were close to the bushes, and we heard the common-keeper say, "They never went over the hill, that's for certain, the little wagrants; they can't be far off—they must be down in the hollow. Come along."

"But I'm blessed if I'm not up to my knees in the bog," cried one of the men; "I'll go no further down, dang me!"

"Well, then let's try the side of the bog," replied the keeper, "I'll show you the way." And the voices retreated, fortunately for us, for there had been a continual struggle between us and the dog for the last minute, I holding his forepaws, and Tom jamming up his mouth. We were now all quiet again, but dare not leave our hiding-place.

We remained there for half-an-hour, when it became nearly dark, and the sky, which had been quite clear when we set out, clouded over. Tom put up his head, looked all round, and perceiving nobody, proposed that we should return as fast as we could; to which I agreed. But we were scarcely clear of the furze in which we had been concealed when a heavy fall of snow commenced, which, with the darkness, prevented us from distinguishing our way. Every minute the snow-storm increased, the wind rose, and hurled the flakes into our faces until we were blinded. Still we made good way against it, and expected every minute to be on the road, after which our task would be easy. On we walked in silence, I carrying the gun, Tom with the hare over his shoulder, and Tommy at our heels. For upwards of an hour did we tread our way through the furze, but could find no road. Above us all was dark as pitch; the wind howled; our clothes were loaded with snow; and we began to feel no inconsiderable degree of fatigue.

At last, quite tired out, we stopped. "Tom," said I, "I'm sure we've not kept a straight course. The wind was on our starboard side, and our clothes were flaked with snow on that side, and now you see we've got it in our quarter. What the devil shall we do?"

"We must go on till we fall in with something, at all events," replied Tom.

"And I expect that will be a gravel-pit," replied I; "but never mind, 'better luck next time.' I only wish I had that rascal of a common-keeper here. Suppose we turn back again, and keep the wind on the starboard side of us as before; we must pitch upon something at last."

We did so, but our difficulties increased every moment; we floundered in the bogs, we tumbled over the stumps of the cut furze, and had I not caught bold of Tom as he was sliding down he would have been at the bottom of a gravel-pit. This obliged us to alter our course, and we proceeded for a quarter of an hour, in another direction, until, worn out with cold and fatigue, we began to despair.

"This will never do, Tom," said I, as the wind rose and roared with double fury. "I think we had better get into the furze, and wait till the storm is over."

Tom's teeth chattered with the cold; but before he could reply, they chattered with fear. We heard a loud scream *overhead*. "What was that?" cried he. I confess that I was as much alarmed as Tom. The scream was repeated, and it had an unearthly sound. It was no human voice—it was between a scream and a creak. Again it was repeated, and carried along with the gale. I mustered up courage sufficient to look up to where the sound proceeded from; but the darkness was so intense, and the snow blinded me so completely, that I could see nothing. Again and again did the dreadful sound ring in our ears, and we remained fixed and motionless with horror; even the dog crouched at our feet trembling. We spoke not a word—neither of us moved; the gun had fallen from my hand; the hare lay at Tom's feet; we held each other's hand in silence, and there we remained for more than a quarter of an hour, every moment more and more sinking under the effects of cold, fatigue, and horror. Fortunately for us the storm, in which had it continued much longer we should, in all probability, have perished, was by that time over; the snow ceased to fall; the clouds were rolled away to leeward; and a clear sky, bespangled with a thousand twinkling lights, roused us from our state of bodily and mental suffering. The first object which caught my eye was a post within two yards of us. I looked at it, followed it up with my eyes, and, to my horror, beheld a body suspended and swinging in chains over our heads.

As soon as I recovered from the shock which the first view occasioned, I pointed it out to Tom, who had not yet moved. He looked up, started back, and fell over the dog—jumped up again, and burst out into as loud a laugh as his frozen jaws would permit. "It's old Jerry Abershaw," said he, "I know him well, and now I know where we are." This was the case; Abershaw had, about three years before, been hung in chains on Wimbledon Common; and the unearthly sound we had heard was the creaking of the rusty iron as the body was swung to-and-fro by the gale. "All's right, Jacob," said Tom, looking up at the brilliant sky, and then taking up the hare, "we'll be on the road in five minutes." I shouldered the gun, and off we set. "By the Lord, that rascally common-keeper was right," continued Tom, as we renewed our steps; "he prophesied we should come to the gallows before long, and so we have. Well, this has been a pretty turn out. Father will be in a precious stew."

"Better luck next time, Tom," replied I; "it's all owing to that turf-and-bog rascal. I wish we had him here."

"Why, what would you do with him?"

"Take down old Abershaw, and hang him up in his place, as sure as my name's Jacob."

Chapter Twenty

We soon recovered the road, and in half-an-hour we were at Putney Bridge; cold, wet, and tired, but not so bad as when we were stationary under the gallows; the quick walking restored the circulation. Tom went in for the bottle of spirits, while I went for the sculls and carried them down to the boat, which was high and dry, and nearly up to the thwarts with snow. When Tom joined me, he appeared with two bottles under his arms. "I have taken another upon tick, Jacob," said he, "for I'm sure we want it, and so will father say, when he hears our story." We launched our boat, and in a couple of minutes were close to the lighter, on the deck of which stood old Tom.

"Boat ahoy! is that you, lads?" cried he.

"Yes, father, all's right," replied Tom, as we laid in our oars.

"Thank God!" replied the old man. "Boys, boys, how you frightened me? where have you been? I thought you had met with some disaster. How have I been peeping through the snow-storm these last two hours, watching for the boat, and I'm as wet as a shag and as cold as charity. What has been the matter? Did you bring the bottle, Tom?"

"Yes, father; brought two, for we shall want them to-night if we go without for a week; but we must all get on dry rigging as fast as possible, and then you shall have the story of our cruise."

In a few minutes we had changed our wet clothes and were seated at the cabin-table, eating our supper, and narrating our adventures to the old man. Tommy, poor fellow, had his share, and now lay snoring at our feet, as the bottles and pannikins were placed upon the little table.

"Come, Jacob, a drop will do you good," said old Tom, filling me one of the pannikins. "A'ter all, it's much better being snug here in this little cabin than shivering with fear and cold under old Abershaw's gallows; and Tom, you scamp, if ever you go gunning again I'll disinherit you."

"What have you got to leave, father, except your wooden legs?" replied Tom. "Your's would be but a *wooden-leg*-acy."

"How do you know but what I can '*post the coal?*'"

"So you will, if I boil a pot o' 'tatoes with your legacy—but it will only be char-coal."

"Well, I believe you are about right, Tom; still, somehow or other, the old woman always picks out a piece or two of gold when I'm rather puzzled how to raise the wind. I never keeps no 'count with her. If I follow my legs before she, I hope the old soul will have saved something; for you know when a man goes to kingdom come, his pension goes with him. However, let me only hold on another five years, and then you'll not see her want; will you, Tom?"

"No, father; I'll sell myself to the king, and stand to be shot at, at a shilling a day, and give the old woman half."

"Well, Tom, 'tis but natural for a man to wish to serve his country; so here's to you, my lad, and may you never do worse! Jacob, do you think of going on board of a man-of-war?"

"I'd like to serve my apprenticeship first, and then I don't care how soon."

"Well, my boy, you'll meet more fair play on board of a king's ship than you have from those on shore."

"I should hope so," replied I, bitterly.

"I hope to see you a man before I die, yet, Jacob. I shall very soon be laid up in ordinary—my toes pain me a good deal lately!"

"Your toes!" cried Tom and I both at once.

"Yes, boys; you may think it odd, but sometimes I feel them just as plain as if they were now on, instead of being long ago in some shark's maw. At nights I has the cramp in them till it almost makes me halloo out with pain. It's a hard thing, when one has lost the sarvice of his legs, that all the feelings should remain. The doctor says as how it's narvous. Come, Jacob, shove in your pannikin. You seem to take it more kindly than you did."

"Yes," replied I, "I begin to like grog now." The *now*, however, might be comprehended within the space of the last twenty-four hours. My depressed spirits were raised with the stimulus, and for a time I got rid of the eternal current of thought which pressed upon my brain.

"I wonder what your old gentleman, the Dominie, as you call him, thought, after he got on shore again," said old Tom. "He seemed to be mighty cut up. I suppose you'll give him a hail, Jacob?"

"No," replied I, "I shall not go near him, nor any one else, if I can help it. Mr Drummond may think I wish to make it up again. I've done with the shore. I only wish I knew what is to become of me; for you know I am not to serve in the lighter with you."

"Suppose Tom and I look out for another craft, Jacob? I care nothing for Mr Drummond. He said t'other day I was a drunken old swab—for which, with my sarvice to him, he lies. A drunken fellow is one who can't, for the soul of him, keep from liquor when he can get it, and who's overtaken before he is aware of it. Now that's not the case with me; I keep sober when there's work to be done; and when I knows that everything is safe under hatches, and no fear of nothing, why then I gets drunk like a rational being, with my eyes open—'cause why?—'cause I chooses."

"That's exactly my notion of the thing," observed Tom, draining his pannikin, and handing it over to his father for a fresh supply.

"Mind you keep to that notion, Tom, when you gets in the king's sarvice, that's all; or you'll be sure to have your back scratched, which I understand is no joke after all. Yet I do remember once, in a ship I was in, when half-a-dozen fellows were all fighting who should be flogged."

"Pray give us that yarn, father; but before you begin just fill my pannikin. I shoved it over half-an-hour ago, just by way of a hint."

"Well then," said old Tom, pouring out some spirits into Tom's pannikin, "it was just as follows. It was when the ship was lying at anchor in Bermuda harbour, that the purser sent a breaker of spirits on shore to be taken up to some lady's house whom he was very anxious to splice, and I suppose that he found a glass of grog helped the matter. Now, there were about twenty of the men who had liberty to go on shore, to stretch their limbs—little else could they do, poor fellows for the first lieutenant looked sharp after their kits to see that they did not sell any of their rigging; and as for money, we had been five years without touching a farthing of pay, and I don't suppose there was a matter of threepence among the men before the mast. However, liberty's liberty after all; and if they couldn't go ashore and get glorious, rather than not go on shore at all, they went ashore and kept sober perforce. I do think, myself, it's a very bad thing to keep the seamen without a farthing for so long—for you see a man who will be very honest with a few shillings in his pocket is often tempted to help himself, just for the sake of getting a glass or two of grog, and the temptation's very great, that's sartain, 'ticularly in a hot climate, when the sun scorches you, and the very ground itself is so heated that you can hardly bear the naked foot to it.

(This has been corrected; the men have for some time received a portion of their pay on foreign stations, and this portion has been greatly increased during Sir James Graham's administration.) But to go on. The yawl was ordered on shore for the liberty men, and the purser gives this breaker, which was at least half full, and I dare say there might be three gallons in it, under my charge as coxswain, to deliver to madam at the house. Well, as soon as we landed, I shoulders the breaker, and starts with it up the hill.

"'What have you there, Tom?' said Bill Short.

"'What I wish I could share with you, Bill,' says I; 'it's some of old Nipcheese's *eights*, that he has sent on shore to bowse his jib up with, with his sweetheart.'

"'I've seen the madam,' said Holmes to me—for you see all the liberty men were walking up the hill at the same time—'and I'd rather make love to the breaker than to her. She's as fat as an ox, as broad as she's long, built like a Dutch schuyt, and as yellow as a nabob.'

"'But old Tummings knows what he's about,' said a Scotch lad of the name of M'Alpine; 'they say she has lots of gold dust, more ducks and ingons, and more inches of water in her tank than any on the island.'

"You see, boys, Bermuda be a queer sort of place, and water very scarce; all they get there is a Godsend, as it comes from Heaven; and they look sharp for the rain, which is collected in large tanks, and an inch or two more of water in the tank is considered a great catch. I've often heard the ladies there talking for a shower:—

"'Good morning, marm. How do you do this fine morning?'

"'Pretty well, I tank you, marm. Charming shower hab last night.'

"'Yes, so all say; but me not very lucky. Cloud not come over my tank. How many inches of water you get last night, marm?'

"'I get good seven inches, and I tink a little bit more, which make me very happy.'

"'Me no so lucky, marm; so help me God, me only get four inches of water in my tank; and dat nothing.'

"Well, but I've been yawing again, so now to keep my course. As soon as I came to the house I knocked at the door, and a little black girl opens the jalousies, and put her finger to her thick lips.

"'No make noise; missy sleep.'

"'Where am I to put this?'

"'Put down there; by-and-by I come fetch it;' and then she closed the jalousies, for fear her mistress should be woke up, and she get a hiding, poor devil. So I puts the breaker down at the door, and walks back to the boat again. Now, you see, these liberty men were all by when I spoke to the girl, and seeing the liquor left with no one to guard it, the temptation was too strong for them. So they looked all about them, and then at one another, and caught one another's meaning by the eye; but they said nothing. 'I'll have no hand in it,' at last says one, and walked away. 'Nor I,' said another, and walked away too. At last all of them walked away except eight, and then Bill Short walks up to the breaker and says—

"'I won't have no *hand* in it, either;' but he gave the breaker a kick, which rolls it away two or three yards from the door.

"'Nor more will I,' said Holmes, giving the breaker another kick, which rolled it out in the road. So they all went on, without having a *hand* in it, sure enough, till they had kicked the breaker down the hill to the beach. Then they were at a dead stand, as no one would spile the breaker. At last a black carpenter came by, and they offered him a glass if he would bore a hole with his gimlet, for they were determined to be able to swear, every one of them; that they had *no hand in it*. Well, as soon as the hole was bored, one of them borrowed a couple of little mugs from a black woman, who sold beer, and then they let it run, the black carpenter shoving one mug under as soon as the other was full, and they drinking as fast as they could. Before they had half finished, more of the liberty men came down; I suppose they scented the good stuff from above as a shark does anything in the water, and they soon made a finish of it; and when it was all finished, they were all drunk, and made sail for a cruise, that they might not be found too near the empty breaker. Well, a little before sunset I was sent on shore with the boat to fetch off the liberty men, and the purser takes this opportunity of getting ashore to see his madam, and the first thing he falls athwart of is his own empty breaker.

"'How's this?' says he; 'didn't you take this breaker up as I ordered you?'

"'Yes, sir,' replied I, 'I did, and gave it in charge to the little back thing; but madam was asleep, and the girl did not allow me to put it inside the door.' At that he began to storm, and swore that he'd find out the malefactors, as he termed the liberty men, who had emptied his breaker; and away he went to the house. As soon as he was gone we got hold of the breaker, and made a *bull* of it."

"How did you manage that?" inquired I.

"Why, Jacob, a *bull* means putting a quart or two of water into a cask which has had spirits in it; and what with the little that may be left, and what has soaked in the wood, if you roll it and shake it well, it generally turns out pretty fair grog. At all events its always better than nothing. Well, to go on—but suppose we fill up again and take a fresh departure, as this is a tolerably long yarn, and I must wet the threads, or they may chance to break."

Our pannikins, which had been empty, were all replenished, and then old Tom proceeded.

"It was a long while before we could pick up the liberty men, who were reeling about every corner of the town, and quite dark before I came on board. The first lieutenant was on deck, and had no occasion to ask me why I waited so long, when he found they were all lying in the stern sheets. 'Where the devil could they have picked up the liquor?' said he, and then he ordered the master-at-arms to keep them under the half-deck till they were sober. The next morning the purser comes off, and makes his complaint on the quarter-deck as how somebody had stolen his liquor. The first lieutenant reports to the captain, and the captain orders up all the men who came off tipsy.

"'Which of you took the liquor?' said he. They all swore that they had no hand in it. 'Then how did you get tipsy? Come now, Mr Short, answer me; you came off beastly drunk—who gave you the liquor?'

"'A black fellow, sir,' replied Short; which was true enough, as the mugs were filled by the black carpenter, and handed by him.

"Well, they all swore the same, and then the captain got into a rage, and ordered them all to be put down on the report. The next day the hands were turned up for punishment, and the captain said, 'Now, my lads, if you won't tell who stole the purser's grog, I will flog you all round. I only want to flog those who committed the theft, for it is too much to expect of seamen that they would refuse a glass of grog when offered to them.'

"Now, Short and the others had a parley together, and they had agreed how to act. They knew that the captain could not bear flogging, and was a very kind-hearted man. So Bill Short steps out, and says, touching his forelock to the captain, 'If you please, sir, if all must be flogged if nobody will peach, I think it better to tell the truth at once. It was I who took the liquor.'

"'Very well, then,' said the captain; 'strip, sir.' So Bill Short pulls off his shirt, and is seized up. 'Boatswain's mate,' said the captain, 'give him a dozen.'

"'Beg your honour's pardon,' said Jack Holmes, stepping out of the row of men brought out for punishment; 'but I can't bear to see an innocent man punished, and since one must be flogged, it must be the right one. It warn't Bill Short that took the liquor; it was I.'

"'Why, how's this?' said the captain; 'didn't you own that you took the liquor, Mr Short?'

"'Why, yes, I did say so, 'cause I didn't wish to see *everybody* flogged — but the truth's the truth, and I had no hand in it.'

"'Cast him loose — Holmes, you'll strip, sir.' Holmes stripped and was tied up. 'Give him a dozen,' said the captain; when out steps M'Alpine, and swore it was him, and not Holmes; and ax'd leave to be flogged in his stead. At which the captain bit his lips to prevent laughing, and then they knew all was right. So another came forward, and says it was him, and not M'Alpine; and another contradicts him again, and so on. At last the captain says, 'One would think flogging was a very pleasant affair; you are all so eager to be tied up; but, however, I shan't flog, to please you. I shall find out who the real culprit is, and then punish him severely. In the meantime, you keep them all on the report, Mr P—,' speaking to the first lieutenant. 'Depend upon it, I'll not let you off, although I do not choose to flog innocent men.' So they piped down, and the first lieutenant, who knew that the captain never meant to take any more notice of it, never made no inquiries, and the thing blew over. One day, a month or two after, I told the officers how it was managed, and they laughed heartily."

We continued our carouse till a late hour, old Tom constantly amusing us with his long yarns; and that night, for the first time, I went to bed intoxicated. Old Tom and his son assisted me into my bed-place, old Tom observing, "Poor Jacob; it will do him good; his heart was heavy, and now he'll forget it all, for a little time, at all events."

"Well but, father, I don't like to see Jacob drunk," replied young Tom. "It's not like him — it's not worthy of him; as for you or me, it's nothing at all; but I feel Jacob was never meant to be a toper. I never saw a lad so altered in a short time, and I expect bad will come of it when he leaves us."

I awoke, as might be supposed, after my first debauch, with a violent headache, but I had also a fever, brought on by my previous anxiety of mind. I rose, dressed, and went on deck, where the snow was nearly a foot deep. It now froze hard, and the river was covered with small pieces of floating ice. I rubbed my burning forehead with the snow, and felt relief. For some time I assisted Tom to heave it overboard, but the fever pressed upon me, and in less than half-an-hour I could no longer stand the exertion. I sat down on the water cask, and pressed my hands to my throbbing temples.

"You are not well, Jacob?" inquired Tom, coming up to me with the shovel in his hand, and glowing with health and exercise.

"I am not, indeed, Tom," replied I; "feel how hot I am."

Tom went to his father, who was in the cabin, padding, with extra flannel, his stumps, to defend them from the cold, which always made him suffer much, and then led me into the cabin. It was with much difficulty I could walk; my knees trembled, and my eyesight was defective. Old Tom took my hand as I sank on the locker.

"Do you think that it was taking too much last night?" inquired Tom of his father.

"There's more here than a gallon of liquor would have brought about," replied old Tom. "No, no—I see it all. Go to bed again, Jacob."

They put me into bed, and I was soon in a state of stupor, in which I remained until the lighter had arrived at the Brentford Wharf, and for many days afterwards.

Chapter Twenty One

When I recovered my senses, I found myself in bed, and Captain Turnbull sitting by my side. I had been removed to his house when the lighter had arrived at the wharf. Captain Turnbull was then talking with Mr Tomkins, the former head clerk, now in charge. Old Tom came on shore and stated the condition I was in, and Mr Tomkins having no spare bed in his house, Captain Turnbull immediately ordered me to be taken to his residence, and sent for medical advice. During the time I had remained in this state old Tom had informed Captain Turnbull, the Dominie, and Mr Tomkins of the circumstances which had occurred, and how much I had been misrepresented to Mr Drummond; and not saying a word about the affair of Wimbledon Common, or my subsequent intemperance, had given it as his opinion that ill-treatment had produced the fever. In this, I believe, he was nearly correct, although my disease might certainly have been aggravated and hastened by those two unmentioned causes. They all of them took my part, and Mr Turnbull went to London to state my condition to Mr Drummond, and also to remonstrate at his injustice. Circumstances had since occurred which induced Mr Drummond to lend a ready ear to my justification; but the message I had sent was still an obstacle. This, however, was partly removed by the equivocating testimony of the young clerk, when he was interrogated by Captain Turnbull and Mr Drummond; and wholly so by the evidence of young and old Tom, who, although in the cabin, had overheard the whole of the conversation; and Mr Drummond desired Captain Turnbull to inform me, as soon as I recovered, that all was forgotten and forgiven. It might have been on his part, but not on mine; and when Captain Turnbull told me so, with the view of raising my spirits, I shook my head as I lay on the pillow. As the reader will have observed, the feeling roused in me by the ill-usage I had received was a *vindictive* one — one that must have been deeply implanted in my heart, although, till then, it had never been roused into action, and now, once roused, was not to be suppressed. That it was based on pride was evident, and with it my pride was raised in proportion. To the intimation of Captain Turnbull, I, therefore, gave a decided dissent. "No, sir, I cannot return to Mr Drummond: that he was kind to me, and that I owe much to his kindness, I readily admit; and now that he has acknowledged his error in supposing me capable of such ingratitude, I heartily forgive him; but I cannot, and will not, receive any more favours from him. I cannot put myself in a situation to be again mortified as I have been. I feel I should no longer have the same pleasure in doing my duty as I once had, and I never could live under the same roof with those who at present serve him. Tell him all this, and pray tell little Sarah how grateful I feel no her for all her kindness to me, and that I shall always think of her with regret, at being obliged to leave her." And at the remembrance of little Sarah I burst into tears, and sobbed on my pillow. Captain Turnbull, whether he rightly estimated my character, or fell convinced that I had made up my mind, did not renew the subject.

"Well, Jacob," replied he, "we'll not talk of that any more. I'll give your messages just in your own words. Now, take your draught, and try to get a little sleep."

I complied with this request, and nothing but weakness now remaining, I rapidly regained my strength, and with my strength, my feelings of resentment increased in proportion. Nothing but the very weak state that I was in when Captain Turnbull spoke to me would have softened me down to give the kind message that I did; but my vindictive mind was subdued by disease, and better feelings predominated. The only effect this had was to increase my animosity against the other parties who were the cause of my ill-treatment, and I vowed that they, at least, should one day repent their conduct.

The Dominie called upon me the following Sunday. I was dressed and looking through the window when he arrived. The frost was now intense, and the river was covered with large masses of ice, and my greatest pleasure was to watch them as they floated down with the tide; "Thou hast had a second narrow escape, my Jacob," said he, after some preliminary observations. "Once again did death (*pallida mors*) hover over thy couch; but thou hast arisen, and thy fair fame is again established. When wilt thou be able to visit Mr Drummond, and be able to thank him for his kindness?"

"Never, sir," replied I; "I will never again enter Mr Drummond's house."

"Nay, Jacob, this savoureth of enmity. Are not we all likely to be deceived—all likely to do wrong? Did not I, even I, in thy presence, backslide into intemperance and folly? Did not I disgrace myself before my pupil—and shalt thou, in thy tender years, harbour ill-will against one who had cherished thee when thou wert destitute, and who was deceived with regard to thee by the base and evil-speaking?"

"I am obliged to Mr Drummond for all his kindness, sir," replied I; "but I never wish to enter his house. I was turned out of it, and never will again go into it."

"*Eheu! Jacobe*, thou art in error; it is our duty to forgive as we hope to be forgiven."

"I do forgive, sir, if that is what is requested: but I cannot, and will not, accept of further favours."

The Dominie urged in vain, and left me. Mr Tomkins also came, and argued the point without success. I was resolved. I was determined to be independent; and I looked to the river as my father, mother, home, and everything. As soon as my health was reinstated, Captain Turnbull one day came to me. "Jacob," said he, "the lighter has returned: and I wish to know if you intend to go on board again, and afterwards go into the vessel into which Mr Drummond proposes to send you."

"I will go into no vessel through Mr Drummond's means or interest," replied I.

"What will you do then?" replied he.

"I can always enter on board a man-of-war," replied I, "if the worst comes to the worst; but if I can serve out my apprenticeship on the river, I should prefer it."

"I rather expected this answer, Jacob, from what you have said to me already; and I have been trying if I cannot help you to something which may suit you. You don't mind being obliged to me?"

"O, no; but promise you will never doubt me—never accuse me." My voice faltered, and I could say no more.

"No, my lad, that I will not; I know you, as I think, pretty well; and the heart that feels a false accusation as yours does is sure to guard against committing what you are so angry at being accused of. Now, Jacob, listen to me. You know old deaf Stapleton, whose wherry we have so often pulled up and down the river? I have spoken to him to take you as his help, and he has consented. Will you like to go? He has served his time, and has a right to take a 'prentice."

"Yes," replied I, "with pleasure; and with more pleasure, from expecting to see you often."

"O, I promise you all my custom, Jacob," replied he, laughing. "We'll often turn old Stapleton out, and have a row together. Is it agreed?"

"It is," replied I; "and many thanks to you."

"Well, then, consider it settled. Stapleton has a very good room, and all that's requisite on shore, at Fulham. I have seen his place, and I think you will be comfortable."

I did not know at the time how much Captain Turnbull had been my friend—that he had made Stapleton take better lodgings, and had made up the difference to him, besides allowing him a trifle per week, and promising him a gratuity occasionally, if I were content with my situation. In a few days I had removed all my clothes to Stapleton's, had taken my leave of Mr Turnbull, and was established as an apprentice to a waterman on the Thames. The lighter was still at the wharf when I left, and my parting with old Tom and his son was equally and sincerely felt on both sides.

"Jacob," said old Tom, "I likes your pride after all, 'cause why, I think you have some right to be proud; and the man who only asks fair play, and no favour always will rise in this world. But look you, Jacob, there's sometimes a current 'gainst a man that no one can make head against; and if so be that should be your case for a time, recollect the old house, the old woman, and old Tom, and there you'll always find a hearty welcome, and a hearty old couple who'll share with you what they have, be it good, bad, or indifferent. Here's luck to you, my boy; and recollect, I means to go to the expense of painting the sides of my craft blue, and then you'll always know her as she creeps up and down the river."

"And Jacob," said young Tom;—"I may be a wild one, but I'm a true one; if ever you want me in fair weather and in foul—good or bad—for fun or for mischief—for a help, or for a friend in need, through thick or thin, I'm yours, even to the gallows; and here's my hand upon it."

"Just like you, Tom," observed his father; "but I know what you mean, and all's right."

I shook hands with them both, and we parted.

Thus did I remove from the lighter, and at once take up the profession of a waterman; I walked down to the Fulham side, where I found Stapleton at the door of the public-house, standing with two or three others, smoking his pipe. "Well, lad, so you're chained to my wherry for two or three years; and I'm to initiate you into all the rules and regulations of the company. Now, I'll tell you one thing, which is, d'ye see, when the river's covered with ice, as it is just now, haul your wherry up high and dry, and smoke your pipe till the river is clear, as I do now."

"I might have guessed that," replied I, bawling in his ear, "without you telling me."

"Very true; but don't bawl in my ear quite so loud, I hears none the better for it; my ears require coaxing, that's all."

"Why, I thought you were as deaf as a post."

"Yes, so I be with strangers, 'cause I don't know the pitch of their voice; but with those about me I hear better when they speak quietly—that's human nature. Come, let's go home, my pipe is finished, and as there's nothing to be done on the river, we may just as well make all tidy there."

Stapleton had lost his wife; but he had a daughter, fifteen years old, who kept his lodgings, and *did for him*, as he termed it. He lived in part of some buildings leased by a boat-builder; his windows looked out on the river; and, on the first floor, a bay-window was thrown out, so that at high water the river ran under it. As for the rooms, consisting of five, I can only say that they could not be spoken of as large and small, but as small and smaller. The sitting-room was eight feet square, the two bed-rooms at the back, for himself and his daughter, just held a small bed each, and the kitchen and my room below were to match; neither were the tenements in the very best repair, the parlour especially, hanging over the river, being lop-sided, and giving you the uncomfortable idea that it would every minute fall into the stream below. Still, the builder declared that it would last many years without sinking further, and that was sufficient. At all events, they were very respectable accommodations for a waterman, and Stapleton paid for them 10 pounds per annum. Stapleton's daughter was certainly a very well-favoured girl. She had rather a large mouth; but her teeth were very fine, and beautifully white. Her hair was auburn—her complexion very fair, her eyes were large, and of a deep blue, and from her figure, which was very good, I should have supposed her to have been eighteen, although she was not past fifteen, as I found out afterwards. There was a frankness and honesty of countenance about her, and an intellectual smile, which was very agreeable.

"Well, Mary, how do you get on?" said Stapleton, as we ascended to the sitting-room. "Here's young Faithful come to take up with us."

"Well, father, his bed's all ready; and I have taken so much dirt from the room that I expect we shall be indicted for filling up the river. I wonder what nasty people lived in this house before us."

"Very nice rooms, nevertheless; ain't they, boy?"

"O yes, very nice for idle people; you may amuse yourself looking out on the river, or watching what floats past, or fishing with a pin at high water," replied Mary, looking at me.

"I like the river," replied I, gravely; "I was born on it, and hope to get my bread on it."

"And I like this sitting-room," rejoined Stapleton; "how mighty comfortable it will be to sit at the open window, and smoke in the summer time, with one's jacket off!"

"At all events you'll have no excuse for dirtying the room, father; and as for the lad, I suppose his smoking days have not come yet."

"No," replied I; "but my days for taking off my jacket are, I suspect."

"O yes," replied she, "never fear that; father will let you do all the work you please, and look on—won't you, father?"

"Don't let your tongue run quite so fast, Mary; you're not over fond of work yourself."

"No; there's only one thing I dislike more," replied she, "and that's holding my tongue."

"Well, I shall leave you and Jacob to make it out together; I am going back to the Feathers." And old Stapleton walked down stairs, and went back to the inn, saying, as he went out, that he should be back to his dinner.

Mary continued her employment of wiping the furniture of the room with a duster for some minutes, during which I did not speak, but watched the floating ice on the river. "Well," said Mary, "do you always talk as you do now? if so, you'll be a very nice companion. Mr Turnbull who came to my father, told me that you was a sharp fellow, could read, write, and do everything, and that I should like you very much; but if you mean to keep it all to yourself, you might as well not have had it."

"I am ready to talk when I have anything to talk about," replied I.

"That's not enough. I'm ready to talk about nothing, and you must do the same."

"Very well," replied I. "How old are you?"

"How old am I! O, then you consider me nothing. I'll try hard but you shall alter your opinion, my fine fellow. However, to answer your question, I believe I'm about fifteen."

"Not more? well, there's an old proverb, which I will not repeat."

"I know it, so you may save yourself the trouble, you saucy boy; but now, for your age?"

"Mine! let me see; well, I believe that I am nearly seventeen."

"Are you really so old? well, now, I should have thought you no more than fourteen."

This answer at first surprised me, as I was very stout and tall for my age; but a moment's reflection told me that it was given to annoy me. A lad is as much vexed at being supposed younger than he really is as a man of a certain age is annoyed at being taken for so much older. "Pooh!" replied I; "that shows how little you know about men."

"I wasn't talking about men, that I know of; but still, I do know something about them. I've had two sweethearts already."

"Indeed! and what have you done with them?"

"Done with them! I jilted the first for the second, because the second was better looking; and when Mr Turnbull told me so much about you, I jilted the second to make room for you: but now I mean to try if I can't get him back again."

"With all my heart," replied I laughing. "I shall prove but a sorry sweetheart, for I have never made love in my life."

"Have you ever had anybody to make love to?"

"No."

"That's the reason, Mr Jacob, depend upon it. All you have to do is to swear that I'm the prettiest girl in the world, that you like me better than anybody else in the world; do anything in the world that I wish you to do—spend all the money you have in the world in buying me ribbons and fairings, and then—"

"And then, what?"

"Why, then, I shall hear all you have to say, take all you have to give, and laugh at you in the bargain."

"But I shouldn't stand that long."

"O, yes, you would. I'd put you out of humour, and coax you in again; the fact is, Jacob Faithful, I made my mind up, before I saw you, that you should be my sweetheart, and when I will have a thing, I will, so you may as well submit to it at once. If you don't, as I keep the key of the cupboard, I'll half starve you; that's the way to tame any brute, they say. And I tell you why, Jacob, I mean that you shall be my sweetheart; it's because Mr Turnbull told me that you knew Latin; now, tell me, what is Latin?"

"Latin is a language which people spoke in former times, but now they do not."

"Well, then, you shall make love to me in Latin, that's agreed."

"And how do you mean to answer me?"

"O, in plain English, to be sure."

"But how are you to understand me?" replied I, much amused with the conversation.

"O, if you make love properly, I shall soon understand you; I shall read the English of it in your eyes."

"Very well, I have no objection; when am I to begin?"

"Why, directly, you stupid fellow, to be sure. What a question!"

I went close up to Mary, and repeated a few words of Latin. "Now," says I, "look into my eyes, and see if you can translate them."

"Something impudent, I'm sure," replied she, fixing her blue eyes on mine.

"Not at all," replied I, "I only asked for this," and I snatched a kiss, in return for which I received a box on the ear, which made it tingle for five minutes. "Nay," replied I, "that's not fair; I did as you desired—I made love in Latin."

"And I answered you, as I said I would, in plain English," replied Mary, reddening up to the forehead, but directly after bursting out into a loud laugh. "Now, Mr Jacob, I plainly see that you know nothing about making love. Bless me, a year's dangling, and a year's pocket-money should not have given you what you have had the impudence to take in so many minutes. But it was my own fault, that's certain, and I have no one to thank but myself. I hope I didn't hurt you—I'm very sorry if I did; but no more making love in Latin. I've had quite enough of that."

"Well, then, suppose we make friends," replied I, holding out my hand.

"That's what I really wished to do, although I've been talking so much nonsense," replied Mary. "I know we shall like one another, and be very good friends. You can't help feeling kind towards a girl you've kissed; and I shall try by kindness to make up to you for the box on the ear; so now, sit down, and let's have a long talk. Mr Turnbull told us that he wished you to serve out your apprenticeship on the river with my father, so that, if you agree, we shall be a long while together. I take Mr Turnbull's word, not that I can find it out yet, that you are a very good-tempered, good-looking, clever, modest lad; and as an apprentice who remains with my father must live with us, of course I had rather it should be one of that sort than some ugly, awkward brute who—"

"Is not fit to make love to you," replied I.

"Who is not fit company for me," replied Mary. "I want no more love from you at present. The fact is that father spends all the time he can spare from the wherry at the ale-house, smoking; and it's very dull for me, and having nothing to do, I look out of the window, and make faces at the young men as they pass by, just to amuse myself. Now, there was no great harm in that a year or two ago; but now, you know, Jacob—"

"Well now, what then?"

"O, I'm bigger, that's all? and what might be called sauciness in a girl may be thought something more of in a young woman. So I've been obliged to leave it off; but being obliged to remain home, with nobody to talk to, I never was so glad as when I heard that you were to come; so you see, Jacob, we must be friends. I daren't quarrel with you long, although I shall sometimes, just for variety, and to have the pleasure of making it up again. Do you hear me—or what are you thinking of?"

"I'm thinking that you're a very odd girl."

"I dare say that I am, but how can I help that? Mother died when I was five years old, and father couldn't afford to put me out, so he used to lock me in all day till he came home from the river; and it was not till I was seven years old, and of some use, that the door was left open. I never shall forget the day when he told me that in future he should trust me, and leave the door open. I thought I was quite a woman, and have thought so ever since. I recollect that I often peeped out, and longed to run about the world; but I went two or three yards from the door, and felt so frightened, that I ran back as fast as I could. Since that I have seldom quitted the house for an hour, and never have been out of Fulham."

"Then you have never been at school?"

"O, no—never. I often wish that I had. I used to see the little girls coming home, as they passed our door, so merrily, with their bags from the school-house; and I'm sure, if it were only to have the pleasure of going there and back again for the sake of the run, I'd have worked hard, if for nothing else."

"Would you like to learn to read and write?"

"Will you teach me?" replied Mary, taking me by the arm, and looking me earnestly in the face.

"Yes, I will, with pleasure," replied I, laughing. "We will pass the evening better than making love, after all, especially if you hit so hard. How came you so knowing in those matters?"

"I don't know," replied Mary, smiling; "I suppose, as father says, it's human nature, for I never learnt anything; but you will teach me to read and write?"

"I will teach you all I know myself, Mary, if you wish to learn. Everything but Latin—we've had enough of that."

"Oh! I shall be so much obliged to you. I shall love you so!"

"There you are again."

"No, no, I didn't mean that," replied Mary, earnestly. "I meant that—after all, I don't know what else to say. I mean that I shall love you for your kindness, without your loving me again, that's it."

"I understand you; but now, Mary, as we are to be such good friends, it is necessary that your father and I should be good friends; so I must ask you what sort of a person he is, for I know but little of him, and, of course, wish to oblige him."

"Well then, to prove to you that I'm sincere, I will tell you something; My father, in the first place, is a very good tempered sort of man. He works pretty well, but might gain more, but he likes to smoke at the public-house. All he requires of me is his dinner ready, his linen clean, and the house tidy. He never drinks too much, and is always civil spoken; but he leaves me too much alone, and talks too much about human nature, that's all."

"But he's so deaf—he can't talk to you."

"Give me your hand—now promise—for I'm going to do a very foolish thing, which is to trust a man—promise you'll never tell it again."

"Well, I promise," replied I, supposing her secret of no consequence.

"Well, then—mind—you've promised. Father is no more deaf than you or I."

"Indeed!" replied I; "why, he goes by the name of Deaf Stapleton?"

"I know he does, and makes everybody believe that he is so; but it is to make money."

"How can he make money by that?"

"There's many people in business who go down the river, and they wish to talk of their affairs without being overheard as they go down. They always call for Deaf Stapleton: and there's many a gentleman and lady, who have much to say to each other, without wishing people to listen—you understand me?"

"O yes, I understand—Latin!"

"Exactly—and they call for Deaf Stapleton; and by this means he gets more good fares than any other waterman, and does less work."

"But how will he manage now that I am with him?"

"O, I suppose it will depend upon his customers; if a single person wants to go down, you will take the sculls; if they call for oars, you will both go; if he considers Deaf Stapleton only is wanted, you will remain on shore; or, perhaps, he will insist upon your being deaf too."

"But I do not like deceit."

"No, it's not right; although it appears to me that there is a great deal of it. Still I should like you to sham deaf, and then tell me all that people say. It would be so funny. Father never will tell a word."

"So far, your father, to a certain degree, excuses himself."

"Well, I think he will soon tell you what I have now told you, but till then you must keep your promise; and now you must do as you please, as I must go down in the kitchen, and get dinner on the fire."

"I have nothing to do," replied I; "can I help you?"

"To be sure you can, and talk to me, which is better still. Come down and wash the potatoes for me, and then I'll find you some more work. Well, I do think we shall be very happy."

I followed Mary Stapleton down into the kitchen, and we were soon very busy, and very noisy, laughing, talking, blowing the fire, and preparing the dinner. By the time that her father came home we were sworn friends.

Chapter Twenty Two

I was rather curious, after the secret confided to me by Mary Stapleton, to see how her father would behave; but when we had sat and talked some time, as he appeared to have no difficulty in answering to any observation in a common pitch of the voice, I observed to him that he was not so deaf as I thought he was.

"No, no," replied he; "in the house I hear very well, but in the open air I can't hear at all, if a person speaks to me two yards off. Always speak to me close to my ear in the open air, but not loud, and then I shall hear you very well." I caught a bright glance from Mary's blue eye, and made no answer. "This frost will hold, I'm afraid," continued Stapleton, "and we shall have nothing to do for some days but to blow our fingers and spend our earnings; but there's never much doing at this time of the year. The winter cuts us watermen up terribly. As for me, I smokes my pipe and thinks on human natur'; but what you are to do Jacob, I can't tell."

"Oh, he will teach me to read and write," replied Mary.

"I don't know that he shall," replied Stapleton. "What's the use of reading and writing to you? We've too many senses already, in my opinion, and if so be we have learning to boot, why then all the worse for us."

"How many senses are there, father?"

"How many! I'm sure I can't tell, but more than enough to puzzle us."

"There are only five, I believe," said I; "first, there's *hearing*."

"Well," replied Stapleton "hearing may be useful at times; but not hearing at times is much more convenient. I make twice as much money since I lost the better part of my hearing."

"Well, then, there's seeing," continued I.

"Seeing is useful at times, I acknowledge; but I knows this, that if a man could pull a young couple about the river, and not be able to see now and then, it would be many a half-crown in his pocket."

"Well, then, now we come to *tasting*."

"No use at all—only a vexation. If there was no tasting we should not care whether we ate brown bread or roast beef, drank water or XX ale; and in these hard times that would be no small saving."

"Well, then, let me see, there's *smelling*."

"Smelling's no use whatever. For one good smell by the river's side there be ten nasty ones; and there is everywhere, to my conviction."

"Which is the next, Jacob?" said Mary, smiling archly.

"*Feeling*."

"Feeling! that's the worst of the whole. Always feel too cold in winter, too hot in summer—feel a blow too; feeling only gives pain; that's a very bad sense."

"Well, then, I suppose you think we should get on better without our senses."

"No, not without all of them. A little hearing and a little seeing be all very well; but there are other senses which you have forgot, Jacob. Now, one I takes to be the very best of the bunch is *smoking*."

"I never heard that was a sense," replied I, laughing.

"Then you haven't half finished your education, Jacob."

"Are reading and writing *senses*, father?" inquired Mary.

"To be sure they be, girl; for without sense you can't read and write; and *rowing* be a sense just as well; and there be many other senses; but, in my opinion, most of the senses be nonsense, and only lead to mischief."

"Jacob," said Mary, whispering to my ear, "isn't *loving* a sense?"

"No, that's nonsense," replied I.

"Well, then," replied she, "I agree with my father that nonsense is better than sense; but still I don't see why I should not learn to read and write, father."

"I've lived all my life without it, and never felt the want of it—why can't you?"

"Because I do feel the want of it."

"So you may, but they leads no no good. Look at those fellows at the Feathers; all were happy enough before Jim Holder, who is a scholar, came among them, and now since he reads to them they do nothing but grumble, and growl, and talk about I don't know what—corn laws, and taxes, and liberty, and all other nonsense. Now, what could you do more than you do now, if you larnt to read and write?"

"I could amuse myself when I've nothing to do, father, when you and Jacob are away. I often sit down, after I've done all my work, and think what I shall do next, and at last I look out of the window and make faces at people, because I've nothing better to do. Now, father, you must let him learn me to read and write."

"Well, Mary, if you will, you will; but recollect, don't blame me for it—it must be all on your own head, and not on my conscience. I've lived some forty or fifty years in this world, and all my bad luck has been owing to having too much senses, and all my good luck to getting rid of them."

"I wish you would tell me how that came to pass," said I; "I should like to hear it very much, and it will be a lesson to Mary."

"Well, I don't care if I do, Jacob, only I must light my pipe first; and, Mary, do you go for a pot o' beer."

"Let Jacob go, father. I mean him to run on all my errands now."

"You mustn't order Jacob, Mary."

"No, no—I wouldn't think of ordering him, but I know he will do it—won't you, Jacob?"

"Yes, with pleasure," replied I.

"Well, with all my heart, provided it be all for love," said Stapleton.

"Of course, all for love," replied Mary, looking at me, "or Latin—which, Jacob?"

"What's Latin?" said her father.

"Oh! that's a new sense Jacob has been showing me something of, which, like many others, proved to be nonsense."

I went for the beer, and when I returned found the fire burning brightly, and a strong *sense* of smoking from old Stapleton's pipe. He puffed once or twice more, and then commenced his history as follows:

"I can't exactly say when I were born, nor where," said old Stapleton, taking his pipe out of his mouth, "because I never axed either father or mother, and they never told me, because why, I never did ax, and that be all agreeable to human natur'." Here Stapleton paused, and took three whiffs of his pipe. "I recollects when I was a little brat about two foot nothing, mother used to whack me all day long, and I used to cry in proportion. Father used to cry shame, and then mother would fly at him; he would whack she; she would up with her apron in one corner and cry, while I did the same with my pinbefore in another; all that was nothing but human natur'." (A pause, and six or seven whiffs of the pipe.)

"I was sent to school at a penny a week, to keep me out of the way, and out of mischief. I larnt nothing but to sit still on the form and hold my tongue, and so I used to amuse myself twiddling my thumbs, and looking at the flies as they buzzed about the room in the summer time; and in the winter, cause there was no flies of no sort, I used to watch the old missus a-knitting of stockings, and think how soon the time would come when I should go home and have my supper, which, in a child was nothing but human natur'." (Puff, puff, puff.) "Father and mother lived in a cellar; mother sold coals and 'tatoes, and father used to go out to work in the barges on the river. As soon as I was old enough, the schoolmissus sent word that I ought to learn to read and write, and that she must be paid threepence a week; so father took me away from school, because he thought I had had education enough; and mother perched me on a basket upside down, and made me watch that nobody took the goods while she was busy down below; and then I used to sit all day long watching the coals and 'tatoes, and never hardly speaking to nobody; so having nothing better to do, I used to think about this, and that, and everything, and when dinner would be ready, and when I might get off the basket; for you see *thinking* be another of the senses, and when one has nothing to do, and nothing to say, to think be nothing more than human natur'." (Puff, puff, and a pause for a drink out of the pot.) "At last, I grew a big stout boy, and mother said that I ate too much, and must earn my livelihood somehow or other, and father for once agreed with her; but there was a little difficulty how that was to be done; so until that was got over I did nothing at all but watch the coals and 'tatoes as before. One day mother wouldn't give me wituals enough, so I helped myself; so she whacked me, so I, being strong, whacked she; so father, coming home, whacked me, so I takes to my heels and runs away a good mile before I thought at all about how I was to live; and there I was, very sore, very unhappy, and very hungry." (Puff, puff, puff, and a spit.) "I walks on, and on, and then I gets behind a coach, and then the fellow whips me, and I gets down again in a great hurry, and tumbles into the road, and before I could get up again, a gemman, in a gig drives right over me, and breaks my leg. I screams with pain, which if I hadn't had the sense of *feeling*, of course I shouldn't have minded. He pulls up and gets out, and tells me he's very sorry. I tells him so am I. His servant calls some people, and they takes me into a public-house, and lays me on the table all among the pots of beer, sends for a doctor, who puts me into bed, and puts my leg right again; and then I was provided for, for at least six weeks, during which the gemman calls and axes how I feel myself; and I says, 'Pretty well, I thanky.'" (Puff, puff—knock the ashes out, pipe refilled, relighted, a drink of beer, and go on.) "So when I was well, and on my pins again, the gentleman says, 'What can I do for you?' and the landlord cuts him short by saying that he wanted a pot-boy, if I liked the profession. Now, if I didn't like the pots I did the porter, which I had no share of at home, so I agrees. The gemman pays the score, gives me half a guinea, and tells me not to be lying in the middle of the road another time. I tells him I won't, so he jumps into his gig, and I never cast eyes upon him since. I stayed three years with my master, taking out beer to his customers, and always taking a little out of each pot for myself, for that's nothing but human natur' when you likes a thing; but I never got into trouble until one day I sees my missus a-kissing in the back parlour with a fellow who travels for orders. I never said nothing at first; but at last I sees too much, and then I tells master, who gets into a rage, and goes into his wife, stays with her half-an-hour, and then comes out and kicks me out of the door, calling me a liar, and telling me never to show my face again. I shies a pot at his head, and showed him anything but my face, for I took to my heels, and ran for it as fast as I could. So much for seeing; if I hadn't seen, that wouldn't have happened. So there I was adrift, and good-bye to porter." (Puff, puff; "Mary, where's my 'baccy stopper?" Poke down, puff, puff, spit, and proceed.) "Well, I walks towards Lunnen, thinking on husbands and wives, porter and human natur', until I finds myself there, and then I looks at all the lighted lamps, and recollects that I haven't no lodging for the night, and then all of a sudden I thinks of my father and mother, and wonders how they be going on. So I thought I'd go and see, and away I went, comes to the cellar, and goes down. There was my mother with a quartern of gin before her, walking to and fro, and whimpering to herself; so says I, 'Mother, what's the matter now?' at which she jumps up and hugs me, and tells me I'm her only comfort left. I looked at the quartern and thinks otherwise; so down I sits by her side, and then she pours me out a glass, and pours out all her grief, telling me how my father had left her for another woman, who kept another cellar in another street, and how she was very unhappy, and how she had taken to gin—which was nothing but human natur', you see, and how she meant to make away with herself; and then she sent for more quarterns, and we finished them. What with the joy of finding me, and the grief at losing my father, and the quarterns of gin, she went to bed crying drunk and fell fast asleep. So did I, and thought home was home after all. Next morning I takes up the business, and finds trade not so bad after all; so I takes the command of all, keeps all the money, and keeps mother in order; and don't allow drinking nor disorderly conduct in the house; but goes to the public-house every night for a pipe and a pot.

"Well, everything goes on very well for a month, when who should come home but father, which I didn't approve of, because I liked being master. So I, being a strong chap, then says, 'If you be come to ill-treat my mother, I'll put you in the kennel, father. Be off to your new woman. Ar'n't you ashamed of yourself?' says I. So father looks me in the face, and tells me to stand out of the way, or he'll make cat's meat of me; and then he goes to my mother, and after a quarter of an hour of sobbing on her part, and coaxing on his, they kiss and make friends; and then they both turns to me, and orders me to leave the cellar, and never to show my face again. I refuses: father flies at me, and mother helps him; and between the two I was hustled out to find my bread how and where I could. I've never taken a woman's part since." (Puff, puff, puff, and a deep sigh.) "I walks down to the water-side, and having one or two shillings in my pocket, goes into a public-house to get a drop of drink and a bed. And when I comes in, I sees a man hand a note for change to the landlady, and she gives him change. 'That won't do,' says he, and he was half tipsy: 'I gave you a ten-pound note, and this here lad be witness.' 'It was only a *one*,' says the woman. 'You're a damned old cheat,' says he, 'and if you don't give me the change, I'll set your house on fire, and burn you alive.' With that there was a great row, and he goes out for the constable and gives her in charge, and gives me in charge as a witness, and then she gives him in charge, and so we all went to the watchhouse together, and slept on the benches. The next morning we all appeared before the magistrate, and the man tells his story and calls me as a witness; but recollecting how much I had suffered from *seeing*, I wouldn't see anything this time. It might have been a ten-pound note, for it certainly didn't look like a one; but my evidence went rather for than against the woman, for I only proved the man to be drunk; and she was let off, and I walked home with her. So says she, 'You're a fine boy, and I'll do you a good turn for what you have done for me. My husband is a waterman, and I'll make you free of the river; for he hasn't no 'prentice, and you can come on shore and stay at the public-house when you ar'n't wanted.' I jumped at the offer, and so, by not *seeing*, I gets into a regular livelihood. Well, Jacob, how do you like it?"

"Very much," replied I.

"And you, Mary?"

"O! I like it very much; but I want father to go on, and to know how he fell in love, and married my mother."

"Well, you shall have it all by-and-by; but now I must take a spell."

Chapter Twenty Three

Old Stapleton finished his pipe, took another swig at the porter, filled, relighted, puffed to try it, cleared his mouth, and then proceeded:—

"Now, you see, Bartley, her husband, was the greatest rogue on the river; he was up to everything, and stood at nothing. He fleeced as much on the water as she did on the land; for I often seed her give wrong change afterwards when people were tipsy, but I made it a rule always to walk away. As for Bartley, his was always night-work, and many's the coil of rope I have brought on shore, what, although he might have paid for, he didn't buy it of the lawful owner, but I never *seed* or *heard*, that was my maxim; and I fared well till I served my time, and then they gave me their old wherry, and built a new one for themselves. So I set up on my own account, and then I seed, and heard, and had all my senses, just as they were before—more's the pity, for no good came of it." (Puff, puff, puff, puff.) "The Bartleys wanted me to join them, but that wouldn't do; for though I never meddled with other people's concerns, yet I didn't choose to go wrong myself. I've seed all the world cheating each other for fifty years or more, but that's no concern of mine; I can't make the world better; so all I thinks about it is to keep honest myself: and if every one was to look after his own soul, and not trouble themselves about their neighbours, why, then, it would be all the better for human natur'. I plied at the Swan Stairs, gained my livelihood, and spent it as I got it; for I was then too young to look out a'ter a rainy day.

"One night a young woman in a cloak comes down to the stairs with a bundle in her arms, and seems in a very great taking, and asks me for a boat. I hauls out of the row alongside of the yard, and hands her in. She trips as she steps in, and I catches to save her from falling, and in catching her I puts my hand upon the bundle in her arms, and feels the warm face of a baby. 'Where am I to go, ma'am?' says I. 'O! pull across, and land me on the other side,' says she; and then I hears her sobbing to herself, as if her heart would break. When we were in the middle o' the stream, she lifts up her head, and then first she looks at the bundle and kisses it, and then she looks up at the stars which were glittering above in the sky. She kisses the child once more, jumps up, and afore I could be aware of what she was about, she tosses me her purse, throws her child into the water, and leaps in herself. I pulls sharp round immediately, and seeing her again, I made one or two good strokes, comes alongside of her, and gets hold of her clothes. A'ter much ado I gets her into the wherry, and as soon as I seed she was come to again, I pulls her back to the stairs where she had taken me from. As soon as I lands I hears a noise and talking, and several people standing about; it seems it were her relatives, who had missed her, and were axing whether she had taken a boat; and while they were describing her, and the other watermen were telling them how I had taken a fare of that description, I brings her back. Well, they takes charge of her, and leads her home; and then for the first time I thinks of the purse at the bottom of the boat, which I picks up, and sure enough there were four golden guineas in it, beside some silver. Well, the men who plied at the stairs axed me all about it; but I keeps my counsel, and only tells them how the poor girl threw herself into the water, and how I pulled her out again; and in a week I had almost forgot all about it, when up comes an officer, and says to me, 'You be Stapleton the waterman?' and I says, 'Yes, I be.' 'Then you must come along with me;' and he takes me to the police-office, where I finds the poor young woman in custody for being accused of having murdered her infant. So they begins to tax me upon my Bible oath, and I was forced to tell the whole story; for though you may loose all your senses when convenient, yet somehow or another, an oath on the Bible brings them all back again. 'Did you see the child?' said the magistrate. 'I seed a bundle,' said I. 'Did you hear the child cry?' said he. 'No,' says I, 'I didn't;' and then I thought I had got the young woman off; but the magistrate was an old fox, and had all the senses at his fingers' ends. So says he, 'When the young woman stepped into the boat did she give you the bundle?' 'No,' says I again. 'Then you never touched it?' 'Yes, I did, when her foot slipped.' 'And what did it feel like?' 'It felt like a piece of human natur'.' says I, 'and quite warm like.' 'How do you mean?' says he. 'Why, I took it by the feel for a baby.' 'And it was quite warm, was it?' 'Yes,' replied I, 'it was.' 'Well then, what else took place?' 'Why, when we were in the middle of the stream she and her child went overboard; I pulled her in again, but could not see the child.' Fortunately for the poor girl, they didn't ask me which went overboard first, and that saved her from hanging. She was confined six months in prison, and then let out again; but you see, if it hadn't been for my unfortunately feeling the child, and feeling it was warm, which proved its being alive, the poor young woman would have got off altogether, perhaps. So much for the sense of feeling, which I say is of no use to nobody, but only a vexation." (Puff—the pipe out, relighted—puff, puff.)

"But, father," said Mary, "did you ever hear the history of the poor girl?"

"Yes, I heard as how it was a hard case, how she had been seduced by some fellow who had left her and her baby, upon which she determined to drown herself, poor thing; and her baby too. Had she only tried to drown her baby I should have said it was quite unnatural; but as she wished to drown herself at the same time, I considers that drowning the baby to take it to heaven with her was quite natural, and all agreeable to human natur'. Love's a sense which young women should keep down as much as possible, Mary; no good comes of that sense."

"And yet, father, it appears to me to be human nature," replied Mary.

"So it is, but there's mischief in it, girl, so do you never have anything to do with it."

"Was there mischief when you fell in love with my mother and married her?"

"You shall hear, Mary," replied old Stapleton, who recommenced.

"It was 'bout two months after the poor girl threw herself into the river that I first seed your mother. She was then mayhap two years older than you may be, and much such a same sort of person in her looks. There was a young man who plied from our stairs, named Ben Jones; he and I were great friends, and used for to help each other, and when a fare called for oars, used to ply together. One night he says to me, 'Will, come up, and I'll show you a devilish fine piece of stuff.' So I walks with him, and he takes me to a shop where they dealed in marine stores, and we goes and finds your mother in the back parlour. Ben sends for pipes and beer, and we sat down and made ourselves comfortable. Now, Mary, your mother was a very jilting kind of girl, who would put one fellow off to take another, just as her whim and fancy took her." (I looked at Mary, who cast down her eyes.) "Now these women do a mint of mischief among men, and it seldom ends well; and I'd sooner see you in your coffin to-morrow, Mary, than think you should be one of this flaunting sort. Ben Jones was quite in for it, and wanted for to marry her, and she had turned off a fine young chap for him, and he used to come there every night, and it was supposed that they would be spliced in the course of a month; but when I goes there she cuts him almost altogether, and takes to me, making such eyes at me, and drinking beer out of my pot, and refusing his'n, till poor Jones was quite mad and beside himself. Well, it wasn't in human natur' to stand those large blue eyes (just like yours, Mary), darting fire at a poor fellow; and when Jones got up in a surly humour, and said it was time to go away, instead of walking home arm in arm, we went side by side, like two big dogs with their tails as stiff up as a crowbar, and ready for a fight; neither he nor I saying a word, and we parted without saying good-night. Well, I dreamed of your mother all that night, and the next day went to see her, and felt worser and worser each time, and she snubbed Jones, and at last told him to go about his business. This was 'bout a month after I had first seen her; and then one day Jones, who was a prize-fighter, says to me, 'Be you a man?' and slaps me on the ear. So, I knowing what he'd been a'ter, pulls off my duds, and we sets to. We fights for ten minutes or so, and then I hits him a round blow on the ear, and he falls down on the *hard*, and couldn't come to time. No wonder, poor fellow! for he had gone to eternity." (Here old Stapleton paused for half a minute, and passed his hand across his eyes.) "I was tried for manslaughter; but it being proved that he came up and struck me first, I was acquitted, after lying two months in gaol, for I couldn't get no bail; but it was because I had been two months in gaol that I was let off. At first, when I came out, I determined never to see your mother again; but she came to me, and wound round me, and I loved her so much that I couldn't shake her off. As soon as she found that I was fairly hooked, she began to play with others; but I wouldn't stand that, and every fellow that came near her was certain to have a turn out with me, and so I became a great fighter; and she, seeing that I was the best man, and that no one else would come to her, one fine morning agreed to marry me. Well, we were spliced, and the very first night I thought I saw poor Ben Jones standing by my bedside, and, for a week or so, I was not comfortable; but, howsomever, it wore off, I plied at the stairs, and gained my money. But my pipe's out, and I'm dry with talking. Suppose I take a spell for a few minutes."

Stapleton relighted his pipe, and for nearly half-an-hour smoked in silence. What Mary's thoughts were I cannot positively assert; but I imagined that, like myself, she was thinking about her mother's conduct and her own. I certainly was making the comparison, and we neither of us spoke a word.

"Well," continued Stapleton, at last, "I married your mother, Mary, and I only hope that any man who may take a fancy to you, will not have so much trouble with his wife as I had. I thought that a'ter she were settled she would give up all her nonsense, and behave herself—but I suppose it was in her natur' and she couldn't help it. She made eyes and gave encouragement to the men, until they became saucy and I became jealous, and I had to fight one, and then the other, until I became a noted pugilist. I will say that your mother seemed always very happy when I beat my man, which latterly I always did; but still she liked to be *fit* for, and I had hardly time to earn my bread. At last, some one backed me against another man in the ring for fifty pound aside, and I was to have half if I won. I was very short of blunt at the time, and I agreed; so, a'ter a little training the battle was fought, and I won easy: and the knowing ones liked my way of hitting so much that they made up another match with a better man, for two hundred pounds;

and a lord and other great people came to me, and I was introduced to them at the public-house, and all was settled. So I became a regular prize-fighter, all through your mother, Mary. Nay, don't cry, child, I don't mean to say that your mother, with all her love of being stared at and talked to, would have gone wrong; but still it was almost as bad in my opinion. Well, I was put into training, and after five weeks we met at Mousley Hurst, and a hard fight it was—but I've got the whole of it somewhere, Mary; look in the drawer there, and you'll see a newspaper."

Mary brought out the newspaper, which was rolled up and tied with a bit of string, and Stapleton handed it over to me, telling me to read it aloud. I did so, but I shall not enter into the details.

"Yes, that's all right enough," said Stapleton, who had taken advantage of my reading to smoke furiously, to make up for lost time; "but no good came of it, for one of the gemmen took a fancy to your mother, Mary, and tried to win her away from me. I found him attempting to kiss her, and she refusing him—but laughing, and, as I thought, more than half-willing; so I floored him, and put him out of the house, and after that I never would have anything more to say with lords and gemmen, nor with fighting either. I built a new wherry, and stuck to the river, and I shifted my lodgings that I mightn't mix any more with those who knew me as a boxer. Your mother was then brought to bed with you, and I hoped for a good deal of happiness, as I thought she would only think of her husband and child; and so she did until you were weaned, and then she went on just as afore. There was a captain of a vessel lying in the river, who used now and then to stop and talk with her; but I thought little about that, seeing how every one talked with her and she with everybody; and besides, she knew the captain's wife, who was a very pretty woman, and used very often to ask Mary to go and see her, which I permitted. But one morning, when I was going off to the boat—for he had come down to me to take him to his vessel—just as I was walking away with the sculls over my shoulder, I recollects my 'baccy box, which I had left, and I goes back and hears him say before I came into the door—'Recollect, I shall be here again by two o'clock, and then you promised to come on board my ship, and see—.' I didn't hear the rest, but she laughed and said yes, she would. I didn't show myself, but walked away and went to the boat. He followed me, and I rowed him up the river and took my fare—and then I determined to watch them, for I felt mighty jealous. So I lays off on my oars in the middle of the stream, and sure enough I see the captain and your mother get into a small skiff belonging to his ship, and pull away; the captain had one oar and one of his men another. I pulled a'ter them as fast as I could, and at last they seed me; and not wishing me to find her out, she begged them to pull away as fast as they could, for she knew how savage I would be. Still I gained upon them, every now and then looking round and vowing vengeance in my heart, when all of a sudden I heard a scream, and perceived their boat to capsize, and all hands in the water. They had not seen a warp of a vessel getting into the row, and had run over it, and, as it tautened, they capsized. Your mother went down like a stone, Mary, and was not found for three days a'terward; and when I seed her sink I fell down in a fit." Here old Stapleton stopped, laid down his pipe, and rested his face in his hands. Mary burst into tears. After a few minutes he resumed: "When I came to, I found myself on board of the ship in the captain's cabin, with the captain and his wife watching over me—and then I came to understand that it was she who had sent for your mother, and that she was living on board, and that your mother had at first refused, because she knew that I did not like her to be on the river, but wishing to see a ship had consented. So it was not so bad a'ter all, only that a woman shouldn't act without her husband—but you see, Mary, all this would not have happened if it hadn't been that I overheard part of what was said; and you might now have had a mother, and I a wife to comfort us, if it had not been for my unfortunate *hearing*—so, as I said before, there's more harm than good that comes from these senses—at least so it has proved to me. And now you have heard my story, and how your mother died, Mary; so take care you don't fall into the same fault, and be too fond of being looked at, which it does somehow or another appear to me you have a bit of a hankering a'ter—but like mother, like child, they say, and that's *human natur'*."

When Stapleton had concluded his narrative, he smoked his pipe in silence. Mary sat at the table, with her hands pressed to her temples, apparently in deep thought; and I felt anything but communicative. In half-an-hour the pot of beer was finished, and Stapleton rose.

"Come, Mary, don't be thinking so much; let's all go to bed. Show Jacob his room, and then come up."

"Jacob can find his own room, father," replied Mary, "without my showing him; he knows the kitchen, and there is but one other below."

I took my candle, wished them good night, and went to my bed, which, although very homely, was at all events comfortable.

Chapter Twenty Four

For many days the frost continued, until at last the river was frozen over, and all communication by it was stopped. Stapleton's money ran short, our fare became very indifferent, and Mary declared that we must all go begging with the market gardeners if it lasted much longer.

"I must go and call upon Mr Turnbull, and ax him to help us," said Stapleton, one day, pulling his last shilling out and laying it on the table. "I'm cleaned out; but he's a good gentleman, and will lend me a trifle." In the afternoon Stapleton returned, and I saw by his looks that he had been successful. "Jacob," said he, "Mr Turnbull desires that you will breakfast with him to-morrow morning, as he wishes to see you."

I set off accordingly at daylight the next morning, and was in good time for breakfast. Mr Turnbull was as kind as ever, and began telling me long stories about the ice in the northern regions.

"By-the-by, I hear there is an ox to be roasted whole, Jacob, a little above London Bridge; suppose we go and see the fun."

I consented, and we took the Brentford coach, and were put down at the corner of Queen Street, from thence we walked to the river. The scene was very amusing and exciting. Booths were erected on the ice, in every direction, with flags flying, people walking, and some skating, although the ice was too rough for that pastime. The whole river was crowded with people, who now walked in security over where they, a month before, would have met with death. Here and there smoke ascended from various fires, on which sausages and other eatables were cooking; but the great attraction was the ox roasting whole, close to the centre pier of the bridge. Although the ice appeared to have fallen at the spot where so many hundreds were assembled, yet as it was now four or five feet thick, there was no danger. Here and there, indeed, were what were called rotten places, where the ice was not sound; but these were intimated by placards, warning people not to approach too near; and close to them were ropes and poles for succour, if required. We amused ourselves for some time with the gaiety of the scene, for the sun shone out brightly, and the sky was clear. The wind was fresh from the northward, and piercing cold in the shade, the thermometer being then, it was said, twenty-eight degrees below the freezing point. We had been on the ice about three hours, amusing ourselves, when Mr Turnbull proposed our going home, and we walked up the river towards Blackfriars Bridge, where we proposed to land, and take the coach at Charing Cross.

"I wonder how the tide is now," observed Mr Turnbull to me; "it would be rather puzzling to find out."

"Not if I can find a hole," replied I, looking for one. "Stop, here is one." I threw in a piece of ice, and found that it was strong ebb. We continued our walk over the ice, which was now very rough, when Mr Turnbull's hat fell off, and the wind catching it, it blew away, skimming across the ice at a rapid rate. Mr Turnbull and I gave chase, but could scarcely keep up with it, and, at all events, could not overtake it. Many people on the river laughed as we passed, and watched us in our chase. Mr Turnbull was the foremost, and, heedless in the pursuit, did not observe a large surface of rotten ice before him; neither did I, until all at once I heard it break and saw Mr Turnbull fall in and disappear. Many people were close to us, and a rope was laid across the spot to designate the danger. I did not hesitate—I loved Mr Turnbull, and my love and my feelings of resentment were equally potent. I seized the bight of the rope, twisted it round my arm, and plunged in after, recollecting it was ebb tide: fortunate for Mr Turnbull it was that he had accidentally put the question. I sank under the ice, and pushed down the stream, and in a few seconds felt myself grappled by him I sought, and at almost the same time, the rope hauling in from above. As soon as they found there was resistance, they knew that I, at least, was attached to it, and they hauled in quicker, not, however, until I had lost my recollection. Still I clung to the rope with the force of a drowning man, and Mr Turnbull did the same to me, and we shortly made our appearance at the hole in which we had been plunged. A ladder was thrown across, and two of the men of the Humane Society came to our assistance, pulled us out, and laid us upon it. They then drew back and hauled us on the ladder to a more secure situation. We were both still senseless; but having been taken to a public-house on the river-side, were put to bed, and medical advice having been procured, were soon restored. The next morning we were able to return in a chaise to Brentford, where our absence had created the greatest alarm. Mr Turnbull spoke but little the whole time; but he often pressed my hand, and when I requested him to drop me at Fulham, that I might let Stapleton and his daughter know that I was safe, he consented, saying, "God bless you, my fine boy; I will see you soon."

When I went up the stairs of Stapleton's lodgings, I found Mary by herself; she started up as soon as she saw me.

"Where *have* you been?" said she, half crying, half smiling.

"Under the ice," I replied, "and only thawed again this morning."

"Are you in earnest, Jacob?" said she; "now don't plague and frighten me, I've been too frightened already; I never slept a wink last night;" I then told her the circumstances which had occurred. "I was sure something had happened," she replied. "I told my father so, but he wouldn't believe it. You promised to be at home to give me my lesson, and I know you never break your word; but my father smoked away, and said, that when boys are amused, they forget their promises, and that it was nothing but human natur'. Oh, Jacob, I'm so glad you're back again, and after what has happened, I don't mind your kissing me for once." And Mary held her face towards me, and returned my kiss.

"There, that must last you a long while, recollect," said she, laughing; "you must not think of another until you're under the ice again."

"Then I trust it will be the last," replied I, laughing.

"You are not in love with me, Jacob, that's clear, or you would not have made that answer," replied Mary.

I had seen a great deal of Mary, and though she certainly was a great flirt, yet she had many excellent and amiable qualities. For the first week after her father had given us the history of his life, his remarks upon her mother appeared to have made a decided impression upon her, and her conduct was much more staid and demure; but as the remembrance wore off, so did her conduct become coquettish and flirting as before; still, it was impossible not to be fond of her, and even with all her caprice there was such a fund of real good feeling and amiableness, which, when called forth, was certain to appear, that I often thought how dangerous and captivating a girl she would be when she grew up. I had again produced the books, which I had thrown aside with disgust, to teach her to read and write. Her improvement was rapid, and would have been still more so if she had not been just as busy in trying to make me fond of her as she was in surmounting the difficulties of her lessons. But she was very young; and although, as her father declared, it was her *natur'* to run after the men, there was every reason to hope that a year or two would render her less volatile, and add to those sterling good qualities which she really possessed. In heart and feeling she was a modest girl, although the buoyancy of her spirits often carried her beyond the bounds prescribed by decorum, and often called forth a blush upon her own animated countenance, when her good sense, or the remarks of others, reminded her of her having committed herself. It was impossible to know Mary and not like her, although, at a casual meeting, a rigid person might go away with an impression by no means favourable. As for myself, I must say, that the more I was in her company the more I was attached to her, and the more I respected her.

Old Stapleton came home in the evening. He had, as usual, been smoking, and thinking of human natur', at the Feathers public-house. I told him what had happened, and upon the strength of it he sent for an extra pot of beer for Mary and me, which he insisted upon our drinking between us—a greater proof of good-will on his part could not have been given. Although Captain Turnbull appeared to have recovered from the effects of the accident, yet it seemed that such was not the case, as the morning after his arrival he was taken ill with shivering and pains in his loins, which ended in ague and fever, and he did not quit his bed for three or four weeks. I, on the contrary, felt no ill effects; but the constitution of a youth is better able to meet such violent shocks than that of a man of sixty years old, already sapped by exposure and fatigue. As the frost still continued, I complied with Captain Turnbull's request to come up and stay with him, and for many days, until he was able to leave his bed, I was his constant nurse. The general theme of his conversation was on my future prospects, and a wish that I would embark in some pursuit or profession more likely to raise me in the world; but on this head I was positive, and also another point, which was, that I would in future put myself under an obligation to no one. I could not erase from my memory the injuries I had received, and my vindictive spirit continually brooded over them. I was resolved to be independent and free. I felt that in the company I was in I was with my equals, or, if there were any superiority, it was on my part, arising from education, and I never would submit to be again in the society of those above me, in which I was admitted as a favour, and by the major part looked down upon, and at the same time liable, as I had once been, to be turned out with contumely on the first moment of caprice. Still, I was very fond of Captain Turnbull. He had always been kind to me, spoke to me on terms of equality, and had behaved with consistency, and my feelings towards him since the accident had consequently strengthened; but we always feel an increased regard towards those to whom we have been of service, and my pride was softened by the reflection that, whatever might be Mr Turnbull's good-will towards me, he never could, even if I would permit it, repay me for the life which I had preserved. Towards him I felt unbounded regard; towards those who had ill-treated me, unlimited hatred; towards the world in general a mixture of feeling which I could hardly analyse; and, as far as regarded myself, a love of liberty and independence, which nothing would ever have induced me to compromise. As I did not wish to hurt Captain Turnbull's feelings by a direct refusal to all his proffers of service, and remarks upon the advantages which might arise, I generally made an evasive answer; but when, on the day proposed for my departure, he at once came to the point, offering me everything, and observing that he was childless, and, therefore, my acceptance of his offer would be injurious to nobody; when he took me by the hand, and drawing me near to him, passed his arm round me, and spoke to me in the kind accents of a father, almost entreating me to consent—the tears of gratitude coursed each other rapidly down my cheeks, but my resolution was no less firm—although it was with a faltering, voice that I replied, "You have been very kind to me, sir—very kind—and I shall never forget it; and I hope I shall deserve it—but—Mr Drummond, and Mrs Drummond, and Sarah, were also kind to me—very kind to me—you know the rest. I will remain as I am, if you please; and if you wish to do me a kindness; if you wish me to love you, as I really do, let me be as I am—free and independent. I beg it of you as the greatest favour that you can possibly confer on me—the only favour which I can accept, or shall be truly thankful for."

Captain Turnbull was some minutes before he could reply. He then said—"I see it is useless, and I will not tease you any more; but, Jacob, do not let the fire of injustice which you have received from your fellow-creatures prey so much upon your mind, or induce you to form the mistaken idea that the world is bad. As you live on, you will find much good; and recollect, that those who injured you, from the misrepresentation of others, have been willing, and have offered, to repair their fault. They can do no more, and I wish you could get over this vindictive feeling. Recollect, we must forgive, as we hope to be forgiven."

"I do sometimes," said I, "for Sarah's sake—I can't always."

"But you ought to forgive, for other reasons, Jacob."

"I know I ought—but if I cannot, I cannot."

"Nay, my boy, I never heard you talk so—I was going to say—wickedly. Do you not perceive that you are now in error? You will not abandon a feeling which your own good sense and religion tell you to be wrong—you cling to it—and yet you will admit of no excuse for the errors of others."

"I feel what you say—and the truth of it, sir," replied I "but I cannot combat the feeling. I will, therefore, admit every excuse you please for the faults of others; but at the same time, I am surely not to be blamed if I refuse to put myself in a situation where I am again liable to meet with mortification. Surely I am not to be censured, if I prefer to work for my bread after my own fashion, and prefer the river to dry land?"

"No, that I acknowledge; but what I dislike in the choice is, that it is dictated by feelings of resentment."

"*What's done can't be helped*," replied I, quickly, wishing to break off the conversation.

"Very true, Jacob; but I follow that up with another of your remarks, which is, 'Better luck next time.' God bless you, my boy; take care of yourself, and don't get under the ice again!"

"For you I would to-morrow," replied I, taking the proffered hand: "but if I could only see that Hodgson near a hole—"

"You'd not push him in?"

"Indeed I would," replied I, bitterly.

"Jacob, you would not, I tell you—you think so now, but if you saw him in distress you would assist him as you did me. I know you, my boy, better than you know yourself."

Whether Captain Turnbull or I were right remains to be proved in the sequel. We then shook hands, and I hastened away to see Mary, whom I had often thought of during my absence.

"Who do you think has been here?" said Mary, after our first greeting.

"I cannot guess," replied I. "Not old Tom and his son?"

"No; I don't think it was old Tom, but it was such an old quiz—with such a nose—O heavens! I thought I should have died with laughing as soon as he went downstairs. Do you know, Jacob, that I made love to him, just to see how he'd take it. You know who it is now?"

"O yes! you mean the Dominie, my schoolmaster."

"Yes, he told me so; and I talked so much about you, and about your teaching me to read and write, and how fond I was of learning, and how I should like to be married to an elderly man who was a great scholar, who would teach me Latin and Greek, that the old gentleman became quite chatty, and sat for two hours talking to me. He desired me to say that he should call here to-morrow afternoon, and I begged him to stay the evening, as you are to have two more of your friends here. Now, who do you think are those?"

"I have no others, except old Tom Beazeley and his son."

"Well, it is your old Tom after all, and a nice old fellow he is, although I would not like him for a husband; but as for his son—he's a lad after my own heart—I'm quite in love with him."

"Your love will do you no harm, Mary; but, recollect, what may be a joke to you may not be so to other people. As for the Dominie meeting old Beazeley and his son, I don't exactly know how that will suit, for I doubt if he will like to see them."

"Why not?" inquired Mary.

Upon a promise never to hint at them, I briefly stated the circumstances attending the worthy man's voyage on board of the lighter. Mary paused, and then said, "Jacob, did we not read the last time that the most dangerous rocks to men were *wine* and *women*?"

"Yes, we did, if I recollect right."

"Humph," said she; "the old gentleman has given plenty of lessons in his time, and it appears that he has received *one*."

"We may do so to the last day of our existence, Mary."

"Well, he is a very clever, learned man, I've no doubt, and looks down upon all of us (not you, Jacob) as silly people. I'll try if *I* can't give him a lesson."

"You, Mary, what can you teach him?"

"Never mind, we shall see;" and Mary turned the discourse on her father. "You know, I suppose, that father is gone up to Mr Turnbull's."

"No, I did not."

"Yes, he has; he was desired to go there this morning, and hasn't been back since. Jacob, I hope you won't be so foolish again, for I don't want to lose my master."

"Oh, never fear; I shall teach you all you want to know before I die," I replied.

"Don't be too sure of that," replied Mary; "how do you know how much I may wish to have of your company?"

"Well, if I walk off in a hurry, I'll make you over to young Tom Beazeley. You're half in love with him already, you know," replied I, laughing.

"Well, he is a nice fellow," replied she; "he laughs more than you do, Jacob."

"He has suffered less," replied I, gloomily, calling to mind what had occurred; "but, Mary, he is a fine young man, and a good-hearted, clever fellow to boot; and when you do know him, you will like him very much." As I said this, I heard her father coming up stairs; he came in high good-humour with his interview with Captain Turnbull, called for his pipe and pot, and was excessively fluent upon *"human natur'."*

Chapter Twenty Five

The afternoon of the next day I heard a well-known voice, which carolled forth, as Mary huddled up her books, and put them out of the way; for at that time I was, as usual, giving her a lesson:—

"And many strange sights I've seen,
  And long I've been a rover,
And everywhere I've been,
  But now the wars are over.
I've been across the line,
  Where the sun will burn your nose off;
And I've been in northern climes,
  Where the frost would bite your toes off.
    Fal de ral, fal de ral, fal de ral de liddy."

"Heave a-head, Tom, and let me stump up at my leisure. It's like warping 'gainst wind and tide with me—and I gets up about as fast as lawyers go to heaven."

I thought when Tom came up first that he had been at unusual trouble in setting off his person, and certainly a better-looking, frank, open, merry countenance was seldom to be seen. In person he was about an inch taller than I, athletic, and well formed. He made up to Mary, who, perceiving his impatience, and either to check him before me, or else from her usual feeling of coquetry, received him rather distantly, and went up to old Tom, with whom she shook hands warmly.

"Whew! what's in the wind now, Jacob? Why, we parted the best friends in the world," said Tom, looking at Mary.

"Sheer off yourself, Tom," replied I, laughing; "and you'll see that she'll come to again."

"Oh, oh! so the wind's in that quarter, is it?" replied Tom. "With all my heart—I can show false colours as well as she can. But I say, Jacob, before I begin my manoeuvres, tell me if you wish me to hoist the neutral flag—for I won't interfere with you."

"Here's my hand upon it, Tom, that the coast is clear as far as I'm concerned; but take care—she's a clipper, and not unlikely to slip through your fingers, even when you have her under your lee, within hail."

"Let me alone, Jacob, for that."

"And more, Tom, when you're in possession of her, she will require a good man at the helm."

"Then she's just the craft after my fancy. I hate your steady, slow-sailing craft, that will steer themselves, almost; give me one that requires to be managed by a man and a seaman."

"If well manned, she will do anything, depend upon it, Tom, for she's as sound below as possible; and although she is down to her bearings on the puff of the moment, yet she'd not careen further."

"Well, then, Jacob, all's right; and now you've told me what tack she's on, see if I don't shape a course to cut her off."

"Well, Jacob, my good boy, so you've been under the water again; I thought you had enough of it when Fleming gave you such a twist; but, however, this time you went to sarve a friend, which was all right. My sarvice to you Mr Stapleton," continued old Tom, as Stapleton made his appearance. "I was talking to Jacob about his last dive."

"Nothing but human natur'," replied Stapleton.

"Well, now," replied old Tom, "I consider that going plump into the river, when covered with ice, to be quite contrary to human natur'."

"But not to save a friend, father?"

"No—because, that be Jacob's nature; so you see one nature conquered the other, and that's the whole long and short of it."

"Well, now, suppose we sit down and make ourselves comfortable," observed Stapleton; "but here be somebody else coming up—who can it be?"

"I say, old codger, considering you be as deaf as a post, you hears pretty well," said old Tom.

"Yes, I hear very well in the house, provided people don't speak loud."

"Well, that's a queer sort of deafness; I think we are all troubled with the same complaint," cried Tom, laughing.

During this remark, the Dominie made his appearance. "*Salve Domine*," said I upon his entering, taking my worthy pedagogue by the hand.

"*Et tu quoque, fili mi, Jacobe!* But whom have we here? the deaf man, the maiden, and—ehu!—the old man called old Tom, and likewise the young Tom;" and the Dominie looked very grave.

"Nay, sir," said young Tom, going up to the Dominie; "I know you are angry with us, because we both drank too much when we were last in your company; but we promise—don't we father?—not to do so again."

This judicious reply of young Tom's put the Dominie more at his ease; what he most feared was raillery and exposure on their parts.

"Very true, old gentleman; Tom and I did bowse our jibs up a little too taut when we last met—but what then?—there was the grog, and there was nothing to do."

"All human natur'," observed Stapleton.

"Come, sir, you have not said one word to me," said Mary, going up to the Dominie. "Now you must sit down by me, and take care of me, and see that they all behave themselves and keep sober."

The Dominie cast a look at Mary, which was intended for her alone, but which was not unperceived by young Tom or me. "We shall have some fun, Jacob," said he, aside, as we all sat down to the table, which just admitted six, with close stowage. The Dominie on one side of Mary, Tom on the other, Stapleton next to Tom, then I and old Tom, who closed in on the other side of the Dominie, putting one of his timber toes on the old gentleman's corns, which induced him to lift up his leg in a hurry, and draw his chair still closer to Mary, to avoid a repetition of the accident; while old Tom was axing pardon, and Stapleton demonstrating that, on the part of old Tom, not to *feel* with a wooden leg, and on the part of the Dominie, to *feel* with a bad corn, was all nothing but "*human natur'*." At last we were all seated, and Mary, who had provided for the evening, produced two or three pots of beer, a bottle of spirits, pipes, and tobacco.

"Liberty Hall—I smokes," said Stapleton, lighting his pipe, and falling back on his chair.

"I'll put a bit of clay in my mouth too," followed up old Tom; "it makes one thirsty, and enjoy one's liquor."

"Well, I malts," said Tom, reaching a pot of porter, and taking a long pull. "What do you do, Jacob?"

"I shall wait a little, Tom."

"And what do you do, sir?" said Mary to the Dominie. The Dominie shook his head. "Nay but you must—or I shall think you do not like my company. Come, let me fill a pipe for you." Mary filled a pipe, and handed it to the Dominie, who hesitated, looked at her, and was overcome. He lighted it, and smoked furiously.

"The ice is breaking up—we shall have a change of weather—the moon quarters to-morrow," observed old Tom, puffing between every observation; "and then honest men may earn their bread again. Bad times for you, old codger, heh!" continued he, addressing Stapleton. Stapleton nodded an assent through the smoke, which was first perceived by old Tom. "Well, he ar'nt deaf, a'ter all; I thought he was only shamming a bit. I say, Jacob, this is the weather to blow your fingers, and make your eyes bright."

"Rather to blow a cloud and make your eyes water," replied Tom, taking up the pot: "I'm just as thirsty with swallowing smoke, as if I had a pipe myself—at all events, I pipe my eye. Jacob," continued Tom, to me apart, "do look how the old gentleman is *funking* Mary, and casting sheeps' eyes at her through the smoke."

"He appears as if he were inclined to board her in the smoke," replied I.

"Yes, and she to make no fight of it, but surrender immediately," said Tom.

"Don't you believe it, Tom; I know her better; she wants to laugh at him—nothing more; she winked her eye at me just now, but I would not laugh, as I did not choose that the old gentleman should be trifled with. I will tax her severely to-morrow."

During all this time old Tom and Stapleton smoked in silence: the Dominie made use of his eyes in dumb parlance to Mary, who answered him with her own bright glances, and Tom and I began to find it rather dull; when at last old Tom's pipe was exhausted, and he laid it down; "There, I'll smoke no more—the worst of a pipe is that one can't smoke and talk at the same time. Mary, my girl, take your eyes off the Dominie's nose, and hand me that bottle of stuff. What, glass to mix it in; that's more genteel than we are on board, Tom." Tom filled a rummer of grog, took half off at a huge sip, and put it down on the table. "Will you do as we do, sir?" said he, addressing the Dominie.

"Nay, friend Dux, nay—pr'ythee persuade me not—avaunt!" and the Dominie, with an appearance of horror, turned away from the bottle handed towards him by old Tom.

"Not drink anything?" said Mary to the Dominie, looking at him with surprise, "but indeed you must, or I shall think you despise us, and do not think us fit to be in your company."

"Nay, maiden, entreat me not. Ask anything of me but this," replied the Dominie.

"Ask anything but this—that's just the way people have of refusing," replied Mary; "were I to ask anything else, it would be the same answer—'ask anything but this.' Now, if you will not drink to please me, I shall quarrel with you. You shall drink a glass, and I'll mix it for you." The Dominie shook his head. Mary made a glass of grog, and then put it to her lips. "Now, if you refuse to drink it, after I have tasted it, I'll never speak to you again." So saying, she handed the glass to the Dominie.

"Verily, maiden, I must needs refuse, for I did make a mental vow."

"What vow was that? was it sworn on the Bible?"

"Nay, not on the sacred book, but in my thoughts most solemnly."

"Oh! I make those vows every day, and never keep one of them; so that won't do. Now, observe, I give you one more chance. I shall drink a little more, and if you do not immediately put your lips to the same part of the tumbler, I'll never drink to you again;" Mary put the tumbler again to her lips, drank a little, with her eyes fixed upon the Dominie, who watched her with distended nostrils and muscular agitation of countenance. With her sweetest smile, she handed him the tumbler; the Dominie half held out his hand, withdrew it, put it down again, and by degrees took the tumbler. Mary conquered, and I watched the malice of her look as the liquor trickled down the Dominie's throat. Tom and I exchanged glances. The Dominie put down the tumbler, and then, looking round, like a guilty person, coloured up to the eyes; but Mary, who perceived that her victory was but half achieved, put her hand upon his shoulder, and asked him to let her taste the grog again. I also, to make him feel more at ease, helped myself to a glass. Tom did the same, and old Tom with more regard to the feelings of the Dominie than in his own bluntness of character I would have given him credit for, said in a quiet tone, "The old gentleman is afraid of grog, because he seed me take a drop too much, but that's no reason why grog ar'n't a good thing, and wholesome in moderation. A glass or two is very well, and better still when sweetened by the lips of a pretty girl; and, even if the Dominie does not like it, he's too much of a gentleman not to give up his dislikes to please a lady. More's the merit; for, if he did like it, it would be no sacrifice, that's sartain. Don't you think so, my old boozer?" continued he, addressing Stapleton, who smoked in silence.

"Human natur'," replied Stapleton, taking the pipe out of his mouth, and spitting under the table.

"Very true, master; and so here's to your health, Mr Dominie, and may you never want a pretty girl to talk to, or a glass of grog to drink her health with."

"Oh, but the Dominie don't care about pretty girls, father," replied Tom; "he's too learned and clever; he thinks about nothing but the moon, and Latin and Greek, and all that."

"Who can say what's under the skin, Tom? There's no knowing what is, and what isn't—Sall's shoe for that."

"Never heard of Sall's shoe, father; that's new to me."

"Didn't I ever tell you that, Tom?—Well, then, you shall have it now—that is, if all the company be agreeable."

"Oh, yes," cried Mary; "pray tell us."

"Would you like to hear it, sir?"

"I never heard of Sall Sue in my life, and would fain hear her history," replied the Dominie; "proceed, friend Dux."

"Well, then, you must know when I was a-board of the Terp-sy-chore, there was a fore-topman, of the name of Bill Harness, a good sort of chap enough, but rather soft in the upper-works. Now, we'd been on the Jamaica station for some years, and had come home, and merry enough, and happy enough we were (those that were left of us), and we were spending our money like the devil. Bill Harness had a wife, who was very fond of he, and he was very fond of she, but she was a slatternly sort of a body, never tidy in her rigging, all adrift at all times, and what's more, she never had a shoe up at heel, so she went by the name of Slatternly Sall, and the first lieutenant, who was a 'ticular sort of a chap, never liked to see her on deck, for you see she put her hair in paper on New Year's day, and never changed it or took it out till the year came round again. However, be it as it may be, she loved Bill, and Bill loved she, and they were very happy together. A'ter all, it ain't whether a woman's tidy without that makes a man's happiness; it depends upon whether she be right within; that is, if she be good-tempered, and obliging, and civil, and 'commodating, and so forth. A'ter the first day or two, person's nothing—eyes get palled, like the cap-stern when the anchor's up to the bows; but what a man likes is, not to be disturbed by vagaries, or gusts of temper. Well, Bill was happy—but one day he was devilish unhappy, because Sall had lost one of her shoes, which wasn't to be wondered at, considering as how she was always slipshod. 'Who has seen my wife's shoe?' says he. 'Hang your wife's shoe,' said one, 'it warn't worth casting an eye upon;' Still he cried out, 'Who has seen my wife's shoe?' 'I seed it,' says another. 'Where?' says Bill. 'I seed it down at heel,' says the fellow. But Bill still hallooed out about his wife's shoe, which it appeared she had dropped off her foot as she was going up the forecastle ladder to take the air a bit, just as it was dark. At last Bill made so much fuss about it that the ship's company laughed, and all called out to each other, 'Who has seen Sall's shoe? — Have you got Sall's shoe?' and they passed the word fore and aft the whole evening, till they went to their hammocks. Notwithstanding, as Sall's shoe was not forthcoming, the next morning Bill goes on the quarter-deck, and complains to the first lieutenant, as how he had lost Sall's shoe. 'Damn Sall's shoe,' said he, 'haven't I enough to look after without your wife's confounded shoes, which can't be worth twopence?' Well, Bill argues that his wife had only one shoe left, and that won't keep two feet dry, and begs the first lieutenant to order a search for it; but the first lieutenant turns away, and tells him to go to the devil, and all the men grin at Bill's making such a fuss about nothing. So Bill at last goes up to the first lieutenant, and whispers something, and the first lieutenant booms him off with his speaking trumpet, as if he were making too free, in whispering to his commanding officer, and then sends for the master-at-arms. 'Collier,' says he, 'this man has lost his wife's shoe: let a search be made for it immediately — take all the ship's boys, and look everywhere for it; if you find it bring it up to me.' So away goes the master-at-arms with his cane, and collects all the boys to look for Sall's shoe — and they go peeping about the maindeck, under the guns, and under the hen-coops, and in the sheep-pen, and everywhere; now and then getting a smart slap with the cane behind, upon the taut part of their trowsers, to make them look sharp, until they all wished Sall's shoe at Old Nick, and her too, and Bill in the bargain. At last one of the boys picks it out of the manger, where it had lain all the night, poked up and down by the noses of the pigs, who didn't think it eatable, although it might have smelt human-like; the fact was, it was the same boy who had picked up Sall's shoe when she dropped it, and had shied it forward. It sartainly did not seem to be worth all the trouble, but howsomever it was taken aft by the master-at-arms, and laid on the capstern head. Then Bill steps out and takes the shoe before the first lieutenant, and cuts it open, and from between the lining pulls out four ten pound notes, which Sall had sewn up there by way of security; and the first lieutenant tells Bill he was a great fool to trust his money in the shoe of a woman who always went slipshod, and tells him to go about his business, and stow his money away in a safer place next time. A'ter, if any thing was better than it looked to be, the ship's company used always to say it was like *Sall's shoe*. There you have it all."

"Well," says Stapleton, taking the pipe out of his mouth, "I know a fact, much of a muchness with that, which happened to me when I was below the river, tending a ship at Sheerness—for at one time, d'ye see, I used to ply there. She was an old fifty-gun ship, called the Adamant, if I recollect right. One day the first lieutenant, who, like yourn, was a mighty particular sort of chap, was going round the maindeck, and he sees an old pair of canvas trowsers stowed in under the trunnion of one of the guns. So says he, 'Whose be these?' Now, no man would answer, because they knowed very well that it would be as good as a fortnight in the black list. With that, the first lieutenant bundles them out of the port, and away they floats astern with the tide. It was about half-an-hour after that, that I comes off with the milk for the wardroom mess, and a man named Will Heaviside says to me, 'Stapleton,' says he, 'the first lieutenant has thrown my canvas trowsers overboard, and be damned to him; now I must have them back.' 'But where be they?' says I: 'I suppose down at the bottom by this time, and the flat-fish dubbing their noses into them.' 'No, no,' says he, 'they wo'n't never sink, but float till eternity; they be gone down with the tide, and they will come back again; only you keep a sharp look-out for them, and I'll give you five shillings if you bring them.' Well, I seed little chance of ever seeing them again, or of my seeing five shillings, but as it so happened next tide, the very 'denticle pair of trowsers comes up staring me in the face. I pulls them in, and takes them to Will Heaviside, who appears to be mightily pleased, and gives me the money. 'I wouldn't have lost them for ten, no, not fur twenty pounds,' says he. 'At all events you've paid me more than they are worth,' says I. 'Have I?' says he; 'stop a bit;' and he outs with his knife, and rips open the waistband, and pulls out a piece of linen, and out of the piece of linen he pulls out a *child's caul*. 'There,' says he, 'now you knows why the trowsers wouldn't sink, and I'll leave you to judge whether they ar'n't worth five shillings.' That's my story."

"Well, I can't understand how it is, that a caul should keep people up," observed old Tom.

"At all events, a *call* makes people come up fast enough on board a man-of-war, father."

"That's true enough, but I'm talking of a child's caul, not of a boatswain's, Tom."

"I'll just tell you how it is," replied Stapleton, who had recommenced smoking; "it's *human natur'*."

"What is your opinion, sir?" said Mary to the Dominie.

"Maiden," replied the Dominie, taking his pipe out of his mouth, "I opine that it's a vulgar error. Sir Thomas Brown, I think it is, hath the same idea; many and strange were the superstitions which have been handed down by our less enlightened ancestors—all of which mists have been cleared away by the powerful rays of truth."

"Well, but, master, if a vulgar error saves a man from Davy Jones's locker, ar'n't it just as well to sew it up in the waistband of your trowsers?"

"Granted, good Dux; if it would save a man; but how is it possible? it is contrary to the first elements of science."

"What matter does that make, provided it holds a man up?"

"Friend Dux, thou art obtuse."

"Well, perhaps I am, as I don't know what that is."

"But, father, don't you recollect," interrupted Tom, "what the parson said last Sunday, that faith saved men? Now, Master Dominie, may it not be faith that a man has in the *caul* which may save him?"

"Young Tom, thou art astute."

"Well, perhaps I am, as father said, for I don't know what that is. You knock us all down with your dictionary."

"Well I do love to hear people make use of such hard words," said Mary, looking at the Dominie. "How very clever you must be, sir! I wonder whether I shall ever understand them?"

"Nay, if thou wilt, I will initiate—sweet maiden, wilt steal an hour or so to impregnate thy mind with the seeds of learning, which, in so fair a soil, must needs bring forth good fruit!"

"That's a fine word, that *impregnate*—will you give us the English of it, sir?" said young Tom to the Dominie.

"It is English, Tom, only the old gentleman *razeed* it a little. The third ship in the lee line of the Channel fleet was a eighty, called the *Impregnable*, but the old gentleman knows more about books than sea matters."

"A marvellous misconception," quoth the Dominie.

"There's another," cried Tom, laughing; "that must be a three-decker. Come, father, here's the bottle, you must take another glass to wash that down."

"Pray what was the meaning of that last long word, sir," said Mary, taking the Dominie by the arm, "mis—something."

"The word," replied the Dominie, "is a compound from conception, borrowed from the Latin tongue implying conceiving; and the *mis* prefixed, which negatives or reverses the meaning; misconception, therefore, implies not to conceive. I can make you acquainted with many others of a similar tendency as *mis*-conception; videlicet, *mis*-apprehension, *mis*-understanding, *mis*-contriving *mis*-applying, *mis*—"

"Dear me, what a many *misses*," cried Mary, "and do you know them all?"

"Indeed do I," replied the Dominie, "and many, many more are treasured in my memory, *quod nunc describere tongum est*."

"I'd no idea that the old gentleman was given to running after the girls in that way," said old Tom to Stapleton.

"Human natur'," replied the other.

"No more did I," continued Mary; "I shall have nothing to say to him;" and she drew off her chair a few inches from that of the Dominie.

"Maiden," quoth the Dominie, "thou art under a mistake."

"Another miss, I declare," cried Tom, laughing.

"What an old Turk!" continued Mary, getting further off.

"Nay, then, I will not reply," said the Dominie indignantly, putting down his pipe, leaning back on his chair, and pulling out his great red handkerchief, which he applied to his nose, and produced a sound that made the windows of the little parlour vibrate for some seconds.

"I say, master Tom, don't you make too free with your betters," said old Tom, when he saw the Dominie affronted.

"Nay," replied the Dominie, "there's an old adage which saith, 'As the old cock crows, so doth the young.' Wherefore didst thou set him the example?"

"Very true, old gentleman, and I axes your pardon, and here's my hand upon it."

"And so do I, sir, and here's my hand upon it," said young Tom, extending his hand on the Dominie's other side.

"Friend Dux, and thou, young Tom, I do willingly accept thy proffered reconciliation; knowing, as I well do, that there may be much mischief in thy composition, but naught of malice." The Dominie extended his hands, and shook both those offered to him warmly.

"There," said old Tom, "now my mind's at ease, as old Pigtown said."

"I know not the author whom thou quotest from, good Dux."

"Author!—I never said he was an author; he was only captain of a schooner, trading between the islands, that I sailed with a few weeks in the West Indies."

"Perhaps, then, you will relate to the company present the circumstances which took place to put old Pegtop's—(I may not be correct in the name)—but whoever it may be—"

"Pigtown, master."

"Well, then—that put old Pigtown's mind at ease—for I am marvellously amused with thy narrations, which do pass away the time most agreeably, good Dux."

"With all my heart, old gentleman; but first let us fill up our tumblers. I don't know how it is, but it does appear to me that grog drinks better out of a glass than out of metal and if it wasn't that Tom is so careless—and the dog has no respect for crockery any more than persons—I would have one or two on board for particular service; but I'll think about that, and hear what the old woman has to say on the subject. Now to my yarn. D'ye see, old Pigtown commanded a little schooner, which plied between the isles, and he had been in her for a matter of forty years, and was as well-known as Port Royal Tom."

"Who might Port Royal Tom be?" inquired the Dominie; "a relation of yours?"

"I hope not, master, for I wanted none of his acquaintance; he was a shark about twenty feet long who rode guard in the harbour, to prevent the men-of-war's men from deserting, and was pensioned by government."

"Pensioned by government! nay, but that soundeth strangely. I have heard that pensions have been most lavishly bestowed, but not that it extended so far. Truly it must have been a *sinecure*."

"I don't know what that last may be," replied old Tom, "but I heard our boatswain, in the *Minerve*, who talked politics a bit, say, 'as how half the pensions were held by a pack of damned sharks;' but in this here shark's case, it wasn't in money, master; but he'd regular rations of bullock's liver to persuade him to remain in the harbour, and no one dare swim on shore when he was cruising round and round the ships. Well, old Pigtown, with his white trousers and straw hat, red nose and big belly, was as well-known as could be, and was a capital old fellow for remembering and executing commissions, provided you gave him the money first; if not, he always took care to forget them. Old Pigtown had a son, a little dark or so, which proved that his mother wasn't quite as fair as a lily, and this son was employed in a drogher, that is, a small craft which goes round to the bays of the island, and takes off the sugars to the West India traders. One fine day the drogher was driven out to sea, and never heard of a'terwards. Now, old Pigtown was very anxious about what had come of his son, and day after day expected he would come back again; but he never did, for very good reasons, as you shall hear by-and-by; and every one knowing old Pigtown, and he knowing everybody, it was at least fifty times a day that the question was put to him, 'Well, Pigtown, have you heard anything of your son?' And fifty times a day he would reply, 'No; and *my mind's but ill at ease.*' Well, it was two or three months afterwards, that when I was in the schooner with him, as we lay becalmed between the islands, with the sun frizzing our wigs, and the planks so hot that you couldn't walk without your shoes, that we hooked a large shark which came bowling under our counter, got him on board and cut him up. When we opened his inside, what should I see but something shining. I took it out, and sure enough it was a silver watch. So I hands it to old Pigtown. He looks at it very 'tentively, opens the outside case, reads the maker's name, and then shuts it up again. 'This here watch,' says he, 'belonged to my son Jack. I bought it of a chap in a South whaler for three dollars and a roll of pigtail, and a very good watch it was, though I perceive it to be stopped now. Now, d'ye see, it's all clear—the drogher must have gone down in a squall—the shark must have picked up my son Jack, and must have *digested* his body, but has not been able to *digest* his watch. Now I knows what's become of him, and so—*my mind's at ease.*'"

"Well," observed old Stapleton, "I agrees with old Poptown, or whatever his name might be, that it were better to know the worst at once than to be kept on the worry all your days; I consider it's nothing but human natur'. Why, if one has a bad tooth, which is the best plan, to have it out with one good wrench, or to be eternally tormented, night and day."

"Thou speakest wisely, friend Stapleton, and like a man of resolve—the anticipation is often, if not always, more painful than the reality. Thou knowest, Jacob, how often I have allowed a boy to remain unbuttoned in the centre of the room for an hour previous to the application of the birch—and it was with the consideration that the impression would be greater upon his mind than even upon his nether parts. All of the feelings in the human breast, that of suspense is—"

"Worse than *hanging*," interrupted young Tom.

"Even so, boy (*cluck, cluck*), an apt comparison, seeing that in suspense you are hanging, as it were, in the very region of doubt, without being able to obtain a footing even upon conjecture. Nay, we may further add another simile, although not so well borne out, which is, that the agony of suspense doth stop the breath of a man for the time, as hanging doth stop it altogether, so that it may be truly said, that suspense is put an end to by suspending." (*cluck, cluck.*)

"And now that you've got rid of all that, master, suppose you fill up your pipe," observed old Tom.

"And I will fill up your tumbler, sir," said Mary; "for you must be dry with talking such hard words."

The Dominie this time made no objection, and again enveloped Mary and himself in a cloud of smoke, through which his nose loomed like an Indiaman in a Channel fog.

Chapter Twenty Six

"I say, Master Stapleton, suppose we were to knock out half a port," observed old Tom, after a silence of two minutes; "for the old gentleman blows a devil of a cloud: that is, if no one has an objection." Stapleton gave a nod of assent, and I rose and put the upper window down a few inches. "Ay, that's right, Jacob; now we shall see what Miss Mary and he are about. You've been enjoying the lady all to yourself, master," continued Tom, addressing the Dominie.

"Verily and truly," replied the Dominie, "even as a second Jupiter."

"Never heard of him."

"I presume not; still, Jacob will tell thee that the history is to be found in Ovid's Metamorphoses."

"Never heard of the country, master."

"Nay, friend Dux, it is a book, not a country, in which thou may'st read how Jupiter at first descended unto Semele in a cloud."

"And pray, where did he come from, master?"

"He came from heaven."

"The devil he did. Well, if ever I gets there, I mean to stay."

"It was love, all-powerful love, which induced him, maiden," replied the Dominie, turning, with a smiling eye, to Mary.

"'Bove my comprehension altogether," replied old Tom.

"Human natur'," muttered Stapleton, with the pipe still between his lips.

"Not the first vessels that have run foul in a fog," observed young Tom.

"No, boy; but generally there ar'n't much love between them at those times. But, come, now that we can breathe again, suppose I give you a song. What shall it be, young woman, a sea ditty, or something *spooney*?"

"Oh, something about love, if you've no objection, sir," said Mary, appealing to the Dominie.

"Nay, it pleaseth me maiden, and I am of thy mind. Friend Dux, let it be Anacreontic."

"What the devil's that?" cried old Tom, lifting up his eyes, and taking the pipe out of his mouth.

"Nothing of your own, father, that's clear; but something to borrow, for it's to be *on tick*," replied Tom.

"Nay, boy, I would have been understood that the song should refer to women or wine."

"Both of which are to his fancy," observed young Tom to me, aside.

"*Human natur'*," quaintly observed Stapleton.

"Well, then, you shall have your wish. I'll give you one that might be warbled in a lady's chamber without stirring the silk curtains:—

> "Oh! the days are gone when beauty bright
>   My heart's chain wove,
> When my dream of life from morn to night
>   Was Love—still Love.
> New hope may bloom, and days may come,
>   Of milder, calmer beam,
> But there's nothing half so sweet in life
>   As Love's young dream;
> Oh! there's nothing half so sweet in life,
>   As Love's young dream."

The melody of the song, added to the spirits he had drunk and Mary's eyes beaming on him, had a great effect upon the Dominie. As old Tom warbled out, so did the pedagogue gradually approach the chair of Mary; and as gradually entwine her waist with his own arm, his eyes twinkling brightly on her. Old Tom, who perceived it, had given me and Tom a wink, as he repeated the two last lines; and then we saw what was going on, we burst into an uncontrollable fit of laughter. "Boys! boys!" said the Dominie, starting up, "thou hast awakened me, by thy boisterous mirth, from a sweet musing created by the harmony of friend Dux's voice. Neither do I discover the source of thy cachinnation, seeing that the song is amatory and not comic. Still, it may not be supposed, at thy early age, that thou canst be affected with what thou art too young to feel. Pr'ythee continue, friend Dux, and, boys, restrain thy mirth."

> "Though the bard to a purer fame may soar
>   When wild youth's past,
> Though he win the wise, who frowned before,

To smile at last,
He'll never meet a joy so sweet
    In all his noon of fame,
As when first he sung to woman's ear
    His soul-felt flame;
And at every close she blush'd to hear
    The once-lov'd name."

At the commencement of this verse the Dominie appeared to be on his guard; but gradually moved by the power of song, he dropped his elbow on the table, and his pipe underneath it; his forehead sank into his broad palm, and he remained motionless. The verse ended, and the Dominie, forgetting all around him, softly ejaculated, without looking up, "Eheu! Mary."

"Did you speak to me, sir?" said Mary, who, perceiving us tittering, addressed the Dominie with a half-serious, half-mocking air.

"Speak, maiden? nay, I spoke not; yet thou mayest give me my pipe, which apparently hath been abducted while I was listening to the song."

"Abducted! that's a new word; but it means smashed into twenty pieces, I suppose," observed young Tom. "At all events, your pipe is, for you let it fall between your legs."

"Never mind," said Mary, rising from her chair, and going to the cupboard; "here's another, sir."

"Well, master, am I to finish, or have you had enough of it?"

"Proceed, friend Dux, proceed; and believe that I am all attention."

"Oh, that hallowed form is ne'er forgot
    Which first love trac'd,
Still it lingering haunts the greenest spot
    On memory's waste.
'Twas odour fled as soon as shed,
    'Twas memory's winged dream,
'Twas a light that ne'er can shine again
    On life's dull stream;
Oh, 'twas light that ne'er can shine again
    On life's dull stream."

"Nay," said the Dominie, again abstracted, "the metaphor is not just. 'Life's dull stream.' 'Lethe tacitus amnis,' as Lucan hath it; but the stream of life flows—ay, flows rapidly—even in my veins. Doth not the heart throb and beat—yea, strongly—peradventure too forcibly against my better judgment? 'Confiteor misere molle cor esse mihi,' as Ovid saith. Yet must it not prevail! Shall one girl be victorious over seventy boys? Shall I, Dominie Dobbs, desert my post?—Again succumb to—I will even depart, that I may be at my desk at matutinal hours."

"You don't mean to leave us, sir?" said Mary, taking the Dominie's arm.

"Even so, fair maiden, for it waxeth late, and I have my duties to perform," said the Dominie, rising from his chair.

"Then you will promise to come again."

"Peradventure I may."

"If you do not promise me that you will, I will not let you go now."

"Verily, maiden—"

"Promise," interrupted Mary.

"Truly, maiden—"

"Promise," cried Mary.

"In good sooth, maiden—"

"Promise," reiterated Mary, pulling the Dominie towards her chair.

"Nay, then, I do promise, since thou wilt have it so," replied the Dominie.

"And when will you come?"

"I will not tarry," replied the Dominie; "and now good night to all."

The Dominie shook hands with us, and Mary lighted him downstairs. I was much pleased with the resolution and sense of his danger thus shown by my worthy preceptor, and hoped that he would have avoided Mary in future, who evidently wished to make a conquest of him for her own amusement and love of admiration; but still I felt that the promise exacted would be fulfilled, and I was afraid that a second meeting, and that perhaps not before witnesses, would prove mischievous. I made up my mind to speak to Mary on the subject as soon as I had an opportunity, and insist upon her not making a fool of the worthy old man. Mary remained below a much longer time than was necessary, and when she re-appeared and looked at me, as if for a smile of approval, I turned from her with a contemptuous air. She sat down, and looked confused. Tom was also silent, and paid her no attention. A quarter of an hour passed, when he proposed to his father that they should be off, and the party broke up. Leaving Mary silent and thoughtful, and old Stapleton finishing his pipe, I took my candle and went to bed. The next day the moon changed, the weather changed, and a rapid thaw took place. "It's an ill wind that blows nobody good," observed old

Stapleton; "we watermen will have the river to ourselves again, and the hucksters must carry their gingerbread-nuts to another market." It was, however, three or four days before the river was clear of the ice, so as to permit the navigation to proceed; and during that time, I may as well observe, that there was dissension between Mary and me. I showed her that I resented her conduct, and at first she tried to pacify me; but finding that I held out longer than she expected, she turned round, and was affronted in return. Short words and no lessons were the order of the day; and as each party seemed determined to hold out, there was little prospect of a reconciliation. In this she was the greatest sufferer, as I quitted the house after breakfast, and did not return until dinner time. At first old Stapleton plied very regularly, and took all the fares; but about a fortnight after we had worked together, he used to leave me to look after employment, and remain at the public-house. The weather was now fine, and, after the severe frost, it changed so rapidly that most of the trees were in leaf, and the horse-chestnuts in full blossom. The wherry was in constant demand, and every evening I handed from four to six shillings over to old Stapleton. I was delighted with my life, and should have been perfectly happy if it had not been for my quarrel with Mary still continuing, she as resolutely refraining from making advances as I. How much may life be embittered by dissension with those you live with, even when there is no very warm attachment; the constant grating together worries and annoys, and although you may despise the atoms, the aggregate becomes insupportable. I had no pleasure in the house; and the evenings, which formerly passed so agreeably, were now a source of vexation, from being forced to sit in company with one with whom I was not on good terms. Old Stapleton was seldom at home till late, and this made it still worse. I was communing with myself one night, as I had my eyes fixed on my book, whether I should make the first advances, when Mary, who had been quietly at work, broke the silence by asking me what I was reading. I replied in a quiet tone.

"Jacob," said she, in continuation, "I think you have used me very ill to humble me in this manner. It was your business to make it up first."

"I am not aware that I have been in the wrong," replied I.

"I do not say that you have; but what matter does that make? You ought to give way to a woman."

"Why so?"

"Why so! don't the whole world do so? Do you not offer everything first to a woman? Is it not her right?"

"Not when she is in the wrong, Mary."

"Yes, when she's in the wrong, Jacob; there's no merit in doing it when she's in the right."

"I think otherwise; at all events, it depends on how much she has been in the wrong, and I consider you have shown a bad heart, Mary."

"A bad heart! in what way, Jacob?"

"In realising the fable of the boys and the frogs with the poor old Dominie, forgetting that what may be sport to you is death to him."

"You don't mean to say that he'll die of love," replied Mary, laughing.

"I should hope not: but you may contrive, and you have tried all in your power, to make him very wretched."

"And, pray, how do you know that I do not like the old gentleman, Jacob? You appear to think that a girl is to fall in love with nobody but yourself. Why should I not love an old man with so much learning? I have been told that old husbands are much prouder of their wives than young ones, and pay them more attention, and don't run after other women. How do you know that I am not serious?"

"Because I know your character, Mary, and am not to be deceived. If you mean to defend yourself in that way, we had better not talk any more."

"Lord, how savage you are! then, suppose I did pay the old gentleman any attention. Did the young ones pay me any? Did either you, or your precious friend, Mr Tom, even speak to me?"

"No; we saw how you were employed, and we both hate a jilt."

"Oh, you do. Very well, sir; just as you please. I may make both your hearts ache for this some day or another."

"Forewarned, forearmed, Mary; and I shall take care that they are both forewarned as well as myself. As I perceive that you are so decided, I shall say no more. Only, for your own sake, and your own happiness, I caution you. Recollect your mother, Mary, and recollect your mother's death."

Mary covered her face and burst into tears. She sobbed for a few minutes, and then came to me. "You are right, Jacob; and I am a foolish—perhaps wicked—girl; but forgive me, and indeed I will try to behave better. But, as father says, it is human nature in me, and it's hard to conquer our natures, Jacob."

"Will you promise me not to continue your advances to the Dominie, Mary?"

"I will not, if I can help it, Jacob. I may forget for the moment, but I'll do all I can. It's not very easy to look grave when one is merry, or sour when one is pleased."

"But what can induce you, Mary, to practise upon an old man like him? If it were young Tom, I could understand it. There might be some credit, and your pride might be flattered by the victory; but an old man—"

"Still, Jacob, old or young, it's much the same. I would like to have them all at my feet, and that's the truth. I can't help it. And I thought it a great victory to bring there a wise old man, who was so full of Latin and learning, and who ought to know better. Tell me Jacob, if old men a how themselves to be caught, as well as young, where is the crime of catching them? Isn't there as much vanity in an old man, in his supposing that I really could love him, as there is in me, who am but a young, foolish girl, in trying to make him fond of me?"

"That may be; but still recollect that he is in earnest, and you are only joking, which makes a great difference; and recollect further, that in trying at all, we very often lose all."

"That I would take my chance of, Jacob," replied Mary, proudly throwing her curly ringlets back with her hand from her white forehead; "but what I now want is to make friends with you. Come, Jacob, you have my promise to do my best."

"Yes, Mary, and I believe you, so there's my hand."

"You don't know how miserable I have been, Jacob, since we quarrelled," said Mary, wiping the tears away, which again commenced flowing; "and yet I don't know why, for I'm sure I have almost hated you this last week—that I have; but the fact is, I like quarrelling very well for the pleasure of making it up again; but not for the quarrel to last so long as this has done."

"It has annoyed me too, Mary, for I like you very much in general."

"Well, then, now it's all over; but Jacob, are you sure you are friends with me?"

"Yes, Mary."

Mary looked archly at me. "You know the old saw, and I feel the truth of it."

"What, 'kiss and make friends?'" replied I; "with all my heart," and I kissed her, without any resistance on her part.

"No, I didn't mean that, Jacob."

"What then?"

"Oh! 'twas another."

"Well, then, what was the other?"

"Never mind, I forget it now," said she laughing, and rising from the chair. "Now, I must go to my work again, and you must tell me what you've been doing this last fortnight."

Mary and I entered into a long and amicable conversation till her father came home, when we retired to bed. "I think," said old Stapleton, the next morning, "that I've had work enough; and I've belonged to two benefit clubs for so long as to 'title me to an allowance. I think, Jacob, I shall give up the wherry to you, and you shall in future give me one-third of your earnings, and keep the rest to yourself. I don't see why you're to work hard all day for nothing." I remonstrated against this excess of liberality; but old Stapleton was positive, and the arrangement was made. I afterwards discovered, what may probably occur to the reader, that Captain Turnbull was at the bottom of all this. He had pensioned old Stapleton that I might become independent by my own exertions before I had served my apprenticeship; and after breakfast, old Stapleton walked down with me to the beach, and we launched the boat. "Recollect, Jacob," said he, "one-third, and honour bright;" so saying, he adjourned to his old quarters, the public-house, to smoke his pipe and think of human natur'. I do not recollect any day of my life on which I felt more happy than on this: I was working for myself, and independent. I jumped into my wherry, and, without waiting for a fare, I pushed off, and, gaining the stream, cleaved through the water with delight as my reward; but after a quarter of an hour I sobered down with the recollection that, although I might pull about for nothing for my own amusement, that as Stapleton was entitled to one-third, I had no right to neglect his interest; and I shot my wherry into the row, and stood with my hand and fore-finger raised, watching the eye of every one who came towards the hard. I was fortunate that day, and when I returned, was proceeding to give Stapleton his share, when he stopped me. "Jacob, it's no use dividing now; once a-week will be better. I likes things to come in a lump; cause, d'ye see—it's—it's—*human natur'*."

Chapter Twenty Seven

I consider that the present was the period from which I might date my first launching into human life. I was now nearly eighteen years old, strong, active, and well-made, full of spirits, and overjoyed at the independence which I had so much sighed for. Since the period of my dismissal from Mr Drummond's my character had much altered. I had become grave and silent, brooding over my wrongs, harbouring feelings of resentment against the parties, and viewing the world in general through a medium by no means favourable. I had become in some degree restored from this unwholesome state of mind from having rendered an important service to Captain Turnbull, for we love the world better as we feel that we are more useful in it; but the independence now given to me was the acme of my hopes and wishes. I felt so happy, so buoyant in mind, that I could even think of the two clerks in Mr Drummond's employ without feelings of revenge. Let it, however, be remembered that the world was all before me in anticipation only.

"Boat, sir?"

"No, thanky, my lad. I want old Stapleton—is he here?"

"No, sir, but this is his boat."

"Humph, can't he take me down?"

"No, sir; but I can, if you please."

"Well, then, be quick."

A sedate-looking gentleman, about forty-five years of age, stepped into the boat, and in a few seconds I was in the stream, shooting the bridge with the ebbing tide.

"What's the matter with deaf Stapleton?"

"Nothing, sir; but he's getting old, and has made the boat over to me."

"Are you his son?"

"No, sir, his 'prentice."

"Humph! sorry deaf Stapleton's gone."

"I can be as deaf as he, sir, if you wish it."

"Humph!"

The gentleman said no more at the time, and I pulled down the river in silence; but in a few minutes he began to move his hands up and down, and his lips, as if he was in conversation. Gradually his action increased, and words were uttered. At last he broke out:— "It is with this conviction, I may say important conviction, Mr Speaker, that I now deliver my sentiments to the Commons' house of Parliament, trusting that no honourable member will decide until he has fully weighed the importance of the arguments which I have submitted to his judgment." He then stopped, as if aware that I was present, and looked at me; but, prepared as I was, there was nothing in my countenance which exhibited the least sign of merriment; or, indeed, of having paid any attention to what he had been saying, for I looked carelessly to the right and left at the banks of the river. He again entered into conversation.

"Have you been long on the river?"

"Born on it, sir."

"How do you like the profession of a waterman?"

"Very well, sir; the great point is to have regular customers."

"And how do you gain them?"

"By holding my tongue; keeping their counsel and my own."

"Very good answer, my boy. People who have much to do cannot afford to loose even their time on the water. Just now I was preparing and thinking over my speech in the House of Commons."

"So I supposed, sir, and I think the river is a very good place for it, as no one can overhear you except the person whose services you have hired— and you need not mind him."

"Very true, my lad; but that's why I liked deaf Stapleton: he could not hear a word."

"But sir, if you've no objection, I like to hear it very much; and you may be sure that I should never say anything about it, if you will trust me."

"Do you my lad? well, then I'll just try it over again. You shall be the speaker—mind you hold your tongue, and don't interrupt me."

The gentleman then began: "Mr Speaker, I should not have ventured to address the House at this late hour, did I not consider that the importance of the question now before it is—so important—no, that won't do—did I not consider that the question now before it is of that, I may say, paramount importance as to call forth the best energies of every man who is a well-wisher to his country. With this conviction, Mr Speaker, humble individual as I am, I feel it my duty, I may say, my bounden duty, to deliver my sentiments upon the subject. The papers which I now hold in my hand, Mr Speaker, and to which I shall soon have to call the attention of the House, will, I trust, fully establish—"

"I say, waterman, be you taking that chap to Bedlam?" cried a shrill female voice close to us. The speech was stopped; we looked up, and perceived a wherry with two females passing close to us. A shout of laughter followed the observation, and my fare looked very much confused.

I had often read the papers in the public-house, and remembering what was usual in the house in case of interruption, called out, "Order, order!" This made the gentleman laugh, and as the other wherry was now far off, he recommenced his oration, with which I shall not trouble my readers. It was a very fair speech, I have no doubt, but I forget what it was about.

I landed him at Westminster Bridge, and received treble my fare. "Recollect," said he, on paying me, "that I shall look out for you when I come again, which I do every Monday morning, and sometimes oftener. What's your name?"

"Jacob, sir."

"Very well; good morning, my lad."

This gentleman became a very regular and excellent customer, and we used to have a great deal of conversation, independent of debating, in the wherry; and I must acknowledge that I received from him not only plenty of money, but a great deal of valuable information.

A few days after this I had an opportunity of ascertaining how far Mary would keep her promise. I was plying at the river side as usual, when old Stapleton came up to me, with his pipe in his mouth, and said, "Jacob, there be that old gentleman up at our house with Mary. Now, I sees a great deal, but I says nothing. Mary will be her mother over again, that's sartain. Suppose you go and see your old teacher, and leave me to look a'ter a customer. I begin to feel as if handling the sculls a little would be of sarvice to me. We all think idleness be a very pleasant thing when we're obliged to work but when we are idle, then we feel that a little work be just as agreeable—that's human natur'."

I thought that Mary was very likely to forget all her good resolutions, from her ardent love of admiration, and I was determined to go and break up the conference. I, therefore, left the boat to Stapleton, and hastened to the house. I did not like to play the part of an eavesdropper, and was quite undecided how I should act; whether to go in at once or not, when, as I passed under the window, which was open, I heard very plainly the conversation that was going on. I stopped in the street, and listened to the Dominie in continuation—"But, fair maiden, *omnia vincit amor*—here am I, Dominie Dobbs, who have long passed the grand climacteric, and can already muster three score years—who have authority over seventy boys, being Magister Princeps et Dux of Brentford Grammar School—who have affectioned only the sciences, and communed only with the classics—who have ever turned a deaf ear to the allurements of thy sex, and ever hardened my heart to thy fascination—here am I, even I, Dominie Dobbs, suing at the feet of a maiden who had barely ripened into womanhood, who knoweth not to read or write, and whose father earns his bread by manual labour. I feel it all—I feel that I am too old—that thou art too young—that I am departing from the ways of wisdom, and am regardless of my worldly prospects. Still, *omnia vincit amor*, and I bow to the all-powerful god, doing him homage through thee, Mary. Vainly have I resisted—vainly have I, as I have lain in bed, tried to drive thee from my thoughts, and tear thine image from my heart. Have I not felt thy presence everywhere? Do not I astonish my worthy coadjutor, Mistress Bately, the matron, by calling her by the name of Mary, when I had always before addressed her by her baptismal name of Deborah? Nay, have not the boys in the classes discovered my weakness, and do they not shout out Mary in the hours of play? *Mare periculosum et turbidum* hast thou been to me. I sleep not—I eat not—and every sign of love which hath been adduced by Ovidius Naso, whom I have diligently collated, do I find in mine own person. Speak, then, maiden. I have given vent to my feelings, do thou the same, that I may return, and leave not my flock without their shepherd. Speak, maiden."

"I will, sir, if you will get up," replied Mary, who paused, and then continued. "I think, sir, that I am young and foolish, and you are old and—and—"

"Foolish, thou wouldst say."

"I had rather you said it, sir, than I; it is not for me to use such an expression towards one so learned as you are. I think, sir, that I am too young to marry; and that perhaps you are—too old. I think, sir, that you are too clever—and that I am very ignorant; that it would not suit you in your situation to marry; and that it would not suit me to marry you—equally obliged to you all the same."

"Perhaps thou hast in thy reply proved the wiser of the two," answered the Dominie; "but why, maiden, didst thou raise those feelings, those hopes in my breast, only to cause me pain, and make me drink deep of the cup of disappointment? didst thou appear to cling to me in fondness, if thou felt not a yearning towards me?"

"But are there no other sorts of love besides the one you would require, sir? May I not love you because you are so clever, and so learned in Latin. May I not love you as I do my father?"

"True, true, child; it is all my own folly, and I must retrace my steps in sorrow. I have been deceived—but I have been deceived only by myself. My wishes have clouded my understanding, and have obscured my reason; have made me forgetful of my advanced years, and of the little favour I was likely to find in the eyes of a young maiden. I have fallen into a pit through blindness, and I must extricate myself, sore as will be the task. Bless thee, maiden, bless thee! May another be happy in thy love, and never feel the barb of disappointment. I will pray for thee, Mary—that Heaven may bless thee." And the Dominie turned away and wept.

Mary appeared to be moved by the good old man's affliction, and her heart probably smote her for her coquettish behaviour. She attempted to console the Dominie, and appeared to be more than half crying herself. "No, sir, do not take on so, you make me feel very uncomfortable. I have been wrong—I feel I have—though you have not blamed me, I am a very foolish girl."

"Bless thee, child—bless thee!" replied the Dominie, in a subdued voice.

"Indeed, sir, I don't deserve it—I feel I do not; but pray do not grieve, sir; things will go cross in love. Now, sir, I'll tell you a secret, to prove it to you. I love Jacob—love him very much, and he does not care for me—I am sure he does not; so, you sir, you are not the only one—who is—very unhappy;" and Mary commenced sobbing with the Dominie.

"Poor thing!" said the Dominie; "and thou lovest Jacob? truly is he worthy of thy love. And, at thy early age, thou knowest what it is to have thy love unrequited. Truly is this a vale of tears—yet let us be thankful. Guard well thy heart, child, for Jacob may not be for thee; nay I feel that he will not be."

"And why so, sir?" replied Mary, despondingly.

"Because, maiden—but nay, I must not tell thee; only take my warning, Mary—fare thee well? I come not here again."

"Good-bye, sir, and pray forgive me; this will be a warning to me."

"Verily, maiden, it will be a warning to us both. God bless thee!"

I discovered by the sound that Mary had vouchsafed to the Dominie a kiss, and heard soon afterwards his steps as he descended the stairs. Not wishing to meet him I turned round the corner, and went down to the river, thinking over what had passed. I felt pleased with Mary, but I was not in love with her.

The spring was now far advanced, and the weather was delightful. The river was beautiful, and parties of pleasure were constantly to be seen floating up and down with the tide. The Westminster boys, the Funny Club, and other amateurs in their fancy dresses, enlivened the scene; while the races for prize wherries, which occasionally took place, rendered the water one mass of life and motion. How I longed for my apprenticeship to be over, that I might try for a prize! One of my best customers was a young man, who was an actor at one of the theatres, who, like the M.P., used to rehearse the whole time he was in the boat; but he was a lively, noisy personage, full of humour, and perfectly indifferent as to appearances. He had a quiz and a quirk for everybody that passed in another boat, and would stand up and rant at them until they considered him insane. We were on very intimate terms, and I was never more pleased than when he made his appearance, as it was invariably the signal for mirth. The first time I certainly considered him to be a lunatic, for playhouse phraseology was quite new to me. "Boat, sir," cried I to him as he came to the hard.

"My affairs do even drag me homeward. Go on; I'll follow thee," replied he, leaping into the boat. "Our fortune lies in this jump."

I shoved off the wherry: "Down, sir?"

"Down," replied he; pointing downwards with his finger, as if pushing at something.

"Down, down to hell, and say I sent you there."

"Thanky, sir, I'd rather not, if it's all the same to you."

"Our tongue is rough, coz—and my condition is not smooth." We shot the bridge, and went rapidly down with the tide, when he again commenced:—

"Thus with imagin'd wing our soft scene flies,
In motion of no less celerity
Than that of thought."

Then his attention was drawn by a collier's boat, pulled by two men as black as chimney-sweeps, with three women in the stern-sheets. They made for the centre of the river, to get into the strength of the tide, and were soon abreast and close to the wherry, pulling with us down the stream.

"There's a dandy young man," said one of the women, with an old straw bonnet and very dirty ribbons, laughing, and pointing to my man.

> "Plead you to me, fair dame? I know you not;
> At Ephesus I am but two hours old,
> As strange unto your town as to your talk."

"Well, he be a reg'lar rum cove, I've a notion," said another of the women, when she witnessed the theatrical airs of the speaker, who immediately recommenced—

> "The barge she sat in, like a burnish'd throne,
> Burn'd on the water—the poop was beaten gold,
> Purple the sails, and so perfumed that
> The winds were love-sick with them; the oars were silver,
> Which to the tunes of flutes kept stroke, and made
> The water, which they beat, to follow faster,
> As amorous of their strokes. For her own person,
> It beggar'd all description."

"Come, I'll be blowed but we've had enough of that, so just shut your pan," said one of the women, angrily.

> "Her gentlewomen, like the Naiades,
> So many mermaids tend her."

"Mind what you're arter, or your mouth will tend to your mischief, young fellow."

> "From the barge
> A strange, invisible perfume hits the sense
> Of the adjacent wharfs."

"Jem, just run him alongside, and break his head with your oar."

"I thinks as how I will, if he don't mend his manners."

> "I saw her once
> Hop forty paces through the public streets."

"You lie, you liver-faced rascal. I never walked the streets in my life. I'm a lawful married woman. Jem, do you call yourself a man, and stand this here?"

"Well, now, Sal, but he's a nice young man. Now an't he?" observed one of the other women.

> "Away,
> Away, you trifler. Love! I know thee not,

I care not for thee, Kate: this is no world
To play with mammets, and to tilt with lips;
We must have bloody noses and cracked crowns."

"I've a notion you will, too, my hearty," interrupted one of the colliers. "That 'ere long tongue of yours will bring you into disgrace. Bill, give her a jerk towards the wherry, and we'll duck him."

"My friend," said the actor, addressing me:—

"Let not his unwholesome corpse come between the wind
And my nobility.

"Let us exeunt, OP."

Although I could not understand his phrases, I knew very well what he meant, and pulling smartly, I shoved towards the shore, and ahead. Perceiving this, the men in the boat, at the intimation of the women, who stood up waving their bonnets, gave chase to us, and my companion appeared not a little alarmed. However, by great exertion on my part, we gained considerably, and they abandoned the pursuit.

"Now, by two-headed Janus," said my companion, as he looked back upon the colliers—

"Nature hath framed strange fellows in her time,
Some that will evermore peep through their eyes,
And laugh like parrots at a bagpiper,
And others of such a vinegar aspect
That they'll not show their teeth by way of smile,
Though Nestor swear the jest be laughable.

"And now," continued he, addressing me, "what's your name, sir? Of what condition are you—and of what place, I pray?"

Amused with what had passed, I replied, "That my name was Jacob—that I was a waterman, and born on the river."

"I find thee apt; but tell me, art thou perfect that our ship hath touched upon the deserts of Bohemia?"

"Do you land at Westminster, sir?"

"No: at Blackfriars—there attend my coming.

"Base is the slave who pays; nevertheless, what is your fare, my lad?

"What money's in my purse? Seven groats and twopence.

"By Jove, I am not covetous of gold,
Nor care I who doth feed upon my cost.

"But—

"I can get no remedy for this consumption of the purse.

"Here my lad—is that enough?"

"Yes, sir, I thank you."

"Remember poor Jack, sir," said the usual attendant at the landing place, catching his arm as he careened the wherry on getting out.

"If he fall in, good-night—or sink or swim.

"Jack, there is a penny for you. Jacob, farewell—we meet again;" and away he went, taking three of the stone steps at each spring. This gentleman's name was, as I afterwards found out, Tinfoil, an actor of second-rate merit on the London boards. The Haymarket Theatre was where he principally performed, and, as we became better acquainted, he offered to procure me orders to see the play when I should wish to go there.

Chapter Twenty Eight

One morning he came down to the hard, and, as usual, I expected that he would go down the river. I ran to my boat, and hauled in close.

"No, Jacob, no; this day you will not carry Caesar and his fortunes, but I have an order for you."

"Thank you; sir; what is the play?"

"The play—pooh! no play; but I hope it will prove a farce, nevertheless, before it's over. We are to have a pic-nic party upon one of those little islands up the river by Kew. All sock and buskin, all theatricals: if the wherries upset, the Hay-market may shut up, for it will be '*exeunt omnes*' with all its best performers. Look you, Jacob, we shall want three wherries, and I leave you to pick out the other two—oars in each, of course. You must be at Whitehall steps exactly at nine o'clock, and I daresay the ladies won't make you wait more than an hour or two, which, for them, is tolerably punctual."

Mr Tinfoil then entered into the arrangement for remuneration, and walked away; and I was conning over in my mind whom I should select from my brother watermen, and whether I should ask old Stapleton to take the other oar in my boat, when I heard a voice never to be mistaken by me—

"Life is like a summer day
Warmed by a sunny ray.

"Lower away yet, Tom. That'll do, my trump.

"Sometimes a dreary cloud,
Chill blast, or tempest loud.

"Look out for Jacob, Tom," cried the old man, as the head of the lighter, with her mast lowered down, made its appearance through the arch of Putney Bridge, with bright blue streaks on her sides.

"Here he is, father," replied Tom, who was standing forward by the windlass, with the fall in his hand.

I had shoved off, on hearing old Tom's voice, and was alongside almost as soon as the lighter had passed under the bridge, and discovered old Tom at the helm. I sprang on the deck, with the chain-painter of the wherry in my hand, made it fast, and went aft to old Tom, who seized my hand.

"This is as it should be, my boy, both on the look-out for each other. The heart warms when we know the feeling is on both sides. You're seldom out of our thoughts, boy, and always in our hearts. Now, jump forward, for Tom's fretting to greet you, I see, and you may just as well help him to sway up the mast when you are there."

I went forward, shook hands with Tom, and then clapped on the fall, and assisted him to hoist the mast. We then went aft to his father and communicated everything of interest which had passed since our last meeting at the house of old Stapleton.

"And how's Mary?" inquired Tom; "she's a very fine lass, and I've thought of her more than once; but I saw that all you said about her was true. How she did flam the poor old Dominie!"

"I have had a few words with her about it, and she has promised to be wiser," replied I; "but as her father says, 'in her it's human natur'.'"

"She's a fine craft," observed old Tom, "and they always be a little ticklish. But, Jacob, you've had some inquiries made after you, and by the women, too."

"Indeed!" replied I.

"Yes; and I have had the honour of being sent for into the parlour. Do you guess now?"

"Yes," said I, a gloom coming over my countenance. "I presume it is Drummond and Sarah whom you refer to?"

"Exactly."

Tom then informed me that Mrs Drummond had sent for him, and asked a great many questions about me, and desired him to say that they were very glad to hear that I was well and comfortable, and hoped that I would call and see her and Sarah when I came that way. Mrs Drummond then left the room, and Tom was alone with Sarah, who desired him to say, that her father had found out that I had not been wrong; that he had dismissed both the clerks; and that he was very sorry he had been so deceived—"and then," said Tom, "Miss Sarah told me to say from herself, that she had been very unhappy since you had left them, but that she hoped that you would forgive and forget some day or another, and come back to them; and that I was to give you her love, and call next time we went up the river for something that she wanted to send to you. So you perceive, Jacob, that you are not forgotten, and justice has been done to you."

"Yes," replied I, "but it has been too late; so let us say no more about it. I am quite happy as I am."

I then told them of the pic-nic party of the next day, upon which Tom volunteered to take the other oar in my boat, as he would not be wanted while the barge was at the wharf. Old Tom gave his consent, and it was agreed he should meet me next morning at daylight.

"I've a notion there'll be some fun, Jacob," said he, "from what you say."

"I think so, too; but you've towed me two miles, and I must be off again, or I shall lose my dinner; so good-bye;" I selected two other wherries in the course of the afternoon, and then returned home.

It was a lovely morning when Tom and I washed out the boat, and, having dressed ourselves in our neatest clothes, we shoved off in company with the two other wherries, and dropped leisurely down the river with the last of the ebb. When we pulled in to the stairs at Whitehall, we found two men waiting for us with three or four hampers, some baskets, an iron saucepan, a frying-pan, and a large tin pail with a cover, full of rough ice to cool the wines. We were directed to put all these articles into one boat; the others to be reserved for the company.

"Jacob," said Tom, "don't let us be kitchen; I'm togged out for the parlour."

This point had just been arranged, and the articles put into the wherry, when the party made their appearance, Mr Tinfoil acting as master of the ceremonies.

"Fair Titania," said he to the lady who appeared to demand, and therefore received, the most attention, "allow me to hand you to your throne."

"Many thanks, good Puck," replied the lady; "we are well placed; but dear me, we haven't brought, or we have lost, our vinaigrette; we positively cannot go without it. What can our women have been about?"

"Pease-blossom and Mustard-seed are much to blame," replied Tinfoil; "but shall I run back for it?"

"Yes," replied the lady, "and be here again ere the leviathan can swim a league."

"I'll put a girdle round the earth in forty minutes," replied the gentleman, stepping out of the boat.

"Won't you be a little out of breath before you come back, sir?" said Tom, joining the conversation.

This remark, far from giving offence, was followed by a general laugh. Before Mr Tinfoil was out of sight, the lost vinaigrette was dropped out of the lady's handkerchief; he was therefore recalled; and the whole of the party being arranged in the two boats, we shoved off; the third boat, in which the provender had been stowed, followed us, and was occupied by the two attendants, a call-boy and scene-shifter, who were addressed by Tinfoil as Caliban and Stephano.

"Is all our company here?" said a pert-looking, little pug-nosed man, who had taken upon himself the part of Quince the carpenter, in the Midsummer Night's Dream. "You, Nick Bottom," continued he, addressing another, "are set down for Pyramus."

The party addressed did not, however, appear to enter into the humour. He was a heavy-made, rather corpulent, white-faced personage, dressed in white jean trousers, white waistcoat, brown coat, and white hat. Whether anything had put him out of humour I know not, but it is evident that he was the butt of the ladies and of most of the party.

"I'll just thank you," replied this personage, whose real name was Winterbottom, "to be quiet, Mr Western, for I shan't stand any of your nonsense."

"Oh, Mr Winterbottom, surely you are not about to sow the seeds of discord so early. Look at the scene before you—hear how the birds are singing, how merrily the sun shines and how beautifully the water sparkles! Who can be cross on such a morning as this?"

"No, miss," replied Mr Winterbottom, "not at all—not at all—only my name's Winterbottom, and not Bottom. I don't wear an ass's head to please anybody—that's all. I won't be *bottom*—that's *flat*."

"That depends upon circumstances, sir," observed Tom.

"What business have you to shove your oar in, Mr Waterman?"

"I was hired for the purpose," replied Tom, dipping his oar in the water, and giving a hearty stroke.

"Stick to your own element, then—shove your oar into the water, but not into our discourse."

"Well, sir, I won't say another word, if you don't like it."

"But you may to me," said Titania, laughing, "whenever you please."

"And to me too," said Tinfoil, who was amused with Tom's replies.

Mr Winterbottom became very wroth, and demanded to be put on shore directly, but the Fairy Queen ordered us to obey him at our peril, and Mr Winterbottom was carried up the river very much against his inclination.

"Our friend is not himself," said Mr Tinfoil, producing a key bugle; "but—

> "Music hath charms to soothe the savage breast,
> To soften rocks, and rend the knotted oak.

"And, therefore, will we try the effect of it upon his senses." Mr Tinfoil then played the air in "Midas":—

> "Pray, Goody, please to moderate," etcetera.

During which Mr Winterbottom looked more sulky than ever. As soon as the air was finished, another of the party responded with his flute, from the other boat—while Mr Quince played what he called base, by snapping his fingers. The sounds of the instruments floated along the flowing and smooth water, reaching the ears and attracting the attention of many who, for a time, rested from their labour, or hung listlessly over the gunnels of the vessels, watching the boats, and listening to the harmony. All was mirth and gaiety—the wherries kept close to each other, and between the airs the parties kept up a lively and witty conversation, occasionally venting their admiration upon the verdure of the sloping lawns and feathering trees with which the banks of the noble river are so beautifully adorned; even Mr Winterbottom had partially recovered his serenity, when he was again irritated by a remark of Quince, who addressed him.

"You can play no part but Pyramus; for Pyramus is a sweet-faced man—a proper man as one shall see on a summer's day; a most lovely, gentleman-like man; therefore, you must needs play Pyramus."

"Take care I don't play the devil with your physiognomy, Mr Western," retorted Winterbottom.

Here Caliban, in the third boat, began playing the fiddle and singing to it—

> "Gaffer, Gaffer's son, and his little jackass,
> Were trotting along the road."

The chorus of which ditty was "Ee-aw, Ee-aw!" like the braying of a jackass.

"Bless thee, Bottom, bless thee; thou art translated," cried Quince, looking at Winterbottom.

"Very well—very well, Mr Western. I don't want to upset the wherry, and therefore you're safe at present, but the reckoning will come—so I give you warning."

"Slaves of my lamp, do my bidding. I will have no quarrelling here. You, Quince, shut your mouth; you, Winterbottom, draw in your lips, and I, your queen, will charm you with a song," said Titania, waving her little hand. The fiddler ceased playing, and the voice of the fair actress rivetted all our attention.

> "Wilt thou waken, bride of May,
> While flowers are fresh, and sweet bells chime,
> Listen and learn from my roundelay
> How all life's pilot boats sailed one day
>   A match with Time!
>
> "Love sat on a lotus-leaf aloft,
> And saw old Time in his loaded boat,
> Slowly he crossed Life's narrow tide,
> While Love sat clapping his wings, and cried,
>   'Who will pass Time?'
>
> "Patience came first, but soon was gone,
> With helm and sail to help Time on;
> Care and Grief could not lend an oar,
> And Prudence said (while he staid on shore),
>   'I wait for Time.'
>
> "Hope filled with flowers her cork-tree bark,
> And lighted its helm with a glow-worm's spark;
> Then Love, when he saw his bark fly past,
> Said, 'Lingering Time will soon be passed,
>   Hope outspeeds time.'
>
> "Wit went nearest Old Time to pass,
> With his diamond oar and boat of glass
> A feathery dart from his store he drew,
> And shouted, while far and swift it flew,
>   'O Mirth kills Time!'
>
> "But Time sent the feathery arrow back,
> Hope's boat of Amaranthus miss'd its track;
> Then Love bade its butterfly pilots move,
> And laughing, said 'They shall see how Love
>   Can conquer Time.'"

I need hardly say that the song was rapturously applauded, and most deservedly so. Several others were demanded from the ladies and gentlemen of the party, and given without hesitation; but I cannot now recall them to my memory. The bugle and flute played between whiles, and all was laughter and merriment.

"There's a sweet place," said Tinfoil, pointing to a villa on the Thames; "Now, with the fair Titania and ten thousand a-year, one could there live happy."

"I'm afraid the fair Titania must go to market without the latter encumbrance," replied the lady; "The gentleman must find the ten thousand a-year, and I must bring as my dowry—"

"Ten thousand charms," interrupted Tinfoil—"that's most true, and pity 'tis 'tis true. Did your fairyship ever hear my epigram on the subject?

> "Let the lads of the East love the maids of *Cash-meer*,
> Nor affection with interests clash;
> Far other idolatry pleases us here,
> We adore but the maids of *Mere Cash*."

"Excellent, good Puck! Have you any more?"

"Not of my own, but you have heard what Winterbottom wrote under the bust of Shakespeare last Jubilee?"

"I knew not that Apollo had ever visited him."

"You shall hear:—

> "In *this here* place the bones of Shakespeare lie,
> But *that ere* form of his shall never die;
> A *speedy end and soon* this world may have,
> But Shakespeare's name shall *bloom* beyond the grave."

"I'll trouble you, Mr Tinfoil, not to be so very witty at my expense," growled out Winterbottom. "I never wrote a line of poetry in my life."

"No one said you did, Winterbottom; but you won't deny that you wrote those lines."

Mr Winterbottom disdained a reply. Gaily did we pass the variegated banks of the river, swept up with a strong flood-tide, and at last arrived at a little island agreed upon as the site of the pic-nic. The company disembarked, and were busy looking for a convenient spot for their entertainment, Quince making a rapid escape from Winterbottom, the latter remaining on the bank. "Jenkins," said he to the man christened Caliban, "you did not forget the salad?"

"No, sir, I brought it myself. It's on the top of the little hamper."

Mr Winterbottom, who, it appears, was extremely partial to salad, was satisfied with the reply, and walked slowly away.

"Well," said Tom to me, wiping the perspiration from his brow with his handkerchief, "I wouldn't have missed this for anything. I only wish father had been here. I hope that young lady will sing again before we part."

"I think it very likely, and that the fun is only begun," replied I. "But come, let's lend a hand to get the prog out of the boat."

"Pat! pat! and here's a marvellous convenient place for our rehearsal. This green plot shall be our stage," cried Quince, addressing the others of the party.

The locality was approved of, and now all were busy in preparation. The hampers were unpacked, and cold meats, poultry, pies of various kinds, pastry, etcetera, appeared in abundance.

"This is no manager's feast," said Tinfoil; "the fowls are not made of wood, nor is small beer substituted for wine. Don Juan's banquet to the Commendador is a farce to it."

"All the manager's stage banquets are farces, and very sorry jokes into the bargain," replied another.

"I wish old Morris had to eat his own suppers."

"He must get a new set of teeth, or they'll prove a *deal* too tough."

"Hiss! turn him out! he's made a *pun*."

The hampers were now empty; some laid the cloth upon the grass, and arranged the plates, and knives and forks. The ladies were as busy as the gentlemen—some were wiping the glasses, others putting salt into the salt-cellars. Titania was preparing the salad. Mr Winterbottom, who was doing nothing, accosted her; "May I beg as a favour that you do not cut the salad too small? It loses much of its crispness."

"Why, what a Nebuchadnezzar you are! However, sir, you shall be obeyed."

"Who can fry fish?" cried Tinfoil. "Here are two pairs of soles and some eels. Where's Caliban?"

"Here I am, sir," replied the man on his knees, blowing up a fire which he had kindled. "I have got the soup to mind."

"Where's Stephano?"

"Cooling the wine, sir."

"Who, then, can fry fish, I ask?"

"I can, sir," replied Tom; "but not without butter."

"Butter shalt thou have, thou disturber of the element. Have we not *Hiren* here?"

"I wasn't *hired* as a cook, at all events," replied Tom: "but I'm rather a *dab* at it."

"Then shalt thou have the *place*," replied the actor.

"With all my heart and *soul*," cried Tom, taking out his knife, and commencing the necessary operation of skinning the fish.

In half-an-hour all was ready: the fair Titania did me the honour to seat herself upon my jacket, to ward off any damp from the ground. The other ladies had also taken their respective seats, as allotted by the mistress of the revels; the tables were covered by many of the good things of this life; the soup was ready in a tureen at one end, and Tom had just placed the fish on the table, while Mr Quince and Winterbottom, by the commands of Titania, were despatched for the wine and other varieties of potations. When they returned, eyeing one another askance, Winterbottom looking daggers at his opponent, and Quince not quite easy even under the protection of Titania, Tom had just removed the frying-pan from the fire with its residuary grease still bubbling. Quince having deposited his load, was about to sit down, when a freak came into Tom's head, which, however, he dared not put into execution himself; but "a nod is as good as a wink to a blind horse," says the proverb. Winterbottom stood before Tom, and Quince with his back to them. Tom looked at Winterbottom, pointing slily to the frying-pan, and then to the hinder parts of Quince. Winterbottom snatched the hint and the frying-pan at the same moment. Quince squatted himself down with a serge, as they say at sea, quoting at the time—"Marry, our play is the most lamentable comedy"—but putting his hands behind him, to soften his fall, they were received into the hot frying-pan, inserted behind him by Winterbottom.

"Oh, Lord! oh! oh!" shrieked Mr Quince, springing up like lightning, bounding in the air with the pain, his hands behind him still adhering to the frying-pan.

At the first scream of Mr Quince, the whole party had been terrified; the idea was that a snake had bitten him, and the greatest alarm prevailed; but when they perceived the cause of the disaster, even his expressions of pain could not prevent their mirth. It was too ludicrous. Still the gentlemen and ladies condoled with him, but Mr Quince was not to be reasoned with. He walked away to the river-side, Mr Winterbottom slily enjoying his revenge, for no one but Tom had an idea that it was anything but an accident. Mr Quince's party of pleasure was spoiled, but the others did not think it necessary that theirs should be also. A "really very sorry for poor Western," and a half-dozen "poor fellows!" intermingled with tittering, was all that his misfortunes called forth after his departure; and then they set to like French falconers. The soup was swallowed, the fish disappeared, joints were cut up, pies delivered up their hidden treasures, fowls were dismembered like rotten boroughs, corks were drawn, others flew without the trouble, and they did eat and were filled. Mr Winterbottom kept his eye upon the salad, his favourite condiment, mixed it himself, offered it to all, and was glad to find that no one would spare time to eat it; but Mr Winterbottom could eat for everybody, and he did eat. The fragments were cleared away, and handed over to us. We were very busy, doing as ample justice to them as the party had done before us, when Mr Winterbottom was observed to turn very pale, and appeared very uneasy.

"What's the matter?" inquired Mr Tinfoil.

"I'm—I'm not very well—I—I'm afraid something has disagreed with me. I'm very ill," exclaimed Mr Winterbottom, turning as white as a sheet, and screwing up his mouth.

"It must be the salad," said one of the ladies; "no one has eaten it but yourself, and we are all well."

"I—rather think—it must be—oh—I do recollect that I thought the oil had a queer taste."

"Why there was no oil in the castors," replied Tinfoil. "I desired Jenkins to get some."

"So did I, particularly," replied Winterbottom. "Oh!—oh, dear—oh, dear!"

"Jenkins," cried Tinfoil, "where did you get the oil for the castors? What oil did you get?—are you sure it was right?"

"Yes, sir, quite sure," replied Jenkins. "I brought it here in a bottle, and put it into the castors before dinner."

"Where did you buy it?"

"At the chemist's, sir. Here's the bottle;" and Jenkins produced a bottle with *castor* oil in large letters labelled on the side.

The murder was out. Mr Winterbottom groaned, rose from his seat, for he felt very sick indeed. The misfortunes of individuals generally add to the general quota of mirth, and Mr Winterbottom's misfortune had the same effect as that of Mr Quince. But where was poor Mr Quince all this time? He had sent for the iron kettle in which the soup had been warmed up, and filling it full of Thames water, had immersed the afflicted parts in the cooling element. There he sat with his hands plunged deep, when Mr Winterbottom made his appearance at the same spot and Mr Quince was comforted by witnessing the state of his enemy. Indeed, the sight of Winterbottom's distress did more to soothe Mr Quince's pain than all the Thames water in the world. He rose, and leaving Winterbottom, with his two hands to his head, leaning against a tree, joined the party, and pledged the ladies in succession, till he was more than half tipsy.

In the space of half-an-hour Mr Winterbottom returned, trembling and shivering as if he had been suffering under an ague. A bumper or two of brandy restored him, and before the day closed in, both Winterbottom and Quince, one applying stimulants to his stomach, and the other drowning his sense of pain in repeated libations, were in a state (to say the least of it) of incipient intoxication. But there is a time for all things, and it was time to return. The evening had passed freely; song had followed song. Tinfoil had tried his bugle, and played not a little out of tune; the flute also neglected the flats and sharps as of no consequence; the ladies thought the gentlemen rather too forward, and, in short, it was time to break up the party. The hampers were repacked, and handed half-empty, into the boat. Of wine there was a little left; and by the direction of Titania, the plates, dishes, etcetera, only were to be returned, and the fragments divided among the boatmen. The company re-embarked in high spirits, and we had the ebb-tide to return with. Just as we were shoving off, it was remembered that the ice-pail had been left under the tree, besides a basket with sundries. The other wherries had shoved off, and they were in consequence brought into our boat, in which we had the same company as before, with the exception of Mr Western, *alias* Quince, who preferred the boat which carried the hampers, that he might loll over the side, with his hands in the water. Mr Winterbottom soon showed the effects of the remedy he had taken against the effects of the castor oil. He was uproarious, and it was with difficulty that he could be persuaded to sit still in the boat, much to the alarm of Titania and the other ladies. He would make violent love to the fairy queen; and as he constantly shifted his position to address her and throw himself at her feet, there was some danger of the boat being upset. At last Tom proposed to him to sit on the pail before her, as then he could address her with safety; and Winterbottom staggered up to take the seat. As he was seating himself, Tom took off the cover, so that he was plunged into the half-liquid ice; but Mr Winterbottom was too drunk to perceive it. He continued to rant and to rave, and protest and vow, and even spout for some time, when suddenly the quantity of caloric extracted from him produced its effect.

"I—I—really believe that the night is damp—the dew falls—the seat is damp, fair Titania."

"It's only fancy, Mr Winterbottom," replied Titania who was delighted with his situation. "Jean trousers are cool in the evening; it's only an excuse to get away from me, and I never will speak again to you if you quit your seat."

"The fair Titania, the mistress of my soul, and body too, if she pleases—has—but to command—and her slave obeys."

"I rather think it is a little damp," said Tinfoil; "allow me to throw a little sand upon your seat;" and Tinfoil pulled out a large paper bag full of salt, which he strewed over the ice.

Winterbottom was satisfied, and remained; but by the time we had reached Vauxhall Bridge, the refrigeration had become so complete that he was fixed on the ice, which the application of the salt had made solid. He complained of cold, shivered, attempted to rise, but could not extricate himself; at last his teeth chattered, and he became almost sober; but he was helpless from the effects of the castor oil, his intermediate intoxication, and his present state of numbness. He spoke less and less; at last he was silent, and when we arrived at Whitehall stairs he was firmly fixed in the ice. When released he could not walk, and he was sent home in a hackney-coach.

"It was cruel to punish him so, Mr Tinfoil," said Titania.

"Cruel punishment! Why, yes; a sort of *impailment*," replied Mr Tinfoil, offering his arm.

The remainder of the party landed and walked home, followed by the two assistants, who took charge of the crockery; and thus ended the pic-nic party, which, as Tom said, was the very funniest day he had ever spent in his life.

Chapter Twenty Nine

It was on the Sunday after the picnic party, when, feeling I had neglected Captain Turnbull, and that he would think it unkind of me not to go near him, after having accompanied Mary to church, I set off on foot to his villa near Brentford. I rang at the porter's lodge, and asked whether he was at home.

"Yes, sir," replied the old woman at the lodge, who was very communicative, and very friendly with me; "and missus be at home too."

I walked up the carriage-drive of one hundred yards, which led to the entrance-door; and when I rang it was opened by a servant I had not seen before as belonging to the establishment. "Where is Mr Turnbull?" inquired I.

"He is in his own room, sir," replied the man; "but you must send up your name, if you please, as every one is not admitted."

I must observe to the reader that I was not dressed in jacket and trousers. The money I earned was more than sufficient to supply all my expenses, and I had fitted on what are called at sea, and on the river, *long togs*. I was dressed as most people are on shore. The servant evidently took me for a gentleman; and perhaps, as far as dress went, I was entitled to that distinction. Many people are received as such in this world with less claims than I had. I gave my name; the man left me at the door, and soon returned, requesting that I would follow him. I must say that I was rather astonished; where were Mr Mortimer and the two men in flaunting liveries, and long cotton epaulettes with things like little marline-spikes hanging to the ends of them? Even the livery was changed, being a plain brown coat, with light blue collar and cuffs. I was, however, soon made acquainted with what had taken place on my entering the apartment of Mr Turnbull—his study, as Mrs T called it, although Mr Turnbull insisted upon calling it his cabin, a name certainly more appropriate, as it contained but two small shelves of books, the remainder of the space being filled up with favourite harpoons, porpoise skulls, sharks' jaws, corals, several bears' skins, brown and white, and one or two models of the vessels which had belonged to his brother and himself, and which had been employed in the Greenland fishery. It was, in fact, a sort of museum of all he had collected during his voyages. Esquimaux implements, ornaments and dresses, were lying about in corners; and skins of rare animals, killed by himself, such as black foxes, etcetera, were scattered about the carpet. His sea-chest, full of various articles, was also one of the ornaments of the room, much to the annoyance of Mrs T, who had frequently exerted her influence to get rid of it, but in vain. The only articles of furniture were two sofas, a large table in the centre, and three or four heavy chairs. The only attempt at adornment consisted in a dozen coloured engravings, framed and glazed, of walrus shooting, etcetera, taken from the folio works of Captains Cook and Mulgrave; and a sketch or two by his brother, such as the state of the *William* pressed by an iceberg on the morning of the 25th of January, latitude —, longitude —.

Captain T was in his morning-gown, evidently not very well, at least he appeared harassed and pale. "My dear Jacob, this is very kind of you. I did mean to scold you for not coming before; but I'm too glad to see you to find the heart now. But why have you kept away so long?"

"I have really been very well employed, sir. Stapleton has given me up the wherry, and I could not neglect his interests, even if I did my own."

"Always right, boy; and how are you getting on?"

"I am very happy, sir; very happy, indeed."

"I'm glad to hear it, Jacob; may you always be so. Now, take the other sofa, and let us have a long palaver, as the Indians say. I have something to tell you. I suppose you observed a change—heh?"

"Yes, sir; I observed that Mr Mortimer was not visible."

"Exactly. Mr Mortimer, or John Snobbs, the rascal, is at present in Newgate for trial: and I mean to send him out on a voyage for the good of his health. I caught the scoundrel at last, and I'll show him no more mercy than I would to a shark that had taken the bait. But that's not all. We have had a regular mutiny and attempt to take the ship from me; but I have them all in irons, and ordered for punishment. Jacob, money is but too often a curse, depend upon it."

"You'll not find many of your opinion, sir," replied I, laughing.

"Perhaps not; because those who have it are content with the importance which it gives to them, and won't allow the damnable fact; and because those who have it not are always sighing after it, as if it were the only thing worth looking after in this world. But now, I will just tell you what has happened since I last saw you, and then you shall judge."

As, however, Captain T's narrative ran to a length of nearly three hours, I shall condense the matter for the information of the reader. It appeared that

Mrs T had continued to increase the lengths of her drives in her carriage, the number of her acquaintances, and her manifold expenses, until Mr T had remonstrated in very strong terms. His remonstrances did not, however, meet with the attention which he had expected; and he found out by accident, moreover, that the money with which he had constantly supplied Mrs T, to defray her weekly bills, had been otherwise appropriated; and that the bills for the two last quarters had none of them been paid. This produced an altercation, and a desire on his part to know in what manner these sums had been disbursed. At first the only reply from Mrs T, who considered it advisable to brazen it out, and, if possible, gain the ascendancy which was necessary, was a contemptuous toss of her head, which undulated the three yellow ostrich feathers in her bonnet, as she walked out of the room and entered her carriage. This, to Mr T, who was a matter-of-fact man, was not very satisfactory; he waited perforce until the carriage returned, and then demanded an explicit answer. Mrs T assumed the highest ground, talked about fashionable expenses, her knowledge of what was due to his character, etcetera. Mr T rejoined about necessary expenses, and that it was due to his character to pay his tradesmen's bills. Mrs T then talked of good-breeding, best society, and her *many plaisers*, as she termed them; Mr T did not know what *many pleasures* meant in French; but he thought she had been indulged in as many as most women since they had come down to this establishment. But to the question: why were not the bills paid, and what had she done with the money? Spent it in *pin money. Pin* money! thirty pounds a-week in *pins*! it would have bought harpoons enough for a three years' voyage. She must tell the truth. She wouldn't tell anything, but called for her salts, and called him a *brute*. At all events, he wouldn't be called a *fool*. He gave her till the next morning to consider of it. The next morning the bills were all sent in as requested, and amounted to six hundred pounds. They were paid and receipted. "Now, Mrs T, will you oblige me by letting me know what you have done with this six hundred pounds?" Mrs T would not—she was not to be treated in that manner. Mr T was not on board a whaler now, to bully and frighten as he pleased. She would have justice done her. Have a separation, alimony, and a divorce. She might have them all if she pleased, but she should have no more money; that was certain. Then she would have a fit of hysterics. So she did, and lay the whole of the day on the sofa, expecting Mr T would pick her up. But the idea never came into Mr T's head. He went to bed; and feeling restless, he rose very early, and saw from his window a cart drive up to the wall, and the parties who came with it leap over and enter the house, and return carrying to it two large hampers. He snatched up one of his harpoons, walked out the other way, and arrived at the cart just as the hampers had been put in, and they were about to drive off; challenged them, and instead of being answered, the horse was flogged, and he nearly run over. He then let fly his harpoon into the horse, which dropped, and pitched out the two men on their heads insensible; secured them, called to the lodge for assistance, sent for constables, and gave them in charge. They proved to be hampers forwarded by Mr Mortimer, who had been in the habit of so doing for some time. These hampers contained his best wine, and various other articles, which also proved that Mr Mortimer must have had false keys. Leaving the culprits and property in charge of two constables, Mr T returned to the house in company with the third constable; the door was opened by Mr Mortimer, who followed him into his study, told him he should leave the house directly, had always lived with *gentlemen* before, and requested that he might have what was due to him. Mr T thought the request but reasonable, and therefore gave him in charge of the constable. Mr Snobbs, rather confounded at such ungentlemanly behaviour, was, with the others, marched off to Bow Street. Mr T sends for the other two servants in livery, and assures them that he has no longer any occasion for their services, having the excessive vulgar idea that this peculation must have been known to them. Pays them their wages, requests they will take off their liveries, and leave the house. Both willing. *They* also had always lived with *gentlemen* before. Mr T takes the key of the butler's pantry, that the plate may not consider him too vulgar to remain in the house, and then walks to the stables. Horses neigh, as if to say they are all ready for their breakfasts; but the door locked. Hails the coachman, no answer. Returning from the stables, perceives coachee, rather dusty, coming in at the lodge gate; requests to know why he did not sleep at home and take care of his horses. He was missus's coachman, not master's, and could satisfy her, but could not satisfy Mr T; who paid him his wages's and, deducting his liveries, sent him after the others. Coachee also was very glad to go—had always lived with *gentlemen* before. Meets the lady's maid, who tells him Mrs T is much too ill to come down to breakfast. Rather fortunate, as there was no breakfast to be had. Dresses himself, gets into a pair-horse coach, arrives at the White Horse Cellar, swallows his breakfast, goes to Bow Street, commits Mr Mortimer, *alias* Snobbs, and his confederates for trial. Hires a job-man to bring the horses up for sale, and leaves his carriage at the coachmaker's. Obtains a temporary footman, and then Mr T returns to his villa. A very good morning's work. Finds Mrs T up in the parlour, very much surprised and shocked at his conduct—at no Mr Mortimer—at no servants, and indebted to her own maid for a cup of tea. More recriminations—more violence—another threat of alimony, and the carriage ordered, that she may seek counsel. No coachman—no carriage—no horses—no nothing, as her maid declares. Mrs T locks herself up in her room, and another day is passed with as little matrimonial comfort as can be expected.

In the meantime, the news flies in every direction. Brentford is full of it. Mr T had been living too fast—is done up—had been had up at Bow Street—creditors had poured in with bills—servants discharged—carriage and horses seized. Mrs T, poor creature, in hysterics, and nobody surprised at it; indeed, everybody expected it. The Peters of Petercumb Hall heard it, and shook their heads at the many upstarts there were in the world. Mr Smith requested the Right Honourable Lord Viscount Babbleton never to mention to his father the Right Honourable Marquis of Spring-guns, that he had ever been taken to see the Turnbulls or that he, Mr Smith, would infallibly lose his situation in *esse*, and his living in *posse*: and Monsieur and Madame Tagliabue were even more astounded; but they felt deeply, and resolved to pay a visit the next morning, at least Monsieur Tagliabue did, and Madame acknowledged to the propriety of it.

The next morning some little order had been restored; the footman hired had been given in charge of a sufficient quantity of plate, the rest had been locked up. The cook was to stay her month; the housemaid had no wish to leave; and as for the lady's maid, she would remain as long as she could to console her poor mistress, and accept what she was inclined to give her in return, in any way of clothes, dresses, etcetera, although, of course, she could not hurt her character by remaining too long in a family where there was no carriage, or gentlemen out of livery. Still Mr T did obtain some breakfast, and had just finished when Monsieur Tagliabue was announced, and was received.

"Ah! Monsieur T, I hope madame is better. Madame Tagliabue did nothing but cry all last night when she heard the very bad news about de debt, and all dat."

"Very much obliged to Madame," replied Turnbull, gruffly; "and now, pray sir, what may be your pleasure?"

"Ah! Monsieur Turnbull, I feel very much for you; but suppose a gentleman no lose his *honour*, what matter de money?" (Mr Turnbull stared.) "You see, Monsieur Turnbull, honour be everything to a gentleman. If a gentleman owe money to one rascally tradesfellow, and not pay him, dat no great matter; but he always pay de debt of honour. Every gentleman pay dat. Here, Monsieur Turnbull," (and the little Frenchman pulled out a piece of paper from his pocket), "be a leetle note of Madame Turnbull, which she gave to Madame Tagliabue, in which she acknowledged she owe two hundred pounds for money lost at *écarté*. Dat you see, Monsieur Turnbull, be what gentlemen call debt of honour, which every gentleman pay, or else he lose de character, and be called one blackguard by all the world. Madame Tagliabue and I too much fond of you and Madame Turnbull not to save your character, and so I come by her wish to beg you to settle this leetle note—this *leetle* debt of *honour;*" and Monsieur Tagliabue laid the note on the table, with a very polite bow.

Mr Turnbull examined the note; it was as described by Monsieur Tagliabue. So, thought he, now the whole story's out; she has been swindled out of her money by this rascally French couple. "Now, Monsieur Tagliabue," said he, "allow me to put a question or two before I pay this money; and if you answer me sincerely, I shall raise no objection. I think Mrs T has already lost about six hundred pounds at *écarté* before?" (Monsieur T, who presumed that Mrs Turnbull had made him acquainted with the fact, answered in the affirmative.) "And I think that two months ago she never knew what *écarté* was."

"Dat is true; but the ladies are very quick to learn."

"Well, but now, do you think that, as she knew nothing about the game, and you and your wife are well acquainted with it, it was honourable on your part to allow her to lose so much money!"

"Ah! Monsieur, when a lady say she will play *comment faire,* what can you do?"

"But why did you never play at this house, Monsieur?"

"Ah! Monsieur Turnbull, it is for de lady of de house to propose de game."

"Very true," replied Mr Turnbull, writing a cheque for the two hundred pounds; "there is your money, Mr Tagliabue; and now that you are paid, allow me to observe that I consider you and your wife a couple of swindlers; and beg that you will never enter my doors again."

"Vat you say, sir! *Swind-lare!* God dam! Sar, I will have satisfaction."

"You've got your money—is that sufficient, or do you want anything else?" replied Mr T, rising from his chair.

"Yes, sar, I do want more—I will have more."

"So you shall, then," replied Mr Turnbull, kicking him out of the room along the passage, and out of the front door.

Monsieur Tagliabue turned round every now and then, and threatened, and then tried to escape, as he perceived the upraised boot of Mr Turnbull. When fairly out of the house he turned round, "Monsieur Turnbull, I will have de satisfaction, de terrible satisfaction, for this. You shall pay. By God, sar, you shall pay—de money for this."

That evening Mr Turnbull was summoned to appear at Bow Street on the following morning for the assault. He met Monsieur Tagliabue with his lawyer, and acknowledged that he had kicked him out of his house for swindling his wife, refused all accommodation, and was prepared with his bail. Monsieur Tagliabue stormed and blustered, talked about his acquaintance with the nobility; but the magistrate had seen too much of foreigners to place much reliance on their asseverations. "Who are you, monsieur?"

"Sar, I am a gentleman."

"What profession are you of, sir?"

"Sar, a gentleman has no profession."

"But how do you live, Monsieur Tagliabue?"

"As a gentleman always does, sar."

"You mentioned Lord Scrope just now as your particular friend, I think?"

"Yes, sar, me very intimate with Lord Scrope; me spend three months at Scrope Castle with mi Lady Scrope; mi Lady Scrope very fond of Madame Tagliabue."

"Very well, Monsieur Tagliabue; we must proceed with another case until Mr Turnbull's bail arrives. Sit down for a little while, if you please."

Another case was then heard, which lasted about half-an-hour; but previous to hearing it, the magistrate, who knew that Lord Scrope was in town, had despatched a runner with a note to his lordship, and the answer was now brought back. The magistrate read it, and smiled; went on with the other case, and when it was finished, said, "Now, M. Tagliabue, you have said that you were intimate with Lord Scrope."

"Yes, sar, very intimate."

"Well, Lord Scrope I have the pleasure of knowing: and, as he is in town, I wrote a note to him and here is his answer. I will read it."

M. Tagliabue turned pale as the magistrate read the following:—

" *Dear Sir* —A fellow of the name you mention came from Russia with me as my valet. I discharged him with dishonesty; after he left, Lady Scrope's attendant, who it appeared was, unknown to us, married to him, left also, and then I discovered the peculations to have been so extensive that had we known where to have laid hold of him, I should certainly have brought them before you. Now the affair is forgotten; but a greater scoundrel never existed;—Yours, *Scrope*."

"Now, sir, what have you to say for yourself?" continued the magistrate in a severe tone. M. Tagliabue fell on his knees and begged for mercy from the magistrate, from Lord Scrope, and lastly, from Mr Turnbull, to whom he proffered the draft for 200 pounds. The magistrate, seeing that Mr Turnbull did not take it, said to him, "Make no ceremony of taking your money back again, Mr Turnbull; the very offer of it proves that he has gained it dishonestly; and 600 pounds is quite enough to have lost." Mr Turnbull then took the cheque and tore it in pieces, and the magistrate ordered M. Tagliabue to be taken to the alien office, and he was sent to the other side of the Channel, in company with his wife, to play *écarté* with whomsoever he pleased. Thus ended the episode of Monsieur Tagliabue.

Chapter Thirty

"And now you see, Jacob, what a revolution has taken place; not very pleasant, I grant, but still it was very necessary. I have since been paying all my bills, for the report of my being in difficulty has brought them in fast enough; and I find that in these last five months my wife has spent a whole year's income; so it was quite time to stop."

"I agree with you, sir; but what does Mrs Turnbull say now—has she come to her senses?"

"Pretty well, I expect, although she does not quite choose to acknowledge it. I have told her that she must dispense with a carriage in future; and so she shall, till I think she deserves it. She knows that she must either have *my company* in the house, or none at all. She knows that the Peters of Petercumb Hall have cut her, for they did not answer a note of hers, sent by the gardener; and Mr Smith has written a very violent answer to another of her notes, wondering at her attempting to push herself into the company of the aristocracy. But what has brought her to her senses more than all is the affair of Monsieur Tagliabue. The magistrate, at my request, gave me the note of Lord Scrope, and I have taken good care that she could read the police report as well; but the fact is, she is so much mortified that I say nothing to her. She has been following the advice of these French swindlers, who have led her wrong, to be able to cheat her of her money. I expect she will ask me to sell this place, and go elsewhere; but at present we hardly exchange a word during the whole day."

"I feel very sorry for her, sir; for I really believe her to be a very good kind-hearted person."

"That's like you, Jacob—and so she is. At present she is in a state to be pitied. She would throw a share of the blame upon other people, and cannot—she feels it is all herself. All her bubbles of grandeur have burst, and she finds herself not half so respectable as she was before her vanity induced her to cut her former acquaintance, and try to get into the society of those who laughed at her, and at the same time were not half so creditable. But it's that cursed money which has proved her unhappiness—and, I may add, mine."

"Well, sir, I see no chance of its ever adding to my misfortunes, at all events."

"Perhaps not, Jacob, even if you ever should get any; but, at all events, you may take a little to-morrow, if you please. I cannot ask you to dine here; it would not be pleasant to you, and show a want of feeling to my wife; but I should like you to come up with the wherry to-morrow, and we'll take a cruise."

"Very well, I shall be at your orders—at what time?"

"Say ten o'clock if the weather is fine; if not the next day."

"Then, sir, I'll now wish you good-bye, as I must go and see the Dominie."

Mr Turnbull took my hand, and we parted. I was soon at Brentford, and was continuing my course through the long, main street, when I met Mr and Mrs Tomkins, the former head clerk who had charge of the Brentford Wharf. "I was intending to call upon you, sir, after I had paid a visit to my old master."

"Very well, Jacob; and recollect we dine at half-past three—fillet of veal and bacon—don't be late for dinner."

I promised that I would not, and in a few minutes more arrived at the Grammar School. I looked at its peaked, antiquated front, and called to mind my feelings when, years back, I had first entered its porch. What a difference between the little uncouth, ignorant, savage, tricked out like a harlequin, and now the tall, athletic, well-dressed youth, happy in his independence, and conscious, although not vain, of his acquirements! and I mentally blessed the founders. But I had to talk to the Dominie, and to keep my appointment with the veal and bacon at half-past three, so I could not spare any time for meditation. I, therefore, unfolded my arms, and making use of my legs, entered the wicket, and proceeded to the Dominie's room. The door was ajar, and I entered without being perceived. I have often been reminded, by Flemish paintings which I have seen since, of the picture which then presented itself. The room was not large, but lofty. It had but one window, fitted with small diamond-shaped panes in heavy wood-work, through which poured a broad, but subdued, stream of light. On one side of the window was an ancient armoire, containing the Dominie's library, not gilt and lettered but well thumbed and worn. On the other his huge chest of drawers, on which lay, alas! for the benefit of the rising generations, a new birch rod, of large dimensions. The table was in the centre of the room, and the Dominie sat at it, with his back to the window, in a dressing-gown, once black, having been a cassock, but now brown with age. He was on his high and narrow-backed chair, leaning forwards, with both elbows on the table, his spectacles on his luxuriant nose, and his hands nearly meeting on the top of his bald crown, earnestly poring over the contents of a book. A large Bible, which he constantly made use of, was also on the table, and had apparently been shoved from him to give place to the present object of his meditations. His pipe lay on the floor in two pieces, having been thrown off without his perceiving it. On one side of him was a sheet of paper, on which he evidently had been writing extracts. I passed by him without his perceiving me, and gaining the back of his chair, looked over his shoulder. The work he was so intent upon was "Ovid's Remedy of Love."

It appeared that he had nearly finished reading through the whole, for in less than a minute he closed the book, and laying his spectacles down, threw himself back in his chair. "Strange," soliloquised the Dominie; "Yet, verily, is some of his advice important, and I should imagine commendable, yet I do not find my remedy therein. '*Avoid idleness*'—yes, that is sage counsel—and employment to one that hath not employed himself may drive away thought; but I have never been idle, and mine hath not been love in idleness; '*Avoid her presence*'—that I must do; yet doth she still present herself to mine imagination, and I doubt whether the tangible reality could be more clearly perceptible. Even now doth she stand before me in all her beauty. '*Read not Propertius and Tibullus*'—that is easily refrained from; but read what I will, in a minute the type passeth from my eyes, and I see but her face beaming from the page. Nay, cast my eyes in what direction I may wist, it is the same. If I looked at the stained wall, the indistinct lines gradually form themselves into her profile; if I look at the clouds, they will assume some of the redundant outlines of her form; if I cast mine eyes upon the fire in the kitchen-grate, the coals will glow and cool until I see her face; nay, but yesterday, the shoulder of mutton upon the spit gyrated until it at last assumed the decapitated head of Mary. '*Think of her faults and magnify them*'—nay, that were unjust and unchristian. Let me rather correct mine own. I fear me that when Ovid wrote his picture he intended it for the use of young men, and not for an old fool like me. Behold! I have again broken my pipe—the fourth pipe that I have destroyed this week. What will the dame say? already hath she declared me demented, and God knows she is not very far from the truth;" and the Dominie covered up his face in his hands. I took this opportunity to step to the door, and appear to enter it, dropping the latch, and rousing the Dominie by the noise, who extended to me his hand. "Welcome, my son—welcome to thine old preceptor; and to the walls which first received thee, when thou wert cast on shore as a tangle weed from the river. Sit, Jacob; I was thinking of thee and thine."

"What, sir? of old Stapleton and his daughter, I suppose."

"Even so; ye were all in my thoughts at the moment that thou madest thy appearance. They are well?"

"Yes, sir," replied I. "I see but little of them; the old man is always smoking, and as for the girl—why, the less one sees of her the better, I should say."

"Nay, Jacob, this is new to me; yet is she most pleasant."

I knew the Dominie's character, and that if anything could cure his unfortunate passion, it would be a supposition on his part that the girl was not correct. I determined at all events to depreciate her, as I knew that what I said would never be mentioned by him, and would therefore do her no harm. Still, I felt that I had to play a difficult game, as I was determined not to state what was not the fact. "Pleasant, sir; yes, pleasant to everybody; the fact is; I don't like such girls as she is."

"Indeed, Jacob; what, is she light?" I smiled and made no answer. "Yet I perceived it not," replied the Dominie.

"She is just like her mother," observed I.

"And what was her mother?"

I gave a brief account of her mother, and how she met her death in trying to escape from her husband. The Dominie mused. "Little skilled am I in women, Jacob, yet what thou sayest not only surpriseth but grieveth me. She is fair to look upon."

"Handsome is that handsome does, sir. She'll make many a man's heart ache yet, I expect."

"Indeed, Jacob. I am full of marvel at what thou hast already told me."

"I have seen more of her, sir."

"I pray thee tell me more."

"No, sir, I had rather not. You may imagine all you please."

"Still she is young, Jacob; when she becometh a wife she might alter."

"Sir, it is my firm opinion (and so it was), that if you were to marry her to-morrow, she would run away from you in a week."

"Is that thy candid opinion, Jacob?"

"I will stake my life upon her so doing, although not as to the exact time."

"Jacob, I thank thee—thank thee much; thou hast opened mine eyes—thou hast done me more good than Ovid. Yes, boy; even the ancients, whom I have venerated, have not done me so kind an act as thou, a stripling, whom I have fostered. Thou hast repaid me, Jacob—thou hast rewarded me, Jacob—thou hast protected me, Jacob—thou hast saved me, Jacob—hast saved me both from myself and from her; for know, Jacob—know—that mine heart did yearn towards that maiden; and I thought her even to be perfection. Jacob, I thank thee! Now leave me, Jacob, that I may commune with myself, and search out my own heart, for I am awakened—awakened as from a dream, and I would fain be quite alone."

I was not sorry to leave the Dominie, for I also felt that I would fain be in company with the fillet of veal and bacon, so I shook hands, and thus ended my second morning call. I was in good time at Mr Tomkins', who received me with great kindness. He was well pleased with his new situation, which was one of respectability and consequence, independently of profit; and I met at his table one or two people who, to my knowledge, would have considered it degrading to have visited him when only head clerk to Mr Drummond. We talked over old affairs, not forgetting the ball, and the illuminations, and Mr Turnbull's *bon mot* about Paradise; and after a very pleasant evening; I took my leave with the intention of walking back to Fulham, but I found old Tom waiting outside, on the look-out for me.

"Jacob, my boy, I want you to come down to my old shop one of these days. What day will you be able to come? The lighter will be here for a fortnight at least, I find from Mr Tomkins, as she waits for a cargo coming by canal, and there is no other craft expected above bridge, so tell me what day will you come and see the old woman, and spend the whole day with us. I wants to talk a bit with you, and ax your opinion about a good many little things."

"Indeed!" replied I, smiling. "What, are you going to build a new house?"

"No, no—not that; but you see, Jacob, as I told you last winter, it was time for me to give up night work up and down the river. I'm not so young as I was about fifty years ago, and there's a time for all things. I do mean to give up the craft in the autumn, and go on shore for a *full due*; but, at the same time, I must see how I can make matters out, so tell me what day you will come."

"Well, then, shall we say Wednesday?"

"Wednesday's as good a day as any other day; come to breakfast, and you shall go away after supper, if you like; if not, the old woman shall sling a hammock for you."

"Agreed, then; but where's Tom?"

"Tom, I don't know; but I think he's gone after that daughter of Stapleton's. He begins to think of the girls now, Jacob; but, as the old buffer, her father, says, 'it's all human natur'.' Howsomever, I never interferes in these matters: they seem to be pretty well matched, I think."

"How do you mean?"

"Why, as for good looks, they be well enough matched, that's sure; but I don't mean that, I mean, he is quite as knowing as she is, and will shift his helm as she shifts hers. 'Twill be a long running fight, and when one strikes, t'other won't have much to boast of. Perhaps they may sheer off after all— perhaps they may sail as consorts; God only knows; but this I knows, that Tom's sweetheart may be as tricky as she pleases, but Tom's wife won't be—'cause why? He'll keep her in order. Well, good-night; I have a long walk."

When I returned home I found Mary alone. "Has Tom been here?" inquired I.

"What makes you ask that question?" replied Mary.

"To have it answered—if you have no objection."

"Oh, no! Well, then, Mr Jacob, Tom has been here, and very amusing he has been."

"So he always is," replied I.

"And where may you have been?" I told her. "So you saw old Dominie. Now, tell me, what did he say about me?"

"That I shall not tell," replied I; "but I will tell you this, that he will not think about you any more; and you must not expect ever to see him again."

"But recollect that he promised."

"He kept his promise, Mary."

"Oh, he told you so, did he? Did he tell you all that passed?"

"No, Mary, he never told me that he had been here, neither did he tell me what had passed; but I happen to know all."

"I cannot understand that."

"Still, it is true; and I think, on the whole, you behaved pretty well, although I cannot understand why you gave him a kiss at parting."

"Good heaven! where were you? You must have been in the room. And you heard every word that passed?"

"Every word," replied I.

"Well," said Mary, "I could not have believed that you could have done so mean a thing."

"Mary, rather accuse your own imprudence; what I heard was to be heard by everyone in the street as well as by me. If you choose to have love scenes in a room not eight feet from the ground, with the window wide open, you must not be surprised at every passer-by hearing what you say."

"Well, that's true. I never thought of the window being open; not that I would have cared if all the world had heard me, if *you* had not."

It never occurred to me till then why Mary was annoyed at my having overheard her, but at once I recollected what she had said about me. I made no answer. Mary sat down, leaned her forehead against her hands, and was also silent. I, therefore, took my candle and retired. It appeared that Mary's pride was much mortified at my having heard her confession of being partial to me—a confession which certainly made very little impression on me, as I considered that she might, a month afterwards, confess the same relative to Tom, or any other individual who took her fancy; but in this I did not do her justice. Her manners were afterwards much changed towards me; she always appeared to avoid, rather than to seek, further intimacy. As for myself, I continued, as before, very good friends, kind towards her, but nothing more. The next morning I was up at Mr Turnbull's by the time agreed upon, but before I set off rather a singular occurrence took place. I had just finished cleaning my boat, and had resumed my jacket, when a dark man, from some foreign country, came to the hard with a bundle under his arm.

"How much for to go to the other side of the river—how much pence?"

"Twopence," replied I; but not caring to take him, I continued, "but you only pay one penny to cross the bridge."

"I know very well, but suppose you take me?"

He was a well-looking, not very dark man; his turban was of coloured cloth—his trousers not very wide; and I could not comprehend whether he was a Turk or not; I afterwards found out he was a Parsee, from the East Indies. He spoke very plain English. As he decided upon crossing, I received him, and shoved off; when we were in the middle of the stream, he requested me to pull a little way up. "That will do," said he, opening his bundle, and spreading a carpet on the stern flooring of the wherry. He then rose, looking at the sun, which was then rising in all its majesty, bowed to it, with his hands raised, three times, then knelt on the carpet, and touched it several times with his forehead, again rose to his feet, took some common field flowers from his vest, and cast them into the stream, bowed again, folded up his carpet, and begged me to pull on shore.

"I say my prayers," said the man, looking at me with his dark, piercing eye.

"Very proper; whom did you say them to?"

"To my God."

"But why don't you say them on shore?"

"Can't see sun in the house; suppose I go out little boys laugh and throw mud. Where no am seen, river very proper place."

We landed, and he took out threepence, and offered it to me. "No, no," said I; "I don't want you to pay for saying your prayers."

"No take money?"

"Yes, take money to cross the river, but not take money for saying prayers. If you want to say them any other morning, come down, and if I am here, I'll always pull you into the stream."

"You very good man; I thank you."

The Parsee made me a low salaam, and walked away. I may here observe that the man generally came down at sunrise two or three days in the week, and I invariably gave him a pull off into the stream, that he might pursue his religious ceremony. We often conversed and at last became intimate.

Mr Turnbull was at the bottom of the lawn, which extended from his house to the banks of the river, looking out for me, when I pulled up. The basket with our dinner, etcetera, was lying by him on the gravel walk.

"This is a lovely morning, Jacob; but it will be rather a warm day, I expect," said he; "come, let us be off at once; lay in your sculls, and let us get the oars to pass."

"How is Mrs Turnbull, sir?"

"Pretty well, Jacob; more like the Molly Brown that I married than she has been for some years. Perhaps, after all, this affair may turn out one of the best things that ever happened. It may bring her to her senses—bring happiness back to our hearth; if so, Jacob, the money is well spent."

Chapter Thirty One

We pulled leisurely up the stream, talking, and every now and then resting on our oars to take breath; for, as the old captain said, "Why should we make a toil of pleasure? I like the upper part of the river best, Jacob, because the water is clear, and I love clear water. How many hours have I, when a boy on board ship, hung over the gunwale of a boat, lowered down in a calm, and watch the little floating objects in the dark blue unfathomable water beneath me; objects of all sizes, of all colours, and of all shapes— all of them beautiful and to be admired; yet of them, perhaps, not one in a hundred millions ever meet the eye of man. You know, Jacob, that the North Seas are full of these animals—you cannot imagine the quantity of them; the sailors call them blubbers, because they are composed of a sort of transparent jelly but the real name I am told is Medusae, that is the learned name. The whale feeds on them, and that is the reason why the whale is found where they are."

"I should like very much to go a voyage to the whale fishery," replied I; "I've heard so much about it from you."

"It is a stirring life, and a hard life, Jacob; still it is an exciting one. Some voyages will turn out very pleasant, but others are dreadful, from their anxiety. If the weather continues fine, it is all very well; but sometimes when there is a continuance of bad weather, it is dreadful. I recollect one voyage which made me show more grey hairs than all the others, and I think I have been twenty-two in all. We were in the drift ice, forcing our way to the northward, when it came on to blow—the sea rose, and after a week's gale it was tremendous. We had little daylight, and when it was daylight, the fog was so thick that we could see but little; there we were tossing among the large drift ice, meeting immense icebergs which bore down with all the force of the gale, and each time we narrowly escaped perishing: the rigging was loaded with ice; the bows of the ship were cased with it; the men were more than half frozen, and we could not move a rope through a block without pouring boiling water through it first, to clear it out. But then the long, dreary, dreadful nights, when we were rising on the mountain wave, and then pitching down into the trough, not knowing but that at each send we might strike upon the ice below, and go to the bottom immediately afterwards. All pitchy dark—the wind howling, and as it struck you, cutting you to the back-bone with its cold, searching power, the waves dancing all black around you, and every now and then perceiving by its white colour and the foam encircling it a huge mass of ice borne upon you, and hurled against you as if there were a demon, who was using it as an engine for your destruction. I never shall forget the *turning* of an iceberg during the dreadful gale which lasted for a month and three days."

"I don't know what that means, sir."

"Why, you must know, Jacob, that the icebergs are all fresh water, and are supposed to have been detached from the land by the force of the weather and other causes. Now, although ice floats, yet it floats deep: that is, if an iceberg is five hundred feet high above the water, it is generally six times as deep below the water—do you understand?"

"Perfectly, sir."

"Now, Jacob, the water is much warmer than the air, and in consequence, the ice under the water melts away much faster; so that if the iceberg has been some time afloat, at last the part that is below is not so heavy as that which is above; then it turns, that is, it upsets and floats in another position."

"I understand you, sir."

"Well, we were close to an iceberg, which was to windward of us, a very tall one, indeed, and we reckoned that we should get clear of it, for we were carrying a press of sail to effect it. Still, all hands were eagerly watching the iceberg, as it came down very fast before the storm. All of a sudden it blew twice as hard as before, and then one of the men shouted out— '*Turning, turning!*'—and sure enough it was. There was its towering summit gradually bowing towards us, until it almost appeared as if the peak was over our heads. Our fate appeared inevitable, as the whole mountain of ice was descending on the vessel, and would, of course, have crushed us into atoms. We all fell on our knees, praying mentally, and watching its awful descent; even the man at the helm did the same, although he did not let go the spokes of the wheel. It had nearly half turned over, right for us, when the ice below, being heavier on one side than on the other, gave it a more slanting impetus, and shifting the direction of its fall, it plunged into the sea about a cable's length astern of us, throwing up the water to the heavens in foam, and blinding us all with the violence with which it dashed into our faces. For a minute the run of the waves was checked, and the sea appeared to boil and dance, throwing up peaked, pointed masses of water in all directions, one sinking, another rising, the ship rocked and reeled as if she were drunk; even the current of the gale was checked for a moment, and the heavy sails flapped and cleared themselves of their icy varnishing—then all was over. There was an iceberg of another shape astern of us, the gale recommenced, the waves pressed each other on as before, and we felt the return of the gale, awful as it was, as a reprieve. That was a dreadful voyage, Jacob, and turned one-third of my hair grey; and what made it worse was, that we had only three fish on board on our return. However, we had reason to be thankful, for eighteen of our vessels were lost altogether, and it was the mercy of God that we were not among the number."

"Well, I suppose you told me that story to prevent my going a voyage?"

"Not a bit, Jacob; if it should chance that you find it your interest to go to the North Pole, or anywhere else, I would say go, by all means; let neither difficulty nor danger deter you; but do not go merely from curiosity; that I consider foolish. It's all very well for those who come back to have the satisfaction to talk of such things, and it is but fair that they should have it; but when you consider how many there are who never come back at all, why, then, it's very foolish to push yourself into needless danger and privation. You are amused with my recollections of Arctic voyages; but just call to mind how many years of hardship, of danger, cold, and starvation I have undergone to collect all these anecdotes, and then judge whether it be worth any man's while to go for the sake of mere curiosity."

I then amused Mr Turnbull with the description of the picnic party, which lasted until we had pulled far beyond Kew Bridge. We thrust the bow of the wherry into a bunch of sedges, and then we sat down to our meal, surrounded by hundreds of blue dragon-flies, that flitted about as if to inquire what we meant by intruding upon their domiciles. We continued there chatting and amusing ourselves till it was late, and then shoved off and pulled down with the stream. The sun had set, and we had yet six or seven miles to return to Mr Turnbull's house, when we perceived a slight, handsome young man in a skiff, who pulled towards us.

"I say, my lads," said he, taking us both for watermen, "have you a mind to earn a couple of guineas with very little trouble?"

"Oh, yes," replied Mr Turnbull, "if you can show us how. A fine chance for you, Jacob," continued he, aside.

"Well, then, I shall want your services, perhaps, for not more than an hour; it may be a little longer, as there is a lady in question, and we may have to wait. All I ask is, that you pull well and do your best. Are you agreed?"

We consented; and he requested us to follow him, and then pulled for the shore.

"This is to be an adventure, sir," said I.

"So it seems," replied Mr Turnbull; "all the better. I'm old now, but I'm fond of a spree."

The gentleman pulled into a little boat-house by the river's side, belonging to one of the villas on the bank, made fast his boat, and then stepped into ours.

"Now, we've plenty of time; just pull quietly for the present." We continued down the river, and after we had passed Kew Bridge, he directed us in shore, on the right side, till we came to a garden sweeping down to the river from a cottage *ornée*, of large dimensions, about fifty yards from the bank. The water was up to the brick-wall, which rose from the river about four or five feet. "That will do, st—, st—, not a word," said he, rising in the stern sheets, and looking over. After a minute or two reconnoitring, he climbed from the boat on to the parapet of the wall, and whistled two bars of an air which I had till then never heard. All was silent. He crouched behind a lilac bush, and in a minute he repeated the same air in a whistle as before; still there was no appearance of movement at the cottage. He continued at intervals to whistle the portion of the air, and at last a light appeared at an upper window: it was removed, and re-appeared three times. "Be ready now, my lads," said he. In about two minutes afterwards, a female, in a cloak, appeared, coming down the lawn, with a box in her hand, panting with excitement.

"Oh, William, I heard your first signal, but I could not get into my uncle's room for the box; at last he went out, and here it is."

The gentleman seized the box from her, and handed it to us in the boat.

"Take great care of that, my lads," said he; "and now, Cecilia, we have no time to lose; the sooner you are in the boat the better."

"How am I to get down there, William?" replied she.

"Oh, nothing more easy. Stop, throw your cloak into the boat, and then all you have to do is, first to get upon the top of the wall, and then trust to the watermen below and to me above for helping you."

It was not, however, quite so easy a matter; the wall was four feet high above the boat, and moreover, there was a trellised work of iron, above a foot high, which ran along the wall. Still, she made every effort on her own part, and we considered that we had arranged so as to conquer the difficulty, when the young lady gave a scream. We looked up and beheld a third party on the wall. It was a stout, tall, elderly man, as far as we could perceive in the dark, who immediately seized hold of the lady by the arm, and was dragging her away. This was resisted by the young gentleman, and the lady was relinquished by the other, to defend himself; at the same time that he called out—"Help, help! Thieves, thieves!"

"Shall I go to his assistance?" said I to Mr Turnbull. "One must stay in the boat."

"Jump up, then, Jacob, for I never could get up that wall."

I was up in a moment, and gaining my feet, was about to spring to the help of the young man, when four servants, with lights and with arms in their hands, made their appearance, hastening down the lawn. The lady had fainted on the grass; the elderly gentleman and his antagonist were down together, but the elderly gentleman had the mastery, for he was uppermost. Perceiving the assistance coming, he called out "Look to the watermen, secure them." I perceived that not a moment was to be lost. I could be of no service, and Mr Turnbull might be in an awkward scrape. I sprang into the boat, shoved off, and we were in the stream and at thirty yards' distance before they looked over the wall to see where we were.

"Stop, in that boat! stop!" they cried.

"Fire, if they don't," cried their master.

We pulled as hard as we could. A musquetoon was discharged, but the shot dropped short; the only person who fell was the man who fired it. To see us he had stood upon the coping bricks of the wall, and the recoil tumbled him over into the river: we saw him fall, and heard the splash; but we pulled on as hard as we could, and in a few minutes the scene of action was far behind us. We then struck across to the other side of the river, and when we had gained close to the shore we took breath.

"Well," said Mr Turnbull, "this is a spree I little looked for; to have a blunderbuss full of shot sent after me."

"No," replied I, laughing, "that's carrying the joke rather too far on the river Thames."

"Well, but what a pretty mess we are in: here we have property belonging to God knows whom; and what are we to do with it?"

"I think, sir, the best thing we can do is, for you to land at your own house with the property, and take care of it until we find out what all this is about; and I will continue on with the sculls to the hard. I shall hear or find out something about it in a day or two; they may still follow up the pursuit and trace us."

"The advice is good," replied Mr Turnbull, "and the sooner we cut over again the better, for we are nearly abreast of my place."

We did so. Mr Turnbull landed in his garden, taking with him the tin-box (it was what they call a deed-box) and the lady's cloak. I did not wait, but boating the oars, took my sculls and pulled down to Fulham as fast as I could. I had arrived, and was pulling gently in, not to injure the other boats, when a man with a lantern came into the wherry.

"Have you anything in your boat, my man?" said he. "Nothing, sir," replied I. The man examined the boat, and was satisfied.

"Tell me, did you see a boat with two men in it as you came along?"

"No, sir," replied I, "nothing has passed me."

"Where do you come from now?"

"From a gentleman's place near Brentford."

"Brentford? Oh, then, you were far below them. They are not down yet."

"Have you a job for me, sir?" said I, not wishing to appear anxious to go away.

"No, my man, no; nothing to-night. We are on the lookout, but we have two boats in the stream, and a man at each landing-place."

I made fast my boat, shouldered my oars and sculls, and departed, not at all sorry to get away. It appeared that as soon as it was ascertained that we were not to be stopped by being fired at, they saddled horses, and the distance by the road being so much shorter, had, by galloping as hard as they could, arrived at Fulham some ten minutes before me. It was, therefore, most fortunate that the box had been landed, or I should have been discovered. That the contents were of value was evident, from the anxiety to secure them; but the mystery was still to be solved. I was quite tired with exertion and excitement when I arrived at Stapleton's. Mary was there to give me my supper, which I ate in silence, complained of a headache, and went to bed.

Chapter Thirty Two

That night I dreamed of nothing but the scene, over and over again, and the two bars of music were constantly ringing in my ears. As soon as I had breakfasted the next morning I set off to Mr Turnbull's, and told him what had occurred.

"It was indeed fortunate that the box was landed," said he, "or you might have now been in prison; I wish I had had nothing to do with it; but, as you say, 'what's done can't be helped;' I will not give up the box, at all events, until I know which party is entitled to it, and I cannot help thinking that the lady is. But, Jacob, you will have to reconnoitre, and find out what this story is. Tell me, do you think you could remember the tune which he whistled so often?"

"It has been running in my head the whole night, and I have been trying it all the way as I pulled here. I think I have it exact. Hear, sir."—I whistled the two bars.

"Quite correct, Jacob, quite correct; well, take care not to forget them. Where are you going to-day?"

"Nowhere, sir."

"Suppose, then, you pull up the river, and find out the place where we landed, and when you have ascertained that, you can go on and see whether the young man is with the skiff; at all events you may find out something— but pray be cautious."

I promised to be very careful, and departed on my errand, which I undertook with much pleasure, for I was delighted with anything like adventure. I pulled up the river, and in about an hour and a-quarter, came abreast of the spot. I recognised the cottage *ornée*, the parapet wall, even the spot where we lay, and perceived that several bricks were detached and had fallen into the river. There appeared to be no one stirring in the house, yet I continued to pull up and down, looking at the windows; at last one opened, and a young lady looked out, who, I was persuaded, was the same that we had seen the night before. There was no wind, and all was quiet around. She sat at the window, leaning her head on her hand. I whistled the two bars of the air. At the first bar she started up, and looked earnestly at me as I completed the second. I looked up; she waved her handkerchief once, and then shut the window. In a few seconds she made her appearance on the lawn, walking down towards the river. I immediately pulled in under the wall. I laid in my sculls, and held on, standing up in the boat.

"Who are you? and who sent you?" said she, looking down on me, and discovering one of the most beautiful faces I had ever beheld.

"No one sent me ma'am," replied I, "but I was in the boat last night. I am sorry you were so unfortunate, but your box and cloak are quite safe."

"You were one of the men in the boat. I trust no one was hurt when they fired at you?"

"No ma'am."

"And where is the box?"

"In the house of the person who was with me."

"Can he be trusted? For they will offer large rewards for it."

"I should think so, ma'am," replied I, smiling; "the person who was with me is a gentleman of large fortune, who was amusing himself on the river. He desires me to say that he will not give up the box until he knows to whom the contents legally belong."

"Good heavens, how fortunate! Am I to believe you?"

"I should hope so, ma'am."

"And what are you, then? You are not a waterman?"

"Yes, ma'am, I am."

She paused, looked earnestly at me for a little while, and then continued, "How did you learn the air you whistled?"

"The young gentleman whistled it six or seven times last night before you came. I tried it this morning coming up, as I thought it would be the means of attracting your attention. Can I be of any service to you, ma'am?"

"Service—yes, if I could be sure you were to be trusted—of the greatest service. I am confined here—cannot send a letter—watched as I move—only allowed the garden, and even watched while I walk here. They are most of them in quest of the tin box to-day, or I should not be able to talk to you so long." She looked round at the house anxiously, and then said, "Stop here a minute, while I walk a little." She then retreated, and paced up and down the garden walk. I still remained under the wall, so as not to be perceived from the house. In about three or four minutes she returned and said, "It would be very cruel—it would be more than cruel—it would be very wicked of you to deceive me, for I am very unfortunate and very unhappy." The tears started in her eyes. "You do not look as if you would. What is your name?"

"Jacob Faithful, ma'am, and I will be true to my name, if you will put your trust in me. I never deceived any one that I can recollect; and I'm sure I would not you—now that I've seen you."

"Yes, but money will seduce everybody."

"Not me, ma'am. I've as much as I wish for."

"Well, then, I will trust you, and think you sent from heaven to my aid; but how am I to see you? To-morrow my uncle will be back, and then I shall not be able to speak to you one moment, and if seen to speak to you, you will be laid in wait for, and perhaps shot."

"Well, ma'am," replied I, after a pause, "if you cannot speak, you can write. You see that the bricks on the parapet are loose here. Put your letter under this brick—I can take it away even in day-time, without being noticed, and can put the answer in the same place, so that you can secure it when you come out."

"How very clever! Good heavens, what an excellent idea!"

"Was the young gentleman hurt, ma'am, in the scuffle last night?" inquired I.

"No, I believe not much, but I wish to know where he is, to write to him; could you find out?" I told her where we had met him, and what had passed. "That was Lady Auburn's," replied she; "he is often there—she is our cousin but I don't know where he lives, and how to find him I know not. His name is William Wharncliffe. Do you think you could find him out?"

"Yes, ma'am, with a little trouble it might be done. They ought to know where he is at Lady Auburn's."

"Yes, some of the servants might—but how will you get to them?"

"That, ma'am, I must find out. It may not be done in one day, or two days, but if you will look every morning under this brick, if there is anything to communicate you will find it there."

"You can write and read, then?"

"I should hope so, ma'am," replied I, laughing.

"I don't know what to make of you. Are you really a waterman?"

"Really, and—" She turned her head round at the noise of a window opening.

"You must go—don't forget the brick;" and she disappeared.

I shoved my wherry along by the side of the wall, so as to remain unperceived until I was clear of the frontage attached to the cottage; and then, taking my sculls, pulled into the stream; and as I was resolved to see if I could obtain any information at Lady Auburn's, I had to pass the garden again, having shoved my boat down the river instead of up, when I was under the wall. I perceived the young lady walking with a tall man by her side; he speaking very energetically, and using much gesticulation, she holding down her head. In another minute they were shut out from my sight. I was so much stricken with the beauty and sweetness of expression in the young lady's countenance that I was resolved to use my best exertions to be of service to her. In about an hour-and-a-half I had arrived at the villa, abreast of which we had met the young gentleman, and which the young lady had told me belonged to Lady Auburn. I could see no one in the grounds, nor indeed in the house. After watching a few minutes, I landed as near to the villa as I could, made fast the wherry, and walked round to the entrance. There was no lodge, but a servant's door at one side. I pulled the bell, having made up my mind how to proceed as I was walking up. The bell was answered by an old woman, who, in a snarling tone, asked me "what did I want?"

"I am waiting below, with my boat, for Mr Wharncliffe; has he come yet?"

"Mr Wharncliffe! No—he's not come; nor did he say that he would come; when did you see him?"

"Yesterday. Is Lady Auburn at home?"

"Lady Auburn—no; she went to town this morning; everybody goes to London now, that they may not see the flowers and green trees, I suppose."

"But I suppose Mr Wharncliffe will come," continued I, "so I must wait for him."

"You can do just as you like," replied the old woman, about to shut the gate in my face.

"May I request a favour of you, ma'am, before you shut the gate—which is, to bring me a little water to drink, for the sun is hot, and I have had a long pull up here;" and I took out my handkerchief and wiped my face.

"Yes, I'll fetch you some," replied she, shutting the gate and going away.

"This don't seem to answer very well," thought I to myself. The old woman returned, opened the gate, and handed me a mug of water. I drank some, thanked her, and returned the mug.

"I am very tired," said I; "I should like to sit down and wait for the gentleman."

"Don't you sit down when you pull?" inquired the old woman.

"Yes," replied I.

"Then you must be tired of sitting, I should think, not of standing; at all events, if you want to sit, you can sit in your boat, and mind it at the same time." With this observation she shut the door upon me, and left me without any more comment.

After this decided repulse on the part of the old woman, I had nothing to do but take her advice—viz., to go and look after my boat. I pulled down to Mr Turnbull's, and told him my good and bad fortune. It being late, he ordered me some dinner in his study, and we sat there canvassing over the affair. "Well," said he, as we finished, "you must allow me to consider this as my affair, Jacob, as I was the occasion of our getting mixed up in it. You must do all that you can to find this young man, and I shall hire Stapleton's boat by the day until we succeed; you need not tell him so, or he may be anxious to know why. To-morrow you go down to old Beazeley's?"

"Yes, sir; you cannot hire me to-morrow."

"Still I shall, as I want to see you to-morrow morning before you go. Here's Stapleton's money for yesterday and to-day and now good-night."

I was at Mr Turnbull's early the next morning, and found him with the newspapers before him. "I expected this, Jacob," said he; "read that advertisement." I read as follows:— "Whereas, on Friday night last, between the hours of nine and ten, a tin box, containing deeds and papers, was handed into a wherry from the grounds of a villa between Brentford and Kew, and the parties who owned it were prevented from accompanying the same. This is to give notice, that a reward of twenty pounds will be paid to the watermen, upon their delivering up the same to Messrs James and John White, of Number 14 Lincoln's Inn Fields. As no other parties are authorised to receive the said tin box of papers, all other applications for it must be disregarded. An early attention to this advertisement will oblige."

"There must be papers of no little consequence in that box, Jacob, depend upon it," said Mr Turnbull; "however, here they are, and here they shall remain until I know more about it; that's certain. I intend to try what I can do myself with the old woman, for I perceive the villa is to be let for three months—here is the advertisement in the last column. I shall go to town to-day, and obtain a ticket from the agent, and it is hard but I'll ferret out something. I shall see you to-morrow. Now you may go, Jacob."

I hastened away, as I had promised to be down to old Tom's to breakfast; an hour's smart pulling brought me to the landing-place, opposite to his house.

Chapter Thirty Three

The house of old Tom Beazeley was situated on the verge of Battersea Fields, about a mile-and-a-half from the bridge bearing the same name; the river about twenty yards before it—the green grass behind it, and not a tree within half-a-mile of it. There was nothing picturesque in it but its utter loneliness; it was not only lonely, but isolated, for it was fixed upon a delta of about half-an-acre, between two creeks, which joined at about forty yards from the river, and ran up through the fields, so that the house was at high water upon an island, and at low water was defended by an impassable barrier of mud, so that the advances to it could be made only from the river, where a small *hard*, edged with posts worn down to the conformation of decayed double-teeth, offered the only means of access. The house itself was one storey high; dark red bricks, and darker tiles upon the roof; windows very scarce and very small, although built long before the damnable tax upon light, for it was probably built in the time of Elizabeth, to judge by the peculiarity of the style of architecture observable in the chimneys; but it matters very little at what epoch was built a tenement which was rented at only ten pounds per annum. The major part of the said island was stocked with cabbage plants; but on one side there was half a boat set upright, with a patch of green before it. At the time that old Beazeley hired it there was a bridge rudely constructed of old ship plank, by which you could gain a path which led across the Battersea Fields; but as all the communications of old Tom were by water, and Mrs Beazeley never ventured over the bridge, it was gradually knocked away for firewood, and when it was low-water, one old post, redolent of mud, marked the spot where the bridge had been. The interior was far more inviting. Mrs Beazeley was a clean person and frugal housewife, and every article in the kitchen, which was the first room you entered, was as clean and as bright as industry could make it. There was a parlour also, seldom used; both of the inmates, when they did meet, which was not above a day or two in three weeks, during the time that old Beazeley was in charge of the lighter, preferring comfort to grandeur. In this isolated house, upon this isolated spot, did Mrs Beazeley pass a life of most isolation.

And yet, perhaps there never was a more lively or a more happy woman than Mrs Beazeley, for she was strong and in good health, and always employed. She knew that her husband was following up his avocation on the river, and laying by a provision for their old age, which she herself was adding considerably to it by her own exertions. She had married old Tom long before he had lost his legs, at a time when he was a prime, active sailor, and the best man of the ship. She was a net-maker's daughter, and had been brought up to the business, at which she was very expert. The most difficult part of the art is that of making large *seines* for taking sea-fish; and when she had no order for those to complete, the making of casting-nets beguiled away her time as soon as her household cares had been disposed of. She made money and husbanded it, not only for herself and her partner, but for her son, young Tom, upon whom she doted. So accustomed was she to work hard and be alone that it was most difficult to say whether she was most pleased or most annoyed when her husband and son made their appearance for a day or two, and the latter was alternately fondled and scolded during the whole of his sojourn. Tom, as the reader may suppose from a knowledge of his character, caring about as much for the one as the other.

I pulled into the *hard*, and made fast my boat. There was no one outside the door when I landed; on entering, I found them all seated at the table, and a grand display of fragments, in the shape of herring-bones, etcetera. "Well, Jacob—come at last—thought you had forgot us; piped to breakfast at eight bells—always do, you know," said old Tom, on my making my appearance.

"Have you had your breakfast, Jacob?" said Mrs Beazeley.

"No," replied I; "I was obliged to go up to Mr Turnbull's, and that detained me."

"No more sodgers, Jacob," said Tom; "father and I eat them all."

"Have you?" replied Mrs Beazeley, taking two more red herrings out of the cupboard, and putting them on the fire to grill; "no, no, master Tom, there's some for Jacob yet."

"Well, mother, you make nets to some purpose, for you've always a fish when it's wanted."

I despatched my breakfast, and as soon as all had been cleared away by his wife, old Tom, crossing his two timber legs, commenced business, for it appeared, what I was not aware of, that we had met on a sort of council-of-war.

"Jacob, sit down by me; old woman, bring yourself to an anchor in the high chair. Tom, sit anywhere, so you sit still."

"And leave my net alone, Tom," cried his mother, in parenthesis. — "You see, Jacob, the whole long and short of it is this—I feel my toes more and more, and flannel's no longer warm. I can't tide it any longer, and I think it high time to lie up in ordinary and moor abreast of the old woman. Now, there's Tom, in the first place, what's to do with he? I think that I'll build him a wherry, and as I'm free of the river he can finish his apprenticeship with my name on the boat; but to build him a wherry would be rather a heavy pull for me."

"If you mean to build it yourself, I think it will prove a *heavy pull* for me," replied Tom.

"Silence, Tom; I built you, and God knows you're light enough."

"And, Tom, leave my net alone," cried his mother.

"Father made me light-fingered, mother."

"Ay, and light-hearted too, boy," rejoined the dame, looking fondly at her son.

"Well," continued old Tom, "supposing that Tom be provided for in that way; then now I comes to myself. I've an idea that I can do a good bit of work in patching up boats; for you see I always was a bit of a carpenter, and I know how the builders extortionate the poor watermen when there's a trifle amiss. Now, if they knew I could do it, they'd all come to me fast enough; but then there's a puzzle. I've been thinking this week how I can make them know it. I can't put out a board and say, Beazeley, *Boat-builder*, because I'm no boatbuilder, but still I want a sign."

"Lord, father, haven't you got one already?" interrupted young Tom; "you've half a boat stuck up there, and that means that you're half a boat-builder."

"Silence, Tom, with your frippery; what do you think. Jacob?"

"Could you not say, 'Boats repaired here?'"

"Yes, but that won't exactly do; they like to employ a builder—and there's the puzzle."

"Not half so puzzling as this net," observed Tom, who had taken up the needle, unseen by his mother, and begun to work; "I've made only ten stitches, and six of them are long ones."

"Tom, Tom, you good-for-nothing—why don't you let my net alone?" cried Mrs Beazeley; "now 'twill take me as much time to undo ten stitches as to have made fifty."

"All right, mother."

"No, Tom, all's wrong; look at these meshes?"

"Well, then, all's fair, mother."

"No, all's foul, boy; look how it's tangled."

"Still, I say, all's fair, mother, for it is but fair to give the fish one or two chances to get away, and that's just what I've done; and now, father, I'll settle your affair to your own satisfaction, as I have mother's."

"That will be queer satisfaction, Tom, I guess; but let's hear what you have to say."

"Then, father, it seems that you're no boat-builder, but you want people to fancy that you are—a'n't that the question?"

"Why, 'tis something like it, Tom, but I do nobody no harm."

"Certainly not; it's only the boats which will suffer. Now, get a large board, with 'Boats *built to order*, and boats repaired, by Tom Beazeley.' You know if any man is fool enough to order a boat, that's his concern; you didn't say you're a boat-builder, although you have no objection to try your hand."

"What do you say Jacob?" said old Tom, appealing to me.

"I think that Tom has given very good advice, and I would follow it."

"Ah! Tom has a head," said Mrs Beazeley, fondly. "Tom, let go my net again, will you? What a boy you are! Now touch it again if you dare," and Mrs Beazeley took up a little poker from the fire-place and shook it at him.

"Tom has a head, indeed," said young Tom, "but as he has no wish to have it broken, Jacob, lend me your wherry for half-an-hour, and I'll be off."

I assented, and Tom, first tossing the cat upon his mother's back, made his escape, crying:

"Lord, Molly, what a fish—"

as the animal fixed in its claws to save herself from falling, making Mrs Beazeley roar out and vow vengeance, while old Tom and I could not refrain from laughter.

After Tom's departure the conversation was renewed, and everything was finally arranged between old Tom and his wife, except the building of the wherry, at which the old woman shook her head. The debate would be too long, and not sufficiently interesting to detail; one part, however, I must make the reader acquainted with. After entering into all the arrangements of the house, Mrs Beazeley took me upstairs to show me the rooms, which were very neat and clean. I came down with her, and old Tom said, "Did the old woman show you the room with the white curtains, Jacob?"

"Yes," replied I, "and a very nice one it is."

"Well, Jacob, there's nothing sure in this world. You're well off at present, and 'leave well alone' is a good motto; but recollect this, that room is for you when you want it, and everything else we can share with you. It's offered freely, and you will accept it the same. Is it not, old lady?"

"Yes, that it is, Jacob; but may you do better—if not, I'll be your mother for want of a better."

I was moved with the kindness of the old couple; the more so as I did not know what I had done to deserve it. Old Tom gave me a hearty squeeze of the hand, and then continued—"But about this wherry—what do you say, old woman?"

"What will it cost?" replied she, gravely.

"Cost; let me see—a good wherry, with sculls and oars, will be a matter of thirty pounds."

The old woman screwed up her mouth, shook her head, and then walked away to prepare for dinner.

"I think she could muster the blunt, Jacob, but she don't like to part with it. Tom must coax her. I wish he hadn't shied the cat at her. He's too full of fun."

As old Beazeley finished, I perceived a wherry pulling in with some ladies. I looked attentively, and recognised my own boat, and Tom pulling. In a minute more they were at the *hard*, and who, to my astonishment, were there seated, but Mrs Drummond and Sarah. As Tom got out of the boat and held it steady against the *hard*, he called to me; I could not do otherwise than go and assist them out; and once more did I touch the hands of those whom I never thought to meet again. Mrs Drummond retained my hand a short time after she landed, saying, "We are friends, Jacob, are we not!"

"Oh, yes, madam," replied I, much moved, in a faltering voice.

"I shall not ask that question," said Sarah, gaily, "for we parted friends."

And as I recalled to mind her affectionate behaviour, I pressed her hand, and the tears glistened in my eyes as I looked into her sweet face. As I afterwards discovered, this was an arranged plan with old and young Tom, to bring about a meeting without my knowledge. Mrs Beazeley courtesied and stroked her apron—smiled at the ladies, looked very *cat*-ish at Tom, showed the ladies into the house, where old Tom assisted to do the honours after his own fashion, by asking Mrs Drummond if she would like to *whet her whistle* after her *pull*. Mrs Drummond looked round to me for explanation, but young Tom thought proper to be interpreter. "Father wants to know, if you please, ma'am, whether, after your *pull* in the boat, you wouldn't like to have a *pull* at the brandy bottle?"

"No," replied Mrs Drummond, smiling; "but I should be obliged for a glass of water. Will you get me one, Jacob?"

I hastened to comply, and Mrs Drummond entered into conversation with Mrs Beazeley. Sarah looked at me, and went to the door, turning back as inviting me to follow. I did so, and we soon found ourselves seated on the bench in the old boat.

"Jacob," said she, looking earnestly at me, "you surely will be friends with *my* father?"

I think I should have shaken my head, but she laid an emphasis on *my*, which the little gipsy knew would have its effect. All my resolutions, all my pride, all my sense of injury vanished before the mild, beautiful eyes of Sarah, and I replied hastily, "Yes, Miss Sarah, I can refuse *you* nothing."

"Why *Miss*, Jacob?"

"I am a waterman, and you are much above me."

"That is your own fault; but say no more about it."

"I must say something more, which is this: do not attempt to make me leave my present employment; I am happy, because I am independent; and that I will, if possible, be for the future."

"Any one can pull an oar, Jacob."

"Very true, Miss Sarah, and is under no obligation to any one by so earning his livelihood. He works for all and is paid for all."

"Will you come and see us, Jacob? Come to-morrow—now do—promise me. Will you refuse your old playmate, Jacob?"

"I wish you would not ask that."

"How then can you say that you are friends with my father? I will not believe you unless you promise to come."

"Sarah," replied I, earnestly, "I will come; and to prove to you that we are friends, I will ask a favour of him."

"Oh, Jacob, this is kind indeed," cried Sarah, with her eyes swimming with tears. "You have made me so—so very happy!"

The meeting with Sarah humanised me, and every feeling of revenge was chased from my memory. Mrs Drummond joined us soon after, and proposed to return. "And Jacob will pull us back," cried Sarah. "Come, sir, look after your *fare*, in both senses. Since you will be a waterman, you shall work." I laughed and handed them to the boat. Tom took the other oar, and we were soon at the steps close to their house.

"Mamma, we ought to give these poor fellows something to drink; they've worked very hard," said Sarah, mocking. "Come up, my good men." I hesitated. "Nay, Jacob, if tomorrow why not to-day? The sooner these things are over the better."

I felt the truth of this observation, and followed her. In a few minutes I was again in that parlour in which I had been dismissed, and in which the affectionate girl burst into tears on my shoulder, as I held the handle of the door. I looked at it, and looked at Sarah. Mrs Drummond had gone out of the room to let Mr Drummond know that I had come. "How kind you were, Sarah!" said I.

"Yes, but kind people are cross sometimes, and so am I—and so was—"

Mr Drummond came in, and stopped her. "Jacob, I am glad to see you again in my house; I was deceived by appearances, and did you injustice." How true is the observation of the wise man, that a soft word turneth away wrath; that Mr Drummond should personally acknowledge that he was wrong to me—that he should confess it—every feeling of resentment was gone, and others crowded in their place. I recollected how he had protected the orphan—how he had provided him with instruction—how he had made *his* house a home to me—how he had tried to bring me forward under his own protection I recollected—which, alas! I never should have forgotten—that he had treated me for years with kindness and affection, all of which had been obliterated from my memory by one single act of injustice. I felt that I was a culprit, and burst into tears; and Sarah, as before, cried in sympathy.

"I beg your pardon, Mr Drummond," said I, as soon as I could speak; "I have been very wrong in being so revengeful after so much kindness from you."

"We both have been wrong—but say no more on the subject, Jacob; I have an order to give, and then I will come up to you again;" and Mr Drummond quitted the room.

"You dear, good boy," said Sarah, coming up to me. "Now, I really do love you."

What I might have replied was put a stop to by Mrs Drummond entering the room. She made a few inquiries about where I at present resided, and Sarah was catechising me rather inquisitively about Mary Stapleton, when Mr Drummond re-entered the room, and shook me by the hand with a warmth which made me more ashamed of my conduct towards him. The conversation became general, but still rather embarrassed, when Sarah whispered to me "What is the favour you would ask of my father?" I had forgotten it at the moment, but I immediately told him that I would be obliged if he would allow me to have a part of the money belonging to me which he held in his possession.

"That I will, with pleasure, and without asking what you intend to do with it, Jacob. How much do you require?"

"Thirty pounds, if there is so much."

Mr Drummond went down, and in a few minutes returned with the sum in notes and guineas. I thanked him, and shortly afterwards took my leave.

"Did not young Beazeley tell you I had something for you, Jacob?" said Sarah, as I wished her good-bye.

"Yes; what is it?"

"You must come and see," replied Sarah, laughing. Thus was a finale to all my revenge brought about by a little girl of fifteen years old, with large dark eyes.

Tom had taken his glass of grog below, and was waiting for me at the steps. We shoved off, and returned to his father's house, where dinner was just ready. After dinner old Tom recommenced the argument; "The only hitch," says he, "is about the wherry. What do you say, old woman?" The old woman shook her head.

"As that is the only hitch," said I, "I can remove it, for here is the money for the wherry, which I make a present to Tom," and I put the money into young Tom's hand. Tom counted it out before his father and mother, much to their astonishment.

"You are a good fellow, Jacob," said Tom; "but I say, do you recollect Wimbledon Common?"

"What then?" replied I.

"Only Jerry Abershaw, that's all."

"Do not be afraid, Tom, it is honestly mine."

"But how did you get it, Jacob," said old Tom.

It may appear strange, but, impelled by a wish to serve my friends, I had asked for the money which I knew belonged to me, but never thought of the manner in which it had been obtained. The question of old Tom recalled everything to my memory, and I shuddered when I recollected the circumstances attending it. I was confused, and did not like to reply. "Be satisfied, the money is mine," replied I.

"Yes, Jacob, but how?" replied Mrs Beazeley; "surely you ought to be able to tell how you got so large a sum."

"Jacob has some reason for not telling, missus, depend upon it; mayhap Mr Turnbull, or whoever gave it to him, told him to hold his tongue." But this answer would not satisfy Mrs Beazeley, who declared she would not allow a farthing to be taken unless she knew how it was obtained.

"Tom, give back the money directly," said she, looking at me suspiciously.

Tom laid it on the table before me, without saying a word.

"Take it, Tom," said I, colouring up. "I had it from my mother."

"From your mother, Jacob!" said old Tom. "Nay, that could not well be, if my memory sarves me right. Still it may be."

"Deary me, I don't like this at all," cried Mrs Beazeley, getting up, and wiping her apron with a quick motion. "Oh, Jacob, that must be—not the truth."

I coloured up to the tips of my ears at being suspected of falsehood. I looked round, and saw that even Tom and his father had a melancholy doubt in their countenances; and certainly my confused appearance would have caused suspicion in anybody. "I little thought," said I, at last, "when I hoped to have so much pleasure in giving, and to find that I had made you happy in receiving the money, that it would have proved a source of so much annoyance. I perceive that I am suspected of having obtained it improperly, and of not having told the truth. That Mrs Beazeley may think so, who does not know me, is not to be wondered at; but that you," continued I, turning to old Tom, "or you," looking at his son, "should suspect me, is very mortifying; and I did not expect it. I tell you that the money is mine, honestly mine, and obtained from my mother. I ask you, do you believe me?"

"I, for one, do believe you, Jacob," said young Tom, striking his fist on the table. "I can't understand it, but I know you never told a lie, or did a dishonourable act since I've known you."

"Thank you, Tom," said I, taking his proffered hand.

"And I would swear the same, Jacob," said old Tom; "although I have been longer in the world than my boy has, and have, therefore, seen more; and sorry am I to say, many a good man turned bad, from temptation being too great; but when I looked in your face, and saw the blood up to your forehead, I did feel a little suspicious, I must own; but I beg your pardon, Jacob; no one can look in your face now and not see that you are innocent. I believe all you say, in spite of the old woman and—the devil to boot—and there's my hand upon it."

"Why not tell—why not tell?" muttered Mrs Beazeley, shaking her head, and working at her net faster than ever.

But I had resolved to tell, and did so, narrating distinctly the circumstances by which the money had been obtained. I did it, however, with feelings of mortification which I cannot express. I felt humiliation—I felt that, for my own wants, that money I never could touch. Still my explanation had the effect of removing the doubts even of Mrs Beazeley, and harmony was restored. The money was accepted by the old couple, and promised to be applied for the purpose intended.

"As for me, Jacob," said Tom, "when I say I thank you, you know I mean it. Had I had the money, and you had wanted it, you will believe me when I say that I would have given it to you."

"That I'm sure of, Tom."

"Still, Jacob, it is a great deal of money, and I shall lay by my earnings as fast as I can, that you may have it in case you want it; but it will take many a heavy pull and many a shirt wet with labour before I can make up a sum like that."

I did not stay much longer after this little fracas; I was hurt—my pride was wounded by suspicion, and fortunate it was that the occurrence had not taken place previous to my meeting with Mrs Drummond and Sarah, otherwise no reconciliation would have taken place in that quarter. How much are we the sport of circumstances, and how insensibly they mark out our career in this world? With the best intentions we go wrong; instigated by unworthy motives, we fall upon our feet, and the chapter of accidents has more power over the best regulated mind than all the chapters in the Bible.

Chapter Thirty Four

I shook hands with Tom, who perceiving that I was vexed, had accompanied me down to the boat, with his usual sympathy, and had offered to pull with me to Fulham, and walk back; which offer I declined, as I wished to be alone. It was a fine moonlight night, and the broad light and shadow, with the stillness of all around, were peculiarly adapted to my feelings. I continued my way up the river, revolving in my mind the scenes of the day; the reconciliation with one whom I never intended to have spoken to again; the little quarrel with those whom I never expected to have been at variance with, and that at the time when I was only exerting myself to serve them; and then I thought of Sarah, as an oasis of real happiness in this contemplated desert, and dwelt upon the thought of her as the most pleasant and calming to my still agitated mind. Thus did I ruminate till I had passed Putney Bridge, forgetting that I was close to my landing place, and continuing, in my reverie, to pull up the river, when my cogitations were disturbed by a noise of men laughing and talking, apparently in a state of intoxication. They were in a four-oared wherry, coming down the river, after a party of pleasure, as it is termed, generally one ending in intoxication, I listened.

"I tell you I can spin an oar with any man in the king's service," said the man in the bow, "Now look."

He threw his oar out of the rowlocks, spun it in the air, but unfortunately did not catch it when it fell, and consequently it went through the bottom, starting two of the planks of the fragile-built boat, which immediately filled with water.

"Hilloa! waterman!" cried another, perceiving me, "quick, or we shall sink." But the boat was nearly up to the thwarts in water before I could reach her, and just as I was nearly alongside she filled and turned over.

"Help, waterman; help me first; I'm senior clerk," cried a voice which I well knew. I put out my oar to him as he struggled in the water, and soon had him clinging to the wherry. I then tried to catch hold of the man who had sunk the boat by his attempt to toss the oar, but he very quietly said, "No, damn it, there's too many; we shall swamp the wherry; I'll swim on shore" — and suiting the action to the word, he made for the shore with perfect self-possession, swimming in his clothes with great ease and dexterity.

I picked up two more, and thought that all were saved, when turning round, and looking towards the bridge, I saw resplendent in the bright beams of the moon, and "round as its orb," the well-remembered face of the stupid young clerk who had been so inimical to me, struggling with all his might. I pulled to him, and putting out my oar over the bow, he seized it after rising from his first sink, and was, with the other three, soon clinging to the side of the wherry.

"Pull me in—pull me in, waterman!" cried the head clerk, whose voice I had recognised.

"No; you will swamp the boat."

"Well, but pull me in, if not the others. I'm the senior clerk."

"Can't help that; you must hold on," replied I, "while I pull you on shore; we shall soon be there." I must say that I felt a pleasure in allowing him thus to hang in the water. I might have taken them all in certainly, although at some risk, from their want of presence of mind and hurry, arising from the feeling of self-preservation; but I desired them to hold on, and pulled for the landing-place; which we soon gained. The person who had preferred swimming had arrived before us, and was waiting on the beach.

"Have you got them all, waterman?" said he.

"Yes, sir, I believe so; I have four."

"The tally is right," replied he, "and four greater galloots were never picked up; but never mind that. It was my nonsense that nearly drowned them; and, therefore, I'm very glad you've managed so well. My jacket went down in the boat, and I must reward you another time."

"Thank you, sir, no occasion for that, it's not a regular fare."

"Nevertheless, give us your name."

"Oh, you may ask Mr Hodgson, the senior clerk, or that full-moon-faced fellow—they know my name."

"Waterman, what do you mean?" replied Mr Hodgson, shivering with cold.

"Very impudent fellow," said the junior of the round face.

"If they know your name, they won't tell it," replied the other. "Now, I'll first tell you mine, which is Lieutenant Wilson, of the navy; and now let's have yours, that I may ask for it; and tell me what stairs you ply from."

"My name is Jacob Faithful, sir," replied I; "and you may ask your friends whether they know it or not when their teeth don't chatter quite so much."

At the mention of my name the senior and junior clerk walked off, and the lieutenant, telling me that I should hear from him again, was about to leave. "If you mean to give me money, sir, I tell you candidly I shall not take it. I hate these two men for the injuries they have heaped on me; but I don't know how it is, I feel a degree of pleasure in having saved them, that I wish for no better revenge. So farewell, sir."

"Spoken as you ought, my lad—that's glorious revenge. Well, then, I will not come; but if ever we meet again I shall never forget this night and Jacob Faithful." He held out his hand, shook mine warmly, and walked away.

When they were gone, I remained for some little time quite stupified at the events of the day. The reconciliation—the quarrel—the revenge. I was still in thought when I heard the sound of a horse's hoofs. This recalled me, and I was hauling up my boat, intending to go home to Stapleton's; but with no great eagerness. I felt a sort of dislike to Mary Stapleton, which I could not account for; but the fact was I had been in company with Sarah Drummond. The horse stopped at the foot of the bridge; and the rider giving it to his servant, who was mounted on another, to hold, came down to where I was hauling up my boat. "My lad, is it too late for you to launch your boat? I will pay you well."

"Where do you wish to go to, sir? It is now past ten o'clock."

"I know it is, and I hardly expected to find a waterman here; but I took the chance. Will you take me about two miles up the river?"

I looked at the person who addressed me, and was delighted to recognise in him the young man who had hired Mr Turnbull and me to take him to the garden, and who had been captured when we escaped with the tin box; but I did not make myself known. "Well, sir, if you wish it, I've no objection," replied I, putting my shoulder to the bow of my wherry, and launching her again into the water. At all events, this has been a day of adventure, thought I, as I threw my sculls again into the water, and commenced pulling up the stream. I was some little while in meditation whether I should make myself known to the young man; but I decided that I would not. Let me see, thought I, what sort of a person this is—whether he is as deserving as the young lady appeared to consider. "Which side, sir?" inquired I.

"The left," was the reply.

I knew that well enough, and I pulled in silence until nearly up to the wall of the garden which ran down to the band of the river. "Now pull in to that wall, and make no noise," was the injunction; which I obeyed, securing the boat to the very part where the coping bricks had been displaced. He stood up, and whistled the two bars of the tune as before, waited five minutes, repeated it, and watched the windows of the house; but there was no reply, or signs of anybody being up or stirring. "It is too late; she is gone to rest."

"I thought there was a lady in the case, sir," observed I. "If you wish to communicate with her, I think I could manage it."

"Could you?" replied he. "Stop a moment; I'll speak to you by-and-by." He whistled the tune once more, and after waiting another ten minutes, dropped himself down on the stern sheets, and told me to pull back again. After a minute's silence he said to me, "You think you could communicate with her, you say. Pray, how do you propose?"

"If you will write a letter, sir, I'll try to let it come to her hand."

"How?"

"That, sir, you must leave me to find out, and trust to opportunity; but you must tell me what sort of a person she is, that I may not give it to another; and also, who there is in the house that I must be careful does not see me."

"Very true," replied he. "I can only say that if you do succeed, I will reward you handsomely; but she is so strictly watched that I am afraid it will be impossible. However, a despairing, like a drowning man, will catch at a straw; and I will see whether you will be able to assist me."

He then informed me that there was no one in the house except her uncle and his servants, all of whom were spies upon her; that my only chance was watching if she were permitted to walk in the garden alone, which might be the case; and perhaps, by concealing myself from eight o'clock in the morning till the evening under the parapet wall, I might find an opportunity. He directed me to be at the foot of the bridge next morning at seven o'clock, when he would come with a letter written for me to deliver, if possible. We had then arrived at Fulham. He landed, and putting a guinea in my hand, mounted his horse, which his servant (had) walked up and down, waiting for him, and rode off. I hauled up my boat and went home, tired with the manifold events of the day. Mary Stapleton who had sat up for me, was very inquisitive to know what had occasioned my coming home so late; but I evaded her questions, and she left me in anything but good-humour; but about that I never felt so indifferent.

The next morning the servant made his appearance with the letter, telling me that he had orders to wait till the evening; and I pulled up the river. I placed it under the loose brick, as agreed upon with the young lady, and then shoved off to the other side of the river, where I had a full view of the garden, and could notice all that passed. In half-an-hour the young lady came out, accompanied by another female, and sauntered up and down the gravel-walk. After a while she stopped, and looked on the river, her companion continuing her promenade. As if without hoping to find anything there, she moved the brick aside with her foot; perceiving the letter, she snatched it up eagerly, and concealed it in her dress, and then cast her eyes on the river. It was calm, and I whistled the bar of music. She heard it, and turning away, hastened into the house. In about half-an-hour she returned, and watching her opportunity, stooped down to the brick. I waited a few minutes, when both she and her companion went into the house. I then pulled in under the wall, lifted up the brick, took the letter, and hastened back to Fulham; when I delivered the letter to the servant, who rode off with it as fast as he could; and I returned home quite pleased at the successful issue of my attempt, and not a little curious to learn the real facts of this extraordinary affair.

Chapter Thirty Five

The next day being Sunday, as usual I went to see the Dominie and Mr Turnbull. I arrived at the school just as all the boys were filing off, two and two, for church, the advance led by the usher, and the rear brought up by the Dominie in person, and I accompanied them. The Dominie appeared melancholy and out of spirits—hardly exchanging a word with me during our walk. When the service was over he ordered the usher to take the boys home, and remained with me in the churchyard, surveying the tombstones, and occasionally muttering to himself. At last the congregation dispersed, and we were alone.

"Little did I think, Jacob," said he, at last, "that when I bestowed such care upon thee in thy childhood, I should be rewarded as I have been! Little did I think that it would be to the boy who was left destitute that I should pour out my soul when afflicted, and find in him that sympathy which I have long lost, by the removal of those who were once my friends! Yes, Jacob, those who were known to me in my youth—those few in whom I confided and leant upon—are now lying here in crumbling dust, and the generation hath passed away; and I now rest upon thee, my son, whom I have directed in the right path, and who hast, by the blessing of God, continued to walk straight in it. Verily, thou art a solace to me, Jacob; and though young in years, I feel that in thee I have received a friend, and one that I may confide in. Bless thee, Jacob! bless thee, my boy! and before I am laid with those who have gone before me, may I see thee prosperous and happy! Then I will sing the *Nunc Dimittis*, then will I say, 'Now, Lord, let thy servant depart in peace.'"

"I am happy, sir," replied I, "to hear you say that I am of any comfort to you, for I feel truly grateful for all your kindness to me; but I wish that you did not require comfort."

"Jacob, in what part of a man's life does he not require comfort and consolation; yea, even from the time when, as a child, he buries his weeping face in his mother's lap till the hour that summons him to his account? Not that I consider this world to be, as many have described it, a 'vale of tears'; No, Jacob; it is a beautiful world, a glorious world, and would be a happy world, if we would only restrain those senses and those passions with which we have been endowed, that we may fully enjoy the beauty, the variety, the inexhaustible bounty of a gracious heaven. All was made for enjoyment and for happiness; but it is we ourselves who, by excess, defile that which otherwise were pure. Thus, the fainting traveller may drink wholesome and refreshing draughts from the bounteous, overflowing spring; but should he rush heedlessly into it, he muddies the source, and the waters are those of bitterness. Thus, Jacob, was wine given to cheer the heart of man; yet, didst not thou witness me, thy preceptor, debased by intemperance? Thus, Jacob, were the affections implanted in us as a source of sweetest happiness, such as those which now yearn in my breast towards thee; yet hast thou seen me, thy preceptor, by yielding to the infatuation and imbecility of threescore years, dote, in my folly, upon a maiden, and turn the sweet affections into a source of misery and anguish." I answered not, for the words of the Dominie made a strong impression upon me, and I was weighing them in my mind. "Jacob," continued the Dominie, after a pause, "next to the book of life, there is no subject of contemplation more salutary than the book of death, of which each stone now around us may be considered as a page, and each page contains a lesson. Read that which is now before us. It would appear hard that an only child should have been torn away from its doting parents, who have thus imperfectly expressed their anguish on the tomb; it would appear hard that their delight, their solace, the object of their daily care, of their waking thoughts, of their last imperfect recollections as they sank into sleep, of their only dreams, should thus have been taken from them; yet did I know them, and Heaven was just and merciful. The child had weaned them from their God; they lived but in him; they were without God in the world. The child alone had their affections, and they had been lost had not He in His mercy removed it. Come this way, Jacob." I followed the Dominie till he stood before another tombstone in the corner of the churchyard. "This stone, Jacob, marks the spot where lies the remains of one who was my earliest and dearest friend—for in my youth I had friends, because I had anticipations, and little thought that it would have pleased God that I should do my duty in that station to which I have been called. He had one fault, which proved a source of misery through life, and was the cause of an untimely death. He was of a revengeful disposition. He never forgave an injury, forgetting, poor, sinful mortal, for how much he had need to be forgiven. He quarrelled with his relations; he was shot in a duel with his friend! I mention this, Jacob, as a lesson to thee; not that I feel myself worthy to be thy preceptor, for I am humbled, but out of kindness and love towards thee, that I might persuade thee to correct that fault in thy disposition."

"I have already made friends with Mr Drummond, sir," answered I; "but still your admonition shall not be thrown away."

"Hast thou, Jacob? then is my mind much relieved. I trust thou wilt no longer stand in thine own light, but accept the offers which, in the fulness of his heart to make redress, he may make unto thee."

"Nay, sir, I cannot promise that; I wish to be independent and earn my own livelihood."

"Then hear me, Jacob, for the spirit of prophecy is on me; the time will come when thou shalt bitterly repent. Thou hast received an education by my unworthy endeavours, and hast been blessed by Providence with talents far above the situation in life to which thou wouldst so tenaciously adhere; the time will come when thou wilt repent, yea, bitterly repent. Look at that marble monument with the arms so lavishly emblazoned upon it. That, Jacob, is the tomb of a proud man, whose career is well known to me. He was in straitened circumstances, yet of gentle race—but like the steward in the Scripture, 'work he could not, to beg he was ashamed.' He might have prospered in the world, but his pride forbade him. He might have made friends, but his pride forbade him. He might have wedded himself to wealth and beauty, but there was no escutcheon, and his pride forbade him. He did marry, and entail upon his children poverty. He died, and the little he possessed was taken from his children's necessities to build this record to his dust. Do not suppose that I would check that honest pride which will prove a safeguard from unworthy actions. I only wish to check that undue pride which will mar thy future prospects. Jacob, that which thou termest *independence* is naught but pride."

I could not acknowledge that I agreed with the Dominie, although something in my breast told me that he was not wrong. I made no answer. The Dominie again spoke.

"Yes; it is a beautiful world for the Spirit of God is on it. At the separation of chaos it came over the water, and hath since remained with us, everywhere, but invisible. We see his hand in the variety and the beauty of creation, but his Spirit we see not; yet do we feel it in the still small voice of conscience, which would lead us into the right path. Now, Jacob, we must return, for I have the catechism and collects to attend to."

I took leave of the Dominie, and went to Mr Turnbull's, to whom I gave an account of what had passed since I last saw him. He was much pleased with my reconciliation with the Drummonds, and interested about the young lady to whom appertained the tin box in his possession. "I presume, Jacob, we shall now have that mystery cleared up."

"I have not told the gentleman that we have possession of the box," replied I.

"No; but you told the young lady, you silly fellow; and do you think she will keep it a secret from him?"

"Very true; I had forgotten that."

"Jacob, I wish you to go to Mr Drummond's and see his family again; you ought to do so." I hesitated. "Nay, I shall give you a fair opportunity without wounding that pride of yours, sir," replied Mr Turnbull; "I owe him for some wine he purchased for me, and I shall send the cheque by you."

To this I assented, as I was not sorry of an opportunity of seeing Sarah. I dined with Mr Turnbull, who was alone, his wife being on a visit to a relation in the country. He again offered me his advice as to giving up the profession of a waterman; but if I did not hear him with so much impatience as before, nor use so many arguments against it, I did not accede to his wishes, and the subject was dropped. Mr Turnbull was satisfied that my resistance was weakened, and hoped in time to have the effect that he desired. When I went home Mary told me that Tom Beazeley had been there, that his wherry was building, that his father had given up the lighter, and was now on shore very busy in getting up his board to attract customers, and obtain work in his new occupation.

I had not launched my wherry the next morning when down came the young gentleman to whom I had despatched the letter. "Faithful," said he, "come to the tavern with me; I must have some conversation with you." I followed him, and as soon as we were in a room, he said, "First, let me pay my debt, for I owe you much;" and he laid five guineas on the table. "I find from Cecilia that you have possession of the tin case of deeds which has been so eagerly sought after by both parties. Why did you not say so? And why did you not tell me that it was you whom I hired on the night when I was so unfortunate?"

"I considered the secret as belonging to the young lady, and having told her, I left it to her discretion to make you acquainted or not as she pleased."

"It was thoughtful and prudent of you, at all events, although there was no occasion for it. Nevertheless, I am pleased that you did so, as it proves you to be trustworthy. Now, tell me, who is the gentleman who was with you in the boat, and who has charge of the box? Observe, Faithful, I do not intend to demand it. I shall tell him the facts of the case in your presence, and then leave him to decide whether he will surrender up the papers to the other party or to me. Can you take me there now?"

"Yes, sir," replied I, "I can, if you please; I will pull you up in half an hour. The house is at the river's side."

The young gentleman leaped into my wherry, and we were soon in the parlour of Mr Turnbull. I will not repeat the conversation in detail, but give an outline of the young man's story.

Chapter Thirty Six

"The gentleman who prevented my taking off the young lady is uncle to both of us. We are, therefore, first cousins. Our family name is Wharncliffe. My father was a major in the army. He died when I was young, and my mother is still alive, and is sister to Lady Auburn. The father and mother of Cecilia are both dead. He went out to India to join his brother, another uncle, of whom I shall speak directly. He has now been dead three years, and out of the four brothers there is only one left, my uncle; with whom Cecilia is living, and whose Christian name is Henry. He was a lawyer by profession, but he purchased a patent place, which he still enjoys. My father, whose name was William, died in very moderate circumstances; but still he left enough for my mother to live upon, and to educate me properly. I was brought up to the law under my uncle Henry, with whom, for some years, I resided. Cecilia's father, whose name was Edward, left nothing; he had ruined himself in England, and had gone out to India at the request of my uncle there, whose name was James, and who had amassed a large fortune. Soon after the death of Cecilia's father, my uncle James came home on furlough, for he held a very high and lucrative situation under the Company. A bachelor from choice, he was still fond of young people; and having but one nephew and one niece to leave his money to, as soon as he arrived with Cecilia, whom he brought with him, he was most anxious to see me. He therefore took up his quarters with my uncle Henry, and remained with him during his sojourn in England; but my uncle James was of a very cold and capricious temper. He liked me best because I was a boy, and one day declared I should be his heir. The next day he would alter his intention, and declare that Cecilia, of whom he was very fond, should inherit everything. If we affronted him, for at the age of sixteen as a boy, and fourteen as a girl, worldly prospects were little regarded, he would then declare that we should not be a shilling the better for his money. With him money was everything: it was his daily theme of conversation, his only passion; and he valued and respected people in proportion to what they were supposed to possess. With these feelings he demanded for himself the greatest deference from Cecilia and me, as his expectant heirs. This he did not receive; but on the whole he was pleased with us, and after remaining three years in England, he returned to the East Indies. I had heard him mention to my uncle Henry his intention of making his will, and leaving it with him before he sailed; but I was not certain whether it had been done or not. At all events, my uncle Henry took care that I should not be in the way; for at that time my uncle carried on his profession as a lawyer, and I was working in his office. It was not until after my uncle James returned to India that he gave up business and purchased the patent place which I mentioned. Cecilia was left with my uncle Henry, and as we lived in the same house, our affections, as we grew up, ripened into love. We often used to laugh at the threats of my uncle James, and agreed that whoever might be the fortunate one to whom he left his property, we would go halves, and share it equally.

"In the meantime I still followed up my profession in another house, in which I at present am a partner. Four years after the return of my uncle James to India news came home of his death; but it was also stated that no will could be found, and it was supposed that he died intestate. Of course my uncle Henry succeeded as heir-at-law to the whole property, and thus were the expectations and hopes of Cecilia and of myself dashed to the ground. But this was not the worst of it: my uncle, who had witnessed our feelings for each other, and had made no comment, as soon as he was in possession of the property, intimated to Cecilia that she should be his heiress, provided that she married according to his wishes; and pointed out to her that a fortune such as she might expect would warrant the alliance of the first nobleman in the kingdom; and he very plainly told me that he thought it advisable that I should find lodgings for myself, and not be any longer an inmate in the same house as was my cousin, as no good would result from it. Thus, sir, we were not only disappointed in our hopes, but thwarted in our affections, which had for some time been exchanged. Maddened at this intimation, I quitted the house; and at the same time the idea of my uncle James having made a will still pressed upon me, as I called to mind what I had heard him say to my uncle Henry previous to his sailing for India. There was a box of deeds and papers, the very box now in your possession, which my uncle invariably kept in his bedroom. I felt convinced that the will, if not destroyed (and I did not believe my uncle would dare to commit an act of felony), was in that box. Had I remained in the house I would have found some means to have opened it; but this was no longer possible. I communicated my suspicions to Cecilia, and begged her to make the attempt, which would be more easy as my uncle would not suspect her of being bold enough to venture it, even if he had the suspicion. Cecilia promised, and one day my uncle fortunately left his keys upon his dressing-table when he came down to breakfast, and went out without missing them. Cecilia discovered them, and opened the box, and amongst other parchments found a document labelled outside as the will of our uncle James; but women understand little about these things, and she was in such trepidation for fear that my uncle should return that she could not examine it very minutely. As it was, my uncle did return for his keys just as she had locked the box and placed the keys upon the table. He asked her what she was doing there, and she made some excuse. He saw the keys on the table, and whether suspecting her, for she coloured up very much, or afraid that the attempt might be made at my suggestion, he removed the box and locked it up in a closet, the key of which, I believe, he left with his banker in town. When Cecilia wrote to me an account of what had passed, I desired her to find the means of opening the closet, that we might gain possession of the box; and this was easily effected, for the key of another closet fitted the lock exactly. I then persuaded her to put herself under my protection, with the determination that we would marry immediately; and we had so arranged that the tin box was to have accompanied us. You are aware, sir, how unfortunately our plan turned out—at least, so far unfortunately, that I lost, as I thought, not only Cecilia, but the tin box, containing, as I expect, the will of my uncle, of which I am more than ever convinced from the great anxiety shown by my uncle Henry to recover it. Since the loss he has been in a state of agitation, which has worn him to a shadow. He feels that his only chance is that the waterman employed might have broken open the box, expecting to find money in it, and being disappointed, have destroyed the papers to avoid detection. If such had been the case, and it might have been had it not fallen into such good hands, he then would have obtained his only wish, that of the destruction of the will although not by his own hands. Now, sir, I have given you a full and honest account of the affair, and leave you to decide how to act."

"If you leave me to decide, I shall do it very quickly," replied Mr Turnbull. "A box has fallen into my hands, and I do not know who is the owner. I shall open it, and take a list of the deeds in contains, and advertise them in the *Times* and other newspapers. If your dead uncle's will is in it it will, of course, be advertised with the others, and after such publicity your uncle Henry will not venture, I presume, to say a word, but be too glad not to be exposed."

Mr Turnbull ordered a locksmith to be summoned, and the tin box was opened. It contained the document of the uncle's purchase of the patent place in the courts, and some other papers, but it also contained the parchment so much looked after—the last will and testament of James Wharncliffe, Esquire, dated two months previous to his quitting England. "I think," observed Mr Turnbull, "that in case of accident, it may be as well that this will should be read before witnesses. You observe, it is witnessed by Henry Wharncliffe, with two others. Let us take down their names."

The will was read by young Wharncliffe, at the request of Mr Turnbull. Strange to say, the deceased bequeathed the whole of his property to his nephew, William Wharncliffe, and his niece, Cecilia, provided they married; if they did not, they were left 20,000 pounds each, and the remainder of the fortune to go to the first male child born after the marriage of either niece or nephew. To his brother the sum of 10,000 pounds was bequeathed, with a liberal arrangement, to be paid out of the estate, so long as his niece lived with him. The will was read, and returned to Mr Turnbull, who shook hands with Mr Wharncliffe, and congratulated him.

"I am so much indebted to you, sir, that I can hardly express my gratitude, but I am still more indebted to this intelligent lad, Faithful. You must no longer be a waterman, Faithful," and Mr Wharncliffe shook my hand. I made no answer to the latter observation, for Mr Turnbull had fixed his eye upon me: I merely said that I was very happy to have been of use to him.

"You may truly say, Mr Wharncliffe," observed Mr Turnbull, "that your future prosperity will be through his means; and, as it appears by the will that you have 9000 pounds per annum safe in the Funds, I think you ought to give a prize wherry, to be rowed for every year."

"And I will take that," replied I, "for a receipt in full for my share in the transaction."

"And now," said Mr Turnbull, interrupting Mr Wharncliffe, who was about to answer me, "it appears to me that it may be as well to avoid any exposure—the case is too clear. Call upon your uncle—state in whose hands the documents are—tell him that he must submit to your terms, which are, that he proves the will, and permits the marriage to take place immediately, and that no more will be said on the subject. He, as a lawyer, knows how severely and disgracefully he might be punished for what he has done, and will be too happy now to accede to your terms. In the meantime I keep possession of the papers, for the will shall never leave my hands until it is lodged in Doctors' Commons."

Mr Wharncliffe could not but approve of this judicious arrangement, and we separated; and, not to interfere with my narrative, I may as well tell the reader at once that Mr Wharncliffe's uncle bowed to circumstances, pretended to rejoice at the discovery of the will, never mentioned the loss of his tin box, put the hand of Cecilia into that of William, and they were married one month after the meeting at Mr Turnbull's, which I have now related.

The evening was so far advanced before this council-of-war was over, that I was obliged to defer the delivery of the cheque to Mr Drummond until the next day. I left about eleven o'clock, and arrived at noon; when I knocked at the door the servant did not know me.

"What did you want?"

"I wanted to speak with Mrs or Miss Drummond, and my name is Faithful."

He desired me to sit down in the hall while he went up; "And wipe your shoes, my lad." I cannot say that I was pleased at this command, as I may call it, but he returned, desiring me to walk up, and I followed him.

I found Sarah alone in the drawing-room.

"Jacob, I'm so glad to see you, and I'm sorry that you were made to wait below, but—if people who can be otherwise will be watermen, it is not our fault. The servants only judge by appearances."

I felt annoyed for a moment, but it was soon over. I sat down by Sarah, and talked with her for some time.

"The present I had to make you was a purse of my own knitting, to put your earnings in;" said she, laughing; and then she held up her finger in mockery, crying, "Boat, sir; boat, sir. Well, Jacob, there's nothing like independence, after all, and you must not mind my laughing at you."

"I do not heed it, Sarah," replied I; (but I did mind it very much) "there is no disgrace."

"None whatever, I grant; but a want of ambition, which I cannot understand. However, let us say no more about it."

Mrs Drummond came into the room and greeted me kindly. "When can you come and dine with us, Jacob? Will you come on Wednesday?"

"Oh, mamma! He can't come on Wednesday; we have company on that day."

"So we have, my dear; I had forgotten it; but on Thursday we are quite alone: will you come, then on Thursday, Jacob?"

I hesitated, for I felt that it was because I was a waterman that I was not admitted to the table where I had been accustomed to dine at one time, whoever might be invited.

"Yes, Jacob," said Sarah, coming to me, "it must be Thursday, and you must not deny us; for although we have greater people on Wednesday, the party that day will not be so agreeable to me as your company on Thursday."

The last compliment from Sarah decided me, and I accepted the invitation. Mr Drummond came in, and I delivered to him Mr Turnbull's cheque. He was very kind, but said little further than that he was glad that I had promised to dine with them on Thursday. The footman came in and announced the carriage at the door, and this was a signal for me to take my leave. Sarah, as she shook hands with me, laughing, asserted that it was not considerate in them to detain me any longer, as I must have lost half-a-dozen good fares already; "So go down to your boat, pull off your jacket, and make up for lost time," continued she; "one of these days mamma and I intend to go on the water, just to patronise you." I laughed and went away, but I was cruelly mortified. I could not be equal to them, because I was a waterman. The sarcasm of Sarah was not lost upon me; still there was so much kindness mixed with it that I could not be angry with her. On the Thursday I went there, as agreed; they were quite alone; friendly and attentive; but still there was a degree of constraint which communicated itself to me. After dinner Mr Drummond said very little; there was no renewal of offers to take me into his employ, nor any inquiry as to how I got on in the profession which I had chosen. On the whole, I found myself uncomfortable, and was glad to leave early, nor did I feel at all inclined to renew my visit. I ought to remark that Mr Drummond was now moving in a very different sphere than when I first knew him. He was consignee of several large establishments abroad, and was making a rapid fortune. His establishment was also on a very different scale, every department being appointed with elegance and conducive to luxury. As I pulled up the river something within my breast told me that the Dominie's prophecy would turn out correct, and that I should one day repent of my having refused the advances of Mr Drummond — nay, I did not exactly know whether I did not, even at that moment, very much doubt the wisdom of my asserting my independence.

And now, reader, that I may not surfeit you with an uninteresting detail, you may allow nearly two years to pass away before I recommence my narrative. The events of that time I shall sum up in one or two pages. The Dominie continued the even tenor of his way — blew his nose and handled his rod with as much effect as ever. I seldom passed a Sunday without paying him a visit, and benefiting by his counsel. Mr Turnbull was always kind and considerate, but gradually declining in health, having never recovered from the effects of his submersion under the ice. Of the Drummonds I saw but little; when we did meet, I was kindly received, but I never volunteered a call, and it was usually from a message through Tom that I went to pay my respects. Sarah had grown a very beautiful girl, and the well-known fact of Mr Drummond's wealth, and her being an only daughter, was an introduction to a circle much higher than they had been formerly accustomed to. Every day, therefore, the disparity increased, and I felt less inclined to make my appearance at their house.

Stapleton, as usual, continued to smoke his pipe and descant upon *human natur'*. Mary had grown into a splendid woman, but coquettish as ever. Poor Tom Beazeley was fairly entrapped by her charms, and was a constant attendant upon her, but she played him fast and loose—one time encouraging and smiling on him, at another rejecting and flouting him. Still Tom persevered, for he was fascinated, and having returned me the money advanced for his wherry, he expended all his earnings on dressing himself smartly, and making presents to her. She had completely grown out of any control from me, and appeared to have a pleasure in doing everything she knew I disapproved; still, we were on fair friendly terms as inmates of the same house.

Old Tom Beazeley's board was up, and he had met with great success; and all day he might be seen hammering at the bottom of boats of every description, and heard, at the same time, lightening his labour with his variety of song. I often called there on my way up and down the river, and occasionally passed a few hours listening to his yarns, which, like his songs, appeared to be inexhaustible.

With respect to myself, it would be more a narrative of feelings than of action. My life glided on as did my wherry—silently and rapidly. One day was but the forerunner of another, with slight variety of incident and customers. My acquaintance, as the reader knows, were but few, and my visits occasional. I again turned to my books during the long summer evenings, in which Mary would walk out, accompanied by Tom and other admirers. Mr Turnbull's library was at my service, and I profited much. After a time reading became almost a passion, and I was seldom without a book in my hand. But although I improved my mind, I did not render myself happier. On the contrary, I felt more and more that I had committed an act of egregious folly in thus asserting my independence. I felt that I was superior to my station in life, and that I had lived with those who were not companions—that I had thrown away, by foolish pride, those prospects of advancement which had offered themselves, and that I was passing my youth unprofitably. All this crowded upon me more and more every day, and I bitterly repented, as the Dominie told me that I should, my spirit of independence—now that it was too late. The offers of Mr Drummond were never renewed, and Mr Turnbull, who had formed the idea that I was still of the same opinion, and who, at the same time, in his afflicted state—for he was a martyr to the rheumatism—naturally thought more of himself and less of others, never again proposed that I should quit my employment. I was still too proud to mention my wishes, and thus did I continue plying on the river, apathetic almost as to gain, and only happy when, in the pages of history or among the flowers of poetry, I could dwell upon times that were past, or revel in imagination. Thus did reading, like the snake which is said to contain in its body a remedy for the poison of its fangs, become, as it enlarged my mind, a source of discontent at my humble situation; but, at the same time, the only solace in my unhappiness, by diverting my thoughts from the present. Pass, then, nearly two years, reader, taking the above remarks as an outline, and filling up the picture from the colours of your imagination, with incidents of no peculiar value, and I again resume my narrative.

Chapter Thirty Seven

"Jacob," said Tom to me, pulling his wherry into the *hard*, alongside of mine, in which I was sitting with one of Mr Turnbull's books in my hand; "Jacob, do you recollect that my time is up to-morrow? I shall have run off my seven years, and when the sun rises I shall be free of the river. How much more have you to serve?"

"About fifteen months, as near as I can recollect, Tom.—Boat, sir?"

"Yes; oars, my lad; be smart, for I am in a hurry. How's tide?"

"Down, sir, very soon; but it's now slack water. Tom, see if you can find Stapleton."

"Pooh! never mind him, Jacob, I'll go with you. I say, Jones, tell old *'human natur'* to look after my boat," continued Tom, addressing a waterman of our acquaintance.

"I thought you had come up to see *her*," said I to Tom, as we shoved off.

"See *her* at Jericho first," replied Tom "she's worse than a dog vane."

"What, are you *two* again?"

"Two indeed—it's all two—we are two fools. She is too fanciful; I am too fond; she behaves too ill, and I put up with too much. However, it's all *one*."

"I thought it was all *two* just now, Tom."

"But two may be made one, Jacob, you know."

"Yes, by the parson: but you are no parson."

"Anyhow, I am something like one just now," replied Tom, who was pulling the foremost oar; "for you are a good clerk, and I am sitting behind you."

"That's not so bad," observed the gentleman in the stern-sheets, whom we had forgotten in the colloquy.

"A waterman would make but a bad parson, sir," replied Tom.

"Why so?"

"He's not likely to practice as he preaches."

"Again, why so?"

"Because all his life he looks one way and pulls another."

"Very good—very good, indeed."

"Nay, sir, good in practice, but still not good *in deed*—there's a puzzle."

"A puzzle, indeed, to find such a regular chain of repartee in a wherry."

"Well, sir, if I'm a regular chain to-day, I shall be like an irregular watch to-morrow."

"Why so, my lad?"

"Because I shall be *out of my time*."

"Take that, my lad," said the gentleman, tossing half-a-crown to Tom.

"Thanky, sir; when we meet again may you have no more wit than you have now."

"How do you mean?"

"Not wit enough to keep your money, sir—that's all!"

"I presume you think that I have not got much."

"Which, sir; wit or money?"

"Wit, my lad."

"Nay, sir, I think you have both: the first you purchased just now; and you would hardly have bought it, if you had not money to spare."

"But I mean wit of my own."

"No man has wit of his own; if he borrows it, it's not his own; if he has it in himself, it's *mother* wit, so it's not his."

We pulled into the stairs near London Bridge, and the gentleman paid me his fare. "Good-bye, my lad," said he to Tom.

"Fare-you-well, for well you've paid your fare," replied Tom, holding out his arm to assist him out of the boat. "Well, Jacob, I've made more by my head than by my hands this morning. I wonder, in the long run, which gains most in the world."

"Head, Tom, depend upon it; but they work best together."

Here we were interrupted—"I say, you watermen, have you a mind for a good fare?" cried a dark-looking, not over clean, square-built, short young man, standing on the top of the flight of steps.

"Where to, sir?"

"Gravesend, my jokers, if you ain't afraid of salt water."

"That's a long way, sir," replied Tom; "and for salt water, we must have salt to our porridge."

"So you shall, my lads, and a glass of grog into the bargain."

"Yes; but the bargain a'n't made yet, sir. Jacob, will you go?"

"Yes, but not under a guinea."

"Not under two guineas," replied Tom, aside. "Are you in a great hurry, sir?" continued he, addressing the young man.

"Yes, in a devil of a hurry; I shall lose my ship. What will you take me for?"

"Two guineas, sir."

"Very well. Just come up to the public-house here, and put in my traps."

We brought down his luggage, put it into the wherry, and started down the river with the tide. Our fare was very communicative, and we found out that he was the master's mate of the *Immortalité*, forty-gun frigate, lying off Gravesend, which was to drop down next morning and wait for sailing orders at the Downs. We carried the tide with us, and in the afternoon were close to the frigate, whose blue ensign waved proudly over the taffrail. There was a considerable sea arising from the wind meeting the tide, and before we arrived close to her we had shipped a great deal of water; and when we were alongside, the wherry, with the chest in her bows, pitched so heavily that we were afraid of being swamped. Just as a rope had been made fast to the chest, and they were weighing it out of the wherry, the ship's launch with water came alongside, and, whether from accident or wilfully, I know not, although I suspect the latter, the midshipman who steered her shot her against the wherry, which was crushed in, and immediately filled, leaving Tom and me in the water, and in danger of being jammed to death between the launch and the side of the frigate. The seamen in the boat, however, forced her off with their oars, and hauled us in, while our wherry sank with her gunwale even with the water's edge, and floated away astern.

As soon as we had shaken ourselves a little, we went up the side, and asked one of the officers to send a boat to pick up our wherry.

"Speak to the first lieutenant—there he is," was the reply.

I went up to the person pointed out to me; "If you please, sir—"

"What the devil do you want?"

"A boat, sir, to—"

"A boat! the devil you do!"

"To pick up our wherry, sir," interrupted Tom.

"Pick it up yourself," said the first lieutenant, passing us, and hailing the men aloft. "Maintop, there, hook on your stays. Be smart. Lower away the yards. Marines and after-guard, clear launch. Boatswain's mate."

"Here, sir."

"Pipe marines and after-guard to clear launch."

"Aye, aye, sir."

"But we shall lose our boat, Jacob," said Tom to me. "They stove it in, and they ought to pick it up." Tom then went up to the master's mate, which he had brought on board, and explained our difficulty.

"Upon my soul, I dar'n't say a word. I'm in a scrape for breaking my leave. Why the devil didn't you take care of your wherry, and haul a-head when you saw the launch coming?"

"How could we, when the chest was hoisting out?"

"Very true. Well, I am very sorry for you, but I must look after my chest." So saying, he disappeared down the gangway ladder.

"I'll try it again, anyhow," said Tom, going up to the first lieutenant. "Hard case to lose our boat and our bread, sir," said Tom touching his hat.

The first lieutenant, now that the marines and after-guard were at a regular stamp and go, had, unfortunately more leisure to attend to us. He looked at us earnestly, and walked aft to see if the wherry was yet in sight. At that moment up came the master's mate, who had not yet reported himself to the first lieutenant.

"Tom," said I, "there is a wherry close to, let us get into it, and go after our boat ourselves."

"Wait one moment to see if they will help us—and get our money, at all events," replied Tom; and we both walked aft.

"Come on board, sir," said the master's mate, touching his hat with humility.

"You've broke your leave, sir," replied the first lieutenant, "and now I've to send a boat to pick up the wherry through your carelessness."

"If you please, they are two very fine young men," observed the mate. "Make capital foretopmen. Boat's not worth sending for, sir."

This hint, given by the mate to the first lieutenant, to regain his favour, was not lost. "Who are you, my lads?" said the first lieutenant to us.

"Watermen, sir."

"Watermen, heh? was that your own boat?"

"No, sir," replied I; "it belongs to the man that I serve with."

"Oh, not your own boat? Are you an apprentice, then?"

"Yes, sir, both apprentices."

"Show me your indentures."

"We don't carry them about with us."

"Then how am I to know that you are apprentices?"

"We can prove it, sir, if you wish it."

"I do wish it; at all events, the captain will wish it."

"Will you please to send for the boat, sir? she's almost out of sight."

"No, my lads, I can't find king's boats for such service."

"Then we had better go ourselves, Tom," said I, and we went forward to call the waterman, who was lying on his oars close to the frigate.

"Stop—stop—not so fast. Where are you going, my lads?"

"To pick up our boat, sir."

"Without my leave, heh?"

"We don't belong to the frigate, sir."

"No; but I think it very likely that you will, for you have no protections."

"We can send for them, and have them down by to-morrow morning."

"Well, you may do so if you please, my lads; but you can not expect me to believe everything that is told me. Now, for instance, how long have you to serve, my lad?" said he, addressing Tom.

"My time is up to-morrow, sir."

"Up to-morrow. Why, then, I shall detain you until tomorrow, and then I shall press you."

"If you detain me now, sir, I am pressed to-day."

"Oh, no! you are only detained until you prove your apprenticeship, that's all."

"Nay, sir, I certainly am pressed during my apprenticeship."

"Not at all, and I'll prove it to you. You don't belong to the ship until you are victualled on her books. Now I sha'n't *victual* you to-day, and therefore you won't be *pressed*."

"I shall be pressed with hunger at all events," replied Tom, who never could lose a joke.

"No you sha'n't; for I'll send you both a good dinner out of the gun-room. So you won't be pressed at all," replied the lieutenant, laughing at Tom's reply.

"You will allow me to go, sir, at all events," replied I; for I knew that the only chance of getting Tom and myself clear was my hastening to Mr Drummond for assistance.

"Pooh! nonsense; you must both row in the same boat as you have done. The fact is, my lads, I've taken a great fancy to you both, and I can't make up my mind to part with you."

"It's hard to lose our bread this way," replied I.

"We will find you bread, and hard enough you will find it," replied the lieutenant, laughing; "it's like a flint."

"So we ask for bread, and you give us a stone," said Tom; "that's 'gainst Scripture."

"Very true, my lad; but the fact is, all the scriptures in the world won't man the frigate. Men we must have, and get them how we can, and where we can, and when we can. Necessity has no law; at least it obliges us to break through all laws. After all, there's no great hardship in serving the king for a year or two, and filling your pockets with prize-money. Suppose you volunteer?"

"Will you allow us to go on shore for half-an-hour to think about it?" replied I.

"No. I'm afraid of the crimps dissuading you. But I'll give you till to-morrow morning, and then I shall be sure of one at all events."

"Thanky for me," replied Tom.

"You're very welcome," replied the first lieutenant, as, laughing at us, he went down the companion-ladder to his dinner.

"Well, Jacob, we are in for it," said Tom, as soon as we were alone. "Depend upon it there's no mistake this time."

"I am afraid not," replied I, "unless we can get a letter to your father, or Mr Drummond, who, I am sure, would help us. But that dirty fellow, who gave the lieutenant the hint, said the frigate sailed to-morrow morning; there he is, let us speak to him."

"When does the frigate sail!" said Tom to the master's mate, who was walking the deck.

"My good fellow, it's not the custom on board of a man-of-war for men to ask officers to answer such impertinent questions. It's quite sufficient for you to know that when the frigate sails you will have the pleasure of sailing in her."

"Well, sir," replied I, nettled at his answer, "at all events you will have the goodness to pay us our fare. We have lost our wherry, and our liberty, perhaps, through you; we may as well have our two guineas."

"Two guineas! It's two guineas you want, heh."

"Yes, sir, that was the fare we agreed upon."

"Why you must observe, my men," said the master's mate, hooking a thumb into each armhole of his waistcoat, "there must be a little explanation as to that affair. I promised you two guineas as watermen; but now that you belong to a man-of-war, you are no longer watermen. I always pay my debts honourably when I can find the lawful creditors; but where are the watermen?"

"Here we are sir."

"No, my lads, you are men-of-war's men now, and that quite alters the case."

"But we are not so yet, sir; even if it did alter the case, we are not pressed yet."

"Well, then, you'll be to-morrow, perhaps; at all events we shall see. If you are allowed to go on shore again, I owe you two guineas as watermen; and if you are detained as men-of-war's men, why then you will only have done your duty in pulling down one of your officers. You see, my lads, I say nothing but what's fair."

"Well, sir, but when you hired us we were watermen," replied Tom.

"Very true, so you were; but recollect the two guineas were not due until you had completed your task, which was not until you came on board. When you came on board you were pressed, and became men-of-war's men. You should have asked for your fare before the first lieutenant got hold of you. Don't you perceive the justice of my remarks?"

"Can't say I do, sir; but I perceive there's very little chance of our being paid," said Tom.

"You are a lad of discrimination," replied the master's mate. "And now I advise you to drop the subject, or you may induce me to pay you 'man-of-war fashion.'"

"How's that, sir?"

"Over the face and eyes, as the cat paid the monkey," replied the master's mate, walking leisurely away.

"No go, Tom," said I, smiling at the absurdity of the arguments.

"I'm afraid it's *no go* in every way, Jacob. However, I don't care much about it. I have had a little hankering after seeing the world, and perhaps now's as well as an other time; but I'm sorry for you, Jacob."

"It's all my own fault," replied I; and I fell into one of those reveries so often indulged in of late, as to the folly of my conduct in asserting my independence, which had now ended in my losing my liberty. But we were cold from the ducking we had received, and moreover, very hungry. The first lieutenant did not forget his promise: he sent us a good dinner, and a glass of grog each, which we discussed under the half-deck, between two of the guns. We had some money in our pockets, and we purchased some sheets of paper from the bum-boat people, who were on the main-deck supplying the seamen, and I wrote to Mr Drummond and Mr Turnbull, as well as to Mary and old Tom, requesting the two latter to forward our clothes to Deal, in case of our being detained. Tom also wrote to comfort his mother, and the greatest comfort which he could give was, as he said, to promise to keep sober. Having entrusted these letters to the bumboat woman, who promised faithfully to put them into the post-office, we had then nothing else to do but to look out for some place to sleep. Our clothes had dried on us, and we were walking under the half-deck: but not a soul spoke to, or even took the least notice of us. In a newly-manned ship just ready to sail there is a universal feeling of selfishness prevailing among the ship's company. Some, if not most, had, like us, been pressed, and their thoughts were occupied with their situation and the change in their prospects. Others were busy making their little arrangements with their wives or relations; while the mass of the seamen, not yet organised by discipline or known to each other, were in a state of disunion and individuality, which naturally induced every man to look after himself without caring for his neighbour. We therefore could not expect, nor did we receive, any sympathy; we were in a scene of bustle and noise, yet alone. A spare topsail, which had been stowed for the present between two of the guns, was the best accommodation which offered itself. We took possession of it, and, tired with exertion of mind and body, were soon fast asleep.

Chapter Thirty Eight

At daylight the next morning we were awakened with a start by the shrill whistles of the boatswain and his mates piping all hands to unmoor. The pilot was on board, and the wind was fair. As the frigate had no anchor down, but was hanging to the moorings in the river, we had nothing to do but to cast off, sheet home, and in less than half-an-hour we were under all sail, stemming the last quarter of the flood tide. Tom and I had remained on the gangway watching the proceedings but not assisting, when the ship being fairly under sail, the order was given by the first lieutenant to coil down the ropes.

"I think, Jacob, we may as well help," said Tom laying hold of the main tack, which was passed aft, and hauling it forward.

"With all my heart," replied I, and I hauled it forward, while he coiled it away.

While we were thus employed the first lieutenant walked forward and recognised us. "That's what I like, my lads," said he; "you don't sulk, I see, and I sha'n't forget it."

"I hope you won't forget that we are apprentices, sir, and allow us to go on shore," replied I.

"I've a shocking bad memory in some things," was his reply, as he continued forward to the forecastle. He did not, however, forget to victual us that day, and insert our names, in pencil, upon the ship's books; but we were not put into any mess, or stationed.

We anchored in the Downs on the following morning. It came on to blow hard in the afternoon, and there was no communication with the shore, except the signal was made, third day, when it moderated, and the signal was made "Prepare to weigh, and send boat for captain." In the meantime several boats came off, and one had a postman on board. I had letters from Mr Drummond and Mr Turnbull, telling me that they would immediately apply to the Admiralty for our being liberated, and one from Mary, half of which was for me, and the rest to Tom. Stapleton had taken Tom's wherry and pulled down to old Tom Beazeley with my clothes, which, with young Tom's, had been despatched to Deal. Tom had a letter from his mother, half indited by his father, and the rest from herself; but I shall not trouble the reader with the contents, as he may imagine what was likely to be said upon such an occasion.

Shortly afterwards our clothes, which had been sent to the care of an old shipmate of Tom's father, were brought on board, and we hardly had received them when the signalman reported that the captain was coming off. There were so many of the men in the frigate who had never seen the captain that no little anxiety was shown by the ship's company to ascertain how far, by the *"cut of his jib,"* that is, his outward appearance, they might draw conclusions as to what they might expect from one who had such unlimited power to make them happy or miserable. I was looking out of the maindeck port with Tom, when the gig pulled alongside, and was about to scrutinise the outward and visible signs of the captain, when I was attracted by the face of a lieutenant sitting by his side, whom I immediately recognised. It was Mr Wilson, the officer who had spun the oar and sunk the wherry, from which, as the reader may remember, I rescued my friends, the senior and junior clerk. I was overjoyed at this, as I hoped that he would interest himself in our favour. The pipe of the boatswain re-echoed as the captain ascended the side. He appeared on the quarter-deck—every hat descending to do him honour; the marines presented arms, and the marine officer at their head lowered the point of his sword. In return, the omnipotent personage, taking his cocked hat with two fingers and a thumb, by the highest peak, lifted it one inch off his head, and replaced it, desiring the marine officer to dismiss the guard. I had now an opportunity, as he paced to and fro with the first lieutenant, to examine his appearance. He was a tall, very large-boned, gaunt man, with an enormous breadth of shoulders, displaying Herculean strength (and this we found he eminently possessed). His face was of a size corresponding to his large frame; his features were harsh, his eye piercing, but his nose, although bold, was handsome, and his capacious mouth was furnished with the most splendid row of large teeth that I ever beheld. The character of his countenance was determination rather than severity. When he smiled the expression was agreeable. His gestures and his language were emphatic, and the planks trembled with his elephantine walk.

He had been on board about ten minutes, when he desired the first lieutenant to turn the hands up, and all the men were ordered on the larboard side of the quarter-deck. As soon as they were all gathered together, looking with as much awe on the captain as a flock of sheep at a strange, mischief-meaning dog, he thus addressed them—"My lads, as it so happens that we are all to trust to the same planks, it may be just as well that we should understand one another. I *like* to see my officers attentive to their duty, and behave themselves as gentlemen. I *like* to see my men well disciplined, active, and sober. What I *like* I *will have*—you understand me. Now," continued he, putting on a stern look—"now, just look in my face, and see if you think you can play with me." The men looked in his face, and saw that there was no chance of playing with him; and so they expressed by their countenances. The captain appeared satisfied by their mute acknowledgments, and to encourage them, smiled, and showed his white teeth, as he desired the first lieutenant to pipe down.

As soon as the scene was over, I walked up to Mr Wilson, the lieutenant, who was standing aft, and accosted him. "Perhaps, sir, you do not recollect me; but we met one night when you were sinking in a wherry, and you asked my name."

"And I recollect it, my lad; it was Faithful, was it not?"

"Yes, sir;" and I then entered into an explanation of our circumstances, and requested his advice and assistance.

He shook his head. "Our captain," said he, "is a very strange person. He has commanding interest, and will do more in defiance of the rules of the Admiralty than any one in the service. If an Admiralty order came down to discharge you, he would obey it; but as for regulations, he cares very little for them. Besides, we sail in an hour. However, I will speak to him, although I shall probably get a rap on the knuckles, as it is the business of the first lieutenant, and not mine."

"But, sir, if you requested the first lieutenant to speak?"

"If I did, he would not, in all probability; men are too valuable, and the first lieutenant knows that the captain would not like to discharge you. He will, therefore, say nothing until it is too late, and then throw all the blame upon himself for forgetting it. Our captain has such interest that his recommendation would give a commander's rank to-morrow, and we must all take care of ourselves. However, I will try, although I can give you very little hopes."

Mr Wilson went up to the captain, who was still walking with the first lieutenant, and, touching his hat, introduced the subject, stating, as an apology, that he was acquainted with me.

"Oh, if the man is an acquaintance of yours, Mr Wilson, we certainly must decide," replied the captain with mock politeness. "Where is he?" I advanced, and Tom followed me. We stated our case. "I always like to put people out of suspense," said the captain, "because it unsettles a man—so now hear me; if I happened to press one of the blood-royal, and the king, and the queen, and all the little princesses were to go down on their knees, I'd keep him, without an Admiralty order for his discharge. Now, my lads, do you perceive your chance?" Then turning away to Mr Wilson, he said, "You will oblige me by stating upon what grounds you ventured to interfere in behalf of these men, and I trust your explanation will be satisfactory. Mr Knight," continued he, to the first lieutenant, "send these men down below, watch, and station them."

We went below by the gangway ladder and watched the conference between the captain and Mr Wilson, who, we were afraid, had done himself no good by trying to assist us. But when it was over the captain appeared pleased, and Mr Wilson walked away with a satisfied air. As I afterwards discovered it did me no little good. The hands were piped to dinner, and after dinner we weighed and made sail, and thus were Tom and I fairly, or rather unfairly, embarked in his majesty's service.

"Well, Tom," said I, "it's no use crying. What's done can't be helped; here we are; now let us do all we can to make friends."

"That's just my opinion, Jacob. Hang care; it killed the cat; I shall make the best of it, and I don't see why we may not be as happy here as anywhere else. Father says we may, if we do our duty, and I don't mean to shirk mine. The more the merrier, they say, and I'll be hanged but there's not enough of us here."

I hardly need say that, for the first three or four days, we were not very comfortable; we had been put into the seventh mess, and were stationed in the foretop; for although we had not been regularly bred up as seaman, the first lieutenant so decided, saying, that he was sure that, in a few weeks, there would be no smarter men in the ship.

We were soon clear of the Channel, and all hands were anxious to know our destination, which, in this almost solitary instance, had been really kept a secret, although surmises were correct. There is one point which, by the present arrangements, invariably makes known whether a ship is "fitting foreign," or for home service, which is, by the stores and provisions ordered on board; and these stores are so arranged, according to the station to which the vessel is bound, that it is generally pretty well known what her destination is to be. This is bad, and at the same time easily remedied; for if every ship, whether for home service or foreign, was ordered to fit foreign, no one would be able to ascertain where she was about to proceed. With a very little trouble strict secrecy might be preserved, now that the Navy Board is abolished; but during its existence that was impossible. The *Immortalité* was a very fast sailing vessel, and when the captain (whose name I have forgotten to mention, it was Hector Maclean) opened his sealed orders, we found that we were to cruise for two months between the Western Isles and Madeira, in quest of some privateers, which had captured many of our outward-bound West Indiamen, notwithstanding they were well protected by convoy, and, after that period, to join the admiral at Halifax, and relieve a frigate which had been many years on that station. In a week we were on our station, the weather was fine, and the whole of the day was passed in training the men to the guns, small arms, making and shortening sail, reefing topsails, and manoeuvring the ship. The captain would never give up his point, and sometimes we were obliged to make or shorten sail twenty times running until he was satisfied.

"My lads," he would say to the ship's company, sending for them aft, "you have done this pretty well; you have only been two minutes; not bad for a new ship's company, but I *like* it done in a minute and a-half. We'll try again." And sure enough it was try again, until in a minute and a-half it was accomplished. Then the captain would say, "I knew you could do it, and having once done it, my lads, of course you can do it again."

Tom and I adhered to our good resolutions. We were as active and as forward as we could be; and Mr Knight, the first lieutenant, pointed us out to the captain. As soon as the merits of the different men were ascertained, several alterations were made in the watch and station bills, as well as in the ratings on the ship's books, and Tom and I were made *second* captains, larboard and starboard, of the foretop. This was great promotion for so young hands, especially as we were not bred as regular sailors; but it was for the activity and zeal which we displayed. Tom was a great favourite among the men, always joking, and ready for any lark or nonsense; moreover, he used to mimic the captain, which few others dared do. He certainly seldom ventured to do it below; it was generally in the foretop, where he used to explain to the men what he *liked*. One day we both ventured it, but it was on an occasion which excused it. Tom and I were aft, sitting in the jolly boat astern, fitting some of her gear, for we belonged to the boat at that time, although we were afterwards shifted into the cutter. The frigate was going about four knots through the water, and the sea was pretty smooth. One of the marines fell overboard, out of the forechains. "Man overboard," was cried out immediately, and the men (became) very busy clearing away the starboard cutter, with all the expedition requisite on such an occasion. The captain was standing aft on the signal chest when the marine passed astern; the poor fellow could not swim, and Tom turning to me said, "Jacob, I should *like* to save that Jolly," and immediately dashed overboard.

"And I should *like* to help you, Tom," cried I, following him.

The captain was close to us, and heard us both. Between us we easily held up the marine, and the boat had us all on board in less than a minute. When we came on deck the captain was at the gangway. He showed his white teeth, and shook the telescope in his hand at us. "I heard you both; and I should *like* to have a good many more impudent fellows like you."

We continued our cruise, looking sharp out for the privateers, but without success; we then touched at Madeira for intelligence, and were informed that they had been seen more to the southward. The frigate's head was turned in that direction until we were abreast of the Canary Isles, and then we traversed east and west, north or south, just as the wind and weather, or the captain's *like* thought proper. We had now cruised seven weeks out of our time without success, and the captain promised five guineas to the man who should discover the objects of our search. Often did Tom and I climb to the mast-head and scan the horizon, and so did many others: but those who were stationed at the look-out were equally on the alert. The ship's company were now in a very fair state of discipline, owing to the incessant practice, and every evening the hands were turned up to skylark—that is, to play and amuse themselves. There was one amusement which was the occasion of a great deal of mirth, and it was a favourite one of the captain's, as it made the men smart. It is called, "Follow my leader." One of the men leads, and all who choose follow him: sometimes forty or fifty will join. Whatever the leader does, the rest must do also; wherever he goes they must follow. Tom, who was always the foremost for fun, was one day the leader, and after having scampered up the rigging, laid out on the yards, climbed in by the lifts, crossed from mast to mast by the stays, slid down by the backstays, blacked his face in the funnel, in all which motions he was followed by about thirty others, hallooing and laughing, while the officers and other men were looking on and admiring their agility, a novel idea came into Tom's head; it was then about seven o'clock in the evening, the ship was lying becalmed, Tom again sprang up the rigging, laid out to the main yard-arm, followed by me and the rest, and as soon as he was at the boom iron, he sprang up, holding by the lift, and crying out, "Follow my leader," leaped from the yard-arm into the sea. I was second, and crying out, "Follow my leader" to the rest, I followed him, and the others, whether they could swim or not, did the same, it being a point of honour not to refuse.

The captain was just coming up the ladder, when he saw, as he imagined, a man tumble overboard, which was Tom in his descent; but how much more was he astonished at seeing twenty or thirty more tumbling off by twos or threes, until it appeared that half the ship's company were overboard. Some of the men who could not swim, but were too proud to refuse to follow, were nearly drowned. As it was, the first lieutenant was obliged to lower the cutter to pick them up, and they were all brought on board.

"Confound that fellow," said the captain to the first lieutenant; "he is always at the head of all mischief. Follow my leader, indeed! Send Tom Beazeley here." We all thought that Tom was about to catch it. "Hark ye, my lad," said the captain; "a joke's a joke, but everybody can't swim as well as you. I can't afford to lose any of my men by your pranks, so don't try that again—I don't *like* it."

Every one thought that Tom got off very cheaply; but he was a favourite with the captain, although that never appeared but indirectly; "Beg pardon, sir," replied Tom, with great apparent humility, "but they were all so dirty—they'd blacked themselves at the funnel, and I thought a little washing would not do them any harm."

"Be off, sir, and recollect what I have said," replied the captain, turning away, and showing his white teeth.

I heard the first lieutenant say to the captain, "He's worth any ten men in the ship, sir. He keeps them all alive and merry, sets such a good example."

Chapter Thirty Nine

In the meantime, Tom had gone up to the fore-royal arm, and was looking round for the five guineas, and just as the conversation was going on, cried out, "Sail ho!"

"Strange sail reported."

"Where," cried the first lieutenant, going forward.

"Right under the sun."

"Mast-head there—do you make her out?"

"Yes, sir; I think she's a schooner; but I can only see down to her mainyard."

"That's one of them, depend upon it," said the captain.

"Up there, Mr Wilson, and see what you make of her. Who is the man who reported it?"

"Tom Beazeley, sir."

"Confound that fellow, he makes all my ship's company jump overboard, and now I must give him five guineas. What do you make of her, Mr Wilson?"

"A low schooner, sir, very rakish indeed, black sides. I cannot make out her ports; but I should think she can show a very pretty set of teeth. She is becalmed as well as we."

"Well, then, we must whistle for a breeze. In the meantime, Mr Knight, we will have the boats all ready."

If you whistle long enough the wind is certain to come. In about an hour the breeze did come, and we took it down with us; but it was too dark to distinguish the schooner, which we had lost sight of as soon as the sun had set. About midnight the breeze failed us, and it was again calm. The captain and most of the officers were up all night, and the watch were employed preparing the boats for service. It was my morning watch, and at break of day I saw the schooner from the foresail-yard about four miles to the North West. I ran down on deck and reported her.

"Very good, my lad. I have her, Mr Knight," said the captain, who had directed his glass to where I pointed; "and I will have her too, one way or the other. No signs of wind. Lower down the cutters. Get the yards and stays hooked all ready. We'll wait a little, and see a little more of her when it's broad daylight."

At broad daylight the schooner, with her appointments, was distinctly to be made out. She was pierced for sixteen guns, and was a formidable vessel to encounter with the boats. The calm still continuing, the launch, yawl, and pinnace were hoisted out, manned, and armed. The schooner got out her sweeps, and was evidently preparing for their reception. Still the captain appeared unwilling to risk the lives of his men in such a dangerous conflict, and there we all lay alongside, each man sitting in his place with his oar raised on end. Cat's-paws of wind, as they call them, flew across the water here and there, ruffling its smooth surface, portending that a breeze would soon spring up, and the hopes of this chance rendered the captain undecided. Thus did we remain alongside, for Tom and I were stationed in the first and second cutters until twelve o'clock, when we were ordered out to take a hasty dinner, and the allowance of spirits was served out. At one it was still calm. Had we started when the boats were first hoisted out the affair would have been long before decided. At last, the captain, perceiving that the chance of a breeze was still smaller then than in the forenoon, ordered the boats to shove off. We were still about the same distance from the privateer, from three-and-a-half to four miles. In less than half-an-hour we were within gun-shot; the privateer swept her broadside to us, and commenced firing guns with single round shot, and with great precision. They *ricochetted* over the boats, and at every shot we made sure of our being struck. At this time a slight breeze swept along the water. It reached the schooner, filled her sails, and she increased her distance. Again it died away, and we neared her fast. She swept round again, and recommenced firing, and one of her shot passed through the second cutter, in which I was stationed, ripping open three of her planks, and wounding two men beside me. The boat, heavy with the gun, ammunition chests, etcetera, immediately filled and turned over with us, and it was with difficulty that we could escape from the weighty hamper that was poured out of her. One of the poor fellows, who had not been wounded, remained entangled under the boat, and never rose again. The remainder of the crew rose to the surface and clung to the side of the boat. The first cutter hauled to our assistance, for we had separated to render the shot less effectual; but it was three or four minutes before she was able to render us any assistance, during which time the other two wounded men, who had been apparently injured in the legs or body, exhausted with loss of blood, gradually unloosed their holds and disappeared under the calm, blue water. I had received a splinter in my left arm, and held on longer than the others who had been maimed, but I could not hold on till the cutter came. I lost my recollection, and sank. Tom, who was in the bow of the cutter, perceiving me go down, dived after me, brought me up again to the surface, and we were both hauled in. The other five men were also saved. As soon as we were picked up, the cutter followed the other boats, which continued to advance towards the privateer. I recovered my senses, and found that a piece of one of the thwarts of the boat, broken off by the shot, had been forced through the fleshy part of my arm below the elbow, where it still remained. It was a very dangerous as well as a painful wound. The officer of the boat, without asking me, laid hold of the splinter and tore it out; but the pain was so great, from its jagged form, and the effusion of blood so excessive after this operation, that I again fainted. Fortunately no artery was wounded, or I must have lost my arm. They bound it up, and laid me at the bottom of the boat. The firing from the schooner was now very warm; and we were within a quarter of a mile of her, when the breeze sprang up, and she increased her distance a mile. There was a prospect of wind from the appearance of the sky, although, for a time, it again died away. We were within less than half-a-mile of the privateer, when we perceived that the frigate was bringing up a smart breeze, and rapidly approached the scene of conflict.

The breeze swept along the water and caught the sails of the privateer, and she was again, in spite of all the exertions of our wearied men, out of gun-shot; and the first lieutenant very properly decided upon making for the frigate, which was now within a mile of us. In less than ten minutes the boats were hoisted in; and the wind now rising fast, we were under all sail, going at the rate of seven miles an hour; the privateer having also gained the breeze, and gallantly holding her own.

I was taken down into the cockpit, the only wounded man brought on board. The surgeon examined my arm, and at first shook his head, and I expected immediate amputation; but on re-examination he gave his opinion that the limb might be saved. My wound was dressed, and I was put into my hammock, in a screened bulk under the half-deck, where the cooling breeze from the ports fanned my feverish cheeks. But I must return to the chase.

In less than an hour the wind had increased, so that we could with difficulty carry our royals; the privateer was holding her own about three miles right a-head, keeping our three masts in one. At sunset they were forced to take in the royals, and the sky gave every prospect of a rough gale. Still we carried on every stitch of canvas which the frigate could bear; keeping the chase in sight with our night-glasses, and watching all her motions.

The breeze increased; before morning there was a heavy sea, and the frigate could only carry top-gallant sails over double-reefed top-sails. At daylight we had neared the schooner, by the sextants, about a quarter of a mile, and the captain and officers went down to take some repose and refreshment, not having quitted the deck for twenty-four hours. All that day did we chase the privateer, without gaining more than a mile upon her, and it now blew up a furious gale: the topgallant sails had been before taken in; the top-sails were close reefed, and we were running at the speed of nearly twelve miles an hour; still so well did the privateer sail, that she was barely within gunshot when the sun went down below the horizon, angry and fiery red. There was now great fear that she would escape, from the difficulty of keeping the glasses upon her during the night, in a heavy sea, and the expectation that she would furl all sail and allow us to pass her. It appeared, however, that this manoeuvre did not enter into the head of the captain of the privateer; he stood on under a press of sail, which even in day-time would have been considered alarming; and at daylight, owing to the steerage during the night never being so correct as during the day, she had recovered her distance, and was about four miles from us. The gale, if anything, had increased, and Captain Maclean determined, notwithstanding, to shake a reef out of the topsails.

In the morning, as usual, Tom came to my cot, and asked me how I was? I told him I was better and in less pain, and that the surgeon had promised to dress my wound after breakfast, for the bandages had not been removed since I had first come on board. "And the privateer, Tom, I hope we shall take her; it will be some comfort to me that she is captured."

"I think we shall, if the masts stand, Jacob; but we have an enormous press of sail, as you may guess by the way in which the frigate jumps; there is no standing on the forecastle, and there is a regular waterfall down in the waist from forward. We are nearing her now. It is beautiful to see how she behaves: when she heels over, we can perceive that all her men are lashed on deck, and she takes whole seas into her fore and aft mainsail, and pours them out again as she rises from the lurch. She deserves to escape, at all events."

She did not, however, obtain her deserts, for about twelve o'clock in the day we were within a mile of her. At two, the marines were firing small arms at her, for we would not yaw to fire at her a gun, although she was right under our bows. When within a cable's length we shortened sail, so as to keep at that distance astern, and the chase, after having lost several men by musketry, the captain of her waved his hat in token of surrender. We immediately shortened sail to keep the weather-gage, pelting her until every sail was lowered down: we then rounded to, keeping her under our lee, and firing at every man who made his appearance on deck. Taking possession of her was a difficult task: a boat could hardly live in such a sea and when the captain called aloud for volunteers, and I heard Tom's voice in the cutter as it was lowering down, my heart misgave me lest he should meet with some accident. At last I knew, from the conversation on deck, that the cutter had got safe on board, and my mind was relieved. The surgeon came up and dressed my arm, and I then received comparative bodily as well as mental relief.

It was not until the next day, when we lay to, with the schooner close to us, that the weather became sufficiently moderate to enable us to receive the prisoners, and put our own men and officers on board. The prize proved to be an American-built schooner, fitted out as a French privateer. She was called the *Cerf Agile*, mounting fourteen guns, of nearly three hundred tons measurement, and with a crew of one hundred and seventy men, of which forty-eight were away in prizes. It was perhaps fortunate that the boats were not able to attack her, as they would have received a very warm reception. Thus did we succeed in capturing this mischievous vessel, after a chase of two hundred and seventy miles. As soon as all the arrangements were made, we shaped our course, with the privateer in company, for Halifax, where we arrived in about five weeks. My wound was now nearly healed, but my arm had wasted away, and I was unable to return to my duty. It was well known that I wrote a good hand, and I volunteered, as I could do nothing else, to assist the purser and the clerk with the ship's books, etcetera.

The admiral was at Bermuda, and the frigate which we were to relieve had, from the exigence of the service, been despatched down to the Honduras, and was not expected back for some months. We sailed from Halifax to Bermuda, and joined the admiral, and after three weeks we were ordered on a cruise. My arm was now perfectly recovered, but I had become so useful in the clerk's office that I was retained, much against my own wishes: but the captain *liked* it, as Tom said and after that there was no more said about the matter.

America was not the seat of war at that period; and, with the exception of chasing French runners, there was nothing to be done on the North American station. I have, therefore, little to narrate during the remainder of the time that I was on board the frigate. Tom did his duty in the foretop, and never was in any disgrace; on the contrary, he was a great favourite both with officers and men, and took more liberties with the captain than any one else dared to have done; but Captain Maclean knew that Tom was one of his foremost and best men, always active, zealous, and indifferent as to danger, and Tom knew exactly how far he could venture to play with him. I remained in the clerk's office, and as it was soon discovered that I had received an excellent education, and always behaved myself respectfully to my superiors, I was kindly treated, and had no reason to complain of a man-of-war.

Such was the state of affairs when the other frigate arrived from the Honduras, and we, who had been cruising for the last four months in Boston Bay, were ordered in by a cutter, to join the admiral at Halifax. We had now been nearly a year from England without receiving any letters. The reader may, therefore, judge of my impatience when, after the anchor had been let go and the sails furled, the admiral's boat came on board with several bags of letters for the officers and ship's company. They were handed down into the gun-room, and I waited with impatience for the sorting and distribution.

"Faithful," said the purser, "here are two letters for you."

I thanked him, and hastened into the clerk's office, that I might read them without interruption. The first was addressed in a formal hand quite unknown to me. I opened it with some degree of wonderment as to who could possibly write to so humble an individual! It was from a lawyer, and the contents were as follows:—

> Sir—We hasten to advise you of the death of your good friend Mr Alexander Turnbull. By his will, which has been opened and read, and of which you are the executor, he has made you his sole heir, bequeathing you, at the present, the sum of 30,000 pounds, with the remainder of his fortune at the demise of his wife. With the exception of 5000 pounds left to Mrs Turnbull for her own disposal, the legacies do not amount to more than 800 pounds. The jointure arising from the interest of the money secured to Mrs Turnbull during her life is 1080 pounds per annum, upon the three per cent, consols, so that at her demise you will come into 36,000 pounds consols, which at 76, will be equal to 27,360 pounds sterling. I beg to congratulate you upon your good fortune, and, with Mr Drummond, have made application to the Admiralty for your discharge. This application, I am happy to say, has been immediately attended to, and by the same mail that conveys this letter is forwarded an order for your discharge and a passage home. Should you think proper to treat our firm as your legal advisers, we shall be most happy to enrol you among our clients.

I am, sir, yours very respectfully, *John Fletcher* .

I must leave the reader to judge of this unexpected and welcome communication. At first I was so stunned that I appeared as a statue, with the letter in my hand, and in this condition I remained until roused by the first lieutenant, who had come to the office to desire me to pass the word for "letters for England," and to desire the sail-maker to make a bag.

"Faithful—why what's the matter? Are you ill, or—?" I could not reply, but I put the letter into his hand. He read the contents, expressed his astonishment by occasional exclamations. "I wish you joy, my lad, and may it be my turn next time. No wonder you looked like a stuck pig. Had I received such news the captain might have hallooed till he was hoarse, and the ship might have tumbled overboard before I should have roused myself. Well, I suppose we shall get no more work out of you—"

"The captain wants you, Mr Knight," said one of the midshipmen, touching his hat.

Mr Knight went into the cabin, and in a few minutes returned, holding the order for my discharge in his hand.

"It's all right, Faithful, here is your discharge, and an order for your passage home."

He laid it on the table, and then went away, for a first lieutenant in harbour has no time to lose. The next person who came was Tom, holding in his hand a letter from Mary, with a postscript from his mother.

"Well, Jacob," said he, "I have news to tell you. Mary says that Mr Turnbull is dead, and has left her father 200 pounds, and that she has been told that he has left you something handsome."

"He has indeed, Tom," replied I; "read this letter."

While Tom was reading, I perceived the letter from Mr Drummond, which I had forgotten. I opened it. It communicated the same intelligence as that of the lawyer, in fewer words; recommended my immediate return, and enclosed a bill upon his house for 100 pounds, to enable me to appear in a manner corresponding to my present condition.

"Well," said Tom, "this is, indeed, good news, Jacob. You are a gentleman at last, as you deserve to be. It has made me so happy; what do you mean to do?"

"I have my discharge here," replied I, "and am ordered a passage home."

"Better still. I am so happy, Jacob; so happy. But what *is* to become of me?" And Tom passed the back of his hand across his eyes to brush away a tear.

"You shall soon follow me, Tom, if I can manage it either by money or any influence."

"I will manage it, if you don't, Jacob. I won't stay here without you, that I am determined."

"Do nothing rashly, Tom. I am sure I can buy your discharge, and on my arrival in England I will not think of anything else until it is done."

"You must be quick, then, Jacob, for I'm sure I can't stay here long."

"Trust to me, Tom; you'll still find me Jacob Faithful," said I, extending my hand. Tom squeezed it earnestly, and with moistened eyes, turned away, and walked forward.

The news had spread through the ship, and many of the officers, as well as the men, came to congratulate me. What would I have given to have been allowed only one half-hour to myself—one half-hour in which I might be permitted to compose my excited feelings—to have returned thanks for such unexpected happiness, and paid a tribute to the memory of so sincere a friend? But in a ship this is almost impossible, unless, as an officer, you can retreat to your own cabin; and those gushings from the heart, arising from grief or pleasure, the tears so sweet in solitude, must be prostituted before the crowd, or altogether repressed. At last the wished-for opportunity did come. Mr Wilson, who had been away on service, came to congratulate me as soon as he heard the news, and with an instinctive perception of what might be my feelings, asked me whether I would not like to write my letters in his cabin, which, for a few hours, was at my service. I thankfully accepted the offer; and, when summoned by the captain, had relieved my overcharged heart, and had composed my excited feelings.

"Jacob Faithful, you are aware there is an order for your discharge," said he, kindly. "You will be discharged this afternoon into the *Astrea*; she is ordered home, and will sail with despatches in a few days. You have conducted yourself well since you have been under my command; and, although you are now in a situation not to require a good certificate, still you will have the satisfaction of feeling that you have done your duty in the station of life to which you have, for a certain portion of it, been called—I wish you well."

Although Captain Maclean, in what he said, never lost sight of the relative situations in which we had been placed, there was a kindness of manner, especially in the last words, "I wish you well," which went to my heart. I replied that I had been very happy during the time I had been under his command, and thanked him for his good wishes. I then bowed and left the cabin. But the captain did not send me on board the *Astrea*, although I was discharged into her. He told the first lieutenant that I had better go on shore, and equip myself in a proper manner; and as I afterwards found out, spoke of me in very favourable terms to the captain of the *Astrea*, acknowledging that I had received the education of a gentleman, and had been illegally impressed; so that, when I made my appearance on board the *Astrea*, the officers of the gun-room requested that I would mess with them during the passage home.

I went on shore, obtained the money for my bill, hastened to a tailor, and with his exertions, and other fitting-out people, procured all that was requisite for the outward appearance of a gentleman. I then returned to the *Immortalité*, and bade farewell to the officers and seamen with whom I had been most intimate. My parting with Tom was painful. Even the few days which I had been away, I perceived, had made an alteration in his appearance.

"Jacob," said he, "don't think I envy you; on the contrary, I am as grateful, even more grateful than if such good fortune had fallen to my own lot; but I cannot help fretting at the thought of being left here without you: and I shall fret until I am with you again."

I renewed my promises to procure his discharge, and forcing upon him all the money I thought that I could spare, I went over the side as much affected as poor Tom. Our passage home was rapid. We had a continuance of North West winds, and we flew before them, and in less than three weeks we dropped our anchor at Spithead. Happy in the change of my situation, and happier still in anticipation, I shall only say that I never was in better spirits, or in company with more agreeable young men than were the officers of the *Astrea*; and although we were so short a time together, we separated with mutual regret.

Chapter Forty

My first object on my return was to call upon old Tom, and assure him of his son's welfare. My wishes certainly would have led me to Mr Drummond's but I felt that my duty required that I should delay that pleasure. I arrived at the hotel late in the evening, and early next morning I went down to the steps at Westminster Bridge, and was saluted with the usual cry of "Boat, sir!" A crowd of recollections poured into my mind at the well-known sound; my life appeared to have passed in review in a few seconds, as I took my seat in the stern of a wherry, and directed the waterman to pull up the river. It was a beautiful morning, and even at that early hour almost too warm—the sun was so powerful; I watched every object that we passed with an interest I cannot describe; every tree, every building, every point of land—they were all old friends, who appeared, as the sun shone brightly on them, to rejoice in my good fortune. I remained in a reverie too delightful to be wished to be disturbed from it, although occasionally there were reminiscences which were painful; but they were but as light clouds, obscuring for a moment, as they flew past, the glorious sun of my happiness. At last the well-known tenement of old Tom, his large board with "Boats built to order," and the half of the boat stuck up on end, caught my sight, and I remembered the object of my embarkation. I directed the waterman to pull to the hard, and, paying him well, dismissed him; for I had perceived that old Tom was at work stumping round a wherry, bottom up; and his wife was sitting on a bench in the boat-arbour, basking in the warm sun, and working away at her nets. I had landed so quietly, and they both were so occupied with their respective employments, that they had not perceived me, and I crept round by the house to surprise them. I had gained a station behind the old boat, where I overheard the conversation.

"It's my opinion," said old Tom, who left off hammering for a time, "that all the nails in Birmingham won't make this boat water-tight. The timbers are as rotten as a pear, and the nails fall through them. I have put in one piece more than agreed for; and if I don't put in another here she'll never swim."

"Well, then, put another piece in," replied Mrs Beazeley.

"Yes; so I will; but I've a notion I shall be out of pocket by this job. Seven-and-sixpence won't pay for labour and all. However, never mind," and Tom carolled forth—

"Is not the sea
Made for the free—
Land for courts and chains alone?
There we are slaves,
But on the waves
Love and liberty's all our own."

"Now, if you do sing, sing truth, Beazeley," said the old woman. "A'n't our boy pressed into the service? And how can you talk of liberty?"

Old Tom answered by continuing his song—

"No eye to watch, and no tongue to wound us;
All earth forgot, and all heaven around us."

"Yes, yes," replied the old woman; "no eye to watch, indeed. He may be in sickness and in sorrow; he may be wounded, or dying of a fever; and there's no mother's eye to watch over him. As to all the earth being forgot, I won't believe that Tom has forgotten his mother."

Old Tom replied—

"Seasons may roll,
But the true soul
Burns the same wherever it goes."

"So it does, Tom—so it does; and he's thinking this moment of his father and mother, I do verily believe, and he loves us more than ever."

"So I believe," replied old Tom—"that is, if he hasn't anything better to do. But there's a time for all things; and when a man is doing his duty as a seaman, he mustn't let his thoughts wander. Never fear, old woman: he'll be back again.

"There's a sweet little cherub that sits up aloft,
To take care of the life of poor Jack."

"God grant it! God grant it!" replied the old woman, wiping her eyes with her apron, and then resuming her netting.

"He seems," continued she, "by his letters, to be over-fond of that girl, Mary Stapleton—and I sometimes think that she cares not a little for him; but she's never of one mind long. I didn't like to see her flaunting and flirting so with the soldiers, and at the same time Tom says that she writes that she cares for nobody but him."

"Women are—women! that's sartin," replied old Tom, musing for a time, and then showing that his thoughts were running on his son, by bursting out—

"Mary, when yonder boundless sea
   Shall part us, and perchance for ever,
Think not my heart can stray from thee,
   Or cease to mourn thine absence—never!
And when in distant climes I roam,
   Forlorn, unfriended, broken-hearted—"

"Don't say so, Tom—don't say so," interrupted the old woman.

Tom continued—

"Oft shall I sigh for thee and home,
   And all those joys from which I parted."

"Aye, so he does, poor fellow, I'll be bound to say. What would I give to see his dear, smiling face!" said Mrs Beazeley.

"And I'd give no little, missus, myself. But still, it's the duty for every man to serve his country; and so ought Tom, as his father did before him. I shall be glad to see him back: but I'm not sorry that he's gone. Our ships must be manned, old woman; and if they take men by force, it's only because they won't volunteer—that's all. When they're once on board they don't mind it. You women require pressing just as much as the men, and it's all much of a muchness."

"How's that Tom?"

"Why, when we make love, and ask you to marry, don't you always pout, and say, 'No!' You like being kissed, but we must take it by force. So it is with manning a ship. The men all say, 'No;' but when they are once there, they like the service very much—only, you see, like you, they want pressing. Don't Tom write and say that he's quite happy, and don't care where he is so long as he's with Jacob?"

"Yes; that's true; but they say Jacob is to be discharged and come home, now that he's come to a fortune; and what will Tom say then?"

"Why, that *is* the worst of it. I believe that Jacob's heart is in the right place; but still, riches spoil a man. But we shall see. If Jacob don't prove 'true blue,' I'll never put faith in man again. But there be changes in this world, that's sartin.

"We all have our taste of the ups and the downs,
As Fortune dispenses her smiles and her frowns;
But may we not hope, if she's frowning to-day,
That to-morrow she'll lend us the light of her ray.

"I only wish Jacob was here—that's all."

"Then you have your wish, my good old friend," cried I, running up to Tom and seizing his hand. But old Tom was so taken by surprise that he started back and lost his equilibrium, dragging me after him, and we rolled on the turf together. Nor was this the only accident, for old Mrs Beazeley was so alarmed that she also sprang from the bench fixed in the half of the old boat stuck on end, and threw herself back against it. The boat, rotten when first put up, and with the disadvantage of exposure to the elements for many years, could no longer stand such pressure. It gave way to the sudden force applied by the old woman, and she and the boat went down together, she screaming and scuffling among the rotten planks, which now, after so many years close intimacy, were induced to part company. I was first on my legs, and ran to the assistance of Mrs Beazeley, who was half smothered with dust and flakes of dry pitch; and old Tom coming to my assistance, we put the old woman on her legs again.

"O deary me!" cried the old woman—"O deary me! I do believe my hip is out! Lord, Mr Jacob, how you frightened me!"

"Yes," said old Tom, shaking me warmly by the hand, "we were all taken aback, old boat and all. What a shindy you have made, bowling us all down like ninepins! Well, my boy, I'm glad to see you, and notwithstanding your gear, you're Jacob Faithful still."

"I hope so," replied I; and we then adjourned to the house, where I made them acquainted with all that had passed, and what I intended to do relative to obtaining Tom's discharge. I then left them, promising to return soon, and, hailing a wherry going up the river, proceeded to my old friend the Dominie, of whose welfare, as well as Stapleton's and Mary's, I had been already assured.

But as I passed through Putney Bridge I thought I might as well call first upon old Stapleton; and I desired the waterman to pull in. I hastened to Stapleton's lodgings, and went upstairs, where I found Mary in earnest conversation with a very good-looking young man, in a sergeant's uniform of the 93rd Regiment. Mary, who was even handsomer than when I had left her, starting up, at first did not appear to recognise me, then coloured up to the forehead, as she welcomed me with a constraint I had never witnessed before. The sergeant appeared inclined to keep his ground; but on my taking her hand and telling her that I brought a message from a person whom I trusted she had not forgotten, he gave her a nod and walked downstairs. Perhaps there was a severity in my countenance as I said, "Mary, I do not know whether, after what I have seen, I ought to give the message; and the pleasure I anticipated in meeting you again is destroyed by what I have now witnessed. How disgraceful is it thus to play with a man's feelings—to write to him, assuring him of your regard and constancy, and at the same time encouraging another."

Mary hung down her head. "If I have done wrong, Mr Faithful," said she, after a pause, "I have not wronged Tom; what I have written I felt."

"If that is the case, why do you wrong another person? why encourage another young man only to make him unhappy?"

"I have promised him nothing; but why does not Tom come back and look after me? I can't mope here by myself; I have no one to keep company with; my father is always away at the alehouse, and I must have somebody to talk to. Besides, Tom is away, and may be away a long while, and absence cures love in men, although it does not in women."

"It appears then, Mary, that you wish to have two strings to your bow, in case of accident."

"Should the first string break, a second would be very acceptable," replied Mary. "But it is always this way," continued she, with increasing warmth; "I never can be in a situation which is not right; whenever I do anything which may appear improper, so certain do *you* make your appearance when least expected and least wished for—as if you were born to be my constant accuser."

"Does not your own conscience accuse you, Mary?"

"Mr Faithful," repeated she, very warmly, "you are not my father confessor; but do as you please—write to Tom if you please, and tell him all you have seen, and anything you may think—make him and make me miserable and unhappy—do it, I pray. It will be a friendly act; and as you are now a great man, you may persuade Tom that I am a jilt and a good-for-nothing."

Here Mary laid her hands on the table and buried her face in them.

"I did not come here to be your censor, Mary; you are certainly at liberty to act as you please, without my having any right to interfere; but as

Tom is my earliest and best friend, so far as his interests and happiness are concerned, I shall carefully watch over them. We have been so long together, and I am so well acquainted with all his feelings, that I really believe that if ever there was a young man sincerely and devotedly attached to a woman, he is so to you; and I will add, that if ever there was a young man who deserved love in return, it is Tom. When I left, not a month back, he desired me to call upon you as soon as I could, and assure you of his unalterable attachment; and I am now about to procure his discharge, that he may be able to return. All his thoughts are upon this point, and he is now waiting with the utmost impatience the arrival of it, that he may again be in your company; you can best judge whether his return will or will not be a source of happiness."

Mary raised her head—her face was wet with tears.

"Then he will soon be back again, and I shall see him. Indeed, his return will be no source of unhappiness, if I can make him happy—indeed, it shall not, Mr Faithful; but pray don't tell him of my foolish conduct, pray don't— why make him unhappy?—I entreat you not to do it. I will not do so again. Promise me, Jacob, will you?" continued Mary, taking me by the arm, and looking beseechingly in my face.

"Mary, I will never be a mischief-maker; but recollect I exact the performance of your promise."

"Oh, and I will keep it, now that I know he will soon be home. I can, I think I can—I'm sure I can wait a month or two without flirting. But I do wish that I was not left so much alone. I wish Tom was at home to take care of me, for there is no one else. I can't take care of myself."

I saw by Mary's countenance that she was in earnest, and I therefore made friends with her, and we conversed for two hours, chiefly about Tom. When I left her she had recovered her usual spirits, and said at parting, looking archly at me, "Now, you will see how wise and prudent I shall be."

I shook my head, and left her that I might find out (my) old friend Stapleton, who, as usual, was at the door of the public-house, smoking his pipe. At first he did not recognise me, for when I accosted him he put his open hand to his ear as usual, and desired me to speak a little louder, but I answered, "Nonsense, Stapleton, that won't do with me." He then took his pipe out of his mouth, and looked me full in the face.

"Jacob, as I'm alive! Didn't know you in your long togs—thought you was a gentleman wanting a boat. Well, I hardly need say how glad I am to see you after so long; that's no more than human natur'. And how's Tom? Have you seen Mary?"

These two questions enabled me to introduce the subject that I wished. I told him of the attachment and troth pledged between the two, and how wrong it was for him to leave her so much alone. The old man agreed with me, and said, that as to talking to the men, that was on Mary's part nothing but "human natur'"; and that as for Tom wishing to be at home and seeing her again, that also was nothing but "human natur'"; but that he would smoke his pipe at home in future, and keep the soldiers out of the house. Satisfied with this assurance I left him, and taking another wherry went up to Brentford to see the Dominie.

Chapter Forty One

I found the worthy old Dominie in the school-room, seated at his elevated desk, the usher not present, and the boys making a din enough to have awaked a person from a trance. That he was in one of his deep reveries, and that the boys had taken advantage of it, was evident. "Mr Dobbs," said I, walking close up to the desk, but the Dominie answered not. I repeated his name in a louder voice.

"Cosine of X plus AB *minus* Z *minus a half*; such must be the result," said the Dominie talking to himself. "Yet it doth not prove correct. I may be in error. Let me revise my work," and the Dominie lifted up his desk to take out another piece of paper. When the desk lid was raised, I removed his work and held it behind me.

"But how is this?" exclaimed the Dominie, and he looked everywhere for his previous calculations. "Nay," continued he, "it must have been the wind;" and then he cast his eyes about until they fixed upon me laughing at him. "Eheu! what do my eyes perceive?—It is—yet it is not—yes, most truly it is, my son Jacob. Welcome, most welcome," cried the old man, descending from his desk, and clasping me in his arms. "Long is it since I have seen thee, my son, *Interea magnum sol circumvolvitur annum*. Long, yes long, have I yearned for thy return, fearful lest, *nudus ignota arena*, thou mightest, like another Palinurus, have been cast away. Thou art returned, and all is well; as the father said in the Scripture: I have found my son which I had lost; but no prodigal thou, though I use the quotation as apt. Now all is well; thou hast escaped the danger of the battle, the fire, and the wreck, and now thou mayest hang up thy wet garment as a votive offering; as Horace hath it, *Uvida suspendisse potenti vestimenta maris Deo*."

During the apostrophe of the Dominie, the boys perceiving that he was no longer wrapped up in his algebra, had partly settled to their desks, and in their apparent attention to their lessons reminded me of the humming of bees before a hive on a summer's day.

"Boys," cried the Dominie, "*nunc est ludendum*; verily ye shall have a holiday; put up your books, and depart in peace."

The books were hastily put up, in obedience to the command; the depart in peace was not so rigidly adhered to—they gave a loud shout, and in a few seconds the Dominie and I stood alone in the school-room.

"Come, Jacob, let us adjourn to my sanctum; there may we commune without interruption. Thou shalt tell me thine adventures, and I will communicate to thee what hath been made known to me relative to those with whom thou wert acquainted."

"First let me beg you to give me something to eat, for I am not a little hungry," interrupted I, as we gained the kitchen.

"Verily shalt thou have all that we possess, Jacob; yet now, I think, that will not be much, seeing that I and our worthy matron did pick the bones of a shoulder of mutton, this having been our fourth day of repast upon it. She is out, yet I will venture to intrude into the privacy of her cupboard, for thy sake. Peradventure she may be wroth, yet will I risk her displeasure." So saying, the old Dominie opened the cupboard, and, one by one, handed to me the dishes with their contents. "Here Jacob are two hard dumplings from yesterday. Canst thou relish cold, hard, dumplings?—but, stop, here is something more savoury—half of a cold cabbage, which was left this day. We will look again. Here is meat—yes, it is meat; but now do I perceive it is a piece of lights reserved for the dinner of the cat to-morrow. I am fearful that we must not venture upon that, for the dame will be wroth."

"Pray put it back, sir; I would not interfere with puss on any account."

"Nay, then, Jacob, I see naught else, unless there may be viands on the upper shelf. Sir, here is bread, the staff of life, and also a fragment of cheese; and now, methinks, I discern something dark at the back of the shelf." The Dominie extended his hand, and immediately withdrew it, jumping from his chair, with a loud cry. He had put his fingers into a rat gin, set by the old woman for those intruders, and he held up his arm and stamped as he shouted out with the pain. I hastened to him, and pressing down the spring, released his fingers from the teeth, which, however, had drawn blood, as well as bruised him; fortunately, like most of the articles of their menage, the trap was a very old one, and he was not much hurt. The Dominie thrust his fingers into his capacious mouth, and held them there some time without speaking. He began to feel a little ease, when in came the matron.

"Why, what's all this!" said she, in a querulous tone. "Jacob here, and all my cupboard on the table. Jacob, how dare you go to my cupboard?"

"It was the Dominie, Mrs Bately, who looked there for something for me to eat, and he has been caught in a rat-trap."

"Serve him right; I have forbade him that cupboard. Have I not, Mr Dobbs?"

"Yea, and verily," quoth the Dominie, "and I do repent me that I took not thine advice, for look at my fingers;" and the Dominie extended his lacerated digits.

"Dear me! well I'd no idea that a rat-trap pinched so hard," replied the old woman, whose wrath was appeased. "How it must hurt the poor things—I won't set it again, but leave them all to the cat; he'll kill them, if he only can get at them." The old lady went to a drawer, unlocked it, brought out some fragments of rags, and a bottle of friar's balsam, which she applied to the Dominie's hand, and then bound it up, scolding him the whole time. "How stupid of you, Mr Dobbs; you know that I was only out for a few minutes. Why didn't you wait—and why did you go to the cupboard? Hav'n't I always told you not to look into it? and now you see the consequences."

"Verily my hand burneth," replied the Dominie.

"I will go for cold water, and it will ease you. What a deal of trouble you do give, Mr Dobbs; you're worse than a charity boy;" and the old lady departed to the pump.

"Vinegar is a better thing, sir," said I, "and there is a bottle in the cupboard, which I dare say is vinegar." I went to the cupboard, and brought out the bottle, took out the cork and smelt it. "This is not vinegar, sir, it is Hollands or gin."

"Then would I like a glass, Jacob, for I feel a sickening faintness upon me; yet be quick, peradventure the old woman may return."

"Drink out of the bottle, sir," said I, perceiving that the Dominie looked very pale, "and I will give you notice of her approach." The Dominie put the bottle to his mouth, and was taking a sufficient draught, when the old woman returned by another door which was behind us; she had gone that way for a wash-basin. Before we could perceive her, she came behind the Dominie, snatched the bottle from his mouth with a jerk that threw a portion of the spirits in his eyes, and blinded him.

"That's why you went to my cupboard, is it, Mr Dobbs?" cried she, in a passion. "That's it, is it? I thought my bottle went very fast; seeing that I don't take more than a tea-spoonful every night, for the wind which vexes me so much. I'll set the rat-trap again, you may depend upon it; and now you may get somebody else to bind your fingers."

"It was I who took it out, Mrs Bately; the Dominie would have fainted with pain. It was very lucky that he has a housekeeper who is careful to have something of the kind in the house, or he might have been dead. You surely don't begrudge a little of your medicine to recover Mr Dobbs?"

"Peace, woman, peace," said the Dominie, who had gained courage by his potation. "Peace, I say; I knew not that thou hadst in thy cupboard either a gin for my hand, or gin for my mouth; since I have been taken in the one, it is but fair that I should take in the other. In future both thy gins will not be interfered with by me. Bring me the basin, that I may appease my angry wounds, and then hasten to procure some viands to appease the hunger of my son Jacob; lastly, appease thine own wrath. *Pax.* Peace, I say;" and the old woman, who perceived that the Dominie had asserted his right of dominion, went to obey his orders, grumbling till she was out of hearing. The application of the cold pump-water soon relieved the pain of the good old Dominie, and with his hand remaining in the basin, we commenced a long conversation.

At first I narrated to him the events which had occurred during my service on board of the frigate. When I told him of my parting with Tom, he observed, "Verily do I remember that young Tom, a jocund, pleasant, yet intrusive lad. Yet do I wish him well, and am grieved that he should be so taken by that maiden Mary. Well may we say of her, as Horace hath of Pyrrha—'*Quis multa gracilis te puer in rosa, perfusis liquidis urgit odoribus, grate, Pyrrha, sub antro. Cui flavam religas comam, simplex munditiis.*' I grieve at it, yea, grieve much. *Heu, quoties fidem mutatosque Deos flebit!* Verily, Jacob, I do prophesy that she will lead him into error, yea, perhaps into perdition."

"I trust not, sir," replied I; but the Dominie made no answer. For half-an-hour he was in deep and serious thought, during which Mrs Bately entered, and spreading a cloth, brought in from the other room some rashers of bacon and eggs, upon which I made a hasty and hearty meal. The old matron's temper was now smoothed, and she welcomed me kindly, and shortly after went out for a fresh basin of cold water for the Dominie to bathe his hand. This roused him, and he recommenced the conversation.

"Jacob, I have not yet congratulated thee upon thy accession to wealth; not that I do not sincerely rejoice in it, but because the pleasure of thy presence has made me unmindful of it. Still, was it fortunate for thee that thou hadst raised up such a friend as Mr Turnbull; otherwise what would have been the result of thy boasted independence? Thou wouldst probably have remained many years on board of a man-of-war, and have been killed, or have returned mutilated, to die unknown."

"You were right, sir," replied I; "my independence was nothing but pride; and I did bitterly repent, as you said I should do, even before I was pressed into the king's service—but Mr Drummond never repeated his offers."

"He never did, Jacob; but as I have since been informed by him, although he was taken by surprise at thy being forced away to serve thy country, still he was not sure that you would accept them; and he, moreover, wished you fully to feel thine own folly. Long before you had made friends with him, he had attested the will of Mr Turnbull, and was acquainted with the contents. Yet, did he watch over thee, and had he thought that thy way of life had led thee into that which was wrong, he would have interfered to save thee; but he considered with Shakespeare that 'sweet were the uses of adversity,' and that thou wouldst be more schooled by remaining some time under her unprepossessing frowns. He hath ever been thy friend."

"I can believe it. I trust he is well, and his family."

"They were well and prosperous, but a little while ago, Jacob; yet I have seen but little of them since the death of Mr Turnbull. It will pain thee to hear that affliction at thy absence hastened his dissolution. I was at his death-bed, Jacob; and I verily believe he was a good man, and will meet the reward of one; yet did he talk most strangely, and reminded me of that remnant of a man you call old Tom. 'It's no use, old gentleman,' said he, as he lay in his bed supported by pillows, for he had wasted away till he was but a skeleton, having broken a blood-vessel with his violent coughing— 'It's no use pouring that doctor's stuff down my throat; my anchor's short stay a-peak, and in a few minutes I shall trip it, I trust for heaven, where I hope there are moorings laid down for me.' 'I would fain comprehend thee,' replied I, 'but thou speakest in parables.' 'I mean to say that death has driven his harpoon in up to the shank, and that I struggle in vain. I have run out all my line. I shall turn up in a few minutes—so give my love and blessing to Jacob—he saved my life once—but now I'm gone.' With these last words his spirit took its flight; and thus, Jacob, did your benefactor breathe his last, invoking a blessing on your head."

I remained silent for a few minutes, for I was much affected by the Dominie's description; he at length resumed the conversation.

"Thou hast not yet seen the Drummonds, Jacob?"

"I have not," I replied, "but I will call upon them tomorrow; but it is time that I should go, for I have to return to London."

"Thou needst not, Jacob. Thine own house is at hand."

"My own house!"

"Yes; by the will of Mr Turnbull, his wife has been left a handsome jointure, but, for reasons which he did not explain, the house and furniture are not left to her, but, as residuary legatee, belong to thee."

"Indeed!—then where is Mrs Turnbull?"

"At Bath, where she hath taken up her residence. Mr Drummond, who hath acted in thy behalf, permitted her to take away such articles as she might wish, but they were but few, chiefly those little objects which filled up rather than adorned the drawing-room. The house is all ready for thy reception, and thou mayst take possession this evening."

"But why did not Mr Turnbull leave it to his widow?"

"I cannot exactly say, but I think he did not wish her to remain in this place. He, therefore, left her 5000 pounds at her own disposal, to enable her to purchase and furnish another."

I then took my leave of the Dominie, and it being rather late, I resolved to walk to the house and sleep there.

Chapter Forty Two

On my arrival the front gates were opened by the gardener's wife, who made me a profound courtesy. The gardener soon afterwards made his appearance, hat in hand. Everything was neat and in good order. I entered the house, and as soon as possible rid myself of their obsequious attentions. I wished to be alone. Powerful feelings crowded on my mind. I hastened to Mr Turnbull's study, and sat down in the chair so lately occupied by him. The proud feeling of possession, softened into gratitude to heaven, and sorrow at his death, came over me, and I remained for a long while in a deep reverie. "And all this, and more, much more, are mine," I mentally exclaimed; "the sailor before the mast, the waterman on the river, the charity-boy, the orphan sits down in quiet possession of luxury and wealth. What have I done to deserve all this?" My heart told me nothing, or if anything, it was almost valueless, and I poured forth my soul in thanks to heaven. I felt more composed after I had performed this duty, and my thoughts then dwelt upon my benefactor. I surveyed the room—the drawings, the furs and skins, the harpoons and other instruments, all remaining in their respective places, as when I last had an interview with Mr Turnbull. I remembered his kindness, his singleness of heart, his honesty, his good sense, and his real worth; and I shed many tears for his loss. My thoughts then passed to Sarah Drummond, and I felt much uneasiness on that score. Would she receive me, or would she still remember what I had been? I recollected her kindness and good-will towards me. I weighed these, and my present condition, against my origin and my former occupation; and could not ascertain how the scale might turn. I shall soon see, thought I. To-morrow, even, may decide the question. The gardener's wife knocked at the door, and announced that my bed was prepared. I went to sleep, dreaming of Sarah, young Tom, the Dominie and Mary Stapleton.

I was up early the next morning, and hastened to the hotel; when, having arranged my person to the best of my power (but at the same time never so little to my satisfaction), I proceeded to the house of Mr Drummond. I knocked; and this time I was not desired to wait in the hall, but was immediately ushered up into the drawing-room. Sarah Drummond was sitting alone at her drawing. My name was announced as I entered. She started from her chair, and blushed deeply as she moved towards me.

We joined hands in silence. I was breathless with emotion. Never had she appeared so beautiful. Neither party appeared willing to break silence; at last I faltered out, "Miss Drummond,"—and then I stopped.

"Mr Faithful," replied she; and then, after a break—"How very silly this is; I ought to have congratulated you upon your safe return, and upon your good fortune; and, indeed, Mr Faithful, no one can do so more sincerely."

"Miss Drummond," replied I, confused, "when I was an orphan, a charity-boy, and a waterman, you called me Jacob, if the alteration in my prospects induces you to address me in so formal a manner—if we are in future to be on such different terms—I can only say that I wish that I were again—Jacob Faithful, the waterman."

"Nay," replied she, "recollect that it was your own choice to be a waterman. You might have been different—very different. You might at this time have been a partner with my father, for he said so but last night, when we were talking about you. But you refused all; you threw away your education, your talents, your good qualities, from a foolish pride, which you considered independence. My father almost humbled himself to you—not that it is ever humiliating to acknowledge and attempt to repair a fault, but still he did more than could be expected from most people. Your friends persuaded you, but you rejected their advice; and what was still more unpardonable, even I had no influence over you. As long as you punished yourself I did not upbraid you; but now that you have been so fortunate, I tell you plainly—"

"What?"

"That it is more than you deserve, that's all."

"You have said but the truth, Miss Drummond. I was very proud and very foolish; but I had repented of my folly long before I was pressed; and I candidly acknowledge that I do not merit the good fortune I have met with. Can I say more?"

"No; I am satisfied with your repentance and acknowledgment. So, now you may sit down, and make yourself agreeable."

"Before I do that, allow me to ask, as you address me as Mr Faithful, how am I to address you? I should not wish to be considered impertinent."

"My name is Miss Drummond, but those who feel intimate with me call me Sarah."

"I may reply that my name is Faithful, but those who feel intimate with me call me Jacob."

"Very true; but allow me to observe that you show very little tact. You should never force a lady into a corner. If I appear affronted when you call me Sarah, then you will do wise to fall back upon Miss Drummond. But why do you fix your eyes upon me so earnestly?"

"I cannot help it, and must beg your pardon; but you are so improved in appearance since I last saw you. I thought no one could be more perfect, but—"

"Well, that's not a bad beginning, Jacob. I like to hear of my perfections. Now follow up your *but*."

"I hardly know what I was going to say, but I think it was that I do not feel as if I ought or can address you otherwise than as Miss Drummond."

"Oh, you've thought better of it, have you? Well, I begin to think myself that you look so well in your present dress, and have become so very different a person, that I ought not to address you by any other name than Mr Faithful. So now we are agreed."

"That's not what I mean to say."

"Well, then, let me know what you did mean to say."

This puzzling question fortunately did not require an answer, for Mr Drummond came into the room and extended his hand.

"My dear Jacob," said he, in the most friendly manner, "I'm delighted to see you back again, and to have the pleasure of congratulating you on your good fortune. But you have business to transact which will not admit of any delay. You must prove the will, and arrange with the lawyers as soon as possible. Will you come now? All the papers are below, and I have the whole morning to spare. We will be back to dinner, Sarah, if Jacob has no other engagement."

"I have none," replied I; "and shall be most happy to avail myself of your kindness. Miss Drummond, I wish you a good morning."

"*Au revoir*, Mr Faithful," replied Sarah, courtesying formally, with a mocking smile.

The behaviour of Mr Drummond towards me was most kind and parental, and my eyes were often suffused with tears during the occupation of the morning. The most urgent business was got through, and an interview with Mr Turnbull's solicitor put the remainder in progress; still it was so late when we had accomplished it, that I had no time to dress. On my return, Mrs Drummond received me with her usual kindness. I narrated, during the evening, my adventures since we parted, and took that opportunity to acknowledge to Mr Drummond how bitterly I had repented my folly, and I may add ingratitude, towards him.

"Jacob," said he, as we were sitting at the tea-table with Mrs Drummond and Sarah, "I knew at the time that you were toiling on the river for shillings that you were the inheritor of thousands; for I not only witnessed but read the will of Mr Turnbull; but I thought it best that you should have a lesson which you would never forget in after life. There is no such thing in this world as independence, unless in a savage state. In society we are all mutually dependent upon each other. Independence of mind we may have, but no more. As a waterman, you were dependent upon your customers, as every poor man must be upon those who have more means; and in refusing my *offers* you were obliged to apply for employment to others. The rich are as entirely dependent upon others as the poor; they depend upon them for their food, their clothes, their necessities, and their luxuries. Such ever will be the case in society, and the more refined the society may be — the more civilised its parts — the greater is the mutual dependence. Still it is an error originating in itself from high feelings, and therefore must be considered as an error on the right side; but recollect how much you might have thrown away had not you, in the first place, secured such a friend as Mr Turnbull; and secondly, if the death of that friend had not so soon put you in possession."

I was but too ready to acknowledge the truth of these remarks. The evening passed away so rapidly that it was midnight before I rose to take my leave, and I returned to the hotel as happy in my mind, and as grateful as ever any mortal could possibly be. The next day I removed to the house left me by Mr Turnbull, and the first order I gave was for a wherry. Such was the force of habit, I could not do without one; and half my time was spent upon the river, pulling every day down to Mr Drummond's, and returning in the evening, or late at night. Thus passed away two months, during which I occasionally saw the Dominie, the Stapletons, and old Tom Beazeley. I had exerted myself to procure Tom's discharge, and at last had the pleasure of telling the old people that it was to go out by the next packet. By the Drummonds I was received as a member of the family — there was no hindrance to my being alone with Sarah for hours; and although I had not ventured to declare my sentiments, they appeared to be well understood, as well by the parents as by Sarah herself.

Two days after I had communicated this welcome intelligence to the old couple, as I was sitting at breakfast, attended by the gardener and his wife (for I had made no addition to my establishment), what was my surprise at the appearance of young *Tom*, who entered the room as usual, laughing as he held out his hand.

"Tom!" exclaimed I, "why, how did you come here?"

"By water, Jacob, as you may suppose."

"But how have you received your discharge? Is the ship come home?"

"I hope not; the fact is, I discharged myself, Jacob."

"What! did you desert?"

"Even so. I had three reasons for so doing. In the first place, I could not remain without you; in the second, my mother wrote to say Mary was taken up with a sodger; and the third was, I was put into the report for punishment, and should have been flogged, as sure as the captain had a pair of epaulettes."

"Well, but sit down and tell me all about it. You know your discharge is obtained."

"Yes, thanks to you, Jacob; all the better, for now they won't look after me. All's well that ends well. After you went away, I presume I was not in the very best of humours; and that rascal of a master's mate who had us pressed, thought proper to bully me beyond all bearing. One day he called me a lying scoundrel; upon which I forgot that I was on board of a man-of-war, and replied that he was a confounded cheat, and that he had better pay me his debt of two guineas for bringing him down the river. He reported me on the quarter-deck for calling him a cheat, and Captain Maclean, who, you know, won't stand any nonsense, heard the arguments on both sides; upon which he declared that the conduct of the master's mate was not that of an officer or a gentleman, and therefore *he* should leave the ship; and that my language to my superior officer was subversive to the discipline of the service, and therefore he should give me a good flogging. Now, Jacob, you know that if the officers don't pay their debts, Captain Maclean always does, and with interest into the bargain; so finding that I was in for it, and no mistake, I swam ashore the night before Black Monday, and made my way to Miramichi, without any adventure, except a tussle with a sergeant of marines, whom I left for dead about three miles out of the town. At Miramichi I got on board of a timber ship, and here I am."

"I am sorry that you deserted, nevertheless," replied I; "it may come to mischief."

"Never fear; the people on the river know that I have my discharge, and I'm safe enough."

"Have you seen Mary!"

"Yes, and all's right in that quarter. I shall build another wherry, wear my badge and dress, and stick above bridge. When I'm all settled, I'll splice, and live along with the old couple."

"But will Mary consent to live there? It is so quiet and retired that she won't like it."

"Mary Stapleton has given herself airs enough in all conscience, and has had her own way quite enough. Mary Beazeley will do as her husband wishes, or I will know the reason why."

"We shall see, Tom. Bachelors' wives are always best managed, they say. But now you want money to buy your boat."

"Yes, if you'll lend it to me; I don't like to take it away from the old people; and I'll pay you when I can, Jacob."

"No; you must accept this, Tom; and when you marry you must accept something more," replied I, handing the notes to him.

"With all my heart, Jacob. I never can repay you for what you have done for me, and so I may just as well increase the debt."

"That's good logic, Tom."

"Quite as good as independence; is it not, Jacob?"

"Better, much better, as I know to my cost," replied I, laughing.

Tom finished his breakfast, and then took his leave. After breakfast, as usual, I went to the boat-house, and unchaining my wherry, pulled up the river, which I had not hitherto done; my attendance upon Sarah having invariably turned the bow of my wherry in the opposite direction. I swept by the various residences on the banks of the river until I arrived opposite to that of Mr Wharncliffe, and perceived a lady and gentleman in the garden. I knew them at once, and, as they were standing close to the wall, I pulled in and saluted them.

"Do you recollect me?" said I to them, smiling.

"Yes," replied the lady, "I do recollect your face—surely—it is Faithful, the waterman!"

"No, I am not a waterman; I am only amusing myself in my own boat."

"Come up," replied Mr Wharncliffe; "we can't shake hands with you at that distance."

I made fast my wherry and joined them. They received me most cordially.

"I thought you were not a waterman, Mr Faithful, although you said that you were," said Mrs Wharncliffe. "Why did you deceive us in that way?"

"Indeed, at that time I was, from my own choice and my own folly a waterman; now I am so no longer."

We were soon on the most intimate terms, and I narrated part of my adventures. They expressed their obligations to me, and requested that I would accept their friendship.

"Would you like to have a row on the water? It is a beautiful day, and if Mrs Wharncliffe will trust herself—"

"Oh, I should like it above all things. Will you go. William? I will run for a shawl."

In a few minutes we were all three embarked, and I rowed them to *my villa*. They had been admiring the beauty of the various residences on the banks of the Thames.

"How do you like that one?" inquired I of Mrs Wharncliffe.

"It is very handsome, and I think one of the very best."

"That is mine," replied I. "Will you allow me to show it to you?"

"Yours!"

"Yes, mine; but I have a very small establishment, for I am a bachelor."

We landed, and after walking about the grounds went into the house.

"Do you recollect this room?" said I to Mr Wharncliffe.

"Yes, indeed I do; it was here that the box was opened, and my uncle's— But we must not say anything about that: he is dead!"

"Dead!"

"Yes; he never held his head up after his dishonesty was discovered. He pined and died within three months, sincerely repenting what he had attempted."

I accepted their invitation to dinner, as I rowed them back to their own residence; and afterwards had the pleasure of enrolling them among my sincerest friends. Through them I was introduced to Lady Auburn and many others; and I shall not forget the old housekeeper recognising me one day, when I was invited to Lady Auburn's villa.

"Bless me! what tricks you young gentlemen do play. Only to think how you asked me for water, and how I pushed the door in your face, and wouldn't let you rest yourself. But if you young gentlemen will disguise yourselves, it's your own faults, and you must take the consequences."

My acquaintances now increased rapidly, and I had the advantage of the best society. I hardly need observe that it was a great advantage; for, although I was not considered awkward, still I wanted that polish which can only be obtained by an admixture with good company. The reports concerning me were various; but it was generally believed that I was a young man who had received an excellent education, and might have been brought forward, but that I had taken a passion for the river, and had chosen to be a waterman in preference to any other employment; that I had since come into a large fortune, and had resumed my station in society. How far the false was blended with the true, those who have read my adventures will readily perceive. For my part, I cared little what they said, and I gave myself no trouble to refute the various assertions. I was not ashamed of my birth, because it had no effect upon the Drummonds; still I knew the world too well to think it necessary to blazon it. On the whole, the balance was in my favour; there was a degree of romance in my history, with all its variations, which interested, and, joined to the knowledge of my actual wealth, made me to be well received, and gained me attention wherever I went. One thing was much to my advantage—my extensive reading, added to the good classical education which I had received. It is not often in society that an opportunity occurs when any one can prove his acquisitions; and thus did education turn the scale in my favour, and every one was much more inclined to believe the false rather than the true versions of my history.

Chapter Forty Three

I had often ruminated in what manner I could render the Dominie more comfortable. I felt that to him I was as much indebted as to any living being, and one day I ventured to open the subject; but his reply was decided.

"I see, Jacob, my son, what thou wouldst wish: but it must not be. Man is but a creature of habit; habit becomes to him not only necessity but luxury. For five-and-forty years have I toiled, instilling precepts and forcing knowledge into the brains of those who have never proved so apt as thou. Truly, it hath been a painful task, yet can I not relinquish it. I might, at one time, that is, during the first ten years, have met the offer with gratitude; for I felt the humiliation and annoyance of wearying myself with the rudiments, when I would fain have commented upon the various peculiarities of style in the ancient Greek and Latin authors; but now, all that has passed away. The eternal round of concord, prosody, and syntax has charms for me from habit: the rule of three is preferable to the problems of Euclid, and even the Latin grammar has its delights. In short, I have a *hujus* pleasure in *hic, haec, hoc; (cluck cluck;)* and even the flourishing of the twigs of that tree of knowledge, the birch, hath become a pleasurable occupation to me, if not to those upon whom it is inflicted. I am like an old horse, who hath so long gone round and round in a mill, that he cannot walk straight forward; and, if it pleases the Almighty, I will die in harness. Still I thank thee, Jacob; and thank God that thou hast again proved the goodness of thy heart, and given me one more reason to rejoice in thee and in thy love; but thine offer, if accepted, would not add to my happiness; for what feeling can be more consolatory to an old man near into his grave than the reflection that his life, if not distinguished, has at least been useful?"

I had not for some time received a visit from Tom; and, surprised at this, I went down to his father's to make inquiry about him. I found the old couple sitting in-doors; the weather was fine, but old Tom was not at his work; even the old woman's netting was thrown aside.

"Where is Tom?" inquired I, after wishing them good morning.

"Oh deary me!" cried the old woman, putting her apron up to her eyes; "that wicked good-for-nothing girl!"

"Good heavens! what is the matter?" inquired I of old Tom.

"The matter, Jacob," replied old Tom, stretching out his two wooden legs, and placing his hands upon his knees, "is, that Tom has 'listed for a sodger."

"'Listed for a soldier!"

"Yes; that's as sartain as it's true; and what's worse, I'm told the regiment is ordered to the West Indies. So, what with fever o' mind and yellow fever, he's food for the land crabs, that's sartain. I think now," continued the old man, brushing a tear from his eye with his fore-finger, "that I see his bones bleaching under the palisades; for I know the place well."

"Don't say so, Tom; don't say so!"

"O Jacob! beg pardon if I'm too free now; but can't you help us?"

"I will if I can, depend upon it; but tell me how this happened."

"Why, the long and the short of it is this: that girl, Mary Stapleton, has been his ruin. When he first came home he was well received, and looked forward to being spliced and living with us; but it didn't last long. She couldn't leave off her old tricks; and so, that Tom might not get the upper hand, she plays him off with the sergeant of a recruiting party, and flies off from one to the other, just like the ticker of the old clock there does from one side to the other. One day the sergeant was the fancy man, and the next day it was Tom. At last Tom gets out of patience, and wishes to come to a fair understanding. So he axes her whether she chooses to have the sergeant or to have him; she might take her choice, but he had no notion of being played with in that way, after all her letters and all her promises. Upon this she huffs outright, and tells Tom he may go about his business, for she didn't care if she never sees him no more. So Tom's blood was up, and he called her a damned jilt, and, in my opinion, he was near to the truth; so then they had a regular breeze, and part company. Well, this made Tom very miserable, and the next day he would have begged her pardon, and come to her terms, for, you see, Jacob, a man in love has no discretion; but she being still angry, tells him to go about his business, as she means to marry the sergeant in a week. Tom turns away again quite mad; and it so happens that he goes into the public-house where the sergeant hangs out, hoping to be revenged on him, and meaning to have a regular set-to, and see who is the best man; but the sergeant wasn't there, and Tom takes pot after pot to drive away care; and when the sergeant returned, Tom was not a little in liquor. Now, the sergeant was a knowing chap, and when he comes in, and perceives Tom with his face flushed, he guesses what was to come, so, instead of saying a word, he goes to another table, and dashes his fist upon it, as if in a passion.

Tom goes up to him, and says, 'Sergeant, I've known that girl long before you, and if you are a man, you'll stand up for her.' 'Stand up for her; yes,' replied the sergeant, 'and so I would have done yesterday, but the blasted jilt has turned me to the right about and sent me away. I won't fight now, for she won't have me—any more than she will you.' Now when Tom hears this, he becomes more pacified with the sergeant, and they set down like two people under the same misfortune, and take a pot together, instead of fighting; and then, you see, the sergeant plies Tom with liquor, swearing that he will go back to the regiment, and leave Mary altogether, and advises Tom to do the same. At last, what with the sergeant's persuasions, and Tom's desire to vex Mary, he succeeds in 'listing him, and giving him the shilling before witnesses; that was all the rascal wanted. The next day Tom was sent down to the depôt, as they call it, under a guard; and the sergeant remains here to follow up Mary without interruption. This only happened three days ago, and we only were told of it yesterday by old Stapleton, who threatens to turn his daughter out of doors."

"Can't you help us, Jacob?" said the old woman, crying.

"I hope I can; and if money can procure his discharge it shall be obtained. But did you not say that he was ordered to the West Indies?"

"The regiment is in the Indies, but they are recruiting for it, so many have been carried off by the yellow fever last sickly season. A transport, they say, will sail next week, and the recruits are to march for embarkation in three or four days."

"And what is the regiment, and where is the depôt?"

"It is the 47th Fusiliers, and the depôt is at Maidstone."

"I will lose no time, my good friends," replied I; "to-morrow I will go to Mr Drummond, and consult with him." I returned the grateful squeeze of old Tom's hand, and, followed by the blessings of the old woman, I hastened away.

As I pulled up the river, for that day I was engaged to dine with the Wharncliffes, I resolved to call upon Mary Stapleton, and ascertain by her deportment whether she had become that heartless jilt which she was represented, and if so, to persuade Tom, if I succeeded in obtaining his discharge, to think no more about her; I felt so vexed and angry with her, that after I landed, I walked about a few minutes before I went to the house, that I might recover my temper. When I walked up the stairs I found Mary sitting over a sheet of paper, on which she had been writing. She looked up as I came in, and I perceived that she had been crying. "Mary," said I, "how well you have kept the promise you made to me when last we met! See what trouble and sorrow you have brought upon all parties except yourself."

"Except myself—no, Mr Faithful, don't except myself, I am almost mad—I believe that I am mad—for surely such folly as mine is madness;" and Mary wept bitterly.

"There is no excuse for your behaviour, Mary—it is unpardonably wicked. Tom sacrificed all for your sake—he even deserted, and desertion is death by the law. Now what have you done?—taken advantage of his strong affection to drive him to intemperance, and induce him, in despair, to enlist for a soldier. He sails for the West Indies to fill up the ranks of a regiment thinned by the yellow fever, and will perhaps never return again—you will then have been the occasion of his death. Mary, I have come to tell you that I despise you."

"I despise and hate myself," replied Mary, mournfully; "I wish I were in my grave. Oh, Mr Faithful, do for God's sake—do get him back. You can, I know you can—you have money and everything."

"If I do, it will not be for your benefit, Mary, for you shall trifle with him no more. I will not try for his discharge unless he faithfully promises never to speak to you again."

"You don't say that—you don't mean that!" cried Mary, sweeping the hair with her hand back from her forehead—and her hand still remaining on her head—"O God! O God! what a wretch I am! Hear me, Jacob, hear me," cried she, dropping on her knees, and seizing my hands; "only get him his discharge—only let me once see him again, and I swear by all that's sacred, that I will beg his pardon on my knees as I now do yours. I will do everything—anything—if he will but forgive me, for I cannot, I will not live without him."

"If this is true, Mary, what madness could have induced you to have acted as you have?"

"Yes," replied Mary, rising from her knees, "madness, indeed—more than madness to treat so cruelly one for whom I only care to live. You say Tom loves me; I know he does; but he does not love me as I do him. O, my God! my heart will break!" After a pause, Mary resumed. "Read what I have written to him—I have already written as much in another letter. You will see that if he cannot get away, I have offered to go out with him as his wife; that is, if he will have such a foolish, wicked girl as I am."

I read the letter; it was as she said, praying forgiveness, offering to accompany him, and humiliating herself as much as it was possible. I was much affected. I returned the letter.

"You can't despise me so much as I despise myself," continued Mary; "I hate, I detest myself for my folly. I recollect now how you used to caution me when a girl. Oh, mother, mother, it was a cruel legacy you left to your child, when you gave her your disposition. Yet why should I blame her? I must blame myself."

"Well, Mary, I will do all I can, and that as soon as possible. To-morrow I will go down to the depôt."

"God bless you, Jacob; and may you never have the misfortune to be in love with such a one as myself."

Chapter Forty Four

I left Mary, and hastened home to dress for dinner. I mentioned the subject of wishing to obtain Tom's discharge to Mr Wharncliffe, who recommended my immediately applying to the Horse Guards; and, as he was acquainted with those in office, offered to accompany me. I gladly accepted his offer; and the next morning he called for me in his carriage, and we went there. Mr Wharncliffe sent up his card to one of the secretaries, and we were immediately ushered up, when I stated my wishes. The reply was:— "If you had time to procure a substitute it would be easily arranged; but the regiment is so weak, and the aversion to the West Indies so prevalent after this last very sickly season, that I doubt if His Royal Highness would permit any man to purchase his discharge. However, we will see. The Duke is one of the kindest-hearted of men, and I will lay the case before him. But let us see if he is still at the depôt; I rather think not." The secretary rang the bell.

"The detachment of the 47th Fusiliers from the depôt—has it marched? And when does it embark?"

The clerk went out, and in a few minutes returned with some a papers in his hand. "It marched the day before yesterday, and was to embark this morning, and sail as soon as the wind was fair."

My heart sank at this intelligence.

"How is the wind, Mr G—? Go down and look at the tell-tale."

The clerk returned. "East North East, sir, and has been steadily so these two days."

"Then," replied the secretary, "I am afraid you are too late to obtain your wish. The orders to the port-admiral are most peremptory to expedite the sailing of the transports, and a frigate has been now three weeks waiting to convoy them. Depend upon it, they have sailed to-day."

"What can be done?" replied I, mournfully.

"You must apply for his discharge, and procure a substitute. He can then have an order sent out, and be permitted to return home. I am very sorry, as I perceive you are much interested; but I'm afraid it is too late now.

However, you may call to-morrow. The weather is clear with this wind, and the port-admiral will telegraph to the Admiralty the sailing of the vessels. Should anything detain them, I will take care that His Royal Highness shall be acquainted with the circumstances this afternoon, if possible, and will give you his reply."

We thanked the secretary for his politeness, and took our leave. Vexed as I was with the communications I had already received, I was much more so when one of the porters ran to the carriage to show me, by the secretary's order, a telegraphic communication from the Admiralty, containing the certain and unpleasant information, "Convoy to West Indies sailed this morning."

"Then it is all over for the present," said I, throwing myself back in the carriage; and I continued in a melancholy humour until Mr Wharncliffe, who had business in the city, put me down as near as the carriage went to the house of Mr Drummond. I found Sarah, who was the depository of all my thoughts, pains, and pleasures, and I communicated to her this episode in the history of young Tom. As most ladies are severe judges of their own sex, she was very strong in her expressions against the conduct of Mary, which she would not allow to admit of any palliation. Even her penitence had no weight with her.

"And yet, how often is it the case, Sarah, not perhaps to the extent carried on by this mistaken girl; but still, the disappointment is as great, although the consequences are not so calamitous. Among the higher classes, how often do young men receive encouragement, and yield themselves up to a passion, to end only in disappointment! It is not necessary to plight troth; a young woman may not have virtually committed herself, and yet, by merely appearing pleased with the conversation and company of a young man, induce him to venture his affections in a treacherous sea, and eventually find them wrecked."

"You are very nautically poetical, Jacob," replied Sarah. "Such things do happen; but I think that women's affections are, to use your phrase, oftener wrecked than those of men. That, however, does not exculpate either party. A woman must be blind, indeed, if she cannot perceive, in a very short time, whether she is trifling with a man's feelings, and base, indeed, if she continues to practise upon them."

"Sarah," replied I, and I stopped.

"Well?"

"I was," replied I, stammering a little—"I was going to ask you if you were blind."

"As to what, Jacob?" said Sarah, colouring up.

"As to my feelings towards you."

"No; I believe you like me very well," replied she, smiling.

"Do you think that that is all?"

"Where do you dine to-day, Jacob," replied Sarah.

"That must depend upon you and your answer. If I dine here to-day, I trust to dine here often. If I do not dine here to-day, probably I never may again. I wish to know, Sarah, whether you have been blind to my feelings towards you; for, with the case of Mary and Tom before me, I feel that I must no longer trust to my own hopes, which may end in disappointment. Will you have the kindness to put me out of my misery?"

"If I have been blind to your feelings I have not been blind to your merit, Jacob. Perhaps I have not been blind to your feelings, and I am not of the same disposition as Mary Stapleton. I think you may venture to dine here to-day," continued she, colouring and smiling, as she turned away to the window.

"I can hardly believe that I'm to be so happy, Sarah," replied I, agitated. "I have been fortunate, very fortunate; but the hopes you have now raised are so much beyond my expectations—so much beyond my deserts—that I dare not indulge in them. Have pity on me, and be more explicit."

"What do you wish me to say?" replied Sarah, looking down upon her work, as she turned round to me.

"That you will not reject the orphan who was fostered by your father, and who reminds you of what he was, that you may not forget at this moment what I trust is the greatest bar to his presumption—his humble origin."

"Jacob, that was said like yourself—it was nobly said; and if you were not born noble, you have true nobility of mind. I will imitate your example. Have I not often, during our long friendship, told you that I loved you?"

"Yes, as a child you did, Sarah."

"Then, as a woman, I repeat it. And now are you satisfied?"

I took Sarah by the hand; she did not withdraw it, but allowed me to kiss it over and over again.

"But your father and mother, Sarah?"

"Would never have allowed our intimacy if they had not approved of it, Jacob, depend upon it. However, you may make yourself easy on that score by letting them know what has passed; and then, I presume, you will be out of your misery."

Before the day was over I had spoken to Mrs Drummond, and requested her to open the business to her husband, as I really felt it more than I could dare to do. She smiled as her daughter hung upon her neck; and when I met Mr Drummond at dinner-time I was "out of my misery," for he shook me by the hand, and said, "You have made us all very happy, Jacob; for that girl appears determined either to marry you or not to marry at all. Come; dinner is ready."

I will leave the reader to imagine how happy I was, what passed between Sarah and me in our *tête-à-tête* of that evening, how unwilling I was to quit the house, and how I ordered a post-chaise to carry me home, because I was afraid to trust myself on that water on which the major part of my life had been safely passed, lest any accident should happen to me and rob me of my anticipated bliss. From that day I was as one of the family, and finding the distance too great, took up my abode at apartments contiguous to the house of Mr Drummond. But the course of other people's love did not run so smooth, and I must now return to Mary Stapleton and Tom Beazeley.

I had breakfasted, and was just about to take my wherry and go down to acquaint the old couple with the bad success of my application. I had been reflecting with gratitude upon my own happiness in prospect, indulging in fond anticipations, and then, reverting to the state in which I had left Mary Stapleton and Tom's father and mother, contrasting their misery with my joy, arising from the same source, when, who should rush into the dining-room but young Tom, dressed in nothing but a shirt and a pair of white trousers, covered with dust, and wan with fatigue and excitement.

"Good heavens! Tom! are you back? then you must have deserted."

"Very true," replied Tom, sinking on a chair, "I swam on shore last night, and have made from Portsmouth to here since eight o'clock. I hardly need say that I am done up. Let me have something to drink, Jacob, pray."

I went to the cellaret and brought him some wine, of which he drank off a tumbler eagerly. During this I was revolving in my mind the consequences which might arise from this hasty and imprudent step. "Tom," said I, "do you know the consequences of desertion?"

"Yes," replied he, gloomily, "but I could not help it. Mary told me in her letter that she would do all I wished, would accompany me abroad; she made all the amends she could, poor girl! and, by heavens, I could not leave her; and when I found myself fairly under weigh, and there was no chance, I was almost mad; the wind baffled us at the Needles, and we anchored for the night; I slipped down the cable and swam on shore, and there's the whole story."

"But, Tom, you will certainly be recognised and taken up for a deserter."

"I must think of that," replied Tom; "I know the risk I run; but if you obtain my discharge, they may let me off."

I thought this was the best plan to proceed upon, and requesting Tom to keep quiet, I went to consult with Mr Wharncliffe. He agreed with me that it was Tom's only chance, and I pulled to his father's, to let them know what had occurred, and then went on to the Drummonds. When I returned home late in the evening the gardener told me that Tom had gone out and had not returned. My heart misgave me that he had gone to see Mary, and that some misfortune had occurred, and I went to bed with most anxious feelings. My forebodings were proved to be correct, for the next morning I was informed that old Stapleton wished to see me. He was ushered in, and as soon as he entered, he exclaimed, "All's up, Master Jacob—Tom's nabbed—Mary fit after fit—*human natur'*."

"Why, what *is* the matter, Stapleton?"

"Why, it's just this—Tom desarts to come to Mary. Cause why?—he loves her—human natur'. That soldier chap comes in and sees Tom, clutches hold, and tries to take possession of him. Tom fights, knocks out sergeant's starboard eye, and tries to escape—human natur'. Soldiers come in, pick up sergeant, seize Tom, and carry him off. Mary cries, and screams, and faints—human natur'—poor girl can't keep her head up—two women with burnt feathers all night. Sad job, Mister Jacob. Of all the senses love's the worst, that's sartain—quite upset me, can't smoke my pipe this morning—Mary's tears quite put my pipe out,"—and old Stapleton looked as if he was ready to cry himself.

"This is a sad business, Stapleton," replied I. "Tom will be tried for desertion, and God knows how it will end. I will try all I can; but they have been very strict lately."

"Hope you will, Mister Jacob. Mary will die, that's sartain. I'm more afraid that Tom will. If one does, t'other will. I know the girl—just like her mother, never could carry her helm amidships, hard a port, or hard a starboard. She's mad now to follow him—will go to Maidstone. I take her as soon as I go back to her. Just come up to tell you all about it."

"This is a gloomy affair, Stapleton."

"Yes, for sartain—wish there never was such a thing as *human natur'*."

After a little conversation, and a supply of money, which I knew would be acceptable, Stapleton went away, leaving, me in no very happy state of mind. My regard for Tom was excessive, and his situation one of peculiar danger. Again I repaired to Mr Wharncliffe for advice, and he readily interested himself most warmly.

"This is, indeed, an awkward business," said he, "and will require more interest than I am afraid that I command. If not condemned to death, he will be sentenced to such a flogging as will break him down in spirit as well as in body, and sink him into an early grave. Death were preferable of the two. Lose no time, Mr Faithful, in going down to Maidstone, and seeing the colonel commanding the depôt. I will go to the Horse Guards, and see what is to be done."

I wrote a hurried note to Sarah to account for my absence, and sent for post-horses. Early in the afternoon I arrived at Maidstone, and finding out the residence of the officer commanding the depôt, sent up my card. In few words I stated to him the reason of my calling upon him.

"It will rest altogether with the Horse Guards, Mr Faithful, and I am afraid I can give you but little hope. His Royal Highness has expressed his determination to punish the next deserter with the utmost severity of the law. His leniency on that point has been very injurious to the service, and he *must do it*. Besides, there is an aggravation of the offence in his attack upon the sergeant, who has irrecoverably lost his eye."

"The sergeant first made him drunk, and then persuaded him to enlist." I then stated the rivalship that subsisted between them, and continued, "Is it not disgraceful to enlist men in that way—can that be called voluntary service?"

"All very true," replied the officer, "but still expediency winks at even more. I do not attempt to defend the system, but we must have soldiers. The seamen are impressed by force, the soldiers are entrapped by other means, even more discreditable: the only excuse is expediency, or, if you like it better, necessity. All I can promise you, sir, is, to allow the prisoner every comfort which his situation will permit, and every advantage at his court-martial, which mercy, tempered by justice, will warrant."

"I thank you, sir; will you allow me and his betrothed to see him?"

"Most certainly; the order shall be given forthwith."

I thanked the officer for his kindness, and took my leave.

Chapter Forty Five

I hastened to the black hole where Tom was confined, and the order for my admission having arrived before me, I was permitted by the sergeant of the guard to pass the sentry. I found Tom sitting on a bench notching a stick with his knife, whistling a slow tune.

"This is kind, Jacob, but not more than I expected of you—I made sure that I should see you to-night or to-morrow morning. How's poor Mary? I care only for her now—I am satisfied—she loves me, and—I knocked out the sergeant's eye—spoilt his wooing, at all events."

"But, Tom, are you aware of the danger in which you are placed?"

"Yes, Jacob, perfectly; I shall be tried by a court-martial and shot. I've made up my mind to it—at all events, it's better than being hung like a dog, or being flogged to death like a nigger. I shall die like a gentleman, if I have never been one before, that's some comfort. Nay, I shall go out of the world with as much noise as if a battle had been fought, or a great man had died."

"How do you mean?"

"Why there'll be more than one *bullet-in*."

"This is no time for jesting, Tom."

"Not for you, Jacob, as a sincere friend, I grant; not for poor Mary, as a devoted girl; not for my poor father and mother—no, no," continued Tom. "I feel for them, but for myself I neither fear nor care. I have not done wrong—I was pressed against the law and Act of Parliament, and I deserted. I was enlisted when I was drunk and mad, and I deserted. There is no disgrace to me; the disgrace is to the government which suffers such acts. If I am to be a victim, well and good—we can only die once."

"Very true, Tom; but you are young to die, and we must hope for the best."

"I have given up all hope, Jacob. I know the law will be put in force. I shall die and go to another and a better world, as the parson says, where, at all events, there will be no muskets to clean, no drill, and none of your confounded pipe-clay, which has almost driven me mad. I should like to die in a blue jacket—in a red coat I will not, so I presume I shall go out of the world in my shirt, and that's more than I had when I came in."

"Mary and her father are coming down to you, Tom."

"I'm sorry for that, Jacob; it would be cruel not to see her—but she blames herself so much that I cannot bear to read her letters. But, Jacob, I will see her, to try if I can comfort her—but she must not stay; she must go back again till after the court-martial, and the sentence, and then—if she wishes to take her farewell, I suppose I must not refuse." A few tears dropped from his eyes as he said this. "Jacob, will you wait and take her back to town?—she must not stay here—and I will not see my father and mother until the last. Let us make one job of it, and then all will be over."

As Tom said this the door of the cell again opened, and Stapleton supported in his daughter. Mary tottered to where Tom stood, and fell into his arms in a fit of convulsions. It was necessary to remove her, and she was carried out. "Let her not come in again, I beseech you, Jacob; take her back, and I will bless you for your kindness. Wish me farewell now, and see that she does not come again." Tom wrung me by the hand, and turned away to conceal his distress. I nodded my head in assent, for I could not speak for emotion, and followed Stapleton and the soldiers who had taken Mary out. As soon as she was recovered sufficiently to require no further medical aid, I lifted her into the post-chaise, and ordered the boys to drive back to Brentford. Mary continued in a state of stupor during the journey; and when I arrived at my own house, I gave her into the charge of the gardener's wife, and despatched her husband for medical assistance. The application of Mr Wharncliffe was of little avail, and he returned to me with disappointment in his countenance. The whole of the next week was the most distressing that I ever passed; arising from my anxiety for Tom, my daily exertions to reason Mary into some degree of submission to the will of Providence—her accusations of herself and her own folly—her incoherent ravings, calling herself Tom's murderer, which alarmed me for her reason; the distress of old Tom and his wife, who, unable to remain in their solitude, came all to me for intelligence, for comfort, and for what, alas! I dare not give them—hope. All this, added to my separation from Sarah during my attendance to what I considered my duty, reduced me to a debility, arising from mental exertion, which changed me to almost a skeleton.

At last the court-martial was held, and Tom was condemned to death. The sentence was approved of, and we were told that all appeals would be unavailing. We received the news on the Saturday evening, and Tom was to suffer on the Tuesday morning. I could no longer refuse the appeals of Mary; indeed, I received a letter from Tom, requesting that all of us, the Dominie included, would come down and bid him farewell. I hired a carriage for old Tom, his wife, Stapleton, and Mary, and putting the Dominie and myself in my own chariot, we set off early on the Sunday morning for Maidstone. We arrived about eleven o'clock, and put up at an inn in close proximity to the barracks. It was arranged that the Dominie and I should see Tom first, then his father and mother, and lastly, Mary Stapleton.

"Verily," said the Dominie, "my heart is heavy, exceeding heavy; my soul yearneth after the poor lad, who is thus to lose his life for a woman—a woman from whose toils I did myself escape. Yet is she exceeding fair and comely, and now that it is unavailing, appeareth to be penitent."

I made no reply; we had arrived at the gate of the barracks. I requested to be admitted to the prisoner, and the doors were unbarred. Tom was dressed with great care and cleanliness in white trousers and shirt and waistcoat, but his coat lay on the table; he would not put it on. He extended his hand towards me with a faint smile.

"It's all over now, Jacob; and there is no hope that I am aware of, and I have made up my mind to die; but I wish these last farewells were over, for they unman me. I hope you are well, sir," continued Tom to the Dominie.

"Nay, my poor boy, I am as well as age and infirmity will permit, and why should I complain when I see youth, health, and strength about to be sacrificed; and many made miserable, when many might be made so happy?" And the Dominie blew his nose, the trumpet sound of which re-echoed through the cell, so as to induce the sentry to look through the bars.

"They are all here, Tom," said I. "Would you like to see them now?"

"Yes; the sooner it is over the better."

"Will you see your father and mother first?"

"Yes," replied Tom, in a faltering tone.

I went out, and returned with the old woman on my arm, followed by old Tom, who stumped after me with the assistance of his stick. Poor old Mrs Beazeley fell on her son's neck, sobbing convulsively.

"My boy—my boy—my dear, dear boy!" said she at last, and she looked up steadfastly in his face. "My God! he'll be dead to-morrow!"

Her head again sank on his shoulder, and her sobs were choking her. Tom kissed his mother's forehead as the tears coursed down his cheeks, and motioned me to take her away. I placed her down on the floor, where she remained silent, moving her head up and down with a slow motion, her face buried in her shawl. It was but now and then that you heard a convulsive drawing of her breath. Old Tom had remained a silent but agitated spectator of the scene. Every muscle in his weather-beaten countenance twitched convulsively, and the tears at last forced their way through the deep furrows on his cheeks. Tom, as soon as his mother was removed, took his father by the hand, and they sat down together.

"You are not angry with me, father, for deserting?"

"No, my boy, no; I was angry with you for 'listing, but not for deserting. What business had you with the pipeclay? But I do think I have reason to be angry elsewhere, when I reflect that after having lost my two legs in defending her, my country is now to take from me my boy in his prime. It's but a poor reward for long and hard service—poor encouragement to do your duty; but what do they care? they have had my servives, and they have left me a hulk. Well, they may take the rest of me if they please, now that they—Well, it's no use crying; what's done can't be helped," continued old Tom, as the tears ran down in torrents; "they may shoot you, Tom; but this I know well, you'll die game, and shame them by proving to them they have deprived themselves of the servives of a good man when good men are needed. I would not have so much cared," continued old Tom, after a pause—"(look to the old woman, Jacob, she's tumbling over to port)—if you had fallen on board a king's ship in a good frigate action; some must be killed when there's hard fighting; but to be drilled through by your own countrymen, to die by their hands, and, worst of all, to die in a red coat, instead of a true blue—"

"Father, I will not die in a red coat—I won't put it on."

"That's some comfort, Tom, anyhow, and comfort's wanted."

"And I'll die like a man, father."

"That you will, Tom, and that's some comfort."

"We shall meet again, father."

"Hope so, Tom, in heaven—that's some comfort."

"And now, father, bless me, and take care of my poor mother."

"Bless you, Tom, bless you!" cried the old man, in a suffocating voice, extending both his hands towards Tom, as they rose up; but the equilibrium was no longer to be maintained, and he reeled back in the arms of me and Tom. We lowered him gently down by the side of his wife; the old couple turned to each other, and embracing, remained sobbing in each other's arms.

"Jacob," said Tom, squeezing me by the hand, with a quivering lip, "by your regard for me, let now the last scene be got over—let me see Mary, and let this tortured heart once more be permitted a respite." I sent out the Dominie. Tom leant against the wall, with his arms folded, in appearance summoning up all his energy for the painful meeting. Mary was led in by her father. I expected she would have swooned away, as before; but, on the contrary, although she was pale as death, and gasping for breath, from intensity of feeling, she walked up to Tom where he was standing, and sat down on the form close to him. She looked anxiously round upon the group, and then said, "I know that all I now say is useless, Tom; but still I must say it—it is I who, by my folly, have occasioned all this distress and misery—it is I who have caused you to suffer a—dreadful death—yes, Tom, I am your murderer."

"Not so, Mary, the folly was my own," replied Tom, taking her hand.

"You cannot disguise or palliate to me, dearest Tom," replied Mary; "my eyes have been opened, too late it is true, but they have been opened; and although it is kind of you to say so, I feel the horrid conviction of my own guilt. See what misery I have brought about. There is a father who has sacrificed his youth and his limbs to his country, sobbing in the arms of a mother whose life is bound up with that of her only son. To them," continued Mary, falling down upon her knees, "to them I must kneel for pardon, and I ask it as they hope to be forgiven. Answer me—oh! answer me! can you forgive a wretch like me?"

A pause ensued. I went up to old Tom, and kneeling by his side, begged him to answer.

"Forgive her, poor thing—yes; who could refuse it, as she kneels there? Come," continued he, speaking to his wife, "you must forgive her. Look up, dame, at her, and think that our poor boy may be asking the same of heaven to-morrow at noon."

The old woman looked up, and her dimmed eyes caught a sight of Mary's imploring and beautiful attitude; it was not to be withstood.

"As I hope for mercy to my poor boy, whom you have killed, so do I forgive you, unhappy young woman."

"May God reward you, when you are summoned before Him," replied Mary. "It was the hardest task of all. Of you, Jacob, I have to ask forgiveness for depriving you of your early and truest friend—yes, and for much more. Of you, sir," addressing the Dominie, "for my conduct towards you, which was cruel and indefensible—will you forgive me?"

"Yes, Mary, from my heart, I do forgive you," replied I.

"Bless thee, maiden, bless thee!" sobbed the Dominie.

"Father, I must ask of you the same—I have been a wilful child—forgive me!"

"Yes, Mary; you could not help it," replied old Stapleton, blubbering; "it was all human natur'."

"And now," said Mary, turning round on her knees to Tom, with a look expressive of anguish and love, "to you, Tom, must be my last appeal. I know *you* will forgive me—I know you have—and this knowledge of your fervent love makes the thought more bitter that I have caused your death. But hear me, Tom, and all of you hear me. I never loved but you; I have liked others much; I liked Jacob; but you only ever did make me feel I had a heart; and alas, you only have I sacrificed. When led away by my folly to give you pain, I suffered more than you—for you have had my only, you shall have my eternal and unceasing love. To your memory I am hereafter wedded, to join you will be my only wish—and if there could be a boon granted me from heaven, it would be to die with you, Tom—yes, in those dear arms."

Mary held out her arms to Tom, who falling down on his knees, embraced her, and thus they remained with their faces buried in each other's shoulders. The whole scene was now at its climax; it was too oppressive, and I felt faint, when I was aroused by the voice of the Dominie, who, lifting up both his arms, and extending them forth, solemnly prayed, "O Lord, look down upon these Thy servants in affliction; grant to those who are to continue in their pilgrimage strength to bear Thy chastening—grant to him who is to be summoned to Thee that happiness which the world cannot give; and O God most mighty, God most powerful, lay not upon us burdens greater than we can bear.—My children let us pray."

The Dominie knelt down and repeated the Lord's prayer; all followed his example, and then there was a pause.

"Stapleton," said I, pointing to Mary. I beckoned to the Dominie. We assisted up old Tom, and then his wife, and led them away; the poor old woman was in a state of stupefaction, and until she was out in the air was not aware that she had quitted her son. Stapleton had attempted to detach Mary from Tom, but in vain; they were locked together as if in death. At last Tom, roused by me, suffered his hold to be loosened, and Mary was taken out in a happy state of insensibility, and carried to the inn by her father and the Dominie.

"Are they all gone?" whispered Tom to me, as his head reclined on my shoulder.

"All, Tom."

"Then the bitterness of death is past; God have mercy on them, and assuage their anguish; they want His help more than I do."

A passionate flood of tears, which lasted some minutes, relieved the poor fellow; he raised himself, and drying his eyes, became more composed.

"Jacob, I hardly need tell my dying request, to watch over my poor father and mother, to comfort poor Mary—God bless you, Jacob! you have indeed been a faithful friend, and may God reward you. And now, Jacob, leave me; I must commune with my God, and pray for forgiveness. The space between me and eternity is but short."

Tom threw himself into my arms, where he remained for some minutes; he then broke gently away, and pointed to the door. I once more took his hand and we parted.

Chapter Forty Six

I went back to the inn, and ordering the horses to be put to, I explained to all but Mary the propriety of their now returning home. Mary was lifted in, and it was a relief to my mind to see them all depart. As for myself, I resolved to remain until the last; but I was in a state of feverish agitation, which made me restless. As I paced up and down the room, the newspaper caught my eye. I laid hold of it mechanically, and looked at it. A paragraph rivetted my attention. "His Majesty's ship *Immortalité* Chatham, to be paid off." Then our ship has come home. But what was that now? Yet something whispered to me that I ought to go and see Captain Maclean, and try if anything could be done. I knew his commanding interest, and although it was now too late, still I had an impulse to go and see him, which I could not resist. "After all," said I to myself, "I'm of no use here, and I may as well go." This feeling, added to my restlessness, induced me to order horses, and I went to Chatham, found out that Captain Maclean was still on board, and took boat off to the frigate. I was recognised by the officers, who were glad to see me, and I sent a message to the captain, who was below, requesting to see him. I was asked into the cabin, and stated to him what had occurred, requesting his assistance, if possible.

"Faithful," replied he, "it appears that Tom Beazeley has deserted twice; still there is much extenuation; at all events, the punishment of death is too severe, and I don't *like* it—I can save him, and I will. By the rule of the services, a deserter from one service can be claimed from the other, and must be tried by his officers. His sentence is, therefore, not legal. I shall send a party of marines, and claim him as a deserter from the Navy, and they must and shall give him up—make yourself easy, Faithful, his life is as safe as yours."

I could have fallen on my knees and thanked him, though I could hardly believe that such good news was true.

"There is no time to lose, sir," replied I, respectfully; "he is to be shot to-morrow at nine o'clock."

"He will be on board here to-morrow at nine o'clock, or I am not Captain Maclean. But, as you say, there is no time to lose. It is now nearly dark, and the party must be off immediately. I must write a letter on service to the commanding officer of the depôt. Call my clerk."

I ran out and called the clerk. In a few minutes the letter was written, and a party of marines, with the second lieutenant, despatched with me on shore. I ordered post-chaises for the whole party, and before eleven we were at Maidstone. The lieutenant and I sat up all night, and, at daylight, we summoned the marines and went to the barracks, where we found the awful note of preparation going forward, and the commanding officer up and attending to the arrangements. I introduced the lieutenant, who presented the letter on service.

"Good heavens, how fortunate! You can establish his identity, I presume."

"Every man here can swear to him."

"'Tis sufficient, Mr Faithful. I wish you and your friend joy of this reprieve. The rules of the service must be obeyed, and you will sign a receipt for the prisoner."

This was done by the lieutenant, and the provost marshal was ordered to deliver up the prisoner. I hastened with the marines into the cell; the door was unlocked. Tom, who was reading his Bible, started up, and perceiving the red jackets, thought that he was to be led out to execution.

"My lads," exclaimed he, "I am ready; the sooner this is over the better."

"No, Tom," said I, advancing; "I trust for better fortune. You are claimed as a deserter from the *Immortalité*."

Tom stared, lifted the hair from his forehead, and threw himself into my arms; but we had no time for a display of feelings. We hurried Tom away from the barracks; again I put the whole party into chaises, and we soon arrived at Chatham, where we embarked on board of the frigate. Tom was given into the charge of the master-at-arms as a deserter, and a letter was written by Captain Maclean, demanding a court-martial on him.

"What will be the result?" inquired I of the first lieutenant.

"The captain says, little or nothing, as he was pressed as an apprentice, which is contrary to Act of Parliament."

I went down to cheer Tom with this intelligence, and taking my leave, set off for London with a light heart. Still I thought it better not to communicate this good news until assurance was made doubly sure. I hastened to Mr Drummond's, and detailed to them all that had passed. The next day Mr Wharncliffe went with me to the Admiralty, where I had the happiness to find that all was legal, and that Tom could only be tried for his desertion from a man-of-war; and that if he could prove that he was an apprentice, he would, in all probability, be acquitted. The court-martial was summoned three days after the letter had been received by the Admiralty. I hastened down to Chatham to be present. It was very short; the desertion was proved, and Tom was called upon for his defence. He produced his papers, and proved that he was pressed before his time had expired. The court was cleared for a few minutes, and then re-opened. Tom was acquitted on the ground of illegal detention, contrary to Act of Parliament, and he was *free*. I returned my thanks to Captain Maclean and his officers for their kindness, and left the ship with Tom in the cutter, ordered for me by the first lieutenant. My heart swelled with gratitude at the happy result. Tom was silent, but his feelings I could well analyse. I gave to the men of the boat five guineas to drink Tom's health, and, hastening to the inn, ordered the carriage, and with Tom, who was a precious deposit, for upon his welfare depended the happiness of so many, I hurried to London as fast as I could, stopped at the Drummond's to communicate the happy intelligence, and then proceeded to my own house, where we slept. The next morning I dressed Tom in some of my clothes, and we embarked in the wherry.

"Now, Tom," said I, "you must keep in the background at first, while I prepare them. Where shall we go first?"

"Oh, to my mother," replied Tom.

We passed through Putney Bridge, and Tom's bosom heaved as he looked towards the residence of Mary. His heart was there, poor fellow! and he longed to fly to the poor girl and dry her tears; but his first duty was to his parents.

We soon arrived abreast of the residence of the old couple, and I desired Tom to pull in, but not turn his head round, lest they should see him before I had prepared them; for too much joy will kill as well as grief. Old Tom was not at his work, and all was quiet. I landed and went to the house, opened the door, and found them both sitting by the kitchen fire in silence, apparently occupied in watching the smoke as it ascended up the spacious chimney.

"Good morning to you both," said I; "how do you find yourself, Mrs Beazeley?"

"Ah, deary me!" replied the old woman, putting her apron up to her eyes.

"Sit down, Jacob, sit down," said old Tom; "we *can* talk of him now."

"Yes, now that he's in heaven, poor fellow!" interposed the old woman.

"Tell me, Jacob," said old Tom, with a quivering lip, "did you see the last of him? Tell me all about it. How did he look? How did he behave? Was he soon out of his pain? And—Jacob—where is he buried!"

"Yes, yes;" sobbed Mrs Beazeley; "tell me where is the body of my poor child."

"Can you bear to talk about him?" said I.

"Yes, yes; we can't talk too much; it does us good," replied she. "We have done nothing but talk about him since we left him."

"And shall, till we sink down into our own graves," said old Tom, "which won't be long. I've nothing to wish for now, and I'll never sing again, that's sartain. We shan't last long, either of us. As for me," continued the old man with a melancholy smile, looking down at his stumps. "I may well say that I've *two* feet in the grave already. But come, Jacob, tell us all about him."

"I will," replied I; "and my dear Mrs Beazeley, you must prepare yourself for different tidings than what you expect. Tom is not yet shot."

"Not dead!" shrieked the old woman.

"Not yet, Jacob;" cried old Tom, seizing me by the arm, and squeezing it with the force of a vice, as he looked me earnestly in the face.

"He lives; and I am in hopes he will be pardoned."

Mrs Beazeley sprang from her chair and seized me by the other arm.

"I see—I see by your face. Yes, Jacob, he is pardoned; and we shall have our Tom again."

"You are right, Mrs Beazeley; he is pardoned, and will soon be here."

The old couple sank down on their knees beside me. I left them, and beckoned from the door to Tom, who flew up, and in a moment was in their arms. I assisted him to put his mother into her chair, and then went out to recover myself from the agitating scene. I remained about an hour outside, and then returned. The old couple seized me by the hands, and invoked blessings on my head.

"You must now part with Tom a little while," said I; "there are others to make happy besides yourselves."

"Very true," replied old Tom; "go, my lad, and comfort her. Come, missus, we mustn't forget others."

"Oh, no. Go, Tom; go and tell her that I don't care how soon she is my daughter."

Tom embraced his mother, and followed me to the boat; we pulled up against the tide, and were soon at Putney.

"Tom, you had better stay in the boat. I will either come or send for you."

It was very unwillingly that Tom consented, but I overruled his entreaties, and he remained. I walked to Mary's house and entered. She was up in the little parlour, dressed in deep mourning; when I entered she was looking out upon the river; she turned her head, and perceiving me, rose to meet me.

"You do not come to upbraid me, Jacob, I am sure," said she, in a melancholy voice; "you are too kind-hearted for that."

"No, no, Mary; I come to comfort you, if possible."

"That is not possible. Look at me, Jacob. Is there not a worm—a canker—that gnaws within?"

The hollow cheek and wild flaring eye, once so beautiful, but too plainly told the truth.

"Mary," said I, "sit down; you know what the Bible says—'It is good for us to be afflicted.'"

"Yes, yes," sobbed Mary, "I deserve all I suffer; and I bow in humility. But am I not too much punished, Jacob? Not that I would repine; but is it not too much for me to bear, when I think that I am the destroyer of one who loved me so?"

"You have not been the destroyer, Mary."

"Yes, yes; my heart tells me that I have."

"But—I tell you that you have not. Say, Mary, dreadful as the punishment has been, would you not kiss the rod with thankfulness, if it cured you of your unfortunate disposition, and prepared you to make a good wife?"

"That it has cured me, Jacob, I can safely assert; but it has also killed me as well as him. But I wish not to live; and I trust, in a few short months, to repose by his side."

"I hope you will have your wish, Mary, very soon, but not in death."

"Merciful heavens! what do you mean, Jacob?"

"I said you were not the destroyer of poor Tom—you have not been; he has not *yet* suffered; there was an informality, which has induced them to revise the sentence."

"Jacob," replied Mary, "it is cruelty to raise my hopes only to crush them again. If not yet dead, he is still to die. I wish you had not told me so," continued she, bursting into tears; "what a state of agony and suspense must he have been in all this time, and I—I have caused his sufferings! I trusted he had long been released from this cruel, heartless world."

The flood of tears which followed assured me that I could safely impart the glad intelligence. "Mary, Mary, listen to me."

"Leave me, leave me," sobbed Mary, waving her hand.

"No, Mary, not until I tell you that Tom is not only alive, but—pardoned."

"Pardoned!" shrieked Mary.

"Yes, pardoned, Mary—free, Mary—and in a few minutes will be in your arms."

Mary dropped on her knees, raised her hands and eyes to heaven, and then fell into a state of insensibility. Tom, who had followed me, and remained near the house, had heard the shriek, and could no longer retain himself; he flew into the room as Mary fell, and I put her into his arms. At the first signs of returning sensibility, I left them together, and went to find old Stapleton, to whom I was more brief in my communication. Stapleton continued to smoke his pipe during my narrative.

"Glad of it, glad of it," said he, when I finished. "I were just thinking how all these senses brought us into trouble, more than all, that sense of love; got me into trouble, and made me kill a man—got my poor wife into trouble, and drowned her—and now almost shot Tom, and killed Mary. Had too much of *human natur'* lately—nothing but moist eyes and empty pipes. Met that sergeant yesterday, had a turn up; Tom settled one eye, and, old as I am, I've settled the other for a time. He's in bed for a fortnight—couldn't help it—human natur'."

I took leave of Stapleton, and calling in upon Tom and Mary, shaking hands with the one, and kissing the other, I despatched a letter to the Dominie, acquainting him with what had passed, and then hastened to the Drummonds and imparted the happy results of my morning's work to Sarah and her mother.

"And now, Sarah, having so successfully arranged the affairs of other people, I should like to plead in my own behalf. I think that after having been deprived almost wholly of your dear company for a month, I deserve to be rewarded."

"You do, indeed, Jacob," said Mrs Drummond, "and I am sure that Sarah thinks so too, if she will but acknowledge it."

"I do acknowledge it, mamma; but what is this reward to be?"

"That you will allow your father and mother to arrange an early day for our nuptials, and also allow Tom and Mary to be united at the same altar."

"Mamma, have I not always been a dutiful daughter?"

"Yes, my love, you have."

"Then I shall do as I am bidden by my parents, Jacob; it will be probably the last command I receive from them, and I shall obey it; will that please you, dear Jacob?"

That evening the day was fixed, and now I must not weary the reader with a description of my feelings, or of my happiness in the preparations for the ceremony. Sarah and I, Mary and Tom, were united on the same day, and there was nothing to cloud our happiness. Tom took up his abode with his father and mother; and Mary, radiant with happiness, even more beautiful than ever, has settled down into an excellent, doting wife. For Sarah, I hardly need say the same; she was my friend from childhood, she is now all that a man could hope and wish for. We have been married several years, and are blessed with a numerous family.

I am now almost at a conclusion. I have only to acquaint the reader with a few particulars relative to my early friends. Stapleton is still alive, and is wedded to his pipe, which, with him, although the taste for tobacco has been considered as an acquired one, may truly be asserted to be human nature. He has two wherries with apprentices, and from them gains a good livelihood, without working himself. He says that the boys are not as honest as I was, and cheat him not a little; but he consoles himself by asserting that it is nothing but human natur'. Old Tom is also strong and hearty, and says that he don't intend to follow his legs for some time yet. His dame, he says, is peaking, but Mary requires no assistance. Old Tom has left off mending boats, his sign is taken down, for he is now comfortable. When Tom married, I asked him what he wished to do; he requested me to lend him money to purchase a lighter; I made him a present of a new one, just launched by Mr Drummond's firm. But old Stapleton made over to him the 200 pounds, left to him by Mr Turnbull, and his mother brought out an equal sum from her hoards. This enabled Tom to purchase another lighter, and now he has six or seven, I forget which; at all events he is well off, and adding to his wealth every year. They talk of removing to a better house, but the old couple wish to remain. Old Tom, especially, has built an arbour where the old boat stood, and sits there carolling his songs, and watching the crafts as they go up and down the river.

Mr and Mrs Wharncliffe still continue my neighbours and dearest friends. Mrs Turnbull died a few months back, and I am now in possession of the whole property. My father and mother-in-law are well and happy. Mr Drummond will retire from business as soon as he can wind up his multifarious concerns. I have but one more to speak of—the old Dominie. It is now two years since I closed the eyes of this worthy man. As he increased in years so did he in his abstractions of mind, and the governors of the charity thought it necessary to superannuate him with a pension. It was a heavy blow to the old man, who asserted his capabilities to continue to instruct; but people thought otherwise, and he accepted my offer to take up his future residence with us, upon the understanding that it was necessary that our children, the eldest of whom, at that time, was but four years old, should be instructed in Latin and Greek. He removed to us with all his books, etcetera, not forgetting the formidable birch; but as the children would not take to the Latin of their own accord, and Mrs Faithful would not allow the rod to be made use of, the Dominie's occupation was gone. Still, such was the force of habit, that he never went without the Latin grammar in his pocket, and I have often watched him sitting down in the poultry-yard, fancying, I presume, that he was in his school. There would he decline, construe, and conjugate aloud, his only witnesses being the poultry, who would now and then raise a gobble, gobble, gobble, while the ducks with their *quack, quack, quack,* were still more impertinent in their replies. A sketch of him, in this position, has been taken by Sarah, and now hangs over the mantel-piece of my study, between two of Mr Turnbull's drawings, one of an iceberg, on the 17th of August '78, and the other showing the dangerous position of the *Camel* whaler, jammed between the floe of ice, in latitude —, and longitude —.

Reader, I have now finished my narrative. There are two morals, I trust, to be drawn from the events of my life, one of which is, that in society we naturally depend upon each other for support, and that he who would assert his independence throws himself out of the current which bears to advancement; the other is, that with the advantages of good education, and good principle, although it cannot be expected that everyone will be so fortunate as I have been, still there is every reasonable hope, and every right to expect, that we shall do well in this world. Thrown up, as the Dominie expressed himself, as a tangled weed from the river, you have seen the orphan and charity-boy rise to wealth and consideration; you have seen how he who was friendless secured to himself the warmest friends; he who required everything from others became in a situation to protect and assist in return; he who could not call one individual his relation, united to the object of his attachment, and blessed with a numerous family; and to amass all these advantages and this sum of happiness, the only capital with which he embarked was a good education and good principles.

Reader, farewell!